I0592567

Titles by Erika Kelly

Praise for the Wild Love series

MINE FOR NOW

"Erika Kelly has a writing style that draws the reader into the story, and I always feel like I'm friends with the heroines and in love with the heroes by the end of her books. *Mine for Now* was just a great love story that had smoking hot romance, an emotional storyline, and great characters." - Reading in Pajamas

"This book had me laughing loudly, it had me crying hard. I swooned big time, I fell in love, I had my heart broken, and then I fell in love all over again. I've read this one twice already and honestly, just writing this review makes me want to read it again. Easily in my top 5 reads of 2016." - Obsessed with Romance

"Turns out, Erika Kelly is a master at bringing out some serious feels. The sexual tension simmers for a while between Dylan and Nicole, and when it finally explodes, it's so, so satisfying." - Krista's Dust Jacket

Praise for the Rock Star Romance series

YOU REALLY GOT ME

"Lovable characters and pulse-pounding chemistry make this one of my favorite reads of the year!"—Laura Kaye, *New York Times* Bestselling Author

"Sexy, lyrical and electric with hot, romantic tension." - NYT and USA Today Bestselling author Lauren Blakely

I WANT YOU TO WANT ME

Booklist calls I WANT YOU TO WANT ME "…steamy, hot, and totally engaging. The characters are realistic, and Kelly paints a vivid picture of what happens behind the scenes in the world of rock."

TAKE ME HOME TONIGHT

All About Romance awards TAKE ME HOME TONIGHT a Desert Isle Keeper review. "All these (characters) are so authentically human they nearly walk off the page. If you like books where real people have real problems and find real love (while having really hot sex)? Pick up **Take Me Home Tonight** and enjoy the ride."

TAKE ME HOME TONIGHT "is emotional and tremendously sexy, with a large cast of characters that readers will adore — Kelly's rendering of Calix's grieving parents is particularly well-done — but it is Mimi's strength that will linger long after the finish." - Sarah MacLean, Washington Post

MINE FOR
THE WEEK

Erika Kelly

ISBN ebook: 978-0-9859904-4-2
ISBN paper: 978-0-9859904-5-9

This book is a work of fiction. Names, characters, places, and
incidents are used fictitiously or are a product of the author's
imagination and any resemblance to actual persons, living or dead,
business establishments, events, or locales is entirely coincidental.

Cover designed by Novak Illustration
Formatting by Polgarus Studio

This book is dedicated to Superman.
You're always there for me. You always come through.

ACKNOWLEDGMENTS

 To Superman, my everything. Thank you for listening to me ramble on for thirty-five minutes and then solving everything in one sentence.

 To Olivia, for sharing this journey with me. And it needs to be said: thank you for looking at every single one of the 3.5 million images I show you while trying to find just the right cover. Your bountiful patience is appreciated.

 To KP, for your kindness and expertise. You make the journey a thousand times better.

 To Sharon, for your friendship and endless support.

 To Kevan, for your guidance.

 To Kristy DeBoer, for taking the time to make my work better.

 To the romance writing community, for your generous support. I couldn't do this without the bloggers and reviewers like Obsessed with Romance, Krista's Dust Jacket, Guilty Pleasures Book Reviews, About That Story, and Reading in Pajamas—to name just a few—whose love of books glitters in their reviews; and my friends in writer groups like the Dreamweavers, CTRWA, WRW, and CoLoNY.

Keep reading for an excerpt from MINE FOR NOW,
the first in the Wild Love series by Erika Kelly

CHAPTER ONE

"Strike!"

Dammit. Ryan O'Donnell swiped the back of his gloved hand across his brow. He stomped on the ground, tapping the bat on his cleat. Hunkering back down, he flexed his fingers on the grip.

Sweat trickled into his eyes. He blinked, keeping his sights on the pitcher's shoulder. The moment the guy took a step back and then rotated his hips, Ryan shifted his gaze to the ball.

Another splitter.

He bent his knees, but as the ball shot forward, Ryan's heart thundered. Blood roared in his ears, and he thought he might pass out. *What the hell's the matter with me?*

His mind sent the signal, but his body didn't swing. At least not soon enough.

"Stee-*rike* two."

Holy shit. The scouts are watching.

He pushed back his shoulders and shook out his arms. *Come on. Focus on the mound.* But even as he thought it, he couldn't resist glancing at his coach. The big man stood like a statue, brow furrowed in confusion and concern over Ryan's performance.

Boos and laughter from the stands trickled into his consciousness.

"Never seen you choke before, O'Donnell," the catcher said.

Block the scouts, block the crowd. Just hit the ball.

The pitcher jerked his knee up, whipped his arm out from behind his back, and in that split second before release, Ryan was pretty sure the guy's fingers shifted into a slider.

I got this.

But his pulse jackhammered. His body felt weak, shaky. Like he hadn't eaten in a while. *Swing.* His arms moved a fraction of a second after his brain had given the command.

"Strike three. You're out."

Ryan hurled the bat. Noise filled his head. He needed to get to the cover of the dugout, away from the eyes of scouts, teammates, and the coach who'd supported him for four years.

Just as he hit the concrete, he caught movement above. Hands gripping the railing, his buddy Jake swung his legs over and dropped to the ground. "Let's go."

He'd known Jake most of his life, so it only took a moment of silent communication to get that his friend had come to save him.

Fuck, yes. A break. Thank Christ his friends had stopped in Florida to catch his game before they headed off on their vacation. He'd take a breather, grab an energy drink.

Coach clapped a hand on his shoulder. "What's going on?"

"Family emergency." Jake didn't betray an ounce of uncertainty. "I've got to get him out of here."

Wait. Was he serious? But Jake wouldn't look at him.

"Can it wait an hour?" Coach looked caught between concern and frustration.

"Absolutely not," Jake said. "We've got to go right now."

If something were really wrong, Jake would say it. *Your dad's in the hospital. Your brother's been in an accident.*

Coach jerked his chin. "Go on."

When Ryan hesitated—because he had no idea where Jake was going with the family emergency ploy—Coach said, "We'll take care of the game, and I'll talk to the scouts." He pointed a finger. "Keep in touch. Let me know what's going on."

Jake grabbed his sleeve and gave a hard shake. "Let's go. *Now.*"

Body still jittery, Ryan dropped his helmet and peeled off his gloves, barely hearing his teammates' solemn voices.

"Hope everything's okay, dude."

"Text me."

His world narrowed to Jake's gray T-shirt, as he followed him into the tunnel.

Something was wrong with his legs. It felt like walking through water. And the pain in his chest...was he having a heart attack? "Jake, man. Hold up."

"No." Jake powered ahead. "Move it."

"What're you doing?"

Jake's stride didn't break. "Getting you out of here before you blow your shot at the Bigs."

The dance floor teemed with grinding bodies—flashes of bare skin, red lipstick, and glittering jewels.

With a cocky grin, Jake jammed his hands into his pockets. "Like shootin' fish in a barrel."

Dixon, another guy he'd known since they were kids, tipped his chin. "I'm going for the hot blonde with the tight ass."

"That narrows it down," Jake said.

Ryan's friends burst out laughing and then spread out to claim their fun for the night.

When he'd left the stadium that morning to find Dixon waiting in a rented Mustang with Ryan's duffle bag stowed in the trunk, he'd jumped right in. At the time he hadn't known he was headed to the airport to join them at an exclusive singles resort.

But his team had lost the game—*because I crapped out*—and Ryan was in a shit mood. He'd let them and himself down.

A hot brunette sitting alone at a table wiggled her fingers to get his attention. He gave her a smile, but...yeah, not feeling it. Maybe a drink first? They'd arrived twenty minutes ago, and he'd been traveling all day. He needed to loosen up a little.

As he headed towards the bar, his phone vibrated in his pocket. He tensed. Pulling it out, he scanned a couple of the most recent texts.

Everything okay?

When you coming back?

Dude, you okay?

Damn, he hated lying to the guys.

When he saw a voicemail from his coach, his chest went tight. Either he returned the call now and made up a story about his family emergency or he ignored it and took this break.

He really needed one. If he'd stayed, he'd have kept fucking up. He needed to shake it off. Take a few days with his buddies. Get back to normal.

"Hey, there."

Ryan's head snapped up at the sound of a sultry voice. The accompanying face and body didn't disappoint. He shoved the phone back in his pocket. "Hey. Ryan O'Donnell."

"Carrie Winters. I saw the three of you standing there." She blew out a slow breath. "The trifecta of holy hotness. It's like winning the lottery."

His smile broadened. As athletes, they tended to get attention like that. Jake, at six-six, with his dark hair and olive skin, had women falling all over him. Dixon might've been shorter than the two of them, but he was a powerhouse of muscle. His blonde hair, shaggy and overgrown like a surfer, got him the attention his height and looks didn't.

"Can I get you something to drink, Carrie?" Unlike most island resorts with tiki lamps and strings of lights, Isla de los Amantes had gleaming black lacquer tables, silver vases filled with exotic orchids, and crystal chandeliers. A safe haven for wealthy singles, it was known for its Vegas attitude. *What happens on Santa Grenada stays on Santa Grenada.*

He made a move to the bar, but she stepped in front of him, planting her hands on his chest.

"Let's just skip to the part where I'm in bed with all three of you at once."

Yup. He really needed that drink. "How about we start with a beer?"

"I've got a better idea. Let's raid my minibar instead." She got up on her toes, her breasts brushing against him, and whispered in his ear. "I just got here." Gliding a hand from his shoulder to his biceps, she gave it a squeeze. "You're seriously the hottest man I've ever seen, and I can't wait to unwrap my welcome-to-paradise present."

Step one in letting loose stood before him. This woman was ready to get down and dirty, no strings attached. He should go for it.

Instead, he stepped sideways and moved around her. "I'm going to grab a beer. You want one?" He pushed through to the bar and lifted a finger to get the bartender's attention.

"You must be a newbie." Carrie cupped his ass and gave it a squeeze. "Because it doesn't work like that here. You don't need to buy me a drink or make small talk. We all want the same thing."

"Yeah? And what's that?"

"An escape from the real world. A chance to just go wild."

He grinned at her. "So, Carrie Winters, where's your real world?"

"Boston. You?"

"I go to school in Michigan." *But I'm supposed to be at a week-long tournament in Florida this week.*

"You're still in school?"

"Senior, but yeah. What do you do?"

"I'm a realtor, and I'm about four years older than you. I've never been a cougar, but that's what I love about this place. I can be whatever I want."

"And what do you want to be?"

An ocean-scented breeze fanned her hair out. Her skin-tight dress revealed a toned body with generous mounds of flesh bursting out of the deep neckline. "When I'm here? Fucking wild. I work in my dad's firm, so I have to be perfect. All the time. And I love it. I'm not complaining. I make a ton of money, and the clients come to me. But sometimes I need to let loose, you know?"

"I do." Christ, did he know.

Her features turned sultry. "Glad to hear we're on the same page. I've been coming to this resort for four years because there's no bullshit. You can just do your thing with anyone, anywhere, anytime. And there's no walk of shame. No worrying if the guy'll call you again. I love it."

He tugged at the collar of his shirt. Was it warm in here? He checked to see if he stood under a heat lamp.

"So, come on, gorgeous. What do you say we take that movie star smile up to my room? As sensational as it is, I'd love to replace it with something a whole lot filthier."

He appreciated her straight-forward approach—he did—but maybe what he needed was a work-out, a hot shower, and a good night's sleep. Start fresh tomorrow.

Just then Jake bustled up to them. "Hey, how's it going?" But before either could respond, he nudged Ryan with his elbow. "Can I talk to you for a sec?" Then, he turned to Carrie. "Will you excuse us?"

"Sure. We'll catch up later." She smiled and headed toward the dance floor.

Jake led him to the side of the outdoor bar. "How's it going?"

"Great, why?"

"Oh, I don't know. Remember when you struck out at the plate this morning?"

Guilt stabbed into him. "Back off, Jake."

"I was kind of hoping that very nice young woman could fuck some sense back into you."

And that's the problem with knowing someone all your life. His friend could see he wasn't into it. "Look, my head's not in it right now. I'm going to hit the gym and crash early."

"That's pretty much what you'd be doing if you were at school. So, yeah, you could go to the gym like you always do. Or, I don't know…" He gave a chin lift to Carrie, who'd already turned her attention to another guy. "You could motorboat the bodacious tits of that woman who clearly wants to climb you like a tree."

Jesus Christ.

"Maybe she's not your type? Not a problem, since you've

basically got a Babes-R-Us selection here. But, hell, man, look around. Every woman you see wants the same thing we do. That's the whole point of coming here—everyone gets what they want without the bullshit. So, come on. Who you bangin' first?" Jake gestured to the crowd like a game show host.

He took a step into Jake's space. "Don't push me."

Jamming his hands deep into his pockets, Jake looked thoughtful for a moment. "You want to know why we took you out of that game?"

The reminder hit like a fastball to the gut. *Christ.* He'd never lied to a coach in his life.

He'd never had to.

It made him sick to think his coach was worried about him, while Ryan was getting his ass groped at a resort.

"'Cause you're gonna blow. That's why. You're on the edge, and it's better to pull your ass out of there than let your coach, your agent, the *scouts*, watch you fuck up." He gave Ryan a meaningful look. "Number one shortstop in the country."

"I hear you. But let me do things my way. I appreciate you guys pulling me out of that disaster, but…" Ryan blew out a breath. "You've got to give me room."

Looking thoughtful, Jake scrubbed his jaw. "Not tellin' you anything you don't already know." He stabbed his finger into Ryan's chest. "But you need to go hard for a few days. Trust me on this. You're too fuckin' controlled. Yeah, all that discipline and focus is great—you wouldn't be a first-round draft pick without it—but you've got to hit that release valve sometimes, man. Take a few days to blow it all off. And, trust me, you need some good, hard fucking to get you loosened up and relaxed."

Damn, that rang true. Just hearing the words relieved

some of the pressure. His friend was right. He did need to go *hard.*

Jake spun around. When he spotted Dixon at the bar, he waved him over.

Dix gave a jerk of his chin in acknowledgment, then whispered in his companion's ear before making his way to them. "What's up?"

"Our man here needs a little help selecting tonight's entertainment." Jake shoved his hands in his pockets and turned to the dance floor. "Who's a good starter chick for a guy who's been monogamous the last six years?"

"Cut the shit." Ryan had ended things with Emma over Christmas break. "I've been single for three months."

They ignored him, as Dixon checked out the dance floor. "You want someone like Emma? Blonde, skinny?"

"I've been with other women besides Emma. We've broken up a lot over the last six years."

"Not the point. You always had Emma in the back of your mind. This time, you're totally free." Jake turned to him. "You are totally free, right?"

"Completely."

"Now that's what I'm talkin' about." Jake pointed to a curvy woman striding around the perimeter of the dance floor. "And see, the thing is, you can have fun with her tonight and not have to hang out with her tomorrow. *She* won't want to." His finger shifted to a woman who looked very much like Emma. Slender, long blonde hair, fragile. "Look at the way she's eyein' you, bro. Hungry little minx. I'll bet she's a tiger in the sack. What do you say? Feel like kickin' back and lettin' her do the work?"

Jake had no idea how appealing that sounded. After six years on-and-off with the same woman, Ryan had had enough of the dead fish routine. He'd loved Emma, of course, but begging for sex? Never again.

"That one." Jake's feral gaze landed on a sexy blonde with an hourglass figure, half-lidded eyes, and shiny red lipstick. "Now that's my kind of woman."

Irritation whipped through him. He'd had enough. "Have at it, man." He stalked off.

With all this energy barreling through him, he needed to go for a long, hard run. The moment he headed out, he saw a dark-haired woman kneeling on a bar stool, surveying the area with a concerned expression. In her white shorts and pale pink tank top, she didn't look anything like the other women in the bar. Her oversized white sweater drooped off one shoulder and didn't cover the ample breasts straining against the top. Her round ass stretched the cotton of her shorts, and when she licked her pink lips, biting down on the bottom one, a jolt of energy blasted through him.

Her.

He got the rules of this place now, understood no one came here for conversation. That suited him just fine.

Bailing on his team might've cost him a shot with the scouts. Bailing on his ex might cost him his lifelong relationship with her family—and her dad was practically a father to him. Even he could see that, for the first time in his life, he wasn't making the smartest decisions. But just then?

This woman with her rosy complexion, sexy as fuck mouth, and body so ripe he wanted to sink his teeth into her ass? He knew exactly what he wanted.

With every step he took toward her, his heart beat faster. When he reached her, electricity flashed across his skin. She was beautiful and undoubtedly the sexiest woman he'd ever seen.

It went against his nature to be so blunt, but what the

hell. He'd play by the resort rules. He stroked a finger down her thigh.

She jerked, looking down at him. "What the hell?"

Holding her fiery gaze, his breath froze in his lungs. "I want you." And, oh, man, did he want her.

"Excuse me?"

Not exactly the reaction he'd expected. *A little outside my comfort zone here.* But he wouldn't give up. "You. I want *you.*"

"Are you high?" She let out a huff of breath, yanking the sweater back up her shoulder. "Wow. That was super classy." Confusion turned to humor. "Yeah, for sure. Let me just shuck off my clothes and we can do it right here. Or did you want to drag me by my hair to the nearest cabana?"

Yes. But the outrage in her eyes doused his lust, leaving him flustered and uncomfortable. "Take it easy. I didn't mean…" He shook his head. "What a night."

She laughed. "Well, if that's been your approach, no wonder your night's not going so well. Little tip for ya? Start off with a simple hello. Then maybe offer to buy a girl a drink. Jeez."

Ryan tipped his head back and dragged a hand through his hair. What the hell was he doing here? He'd rather be sitting alone in his room working on code than trying to navigate the waters of an exclusive singles resort.

"Fuck it. Never mind." He struck off, thinking he'd check with the concierge for a good running route. But he didn't get more than a few feet before he realized he'd been a jerk. He turned back to apologize and found her climbing off the stool, her round ass hoisted high, her leg reaching for the floor. He took her arm, helping her.

Once she had her footing, she looked up at him. "Thank you."

Her long, dark hair gleamed in the yellow lights, and her

blue eyes were lit with intelligence and an irresistible spark. And he felt like a total ass for treating her the way he had. "Look, I'm sorry for touching you. I don't…I'm not like that." He let out a breath and scratched the scruff on his chin. "Can I buy you a drink?"

Her good humor seemed to fade. "Three things. I don't drink, I have zero interest in a one-night stand, and I really need to find my friend right now." Her phone clattered to the wood floor, and they both crouched at the same time to retrieve it. When she leaned forward, her breasts plumped in the top, and a surge of lust rushed him so hard his dick pressed uncomfortably against the buttons of his jeans.

He handed her the phone, his whole world narrowing to this woman who smelled like vanilla and flowers and looked so luscious he wanted to do filthy things to her.

She gave him a distracted, "Thank you," before touching the screen of her phone as she stood.

Following her out of the bar, he couldn't help catching her conversation. "Hey. I don't see Laura anywhere, and she's not answering her phone." She paused. "I said I can't find Laura." She was nearly shouting now. "I know, but she's got my wallet." Another pause. "I handed her my bag when we got off the boat so I could take some pictures. Anyhow, I'll go to the front desk and see if they'll loan me some cash, but then I'll jump in a taxi and come get you. Are you going to be all right until I get there?"

They were both headed to the lobby, so he couldn't miss the way her shoulders hunched and her arm wrapped across her stomach. "God, Kat. I can't believe this. Can you talk to the bartender? Is there someone there you can trust? Yeah, yeah, okay, don't worry. Let me get some money, and then I'm on my way."

Ryan stepped up to her. "What do you need?"

She lowered the phone from her mouth. "I'm seriously not interested. I mean, at *all*." Striding down the stone walkway, she continued her conversation. "You sure you don't want to call the police?"

"I'm not trying to hit on you. You obviously need help." But she ignored him. *Well, Christ.* When did he become the creep a girl had to get away from?

All right, enough. Time to put an end to this day. Screw the concierge. He'd head up to his room and change into gym shorts.

"Kat, I *am* hurrying. But I need cash for a cab, and I think town's at least twenty minutes away."

They'd reached the door to the lobby, so he held it open. Blocking her way, he pulled out his wallet, yanked out some bills, and thrust them at her.

She stopped, gazing up at him as though trying to figure out his motives. "Hang on a second," she said into the phone. "Are you sure? I mean, why are you doing this?"

"I'm paying for sex. How much will this get me?"

When her jaw dropped and her eyes went round, he gave her a disbelieving look. *Really?* She thought he was capable of *that?* "You need some cash. I'm happy to give you some."

"Kat? I'm good. I got it, so I'm on my way." She started to lower the phone, but then jerked the phone back to her ear. "Wait, Kat? Listen. Stay in the bathroom until I get there. Promise me you'll lock yourself in a stall. Okay, see you." She took the money. "I don't know what to make of you, but I need this, so, thank you. I'll pay you back tomorrow."

Ryan shoved his wallet back in his pocket. "Not necessary." He stepped aside, letting her go through the doors. She breezed past, leaving him in a cloud of her sweet scent.

He followed behind her. "Is your friend all right? I heard you talking."

"She went into town with some guy she met here." She glanced at him over her shoulder, as she headed across the wide-planked wood floor of the vast lobby. "He dumped her for someone else, and now she's stuck in a really scary bar. You know it's DJ week on the island, right? So the town's jammed with people, everyone partying like it's the end of the world, and she's scared to death."

"Is she in danger?"

"A bunch of drunken idiots had her backed against a wall. She managed to run into the bathroom, but she's afraid to come out. She can hear them outside the door."

"Do you need me to come with you?"

"I...what?"

Why did she still look like she couldn't trust him? *Him*, for Christ's sake.

Right. Because he'd touched her. Told her he wanted her. Had he really done that? He was more fucked up than he realized. "Do you have a plan for how you're going to help your friend against those guys?"

Her features fell. "I didn't really think about it, but no, I guess not."

"Then I'll go with you."

"I don't have time to argue, and I really could use the help of those nice muscles you've got there, so I'm not going to argue if you want to come." She strode forward, heading outside.

"I'll get a cab." As he made his way to the valet station, he thought about all those women in the bar down to party with him right then. He could be pounding babes and brews, just like his friends.

Instead, he was heading into town with the one woman at the resort who had no interest in him.

CHAPTER TWO

Five minutes later, they were on the road.

"Thank you for doing this. I'm Sophie Valentine, by the way."

"Ryan O'Donnell." He couldn't believe he'd come onto her the way he had. When he rubbed the scruff on his chin, he remembered what he looked like. Over the past three months, he'd let himself go. Let his hair grow out. He'd even grown chin whiskers. He was so used to being clean-cut he forgot he might look a little sketchy.

He wished like hell he'd gone with his own instincts tonight instead of being so forward. "Sophie, listen, I'm sorry for hitting on you like that."

"Yeah, what was that all about?"

He blew out a breath. "I don't know. Everyone keeps telling me how this place works, so I went along with it. I thought..." He shrugged.

"What do you mean *how this place works*? It's a resort on Santa Grenada. The rules of civility don't apply?"

"You do know what kind of resort this is, right?"

She leaned back in her seat, looking a little uncomfortable. "I mean, it's a singles resort. I get that. But you don't just touch a woman's *leg*. That's kind of skeezy, right?"

They'd reached the end of the golf course. Ryan watched out the window as the driver turned onto the dark road toward town. "Yeah, it's skeezy. I'm not usually like that. I'm sorry."

"It's okay." She reached for her phone. "I'm going to check in with my friend." Her thumb pressed the key pad. "Hey, how's it going?" The large sweater slid off her shoulder, but she didn't seem to notice as she wound a strand of dark hair around a finger. "I know I don't have to, but I'm worried about you. If you don't want me to keep calling, then send me a text every few minutes, so I know you're okay. I'm kind of freaking out here." She shot a look his way and gave him a soft smile. "But I'm bringing muscle, so it should be all right." And then she made a face and rolled her eyes. "Actually, yeah, I think he's exactly your type."

Pawning him off on another woman pissed him off, so he looked away and pulled out his phone. Time to listen to Coach's message. But before he could punch the button, a text came in. *Emma.*

He didn't want to deal with his ex.

Thinking about coming to see u. Been too long and I miss u.

Breaking up with someone he'd known since they were kids hadn't been easy, especially because he'd meant it this time. So, to keep things pleasant, he'd told her they could stay friends. It wasn't like he could cut her off. Not entirely. Her dad—his old Little League coach—meant a lot to him. Always would.

But damn. Flying in from Europe to see him? She knew he was in the middle of his season. Then again, she'd skipped college to take advantage of modeling contracts, so she'd never been in touch with college schedules.

"She's okay." Sophie pulled the sweater up over her shoulder and set the phone on her bare thigh. "She'll text to let me know how it's going."

He nodded, but his mind was on Emma. He suspected she didn't believe they were really over. They'd always gotten back together before, so her text probably launched her latest reunion plan.

But he didn't want her to even consider coming to see him. If they happened to be in town at the same time, that would be fine. But she needed to know the days when she could visit him at school were over.

He texted back. *Not a good idea. Sorry.*

"You okay?" Sophie's soft voice brushed across his skin like a feather, making it erupt in chill bumps.

He looked up. "Yeah, sure." He didn't want to deal with Emma just then, so he set his phone aside. "So what brings you to Isla de los Amantes?"

"Are you saying I don't look like the type who'd spend a week at a playground for rich twenty-somethings where anything goes?"

He grinned. "My ego's already taken a hit tonight. I'll pass on answering that one."

She gave him a blisteringly sexy smile. "Actually, I'm a last minute addition to my friends' spring break plans. Kat's the one who booked the trip."

"So it's Kat who wants to get funky?"

"Well, you'll have to ask her that, but I'm pretty sure that's not quite what she came here for. But she's great. You'll love her. She's beautiful and fun. You'll see."

"Sophie."

She looked up abruptly.

He must've sounded harsher than he'd intended. "Don't hook me up with your friend, okay?

Her lips parted softly, as she watched him, as though trying to figure out what he really meant. *Good.* He'd tell her. "I'm not a player. Never have been. Do me a favor and forget how we first met, okay?"

"Okay." Her phone buzzed, and she checked it.

Which gave him a chance to check his. Another text from Emma, dammit.

Are you mad at me? We've barely talked. I want to see you, ok?

Hell. For five minutes there, he'd actually forgotten about his troubles.

Sophie reached across the seat for him, her hand stopping just short of contact. "She says two women just came in fighting over which one gets stuck with the short guy. One of the girls says she's tired of always winding up with the fugly one." Her smile lit up the cab and sent a rush of warmth through him.

And then it struck him. He'd come for a break. He *needed* this break. So what the hell was he doing checking his phone, letting his real life intrude?

If he didn't take advantage of his time here, he'd go back to school as messed up as when he'd left. And then lying to his coach and teammates would have been for nothing.

He sent Emma a final text. *Not possible to see you this week. Won't be checking my phone much either. Talk later.*

Done. No more dealing with his ex till he got back to school.

Holding his finger down on the volume button, he silenced it. "So. Last minute addition? Your other plans fell through?"

The prettiest pink flared across her cheeks, and she looked away. "No, I got some really weird news and I just…I wanted to get out of town. And I've always wanted to come to Santa Grenada. There's so much to do here."

"Yeah? Like what?"

"Oh, this island's amazing. Did you know it has an active volcano?"

He shook his head. He knew nothing about it.

"And the resort's about twelve miles away from some great surfing. Well, depending on the season. So, I'ma get me some of that."

"Some surfing? Or surfers?"

"Please. I'm from LA. I got surfers on speed dial."

"Okay. And the weird news? Does it involve a surfer?"

"Oh." Anger drew her brows in. She waved a hand dismissively. "Not at all."

He waited for more, but she just said, "Long story."

He settled back in his seat and glanced pointedly out the window. Moonlight lent the forested landscape an eerie, ominous feel. No houses or streetlamps meant they were still miles outside of town.

She laughed. "Yeah, okay. What the hell, you're just a…"

He tensed. "What? A jock?" He didn't know why it mattered what she thought of him.

She waved a hand at him. "Oh, come on. I don't even know you." But her gaze lowered to his biceps. "You're a jock?"

"I play baseball for Michigan."

"Ah."

"So what, then? A skeez?"

She smiled. "No, I was just going to say you're someone I'll never see again, but that seemed rude, so I didn't say it."

"You're right. We'll never see each other again. So, go on."

"I'm sorry if I hurt your feelings."

God, she was cute. "You didn't."

"I know I did."

"I promise you my feelings weren't hurt."

"But you flinched. So, yeah, they were."

"I didn't flinch. Go on."

"Way to be self-aware." Her teasing smile did funny things inside his chest. "Okay, so, bottom line, my sister and brothers want to make some changes to our family business."

"And you don't?"

"Not at all. Our business has been around…well, let's just say that the core product we sell? My great, great, great, great, great grandmother started making it in Manchester, England in the eighteen hundreds. Don't bother counting my greats. I suck at math."

"And your parents? What do they want?"

"My parents passed away a while ago."

"I'm sorry to hear that."

"Yeah, sucks. But thanks."

"So, when you say family, you mean just the siblings?"

She nodded. "There're five of us.

"Anyone else against the changes? Or just you?"

Her phone buzzed, and she picked it up. "Just me." She smiled as she read the text. "Apparently, women can pee like race horses, too."

"Good to know." He waited while she responded to her friend. And then he pushed for more information. "What kind of changes?"

"We sell a variety of…products. They want to sell off the one that started everything."

"Why?"

She looked away. "You don't want to hear my crap. And I can't believe I took you away from tonight's fun. I'm sorry. I wasn't thinking."

"You were thinking about your friend. That's nice. And I wasn't having fun."

"Yeah, 'cause I cock-blocked you."

Watching those sexy lips form the word "cock" sent a rush of heat through him. A flash of her on her knees, his cock in her mouth, shot a punch of lust through his system.

She gave him a once-over. "I'm guessing no one can really block you, though. You probably get every girl you want." And then her eyes went wide. "Why on earth did you proposition *me?*"

"Because you're gorgeous." Heat flamed up his neck, burning his ears. *Smooth.*

The nearly full moon splashed its light onto her skin, making it glow. He spotted a house, set back a good bit from the road. Up ahead, lights from a gas station appeared. They'd hit the outskirts of town.

The screen of his phone lit up, and he looked down to see his teammate's name. If he read the text, he'd have to respond. He'd have to lie.

A warm hand settled on his, resting on the seat next to him. "Are you all right?"

He nodded, swiping his other hand across the dampness on his forehead. "Great." But when he looked at Sophie and saw the warmth in her eyes, it loosened something in him. "Ball players don't get spring break. We've got some important games this week." The way she looked at him, the intense focus, made him feel a closeness to her that made no sense.

He scrubbed a hand over his face. Why was he telling her this shit? He *didn't* know her. "The scouts come to Florida." His pulse jackhammered. "They're finalizing their lists. I should be there." His agent believed he'd be a first-round pick.

"But you're not?" Her voice softened.

"I'm not."

"Are you going to be kicked off the team?"

"Nah. My coach won't kick me off for this. But he'll do something."

"Why'd you do it?"

He never shared his shit. Didn't even talk to his closest friends about it. "I don't know. I just…"

"You just what?"

"I need a break. Training's year-round." A band tightened around his lungs, making it difficult to draw a full breath. "I've played baseball all my life, and once I sign, I'll be playing at a whole other level. I just wanted a break. A couple days to not be disciplined and focused and…perfect." Jesus, he could not *believe* he'd said all that to a stranger. He hadn't even said it to himself.

"So, before you get locked into your future, you want an escape from reality?"

He shot her a look. "Yes." He stuttered out a laugh. "*Yes.*"

She had the softest, sweetest smile. Nothing frantic or manipulative. Just warm. Engaged. "Well, I don't know. In the scheme of things, bailing for a few days isn't such a big deal, right?"

It could cost him the reputation he'd spent a lifetime building. But saying the words out loud would probably give him a heart attack. "I lied. To my coach, my teammates. I don't do that."

Her eyes warm with concern, she leaned closer. "So, if he's not going to cut you from the team, tell him the truth."

"He'll make me come back."

"With handcuffs? A SWAT team?" She gave his hand a squeeze. "Come clean. Tell him you're messed up in the head and you need this break. When you get back, you'll give him a hundred and ten percent."

The weight of sand bags lifted off his chest. He knew she was right. Even if he didn't do it right away, coming clean was the right answer. "I'm going to."

She unbuckled her seat belt and shifted closer to him. "It'll be okay, you know."

The sweater had slipped off her shoulder again. Streetlamps spilled pale yellow light onto her creamy white skin. Her breasts wobbled from the motion of the tires jolting over rutted roads.

With her sitting this close, his body heated up. She was beautiful, yes, but she was so fucking real, so warm and compassionate, so in the moment with him that he wanted to haul her onto his lap and kiss her.

"Everything always works out." Her voice was gentle, warm. "You know that, right?"

He nodded, completely captivated by her. He just...fuck, she was so sexy and soft and sweet.

"Do you want to play baseball? I mean, is this the future you want?"

That snapped him out of his lust-fog. "Of course. It's what I've worked for." He thought of his dad—all the time and money he'd put into building Ryan's future as a ball player. Quitting three months before grabbing the brass ring? *Not gonna happen.*

"You're sweating. Do you want to open your window?"

He didn't feel hot. He felt clammy. But he cracked it anyway, and the moist island air rushed in.

She watched him curiously, as if trying to figure him out. "If you didn't play, what would you do?"

"I'm *going* to play. That's not the point. I just want a break. That's all."

"You seem a little anxious."

He shrugged, tamping down the anxiety. "There'll be consequences for what I've done. And I don't know what they are yet."

"Okay. But, you know, just to throw it out there, lots of people play sports all the way through college but don't go pro. Maybe you worked so hard to be All American in high school and starting pitcher in college or whatever. If you've hit those marks, you don't necessarily have to keep doing it the rest of your life."

"No, I'm pretty sure I worked hard so I could make the majors." He gave her a smile, when what he really wanted to do was throw open the door and start running. Back to the bar. For that cold beer he never got. He cleared his throat, needing to talk about something else. "What about you? Are you expected to go into the family business?"

"I *want* to."

He loved the fierceness in her eyes. "So what will you do?"

"Hah." She tugged the sweater back up.

"What?"

"Nothing, it's just…" She gave him a mischievous smile. "You're entering dangerous territory."

"Hey, I just shared my crap with you. Come on. Your turn."

"You know this is a pretty serious conversation for people who literally just met."

He checked the driver's GPS. "We've got seven more minutes. Let's see just how deep we can go."

She smiled, and he felt the warmth of it down to his bones. "Fine. What will I do? Well, we haven't figured that out yet." She let out a frustrated breath. "Okay, it's like this. I'm the youngest. And when I say youngest, I mean my sister is eight years older than me. My parents popped out four kids, and then eight years later I came along. Which means my siblings have been running the company without me for a long time."

"Are you saying they don't have a job for you?"

"They'll *find* one for me." Her forehead creased. "But who wants to be given a token job? I graduate in two months, and they still haven't figured out what I'm going to do. If they think I'm going to hang out at the beach or…or spend my days shopping while they figure it out…well, that's not going to happen."

"What role do you want?"

For the first time, she looked at him with a tortured expression. "I don't know." She said it quietly, looking at him like she was completely lost. "I want to take my place in the company just like them. It's not like any of them were groomed for a specific role. I mean, my parents died, so my oldest brother took over as CEO. My second oldest brother took over my mom's IT job. The others just fell into place. But with me…there's no specific place." And then she gave a weak smile. "I suppose I could be a greeter. You know, wear a red vest and stand out front and hand out cookies every morning."

"Somehow I think you'd be wasted in that role. How do they see you?"

Her features pulled in, and she looked uncomfortable. "I don't know if they see me at all. I mean, they've always been in totally different phases of life than me."

"Didn't you say they wanted to sell the family business?"

"Just one part of it." She looked like she wanted to say more, so he waited. After a moment, she said, "Can you keep a secret?"

"I can."

She leaned toward him—even closer—exposing her inner wrist. That delicious vanilla and floral scent swirled around him. Holy shit, she smelled good. And then she tapped the tattoo. It took him a moment to make sense of it. "It's a heart."

"It's a *Crazy* Heart."

Valentine. "You're *that* Valentine?" Crazy Hearts were to Valentine's Day what Peeps were to Easter. It was *that* big a deal.

She glanced into the rear-view mirror, but the driver was now negotiating traffic, his features set in a scowl. "Shh."

Now the ink made sense. Heart-shaped, the cookie was a silvery gray—confectioner's sugar—with a raspberry jam heart in the center.

Her sweater fell off the other shoulder, too, so now all that bare skin was *right there*. And since she sat so close, he could see right down her tank top into the deep valley of her breasts. Desire pulsed through his cock. Honestly, it wasn't the spectacular tits. It was *her*. Everything about her. And now that he'd gotten to know her a little, he wanted her even more.

"So you're Crazy Hearts?" he asked, just to shake off the grip of lust.

She nodded. "We make more than just Crazy Hearts, of course." Her gaze narrowed. "Promise I can trust you?"

"Absolutely." She didn't know him, but not only didn't he talk about his own shit, he didn't talk about his friends', either.

"I shouldn't say anything, obviously. Your dad's probably the head of some venture capital firm that does corporate take-overs in the food industry. Which would explain why a guy your age is at an exclusive resort." She sighed. "I really should keep my mouth shut."

"My dad's in wealth management, so you don't have to worry about me."

"Wealth management means he handles money for those venture capitalists in the food industry."

"Good point. You still don't need to worry about me. My dad and I don't talk about things like that." But he missed the whispering, so he steered the conversation back. "It's not Crazy Hearts they want to sell, is it?"

She nodded, gaze flicking back to the rearview mirror. "You can't say anything, okay?"

"I won't."

"So you know how I said my siblings are so much older than I am? Well, they've all got kids now. They want to shift our focus to healthy snacks. They want to go green and be responsible guardians of the planet and all that."

"So make Crazy Hearts healthy."

She drew back from him. "No. They're perfect just as they are."

"They're processed shit made in a factory."

Her brilliant smile gave him a jolt. "Aren't they delicious?"

"I don't eat crap like that."

"Right. Athlete."

He nodded. "In high school, the baseball team used to sell Crazy Hearts. We'd deliver the orders ourselves."

"Of course you did. You must've made a killing."

"We did. Girls love a jersey."

"Please. Girls love all this." She waved a hand at him, taking him in from head to toe.

"Sophie Valentine. Did you just say I'm hot?"

"Well, yeah." She reached for his biceps and squeezed it. "What does it take to make something like this?"

"A lot of dedication. And no Crazy Hearts."

"When we get back to the resort, I'm going to give you one."

Why did that sound so salacious? "One what?"

"A Crazy Heart. What did you think I meant?"

"You bring them with you?" The cab braked, jerking them forward. When he looked out the window, he saw they'd hit a red light. Which meant they were in town. Disappointment slammed him. He'd enjoyed his time with her more than anything he could remember in a long time.

"Oh, sure. I learned early on that anywhere I go where people will figure out who I am, they'll be asking for Crazy Hearts. So I bring some and hand them out. Leave them for the cleaning staff and valets. They love it."

Her pride shifted his energy into a higher gear. "You shouldn't sell it."

"What can I do? I'm one vote out of five."

"Fuck that. They're your family. Convince them."

"They have an offer." She leaned so close he could smell the shampoo in her hair. "And it's really big. I mean, too-big-to-turn-down big." She clapped a hand over her mouth, eyes going wide. "I can't believe I told you that. Please don't tell anyone."

He tipped her chin, forcing her to look him in the eye. "*You* have an offer."

"What?"

"You. Not they. This is your family. You have a say."

Her eyes rounded. "Isn't it funny that I never thought of it like that? I just gave them all the power. But you're absolutely right." Her mouth softened, lips parting.

Oh, fuck, did he want to kiss this woman. His breath hitched. It was killing him to keep fighting off his hard-on.

Even after the light had turned green, the cab remained stationary. The boulevard was jammed with red taillights, the sidewalks packed with partiers.

"Get a lawyer."

She stiffened. "Against my family? I can't do that. I can't ruin my relationship with them over this."

"No, get a lawyer to brainstorm options. It's not black and white. It never is."

"What do you mean?"

She looked so hopeful. He wanted to fix her problem right then and there. "I mean there are creative solutions to every business deal. You just have to hire the right people to find them."

"Are you a business major?"

"Yeah." He shoved aside the familiar rise of irritation at his major. "And I'll bet you can find a way to make everyone happy."

"Like?"

"Like buying them out."

"I could never match the offer."

"You might not have to, depending on what rights you have. But maybe not all four of them are set on selling off Crazy Hearts. Talk to each one individually. Stop thinking about this as you against the block of them. Maybe one or two of them agree with you. Who's leading the charge on this? Is it one person or all of them together?"

"It's my sister. She just had her first baby. All through her pregnancy she was talking about how our processing affects the environment, how irresponsible we are, how we're poisoning children with hydrogenated oils. And then about a week ago, at my niece's birthday party, she announced the deal. She said it was an offer they couldn't refuse."

"The four of them took this action without you?"

"Yes, but I don't work at corporate yet, so why would they include me?"

He held her gaze so she heard him. "Because you're one of them. You're not an outsider, Soph. Look into it. See what the options are."

Those blue eyes warmed. "I will." Her hand wrapped around his wrist.

Lights from the city flashed into the car, splattering color all over them. He wanted to kiss that mouth, run his fingers through her hair. An image flashed in his mind of him thrusting into her from behind. Her long, dark hair wrapped around his hand, as he pulled her back for a deep, carnal kiss.

Jesus. He'd just met her. *Get a grip.*

Sophie pulled back a little, so he dropped his hand. "It's weird that I never thought about my options. I've just always seen it as me against them. But you're right. I'll talk to our lawyer. Thank you." She smiled up at him like he was some kind of hero, and not some guy who wanted to plough into her.

What would she be like in bed? He'd never get to find out, but he wondered what she'd look like on her back, stripped of her tank top and shorts.

Oh, fuck. He could see it so clearly—her dark hair splayed on the white pillowcase, her full breasts bouncing—he went hard as a pipe.

The cab jerked to a stop. Nothing but headlights and traffic everywhere.

She looked around, distraught. "Oh, no. This is terrible. How far are we?"

He checked the dashboard GPS. "Not far." He pulled a bill out of his front pocket and handed it to the driver. "We'll get out here." The driver eyed him questioningly but took the cash.

Ryan got out, reaching back to help her out of the cab.

"We don't even know where it is." She looked around.

"Two blocks away."

"Are you sure?"

He slammed the door behind him, took her hand, and they wove through traffic to the sidewalk. "Positive. Saw it on his GPS."

She stopped just for a moment to take it all in. "Oh, my God."

Everywhere around them people spilled out of bars and danced in the streets. Locals leaned out apartment windows shouting at passersby. There was beauty in the chaos, though. The blue, gold, and red flag of Santa Grenada hung off street lights, and banners filled shop windows. Everything throbbed with color and life.

"What kind of festival is this?" he asked.

"Electronic music. All the big DJs come here for it. It's not as big as Ibizia, but it's pretty close."

She pulled out her phone, punched a number, and waited. "Hey, Kat, we're here, just getting out of the cab. Be there in five minutes."

As they made their way through the mob, Ryan found himself clutching her hand more tightly. He didn't want to lose her.

No, but really. Even though he'd just met her, he didn't want to lose her.

CHAPTER THREE

Sophie Valentine took one look at the run-down, dirty bar and wondered what she'd have done without Ryan. What had she been thinking, charging out here on her own?

Dozens of people lined up on the sidewalk waiting to get in. "Should we go in the back way?"

He couldn't hear her over the noise. Cars barely moved down the crowded street; bass thumped out of them, each blasting a different tune. The people looked rough, happy, and completely wasted.

She got up on her toes, holding onto his shoulder. "Go around back?"

He leaned down, mouth right near her ear. "Not walking down an alley in this neighborhood. Let's just go in."

She gazed up at the tall, muscled guy who'd given up his plans to help her. Touching his arm, she pulled him closer, making sure she had his attention. "Thank you. For coming with me." She gestured to the rough crowd. "You were right. I shouldn't have tried to come alone."

This man, with his devastating smile and movie star good looks, stood apart from everyone else. His hard body, sculpted muscles, and broad shoulders made him look pure badass. But when he looked at her, something changed, his expression softened. A hint of vulnerability that made it seem like she somehow affected him.

He didn't answer her, just nodded, looking a little flustered.

Letting him go, she drew in a breath and faced the entrance. "Let's do this."

"Wait. Give me your cell phone." She handed it over, and he punched in his number. Finished, he shoved the phone into the pocket of his worn jeans.

He reached for her elbows, drawing her to him. Standing close enough to feel the heat of his body and smell the soap on his skin made her breath catch in her throat.

"Stay with me. At all times, I want your hand in mine, got it?"

With his intimidating height, not to mention powerful muscles, she wasn't about to argue. He was her best line of defense. Hell, he was her *offense*. "Got it."

As she gazed up at this incredibly good-looking man—a man hot enough and cocky enough to be a model—she knew Kat would go crazy for him. And, since Sophie wasn't into hookups, she might have to hear all about Kat's *funky* adventures with the hot baseball player over the next few days.

"Um, before we go in there and…" *You meet my gorgeous, sexy friend.* "I just want to say that I hope everything works out for you."

His features pulled in tight. "Aren't we going to see each other again?"

"I've got plans, like, every day. And you're…we'll be doing different things."

He clearly didn't like what she was saying, but his hand slid down her arm to grasp hers, and then he used his bulk to push through the crowd. Body odor, booze, and cologne assaulted her as she released his hand to push her arm through his, locking her body against him.

Once inside, the music and roar of conversation hit her. Together, they made their way through the crowd to the bathrooms. Letting him go, she pushed the dirty, sticky door open and called, "Kat?"

"Oh, my God." Her friend knocked the door of the stall open so hard it jerked on its hinges and slammed back shut. Kat raced toward her, throwing herself into Sophie's arms. "Get me out of here."

"Are you all right?" Sophie pulled back to look at her, noticing the way her silk blouse hung oddly off her shoulder. "What happened?"

"They were drunk and pawing at me. When I ran off, one of the guys grabbed my shirt. I got away, but they scared the crap out of me. God, Sophie. It was horrible. I'm so glad you're here."

Her friend looked pale, in spite of the perfect make-up she always wore. "Okay, let's go."

"What if they're still there?"

"It's so crowded they'll never even notice you."

Her friend looked hesitant. "I kind of kicked one of them in the junk."

"Of course you did." She smiled. "But don't worry. I've got some muscle with me."

She stepped out of the bathroom to find her big, hulk of a friend waiting right there. God, he looked hot, standing there in his snug black Polo with his arms folded over his formidable chest.

"That's him?" Kat unabashedly checked him out. "Holy shit."

"I know."

But Ryan didn't look amused. "Ready?"

"Can I have a minute to take in all the hotness that's you?" With a shake of her long, blonde hair, Kat gave him a teasing look.

"Are you kidding me right now?" Sophie nudged her. "You've been hiding out in a bathroom stall for an hour, and you're hitting on my new friend? He gave up his night to help us out."

She saw the way Ryan's features changed, softened with appreciation, as he looked at her.

"Fine, let's get out of here." Kat pushed forward. "But I don't know what you expected me to do when you brought me a guy like that."

"He's not your blind date. Let's go, so he can get back to what he was doing."

Her friend grabbed her arm, leaning close to her ear for a private conversation. "Okay, but once we're out of here, I'm naming you godmother of our firstborn."

Ryan reached a hand around Sophie's waist, pulling her hard up against him. "Everything all right?"

"She's shaken up, but yeah." She stepped back a little. "Kat, this is Ryan O'Donnell."

Kat held out a hand. "Thanks so much for coming."

"Oh, my God, this isn't a cocktail party." She'd known Kat would be all over Ryan, so it really shouldn't bother her. She wouldn't let it. She headed down the hallway.

But Ryan grabbed her hand. "What'd I tell you?"

She looked up at him, a little surprised to see him so serious, but then she saw Kat on his other side, equally close, and she just nodded. Whatever. It wasn't like she wanted to hook up with him anyway. *Kat* had come here to meet guys. *Not me.*

Wrapping an arm around her shoulders, Ryan held her close to his body and maneuvered the three of them toward the door.

A guy stepped forward, blocking their way. "There she is." Within seconds, they found themselves surrounded by a bunch of scary looking dudes.

"You're not leaving, are you?" One of them reached for Kat.

Ryan shifted her slightly behind him. He didn't say a word, just stared at the guy. If anyone looked at her like that, she'd probably pee in her pants. But Ryan didn't betray an ounce of fear. He looked alert, assessing.

"Hey, man." With his long hair, leather vest, and heavy boots, the guy looked like a biker. "Looks like you got a bitch of your own. You're not gonna get greedy and keep two of 'em, are ya?"

Another of the guys stepped forward, a hard gleam in his eye. "She's not leaving until I get my dance."

Kat stepped closer. "He's the one I kicked in the junk."

The muscles in Ryan's arm tensed, so he must've heard. She didn't know how to call the police in Santa Granada, and things were about to get out of hand. Sophie scanned the area for help. Were there bouncers? A bar this crowded must have security of some kind.

Ryan squeezed her hand, and she looked up at him.

Quietly, he said, "On the count of three, take her and run out the back. Go to the same place the cab dropped us and wait for me."

"I'm not leaving you alone here—"

He flashed her a look that brooked no resistance, and she understood. If he had to worry about them, he stood no chance of escaping himself.

"One, two…" He released both of them, pulled a chair out from under a guy, and held it in front of him, blocking the attack of five angry drunks.

"Oh, my God." Kat stood there frozen, horrified.

Just as quickly, Ryan grabbed a second chair, wielding one in each hand, as the guys moved in.

"Let's go." But Kat wouldn't budge. Sophie grabbed her arm and towed her as she fought her way through the crowd. They slammed through the emergency exit at the back of a long hallway and found themselves in a filthy alley that smelled of rotten garbage.

Shaking, Sophie forced herself to think which way she needed to go.

"Is he going to be okay?" Kat had her eye on the door, and Sophie worried she'd go back in.

"He's better off by himself than burdened by us."

"But he's all frat boy, you know? He doesn't stand a chance with those guys. They're, like, bikers or something."

"He told us to go, so we're going. That's the only thing we can do. Even if I could call the police, by the time they got here, the fight would be over. Now, let's go." She took off down the alley, Kat stumbling along in her wedges beside her. Fear squeezed her lungs, making it hard to catch her breath.

Just as she hit the boulevard at the end of the alley, she glanced behind her.

Ryan. All that hard-packed muscle bunched as he hauled ass toward her. God, he even ran like a movie star in a chase scene.

She started back for him, but he waved her on. Trusting him, she grabbed Kat's hand and turned onto the main boulevard.

As soon as she got to the spot where the cab had dropped them, she stepped into the street to flag a taxi. Kat leaned against the side of the building, bent over, chest heaving. "Are you all right?" Sophie called.

Her friend waved her off.

Ryan caught up with them seconds later. It looked like he was coming straight for her, but at the last minute, he veered and went to Kat instead.

A rush of humiliation stung her nerves. *This isn't a competition, you idiot.* Sophie was obviously fine, while Kat crouched on the sidewalk, head between her knees.

And then she saw a car door open just down the street. The lighted box on top flipped on. "Got one." She took off to claim the cab before someone else did.

As soon as the couple got out, Sophie slid right in. "Can you please take us to Isla de los Amantes?"

The eyes peering at her in the rear-view mirror met hers in acknowledgment.

Kat, looking flushed and slightly disheveled, slid into the middle seat. And again Sophie felt that pang of jealousy that Kat would get to sit next to Ryan. Which, of course, was completely stupid. He'd come to the resort to get laid. So Sophie could get with him if she wanted. *He's obviously interested.*

You. I want you.

Funny how when he'd said those words to her, she'd thought he was a complete dick. And now...now those words slid into her system all hot and spicy.

But then the car door slammed.

"Where's he going?" Kat swiveled around to watch him jog around the back of the cab and open the door on Sophie's side.

He nudged her over. With a confused expression, Kat shifted over. And then Sophie was sandwiched between them. His big body pressed against hers, a wall of heat.

"Well, hello, Awesome." Sophie looked him over to make sure he was all right. He sat close enough that she could feel his heavy breaths. "Are you hurt?"

"Nah."

Thrilled beyond reason that he'd chosen to sit beside her, she couldn't keep the grin off her face. "Now aren't you glad you train so hard?"

"Hey, thank you so much." Kat leaned across her, letting her shiny, straight hair spill forward. "I can't believe you did that for me."

"No problem." He barely even looked at Kat.

Noticing a smudge at the side of his head, Sophie scraped his disheveled hair back to see it more clearly. "You got clocked."

"It was nothing."

"Are you sure?" God, what if those men had had *knives*? She glanced at the hand resting on his thigh. Were his knuckles bleeding? She leaned across him, and he drew a sharp breath. "Your ribs?"

He shook his head. Lifting his hand, she checked the knuckles. They looked swollen and red. "Did they hurt you?"

"Don't worry about it." He said it evenly, but she wasn't convinced he wasn't hurt.

She let go of him. "Okay, but that was a big thing you did for us."

"I'm fine." He tilted his head back and closed his eyes.

She took in his incredibly fit body, the thick biceps, broad shoulders, and tapering waist. And…holy cow. It was impossible not to notice the very large bulge in his jeans.

She jerked back, flashing a look at Kat, who just smiled at her. She gave Kat a *What the hell* look. Did fighting get a guy hard? Or was it her?

He opened one eye. "You tell the driver where we're going?"

"Of course."

He reached for her hand and put it on his thigh. The simple gesture sent a wash of warmth through her. She didn't understand this...*thing* between them.

Kat leaned forward again, touching his arm. "I can't believe you took on five guys."

"I didn't. I held them off with a chair." He opened one eye. "And then I ran like a girl."

Both she and Kat burst out laughing. Not what they expected to hear from a wall of muscle like him. And then he sat up. A big warm arm wrapped around her shoulders. She breathed in the clean cotton of his shirt and something masculine that was uniquely him.

"And what if I'd lost the fight?"

She gazed up at him, at that delectable mouth and those warm brown eyes, and a shock of connection struck the center of her chest. "Not possible."

"Yeah? What makes you so sure?"

"Oh, come on. You've got winner written all over you."

That sensual mouth curved into a smile, and he started to speak, when Kat said, "Oh, my God, what is going on here? This is unbelievable. We're never going to get back to the hotel."

Sophie looked out the window. They hadn't even reached the end of the street. "I told you about the festival."

"I know, but I didn't think it would cover the entire town. I thought it'd be at some stadium or something. God, what a mistake. I don't even know what I was thinking going off with some guy. I'm at this amazing resort, where I can have anything I want, and I wind up ditched at a disgusting bar. I'm seriously going to find a chaise and plant myself in it for the rest of the week."

"You're not coming with me tomorrow night?"

Kat turned toward her. "You are *not* going to the festival. You see the type of people here."

"I want to check it out."

Ryan's body tensed beside her. "Soph."

God, did he hear himself? *Soph*. He talked to her like they were old friends. "What?" She caught his expression of disapproval and said, "I'm sure lots of people will be going to it. I'll check with the concierge."

"You should just stay at the resort," Kat said. "That's the whole point of coming to a place like this."

She leaned into her friend. "I don't think we're here for the same reasons."

With his eyes closed, Ryan said, "What're you here for?"

Since she'd already told him about her plans, she assumed he was talking to Kat. She glanced out the window. Fortunately, the driver had turned onto a less crowded street. They seemed to be out of the worst of the traffic now.

"We've never really done a legit spring break before, and this is our last chance before we graduate." Kat shrugged. "I looked into a ton of resorts, but this place seemed perfect. It's a more upscale way to hang out with the right kind of guys."

"I'm not sure they want to hang out for the same reason you do, Kat."

"What does that mean?"

"I'm just saying people are here to party. Let loose. They're not looking for anything serious."

Ryan leaned forward. "They wanna fuck."

Kat's eyes flared. "Why do you say it like that?"

"A guy basically told me he wanted to have sex with me. Like, instantly. No, *Hey, how ya doin*? Or, *Can I buy you a drink*? Just, *Hey, let's do it.*"

"Are you serious?" She seemed flustered. "That's not...I mean, come on, that was *one* guy. Not everyone's like that. You meet losers in bars all the time. He's probably just a jerk."

"I had the same experience." Ryan didn't seem the least bit affected by her commentary.

Sophie laughed at her friend's horrified expression. "Whatever. We're still going to have fun."

"I can't believe it." When they both just looked at Kat, color rose in her cheeks. "That's so not what I wanted."

"It's not big a deal." But she knew for Kat it was. They graduated in two months, and Kat didn't want to go out into the world alone. She wanted to find love…at a singles resort. "We'll hang out, relax. Come on, it's a gorgeous island. We'll make the best of it."

"I'm not here to relax."

"I know that." She gave her friend's hand a squeeze. "You still might meet someone. You never know."

"Not if they just want to hook up with me and move onto the next girl. God, what a waste of time."

"What am I missing here?" Ryan asked.

Sophie wondered how Kat would answer.

"I'm twenty-one and I'm still single." She shot Ryan a look. "And don't give me any feminist crap. The ladies fought for our right to choose, and I want to be in a relationship." She stared at the palms of her hands. "I'm graduating college, and I don't even have a job lined up. I'm just…I don't even know what I'm doing with my life. And I just thought if I put myself in a target-rich environment—"

"A what?" Ryan looked totally confused.

"You know. A place where you'll meet people who're similar to you. An exclusive singles resort seems like the perfect place for me to meet a guy." Kat rested her head against the window. "I'm going to become one of those pushy Beverly Hills real estate agents, aren't I?"

"What's your major?" Ryan asked.

Kat rolled her eyes. "Psychology. But I don't want to be a therapist anymore."

"Go to graduate school," Ryan said. "Be a lawyer or get an MBA. That'll put you in a very specific pool of men."

"That's a good point. I just…in a million years I never would have imagined graduating college with nothing to show for it." She tilted her head back and shielded her eyes with a hand. "Seriously, you guys. What am I going to do? I am *not* moving back in with my mom."

"You can work for us," Sophie said. "Meanwhile, apply to graduate programs for next year."

"Work in a factory? In Long Beach?"

Sophie burst out laughing. "We have administrative offices, too, you know. But, yes, they're in Long Beach." When she leaned back, she kind of melted into the space Ryan made under his arm. A strand of hair fell onto her cheek, and he gently stroked it off her face.

Kat noticed, and she waved a finger between them. "What's going on with you two? Do you know each other?"

Sophie pulled away from him. "Of course not."

"I'm the one who wanted to fuck her."

His deep voice made the statement sound even harsher than he might have intended. Heat flamed up her neck, and Kat looked comical in her shock.

"But she put me in my place." The arm already wrapped around her shoulders squeezed.

She gave Kat a reassuring smile. "And now we're just friends."

He hitched an eyebrow, but she pressed her lips together and gave him a look that said, *Don't be getting any ideas, buddy.*

"Okay." Kat didn't sound like she believed her.

Oh, please. She'd never had a one-night stand in her life. And she certainly wouldn't start now.

CHAPTER FOUR

As the cab turned into the resort, Sophie's heart squeezed. Her time with Ryan was up. Once they got out of the cab, they'd go their separate ways. She'd go off on her adventures, and he'd get lost in a sea of willing women.

Whatever. She couldn't think about it. She had a week to enjoy herself. And, better still, she might be able to save Crazy Hearts. As soon as she got to her room, she'd call Barry. See if there was anything she could do to prevent the sale.

The moment the cab came to a stop under the portico, Kat got out. Ryan kept his arm around Sophie, leaning down like he was about to say something, but she didn't want to hear it. She didn't want to look into those beautiful topaz eyes—the vulnerability that belied his gorgeous features and outrageously masculine build.

So, she slid out after Kat and followed her friend into the lobby. With every step she took away from him, panic grew. She didn't want to leave him. She wanted to grab his hand and whisk him off to her room. Order room service, laugh under the covers, and stay up all night talking.

Gah. Stop it. She didn't even know the guy.

She started off toward the elevators, just wanting to get

away from him, but seriously, how rude was that? Racing off without saying goodbye? She turned back and stepped right into Ryan's solid chest. She retreated so quickly her butt slammed into the edge of the concierge's desk. "Hey, so, thank you again. I owe you a lot."

"Pay it to me in Crazy Hearts."

"You don't eat Crazy Hearts."

"Tonight I do. Shaking things up, remember?"

Kat joined them, resting her hand on Ryan's arm. "You guys heading to the bar?"

She had to consciously squelch the stab of jealousy at seeing her friend touch him. *See, that's exactly why I don't do hookups.* She got too emotionally attached. When she loved, she loved with everything in her.

"I am." He looked at Sophie intently.

"I'm going to finish unpacking." She gave Ryan what she hoped was a sincere smile. "Thanks for talking to me tonight. You gave me some great ideas. Anyhow, I'll see you guys later. Goodnight." She started for the bank of elevators, when she heard Ryan call her name.

God, what did he want? He needed to leave her alone. Because, no, she didn't do hookups, but maybe that was because she'd never been tempted before.

But she wouldn't give in because she could guarantee that tomorrow he'd be unleashing all that intensity, all that intimacy, on another girl.

Keep walking.

The click clack of heels on wood snapped her out of her thoughts. "Sophie, wait up."

At the sound of her friend's voice, she slowed.

"Sweetie, what's going on?" Kat touched Sophie's shoulder.

"Nothing. I've been traveling all day. I just want to unwind a little and go to bed."

"Oh, come on. I saw you."

"Saw what?"

"With him. Don't pretend nothing's going on with you and Zac Efron back there."

"Zac Efron?"

"As if Ryan isn't an even better version? Zac, only hotter, taller, and bigger? And he's so obviously into you."

"*If* he's interested, he wants to have *sex* with me."

"Yeah, I got that." She fanned herself. "Has any guy ever said it to you like that?"

I'm the one who wanted to fuck her. He'd said it with such intensity. "No. But so what? You're saying I should be flattered because a really hot guy wants to do me?"

"Uh, yeah." She laughed. "Come on, we're at Isla de los Amantes. And don't tell me you're here to explore the island, Soph. Because you're not going to be on your death bed recalling that time you snorkeled on Santa Grenada. You're going to remember that incredibly gorgeous, hard-bodied guy who lusted after you and took you so hard you saw stars." She glanced over her shoulder, but Ryan was gone.

"Well, when you put it *that* way." She tried to laugh, but she wasn't good at faking. "Come on, you know me better than that. I'll pass."

"You could be walking away from the love of your life. And you'll never know unless you take a chance. There *is* something between you two. Anyone can see it. What do you have to lose?"

Her heart. She wasn't like Kat, who slept with a guy hoping it would turn into a relationship. Sophie was the opposite. She'd only sleep with someone after she got to know him. "I think you know me well enough to know that if I had sex with him, I'd feel like crap the next day. There's just no way I can watch him getting busy with other girls the rest of the week." She drew a breath, held it, before saying, "But you should go for it."

Kat seemed to think about it. "Are you sure?"

Was she sure? What if Kat was right? What if she and Ryan did have some special connection? If she gave it a few more days…*Oh, my God. Listen to me trying to turn an island hookup into a happily ever after.* She graduated college in two months. She wasn't even looking for "The One."

She shook it off. "Positive. Go get him."

At home when she couldn't sleep, Sophie got up, checked her emails, Facebook, and Snapchat, and then climbed back into bed. After that, she'd usually drop like a stone. But, with the time change and the news she'd gotten from Barry, she'd gotten way too energized.

She'd needed to get out of her room.

But now, stepping out of the elevator, she hesitated. What if by some fluke she happened to pass Ryan and some woman making out? Or Ryan and *Kat*?

Oh, come on. Would she really let that possibility limit her this week? *Not a chance.*

What was the big deal anyway? She'd known him all of an hour.

As she pushed through the doors that led to the pool, the smell of chlorine overwhelmed the island air. Laughter caught her attention, and she realized the place was hopping even at two in the morning. As she passed the huge pool, with its caves and waterfalls, she heard the sound of water slapping against tile and the gentle moans of a man and a woman in a serious clutch.

She focused on getting down to the beach. With the news she'd gotten from Barry, she needed to call her sister and have the conversation she should have had instead of booking a flight to the island.

Another burst of laughter and a feminine squeal had her glancing over to see a group of people inside a hot tub. A woman straddled a guy's lap, while the others chatted and drank beer. The water bubbled like a cauldron, while steam swirled into the air.

She'd seen Kat in action so many times—the way she threw herself at a guy as if she'd known him forever. Most guys jumped right in, playing along with the instant intimacy. Usually, they took what she offered and never called again.

Sophie never wanted to be that girl. Just as she passed the hot tub, a pair of eyes looked up and met hers.

Ryan. Surrounded by women. Guys, too, but Sophie only saw the two women plastered to his sides. The shock of it traveled along her nerves.

Just what she'd expected him to be doing. But seeing it?

Anxiety quickened her step until she finally made it to the archway where pavement gave way to beach, and the smell of chlorine gave way to salty ocean air. The minute her toes hit the still-warm sand, they curled.

It hurt to see him like that but, really, it was exactly what she needed to finally put the whole Ryan O'Donnell thing to rest.

A row of double-wide chaises lined up on the beach beckoned her. She needed to wipe the image of him in the hot tub from her mind or else it would play on repeat for the next six days.

He'd never misled her. She'd known exactly why he and his friends had come here. So it was done. She could blot Ryan O'Donnell out of her mind for good. Concentrate on all the fun plans she'd made.

She stretched out on one of the teak chaises, the cushion

damp from the moist air. The steady sound of waves hissing against the shore calmed her down. She gazed up at the perfectly clear sky, glittering with millions of stars, and let the sea spray spatter over her bare skin.

"Sophie?" That familiar deep voice set her body humming.

Her legs stretched out, and she turned to Ryan with a forced smile. "Hey."

He stood before her in nothing but a wet T-shirt and board shorts that clung to his body so tightly she could see every angle of his musculature. The moment she realized she could see the outline of his semi, heat exploded in her chest.

She tore her gaze away.

"Everything okay?"

"Sure." She seriously had to get away from him. But when she started to get up, he motioned her to stay put.

Sitting down on the edge of her chaise, he pulled the clinging shirt away from his body. "Can't sleep?"

"Did you hook up with Kat?"

He reared back. "No. I…" He blew out a breath, shaking his head. "Can we not talk about who I'm going to hook up with?"

Okay, she'd just been friend-zoned. And that was good, right? He was being respectful. He understood she wouldn't sleep with him, and he still wanted to hang out with her. That was nice.

She needed to buck up because they'd be around each other the rest of the week. Pushing past her disappointment, she focused on her good news. "Guess what?"

He shifted, lifting a knee onto the edge of the chaise and clasping his ankle. "What?"

Energy sparked and snapped between them. By his bright smile, she knew he felt it, too. "I talked to our lawyer.

He told me the company's run by a family trust. And it's set up that way for this very reason, so that one generation can't undo the work of the generations before it. He said my sister would need one hundred percent agreement of the beneficiaries of the trust. Meaning, my vote is as powerful as each of theirs. It can't be four against one. Isn't that cool?"

"Very cool."

"He also said that the trust only distributes half the profits to us each year. The other half goes into the trust, so he thinks it may be possible for me to take out my share and buy out the ones who don't want to own Crazy Hearts. And the thing is." She sat up in her excitement. She started to speak, but she didn't anticipate his fingers sliding into the hair at her temple, stroking it away from her face.

She swallowed, her breathing turning shallow. She wished he wouldn't do that.

"Go on."

"Um…what was I saying?"

He smiled. "The other half of the trust."

"You were listening."

"Of course."

"My family never really listens to me. They're great, don't get me wrong, but they just don't have time to talk beyond getting the basic facts. Plus, of course, three of them are men, so they're all, Can you just get to the point? Anyway, I—"

"I like listening to you. You're full of life. And you're smart." He paused. "And you're incredibly beautiful."

She had no words. After the blood pounding in her ears subsided, she said, "Do you have a girlfriend?"

"What? No." He rubbed the back of his neck, looking uncomfortable. "Why would you ask that?"

Because he was getting her all stirred up, making her want what she couldn't have.

Yeah, the whole friends thing? Not possible. She was too attracted to him. She'd chat with him for a few minutes and then go back to her room. And then avoid him the rest of the week. "I just wondered. You said you weren't a horndog, and yet…" She tipped her head, indicating what she'd seen in the hot tub.

"I just got out of a six-year relationship. I'm trying to have some fun."

"Six years? That's…wow. That's a long time."

"Yeah."

"Why'd you break up?"

If he looked uncomfortable before, now he looked like she'd put spiders on his feet. "It was time."

"Can I see her?"

"No." He tensed. "Why?"

"I just want to see the woman you loved for six years."

He searched her expression, and she saw the moment he gave into her. He pulled his phone out of his board shorts and started scrolling through pictures. "Here."

She had to lift the screen away from the resort lights behind them. When she got a good angle, she saw a model. Not just a good-looking woman, but an actual model posing in a swimsuit. "Cute. Let me see your real girlfriend. Not the fantasy version."

"That's her. She's a model."

"Of course she is." She threw herself back down on the chaise. "She's gorgeous."

He turned to stretch his long body out beside her, nudging her to give him more room. "You know what's funny? After six years with someone you don't see her physical beauty. I've actually known her most of my life. She's my coach's daughter."

"Your Mich U coach?"

"No. Her dad coached Little League. He's the reason I chose baseball."

"That's so nice. Did you ever tell him that? I bet he'd love to know how he inspired one of his players."

"Oh, he knows. He practically raised me."

She supposed that could mean a lot of things, but she wouldn't press.

"Things weren't so great at home, so he took me in. Fed me, helped me with my homework. He's a good guy."

"You're lucky you had him. Are you not close with your parents?"

The silence that followed was weighted enough to make her worry about his family life. He sighed. "My mom's an alcoholic."

"I'm sorry." She said it so quietly it got snatched under the sound of a crashing wave. But she knew he heard because his features softened.

"She's truly a victim of her disease, so we don't see her anymore. But when I was a kid, it was bad. She and my dad...there was a lot of fighting. Home wasn't a good place to be. I think Coach Ed got what was going on. Actually, I don't know what he got. Funny how I never really thought about that. I guess when no one came to pick me up enough times he got tired of waiting around and just took me home with him."

"He probably liked you. He cared."

"Yeah. Maybe. Anyway, so, I grew up with Emma. As a kid, she was all legs and crooked teeth. But by the time we hit high school, she'd turned into a beauty. It changed her. She got a lot of attention for her looks."

"I can imagine. Does she work a lot?"

"She does, but it's not the high end stuff. She works in Europe and Africa, mostly."

"Is that why you broke up?"

"Yes. I only date high-end models."

His delivery was so serious it took her a moment to realize he was kidding. And when she did, she burst out laughing. But then he watched her with this look in his eyes—all hunger and awe—and it sobered her right up. She cleared her throat. "I *meant* did you break up because you don't see each other enough?"

"Not at all."

Again, she waited. But this time she didn't think he'd answer.

"We broke up a lot."

"What made it permanent?"

He seemed really uncomfortable. She was pushing for answers he didn't want to give. "It's okay. I'm being nosy." Reaching for her phone, she started to get up.

Ryan clamped a big palm on her thigh. "I don't like to talk about her. It's not cool."

"That's about the nicest thing I've ever heard. Most guys I know don't have any problem trashing an ex."

"Yeah, well. She's not a bad person. She's just…" He blew out a breath.

"You miss her?"

He gazed up at the sky. "God, no."

"I heard somebody say you shouldn't break up until you've resolved all the emotional issues."

"It's over. Trust me on that."

She wondered what he wasn't saying. Had Emma done something? "Are you trying to convince me or yourself?"

"No, Jesus. It's over. You can't imagine how glad I am it's over. But everyone knows us together, and they can't see me as separate. So they bring her up all the time." He swung his legs off the chaise, turning his back to her. Hands roughing up the hair at the back of his neck, he stared out at the sea. "How's Emma? When you getting back with Emma? Drives me fucking crazy."

So under that calm façade, that shiny surface, roiled a very complicated man. Why did he hold so much inside?

After a few moments, he got up, dug some pebbles out of the sand, and hurled them, one by one, into the ocean. And then he turned to her with a wild look in his eye. "I don't love her like that."

"Like what?"

"Like a boyfriend. I was with her six years. I'm close to her family. It's not easy to break up with someone you've known that long. She's got issues. She needs me."

"You like to be needed?"

"No, it's not that. Don't you have friends you've known a long time, and when they need you, you just have to be there?"

"Yes, definitely. But I don't think you have to stay romantically tied to her. That isn't fair to either of you."

"I know that." He crashed onto the chaise, and he stretched out alongside her. "Of course I know that. She just has a way of getting to me."

"You mean she manipulates you?"

"I don't want to talk about this shit. It drives me crazy."

"A lot of things drive you crazy right now."

"Exactly."

"So maybe you shouldn't break up with her. Not until you feel less crazy."

He rolled to his side, looking all fierce and badass. "You think I broke up with her rashly? Are you kidding me? She's got so many damn issues I can't stand it. She won't eat anything, so she gets bitchy and depressed. She takes forever to get ready—she won't just go somewhere spontaneously.

Ever. And even when she's ready, she's worrying about how she looks. Drives me up a fucking wall. So I get sick of her shit, I break up with her, and then she reels me back in. She gets all sweet and loving, but you know what? That's not who she is. She isn't sweet and loving. She's neurotic." He lowered his head, swearing under his breath. "I'm being an asshole. Making her sound like a bitch. She's not a bitch. But she's got a lot of issues... You know what? She's a great girl, but I don't love her. And that's it. I just don't love her."

"You feel guilty about breaking up with her, don't you?"

"Yes. Fuck, yes."

"So maybe there's more to it. Are you afraid of letting her dad down? He was like a dad to you, so maybe you think you're losing a dad, too?"

"I have a dad." But he said it quietly, the fire in him doused. He looked out to sea, pulling on his chin whiskers. "But, yeah, you're right. Breaking up with Emma will hurt my relationship with her family. She says she wants to stay friends and, because of her dad, I told her that was fine."

"But you don't want to be friends?"

"She doesn't really want to be friends. She wants me back, so we can continue on exactly the way we were. And that is not going to happen. Ever. I can't..."

"What?"

"I can't be with her. I don't want to recycle the same damn stories from our childhood. I don't want to listen to her experiences in clubs or what the photographer on her shoot made her do. I don't want to pretend I'm interested in what she has to say. I don't want to be so fucking careful with her. I want more. I want to feel something. I don't want to fuck a rag doll."

Whoa. Wow. She tried not to show any emotion. She didn't want to stop him from venting. Clearly, he needed it.

His eyes closed and he rammed his hands through his hair. "I'm such a piece of shit. I shouldn't be talking about her like this."

Sophie smoothed a hand up his arm. "Hey, it's okay. I don't know her. I don't know your friends. We live on opposite ends of the country. You can say anything you want."

"It's not her fault."

"It's no one's fault. You're twenty-one. You had six years with her. That's a really long time."

"Yeah."

"So, to recap, it sounds like you're done with her, but she doesn't want to let you go, and you're afraid to cut her loose because she'll go crying to her dad, the man who's like a dad to you, and then she's going to turn her family against you, shutting you out. And you've worked really hard to be the good guy, and she's going to destroy all that, turning you into the asshole boyfriend that broke her heart and carelessly tossed away everything she and her dad did to help make you into the man you are today, and *that's* what's making you crazy."

He looked at her a long time, revealing nothing. And then a slow smile spread across his unbearably handsome features. "Yes."

"Why do you look surprised?"

"Because I didn't know that."

"You don't know a lot about yourself."

"I'm beginning to see that."

CHAPTER FIVE

Electricity arced between them.

The way he looked at her mouth sent a sizzle down Sophie's spine, and she thought he might kiss her.

But he didn't. He just blew out a breath and looked away. "I don't want to talk about me anymore."

"Okay."

"Tell me what happened to you after your parents died. Your sister was eight years older than you, so who took care of you?"

She loved that he remembered so much of what she'd said. "My sister had graduated business school a year earlier, which made her really happy, since my parents got to see her turn out just how they wanted. She wasn't exactly up for raising a sixteen-year-old, but she moved back home with me anyway. A few months later my aunt Georgie came for a visit and saw how I was living, how Abby was partying and all that, and she moved in. Which was great. My aunt's amazing. She lives in Montana, in a really cool ski town."

She rarely talked about this stuff, since it was personal business and she didn't like to badmouth her own family. "Sometimes I feel closer to her than my own mom. My mom and I didn't have much in common. She and my sister would go shopping and to the spa. They both ate the same way—coffee for breakfast, lettuce leaves for lunch." Guilt boxed her ears, and she cringed. "Promise you won't say anything?"

"Promise."

She held out her pinkie. "Pinkie swear. Everything we say tonight stays between us."

He lifted his pinkie, and they hooked together. His heated gaze made her heart pound. "You can count on me, Soph."

"Now I know how you felt talking about Emma. It feels disloyal to say I felt closer to my aunt than my mom. I've never said that before. But since I'm on a roll, I can tell you I'm the opposite of my mom and my sister."

"Yeah? How?"

"I'm independent. I eat. I'm low-maintenance."

"Is that right?"

"Wait, does it sound like I'm selling myself to you? I'm not, I swear. I mean, obviously, I'm not your type."

"I don't have a type."

"Well, I mean, you're an athlete. Fitness is essential to you and Emma. And that's just not my thing."

"Emma's not fit. She's thin. She doesn't eat."

"I know. I'm just saying."

"What're you saying?"

"Just that, obviously, I like to eat."

He smiled.

"I like to eat more than I like to wear skinny jeans."

His smile broadened.

"I mean, of course I want to be thinner. Who wouldn't, right? But I really love food. I'm not disgusting. I eat good food. I just *eat*. I think about my next meal. I plan it. I think about everything that goes into my mouth."

His features hardened and his hips shifted. "Sophie."

"I didn't mean it like that, perv."

"I'm not a perv." His gaze remained fixed on her mouth. "I don't have a type, Sophie. Just because I dated Emma for so long doesn't mean she's my type. But there's something about you..." He seemed surprised by his own admission. But then he just shrugged. "It's more than your body. Well, it's your body, too, but I like *you*."

"That's probably my cue to go."

"No." He grabbed her arm.

"Ryan...I'm not going to have sex with you. I mean, sure, I'm attracted to you, but if I did, then tomorrow I'd have to watch you hooking up with someone else. And that would make me feel bad."

"Okay." A flash of need was quickly replaced with his dazzling smile.

She wondered if he knew he didn't need that phony smile to charm people. "Okay what?"

"Okay, I understand. I don't want you to feel bad." He didn't say it like some charmer. He said it with sincerity.

She believed him. "You're awfully nice."

"I'm a very nice guy. Ask anyone. I'm nice." There was a little acid in that last word.

She was starting to figure him out. "Are you tired of being nice, Ryan?"

He nodded, and she could see a hint of not-so-nice burning in those eyes.

"I see why your friends brought you here. They're right. You do need a place like this. You need to let go. And I get the feeling with these women you don't need to be so nice." She drew in a breath. "I suspect you can just fuck them."

His gaze fixed on her mouth. "Say that word again. Slowly."

"See? You *are* a perv." She nudged him. "You should

take what these women want, Ryan. Because…I don't want that." She sat up, ready to go back to her room.

His grip tightened on her wrist, but she shook her head. She got it now. "If you hang out with me, you'll just have to be nice. And that's not why you came here. Go back with your friends. Get rid of some of the crazy before you go back to school. Goodnight, Ryan." The panic she saw in his eyes matched what she felt inside. But it didn't matter. What he needed, she couldn't provide.

On shaky legs, she hurried to the path. The ocean breeze cooled her skin, and she filled her lungs with the humid air. Once on the pavement, she clapped her flip flops together and shoved her feet inside them.

And then she heard his voice. "Wait up."

Once he caught up with her they walked in silence past the hot tub, the pool, and the tables. Flashes of bare skin in her peripheral vision kept her focused on the hotel doors.

The beat of attraction still pulsed in her veins. Really, the sooner she got away from him the better. She reached for the door, but he got there first, pulling it open for her. Drawing in a shaky breath, she gave him a smile. "I'll, um, I'll see you around."

"I'm walking you to your room."

"Oh, God no." That was the last thing she needed.

"It's nearly three in the morning. People are drunk. I want to make sure you get in safely."

"It's a resort. I'm perfectly safe."

"I disagree, but you owe me a Crazy Heart anyway, so I'm collecting."

The way he looked at her, the warmth, the intimacy, the *need*, sent her pulse skittering out of control. He was not making it easy to walk away from him. "Okay, sure."

Brushing past him, she entered the quiet hotel, the slap

of her flip flops against the soles of her feet distinctly loud in the carpeted corridor.

The elevator bank was straight ahead, the restaurant, which was open twenty-four-seven, to her right. "I have to order breakfast, so I can just leave some Crazy Hearts for you at the desk."

"Walking you to your room."

"Right." As long as he didn't think walking her to her room was code for banging her in the hallway. Desire roared through her at the image of his hands grasping her bottom, lifting her, and slamming her back against a wall. She could just feel his erection between her legs, his hard chest pinning her.

Holy hell, she'd *never* felt this kind of attraction before.

Finding the hostess at the podium, she said, "Can I please order breakfast in my room tomorrow morning? Well, I guess this morning."

"Sure thing." She reached underneath and pulled out an order form. "What time?"

"I'm taking a boat out at nine, so…how about eight?"

"Sounds good. Would you like to see a menu?"

"No, that's all right. I looked at it in my room. I'd like a spinach and cheddar omelet, whole grain toast with butter and strawberry jam, a mango juice, and a papaya juice."

"You got it. Is that it?"

"Yes, thank you."

"Room number?"

"Six-thirty-two."

"All set."

Sophie turned to find Ryan leaning against the wall, bare foot propped on it. He looked so freaking handsome her mind started blasting out warning signals. *Do not let this man into your room. Repeat: keep him out of the room with the very large and comfortable bed inside it.*

She breezed right by him, but of course he fell into step beside her. She pushed the call button. The doors opened immediately, and they got in. His presence filled the space, his intense energy closing in on her. She could see him from every angle in the mirrors—his broad shoulders, the thick muscles of his biceps, the strong jaw and golden brown eyes. He seemed coiled, his energy restrained.

She looked away. "Someone needs a cookie."

"Pretty sure it's not a cookie I need."

"That's because you haven't had one in a long time. You've forgotten the simple magic of a Crazy Heart."

He shifted restlessly, color rising in his cheeks. "I think you're right."

She had the feeling he'd missed out on a lot of things people their age took for granted.

With a ping, the doors opened, and she quickly strode out. Pulling her key card from her pocket, she moved down the plushly-carpeted hall. Crystal sconces lit the path to her suite.

Once at her door, she swiped the card. "Hang tight. I'll grab your cookie." She stepped into the room, and then hesitated. Was she really going to keep him in the hallway? She quickly swung around to catch the door before it closed but found his hand on it, keeping it open. "Come on in."

The door slammed hard behind them. Her huge corner-suite smelled like her vanilla and gardenia body lotion.

He stood there, this big, powerful guy, watching her with a vulnerability in his eyes that touched her. "I'll just…Give me one second."

She'd unpacked, stowed her luggage in the walk-in closet, but she'd left the carry-on filled with cookies on the other side of the desk. Unzipping it, she pulled one out, and then handed it to him.

He took it. "I haven't had one of these since high school."

"Then my timing's excellent, what with you going rogue this week and all."

"I can only do this if you share it with me." His lips parted, the corners curling, and then his features bloomed into a devastating smile. "One bite?"

Her body went hot and electric. The curve of his mouth, his penetrating gaze, the sheer masculinity of him—he just overwhelmed her. "I'm not the one with issues. I can eat the whole thing."

Heat flared in his eyes. He kicked the chair back, dropped into it, and then patted his thigh.

Oh, no. She wasn't sitting on his lap. When she swallowed, it sounded like an aluminum can crumpling in her ears.

After ripping open the plastic wrapper, he pulled the cookie out. The powdered sugar drifted onto his board shorts. Tossing the wrapper onto the desk, he reached for her hand and gave it a tug.

Okay, fine, she'd sit on his lap. Just while he ate the cookie. Perched on his strong thigh, she nearly swooned when his arm banded around her waist. She tried to tear her gaze away, tried to focus on the cookie, but his body was so hard and his gaze so filled with want, she just couldn't.

And, oh, God, was she squirming on his thigh?

He lowered the cookie, wrist propped on his thigh. "Hey, so why don't you drink?"

She shot him a look. Where had *that* come from?

"Earlier tonight." He gave her thigh a squeeze. "You said three things about you. You don't drink, you don't do one-night stands, and you needed to find your friend."

Did he remember *everything* she said? She seriously wanted to kiss this man.

No, that was a lie. With the way he looked at her, the curve of his sensuous mouth, the heat in his eyes, she wanted so much more. Would it be so terrible to have one night with him?

Yeah, actually, it would. "It's not a big deal. Just a preference."

"I don't know many people who don't drink, so I'm curious."

"I guess it was just watching my brothers and sister get in trouble all the time. My parents were always yelling at them, grounding them. Obviously, they all pulled it together and they're not like that anymore, but watching them...I can't even tell you..." She stopped when she realized he knew exactly what she was talking about. He'd grown up with an alcoholic mom. "Well, you know. The throwing up, the hangovers, the totaled cars."

"I do know."

"They scared me. I remember this one morning, New Year's Day. Abby didn't come home from a party until six in the morning. And my parents were crazy mad. They started in on her, but she just ignored them. Kicked off her heels and passed out on the couch, while the rest of us watched football. And then she woke up, looking completely wrecked, and stumbled into the kitchen. And all of a sudden she dropped to her hands and knees and threw up all over the floor."

"Attractive."

"Yeah, and I'll never forget my mom watching with her hands on her hips, and she goes, Is this the woman you always wanted to be?"

Ryan smiled. "I like your mom."

"Yeah, I wish I still had her. But even when I got older and watched my friends doing the same things, I just thought it looked boring and stupid. I mean, I'll go to frat parties, but I'm the first to leave. What about you? I mean, with your mom, how did that affect you? Do you drink?"

"My brother, sister, and I are like the Three Bears. I'm a social drinker. I drink but not enough to get drunk. My brother drinks a lot, and my sister has no interest in partying whatsoever."

"Oh, I think I'd like her. She doesn't happen to go to school on the West Coast, does she?"

"You'd love her, but no, she's a freshman at Wilmington."

"Really? Wow. Smart girl. What's she studying?"

"No idea."

He must've noted her surprise, because he shrugged. "I'm not close to either of them."

"That's too bad."

"Soph?" His arm banded around her, and he hauled her closer to his chest. He looked like he wanted to say something, but he stopped himself. He watched her with an unnerving intensity.

"Yes?" she said, barely able to speak. Was he going to kiss her?

But he just leaned his forehead against hers and let out a slow breath. "I'm about to defile my body, and I need your support."

"Crazy Hearts are all about the lovin'."

He fought a smile. "We'll see about that." He brought the cookie to his mouth and took a small bite. Immediately, his mouth puckered. He coughed, blowing the powdered sugar all over the desk. "That's terrible."

"No, it's not. It's beloved."

"It's like eating a mouthful of sugar. Is that the only ingredient?"

"Of course not. There's also corn syrup, hydrogenated

oil, artificial coloring, and some benzoate preservatives."

"Jesus, Soph. You trying to kill me?"

"And, look, it's not just a cookie." She pulled his hand toward her, licking her lips before pressing them into the confectioner's sugar. "It's lipstick, too."

He looked at her like she made him happy. "Everyone used to do that in middle school. I don't know why it didn't have this effect on me then."

"What effect?"

"Makes me want to kiss you."

"I know. I'm a sexy beast."

"You are so fucking sexy." He leaned in, lips parted, and he stayed right there, so close she could smell the cookie on his breath. Was he asking for permission? She didn't know. All she knew was that one moment her breath was trapped in her throat and the next his tongue swept along her lips. Arousal streaked through her so hot and fast the soles of her feet burned.

"Delicious," he murmured, before tipping her chin. And then he kissed her. The moment their mouths met, he moaned, his arms wrapping even more tightly around her. "You light me up."

His mouth opened hungrily, his tongue sliding in and seeking hers. She couldn't resist. She wrapped her arms around his neck and kissed him right back.

Yes, oh, yes. Sensation spread from her center, a warm, thrilling rush that pulled her under. His hand went to the small of her back, pressing, and his kiss grew hungrier, more carnal.

"Damn." His other hand gripped her thigh, and he shifted her, spreading her legs so she straddled him. And once he had her right *there*, pressed up tight against him, his hips rocked up.

And, God, the heat of his body, the silky softness of his hair. The urgency of his kiss. She slid her hands under his T-shirt, caressing the smooth skin and hard muscles of his chest. His stomach contracted, his arms tightened around her back, and his kiss turned voracious. She moaned into his mouth because nothing had ever felt so good.

And then his hands cupped her ass, and he lifted her. Air rushed over her and she started to tip, but before he could lower her to the bed, she twisted away from him.

A new kind of energy blew through her, turning her cold. "Stop."

His forehead rested on her shoulder, as he drew in quick, shallow breaths.

Gently, she pulled out of his arms. He cupped her elbows as she found her footing, keeping her close.

"I don't want this," she whispered. And even as she took a step back, her body cried out for him.

No, she didn't want a hookup, but she wanted *him*. It was an ache, deep and raw, and nothing she could ever fulfill.

Because she couldn't give herself away like that. Not without getting something in return. And Ryan O'Donnell had nothing to give beyond this one moment.

Moving to the door, she unlocked it, held it open. "I'll see you around, okay?"

For one brief moment, his expression revealed everything. Confusion, regret, and a yearning so vivid she felt it in her own her heart.

And then he shut down. Erased everything. "Sure. Yeah." In three quick strides he was at the door.

But instead of leaving, he stopped. Thumb softly stroking her jaw, he said, "Goodnight, Sophie Valentine."

CHAPTER SIX

Hitting the sand after a twelve-mile run around the golf course, up the road a ways, and back again, Ryan leaned over, hands on his knees, to catch his breath.

A solid twelve miles. So why the hell did he *still* have all this fucked-up energy?

He'd tried to block shit out, but he kept remembering that kiss. The grip she'd had on his hair, the rhythmic friction of her hips. This thing they had—it was intense. He'd never felt anything like it before.

But, yeah, he got it. She didn't do hookups.

Spying a chaise, he headed toward it. A strong breeze cooled the perspiration on his skin, and he looked up at a blue sky. But he only saw Sophie, her lips coated with sugar. And then he remembered swiping his tongue across them, tasting that sweetness, the flood of heat that had rushed his body.

A familiar laugh spiked his pulse. He propped up on his elbows to find Sophie on a Hobie Cat, grabbing hold of the mast as the guy at the boat rental stand launched her into the water. She waved at the attendant, kneeling on the trampoline in her red bikini, and then turned to navigate her way into the ocean.

She pushed the tiller, watching the sails until they snapped and billowed. Her hair lifted in the breeze, whipping around her face. All alone on her Hobie, laughing like that—man, she didn't need anything or anyone to make her happy.

Christ. He had to stop thinking about her.

Besides, he had to deal with his shit. Reaching for his phone, he tapped the screen to find yet another text from Emma.

Coming to see you. We need to talk.

She pulled this shit all the time. Never listened to a damn thing. Well, screw it. He was not getting into this drama with her. He'd already told her not to come.

One last message, and then he was done. *I told you I can't see you this week. I'll talk to you after the break.*

He kept his gaze on Sophie, as she struggled with the choppy water. The wind looked a little rough out there.

He forced himself to look away. Not only didn't she need his help, but he needed to take care of his own mess. He still hadn't called his coach back.

Time to man up. But something stopped him. He wasn't ready to go back yet, and as soon as he came clean with his coach, he'd have to get his ass back there. What would it hurt to take the weekend off? They didn't have another game until Tuesday.

Ryan didn't confide in many people, so he didn't have many to turn to for help. But he did have his dad. He punched his dad's speed dial.

Big Bill answered on the second ring. "Yello. Bill here."

"Hey, Dad."

"Ah, my favorite son." His dad called all of them his favorites. "Saw you lost the game against Oregon."

Wind whipped his hair across his face. He'd kept it short all his life, so he still wasn't used to this new length. "Yeah. About that." He'd never let his dad down. Always had good grades, always made MVP, treated everyone with respect. He was the kid adults patted on the head, as they told his dad what a great kid he had there.

"I'm listening."

How come he knew he could count on his dad, and yet he never talked to him? "I fucked up."

After a pause, his dad said, "Go on."

"I'm in the Caribbean."

"You're…" He let out a breath into the receiver. "Okay."

"I told Coach I had a family emergency."

"There something I don't know about?"

"No." Not about his family anyway.

"Okay. You tellin' me this because I'm about to get a call from him?"

"No. I'm telling you because I feel like shit about it."

"Ah. Got it. You wanna tell me why you skipped out on your team?"

The punch of guilt made him wince. "Not really."

His dad barked out a laugh. Ryan pulled the phone from his ear. A gust of wind plastered his gym shorts to his thighs, reminding him about Sophie. When he looked up, he saw her skidding across the water—heading toward open ocean. "Hang on a sec." Lowering the phone, he called out to the guy at the boat stand. "Hey. She knows not to leave the lagoon, right?"

"Of course." The guy shielded his eyes with a hand to look for her. "Whoa. Wind picked up."

While the attendant stepped around the counter and hoisted a red flag up a pole, Ryan made a quick scan of the water. A couple pulled in the furling line, as their leeward pontoon dug into the water. But they had each other, so if their boat flipped, they'd be okay. Sophie was out there alone.

"Ryan?" he heard his dad shout.

Hopefully, she'd notice the flag. *Not his business.* "Yeah, sorry."

"You called me for a reason. So what're you looking for here? Me to kick your ass? Or to be okay with it?"

"I don't think I can get you to be okay with it."

"Nope. You got a responsibility to your coach and teammates."

He knew that. "Yeah."

"Lotta people dependin' on you. You can't just bail on 'em." His dad blew out a breath. "This isn't like you at all. You worked your ass off to get to this point. What's going on?"

Anxiety thrummed his nerves. He sat forward, curling his toes in the sand. "I just…"

"You just what?"

"I just needed a break. For once in my fucking life, I wanted a break."

"Three months before the draft?" His voice was like a sonic boom in his ear.

Ryan let out a shaky breath. "Pretty much."

"You been dreading this?" His dad's tone gentled.

"Yes." Energy rushed through him, blowing out the dark, heavy clouds. His dad got it. "*Yes.*"

"You got any sense of why? Something happen?"

"No. Nothing happened." He closed his eyes against a spray of grit. "What I know is that I like baseball. I like my coach and my teammates. I like winning. But I just don't want to be on the field. And I came here to figure out why."

"Got you."

When his dad didn't say anything more, Ryan kicked the sand off his foot. "What do you think?"

"I think right now it's not about you. You're in the middle of your damn season. You're the star of the team."

Not helping. "Yeah, I know that. But I'm the reason we lost to Oregon. And it wasn't just that game. It's been getting worse. *I've* been getting worse."

"So you didn't want the scouts to see you screw up?"

"Yeah, that, too."

His dad chuckled.

"Dad, I…I think I was having a panic attack."

"You talk to your coach about it?"

"No."

"Shit time to blow yourself up. Not a lot of kids get this shot, so you gotta think hard about skipping out on this week. You blow it, and there won't be any going back."

"Missing this week won't kill my chances in the draft. The scouts think I had a family emergency."

"You gonna keep lyin' to your coach?"

"No." Shame slammed him.

"Look, son. You need to call him right now and let him know what's been going on with you."

Noticing Sophie's Hobie bouncing over growing chop, Ryan shot off the chaise. *Oh, hell.* She was too busy trying to keep the bow out of the water to notice the flag had gone up.

And why the hell was she heading for the ocean?

"Dad, I gotta go." He headed down to the boat rental stand. "But, yeah, I'll call Coach. Let you know how it goes."

"You do that. I'm here if you want to talk."

"Thanks, Dad." He slapped his phone on the desk and quickly read the guy's name tag. "Hey, Sam. You think you can take me out there? Looks like she's having a hard time."

"What? Who?" Sam looked up from his cell phone, scanning the ocean. "Yeah, that wind's knockin' all right." He leaned down and pulled out a sign, setting it on the counter.

Closed temporarily due to weather.

"I need to get to her." *Now.* "Before she leaves the lagoon."

Shielding his eyes, Sam tracked Sophie's progress. "Nah, she wouldn't do that. She said she's done this a hundred times."

"Look, she's out there alone. If she flips, she's not gonna be able to get the boat back up by herself. Can you just get me out there?"

The guy watched her for a few moments, and then scanned the water. Several boats were already heading back to shore. "Okay, but let's make it quick." He pulled up his walkie talkie. "It's Sam. Wind's picked up. You want send someone down here to help me out?"

"Copy that."

Ryan jumped into the dinghy before Sam. Once in, the guy locked the lift level, put the engine in neutral, and shifted the throttle into position. Ryan pulled the starter cord, and they took off.

Rough seas made the ride choppy, and they caught air a bunch of times, slamming down hard enough to rattle teeth.

As they neared the Hobie, Ryan waved to get her attention. "Sophie. *Soph.*" But her features were scrunched in concentration, her arms pulling the ropes taut, trying to get control of the sail. "Dammit, Sophie." He watched her stand up on the trampoline.

He hoped like hell the Hobie didn't tip. If it did, she'd…*Fuck*. He had to get to her.

"Hurry up." The wind swallowed his shout to Sam.

And then the Hobie flew a hull. With a hand on the tiller, Sophie clung to the rail.

Anxiety ripped across his skin like fire, and he wanted to dive into the water right then. "Sophie!"

But she dumped wind and slowed down—and *thank Christ*—the hull dropped back to the water.

"Close one," Sam said.

Ryan needed to get her attention. Needed to get on that boat with her.

"Almost got her." Sam had the dinghy almost parallel with the Hobie.

She was heading out of the lagoon. "Get me closer, dammit." Once she got caught in the pull of two opposing currents, she'd lose control of the boat. "Sophie." He barked so loudly, he finally got her attention.

She whipped around toward him, eyes wide in shock.

"Turn into the wind *now*."

After a moment of alarm, she quickly turned and pushed the tiller away from her body. The boat came around and instantly stopped. Ryan dove into the water. Momentarily lost in the quiet and blur of submersion, he imagined her ignoring him and just continuing into open ocean.

Panic had him powering to the surface. Shaking his hair out of his eyes, he found her watching him with concern. "Dammit, Sophie."

"Hey," Sam called. "You need me?"

"No, thanks." Ryan stroked hard until he reached her.

She stood up, and the lightweight boat rocked. "What're you doing here?"

Lunging forward, he grabbed the fiberglass hull and hoisted himself aboard. "Sit down. I don't want you to flip this thing."

Surprise turned to anger. "I'm not going to *flip* it."

His heart pounded like a drum. He grabbed the tiller, adjusted the sail, and turned the boat back to shore.

"*Hey.* You can't just take over."

Wind batted his ears, and cold water crashed over the trampoline.

"I'm not going back yet. What is your problem?"

"See the red flag?" He gestured to shore. "It's too windy out here for a Hobie, and you were heading out of the lagoon."

She looked at him like he was crazy. "No, I wasn't." One hand pulled the hair off her face, the other pointed toward the beach. "I was going into that inlet."

He glanced over his shoulder to see the odd little cove that looked like a giant had shoved a finger into the sandy coastline. The water glowed a brilliant turquoise. He hadn't seen the inlet from shore.

But that wasn't the point. "It's still too windy to be out here right now." He drew in a deep breath to settle his nerves but got another jolt when he recalled how close she'd come to the riptide. "And you got way too close to open ocean."

"I was *turning.*" She crawled over to him, unsteadily. As she reached him, she tried to pull on his arm. "Can you please let go? I'm going into that cove." But when he wouldn't budge, she shouted, "What is the matter with you?"

"What's the matter? Jesus, Soph, you scared the shit out of me." When he saw her baffled expression, he forced himself to calm down. "It looked like you were having a hard time controlling the boat. The wind's bad enough, but you were getting way too close to the rip." He blew out a breath, as he managed the light craft in a strong wind.

"Are you out of your mind?" She sounded incredulous.

The Hobie pitched deep, right up to the crossbar. "Up on the hull, Soph. Hold on and lean back."

As soon as the craft stabilized, he cast a glance over his shoulder, relieved to see she'd done as he'd asked. She'd also lost some of her outrage. "Okay, yes, I was definitely struggling there for a minute, but I was heading into the cove to get out of the wind. So, thank you, but I'm fine now." The choppy water had her breasts bouncing wildly.

Now was not the time to notice her breasts in the red bikini. Unlike most women at the resort who wore little scraps of material, Sophie's swimsuit had decent coverage. But nothing could hide the fullness—the absolute ripeness of hers—the hard points of her nipples, the beads of water on her skin. He had to look away. With a chin lift, he said, "Everyone's heading in."

"Okay, cool, but *I'm* heading into that nice, quiet cove over there. So please get off my boat. Go swim back to shore. I'm serious, Ryan." She crawled toward him and pushed his shoulders. "Get off."

He watched her face screw up with the effort it took to push him over, and he burst out laughing.

"Don't be a jerk."

He turned fully to her. "I'm not a jerk. I just saved your life."

"I'm on a *Hobie*. In a *lagoon*." She blew out an exasperated breath. "I would've been fine."

He gestured toward the other boats in the lagoon. "Everyone's going back in."

As she stood there watching the others heading back to shore, her long hair fluttered out behind her, and she looked like a warrior queen. That sexy mouth, those brilliant blue eyes, and that lush body made him want her with a fierceness that completely undid him.

"Stop looking at me like that." She stepped back, losing her balance and nearly toppling over.

He grabbed her arm, steadying her. "Can you please sit down so I can get us safely to shore?"

She jerked out of his hold. "I can get myself back to shore."

"In normal conditions you can. But with this wind you could flip. And you'd never get this thing back up by yourself."

"God, would you stop with the flipping? I wasn't going to *flip*."

"You've never done this before, have you?"

She looked away. "Of course I have."

"Great, Soph. You lied to Sam."

"I didn't lie."

He gave her a weighted look.

"I went to camp on Catalina Island. I took a Hobie out. I think it was a Hobie."

"When you were twelve?"

She held onto the rail, her hair whipping like ribbons in the wind. Fuck, she was hot. Fierce, sexy, and wildly independent.

"So, fine, thank you for saving me. Now, if you'll jump off and get back to your day of banging women, we'll both be happy."

"Christ." He'd hurt her. "I'm sorry about last night. I got carried away. You're a beautiful woman, and I'm obviously attracted to you. I'm sorry I pushed it so far."

She looked at him for a moment, as though measuring his sincerity. "I don't blame you for anything other than pirating my boat. Just go, okay? And let me get back to my fun."

"Take the boat out later with your friends."

"You know, if I waited for people to do things with me, I'd never do anything. Look, I get it now. It did get a little scary there. But I'm good now. Thank you for helping me, but I'm going to head into that cove and wait out the wind."

"Soph, I'm not trying to be a dick, but I grew up around boats. I'm serious when I tell you the Hobie's not safe in these conditions. That's why he put up the red flag. Let me just get you back to shore, and you can take it out another day. Okay?" The wind whipped his words right back into his face like a hard slap. He should be with his friends. Getting with girls like Carrie. Not fucking up Sophie Valentine's life.

He had to point a little further away from the wind after the tack so he could gain some speed before heading up to the beach. "Can you please just sit on the trapeze so I can bring her in?"

"You completely ruined my morning adventure. So, screw you." She shoved him, hard, and he lost his footing but didn't fall in. "What are you, a duck? Do you have webbed feet? Get off my boat!"

"I'm about to, and so are you. Now jump off and get onto shore so I can bring the boat in." Ryan motioned for Sam to come and help him, as the boat ground into the sand.

"You *suck*." Sophie jumped off and strode away. Her feet left an imprint on the wet sand.

Anger pulsed under his skin, as he helped Sam drag the boat onto shore. Heat prickled under his armpits and sweat popped out on his forehead. He wasn't normally an asshole.

He didn't know why he was one now.

When they'd finished, Sam jogged over to help another guest. Ryan flexed his fingers, needing to hurl something. But instead he looked around for Sophie, found her storming across the beach. Where the hell was she going? She hadn't even bothered to pick up her key card and phone.

Watching her stride away, Ryan's anger mounted. Too impatient to wait for Sam to finish with the guests, Ryan interrupted. "Hey, can I get my phone?" He glanced over his shoulder to find Sophie hauling it up the beach. "And her stuff?"

"Sure. Yeah."

He saw the way they all looked at him, like he was some rude prick. But he didn't care. He had to catch up with her. Sam headed for his desk, reached into a cubby, and handed him her key card and white cover-up, along with Ryan's own belongings.

"Thanks." Pocketing his phone, Ryan took off after her.

The beach was empty at this hour, just some workers setting up umbrellas and beach chairs. So he hollered for her. "Sophie."

She ignored him, sand kicking out with each aggressive stride she took. The round globes of her ass shaking with each hurried step drove him out of his mind. He followed her, the noise in his head so loud he couldn't think.

He'd give her the damn key card and cover-up, take a shower, and go back to bed. What the hell was he doing getting up so early anyhow? He was on vacation. He rarely had a chance to sleep late.

She hit the arched walkway that led to the pool and disappeared.

"Sophie, dammit." Fuck him. Fuck this noise in his head. He could leave her stuff at the front desk. It didn't matter. *She* didn't matter.

The moment his feet hit the pavement, he remembered he'd left his gym shoes by the chaise. Which meant he had to turn around, and that just pissed him off even more. *Dammit.* He didn't want to turn back and get his damn shoes.

And where the hell had Sophie gone? Didn't she want her

keycard? He didn't see that bouncing, round ass anywhere. But, holy shit, he could feel her clutching him, feel the press of her body against his. Desire burned through him. She'd been so fucking responsive last night. That's what it was, really, what had made him so wild. Her response to him.

It was *them. Combustible.*

He remembered tucking his face into her neck, being surrounded by her scent, her silky hair. Her hands reaching under his shirt—her touch so hungry. *Oh, Christ.*

His heart pounded. Need burned a fiery path through his limbs. Where the hell had she gone?

He scanned the empty pool, the chaises, and the path to the terrace grill. Stalking towards the hotel, he peered through the glass doors but didn't see anyone inside. She couldn't have made it to the elevator that quickly.

The sound of water hitting pavement snapped his attention to the side of the building. To the outdoor showers.

An image sprang to mind. Sophie, naked, water glistening on that peachy skin.

Desire charged through him. *Don't do it.* If he went in there, he'd touch her. And he couldn't do that. She didn't want it.

Go to your room.

Fuck that. Go to the gym. Work this crazy shit out of you.

He stood outside the hotel, every muscle tensed. A worker rolled a cart of clean towels out a side door and wheeled it toward the wicker towel stand.

But all he could focus on was the water splattering on concrete. Had she taken off her bikini?

None of your damn business. He turned away from the worker, but instead of opening the door to the hotel, he found his feet eating up the path, taking him toward the row of outdoor showers.

He'd just give her the key card and cover-up, and then he'd go. Leave her alone.

Water pooled outside a stall. "Soph?" He knocked, and then called for her again.

The door swung open, and she stood there in her red bikini, soap suds streaming down her gleaming body. Her features softened when she saw the cover-up and phone he held out to her.

Taking them out of his hand, she set them on a wooden shelf. "Thank you." Then, she stepped under the spray and tilted her head back, her long dark hair streaming over her shoulders.

Holy hell. Desire rushed him so hard his breath went choppy, his knees weak. He closed and locked the door, heading right for her. Her eyes flared with surprise, but she didn't stop him. The look in her eyes set his blood roaring. Heat, need, *want* burst inside him.

Her chest rose and fell with her rapid breathing. He moved toward her, crowding into her space, needing to touch her more than he needed air.

"I can't believe you pirated my boat."

Water splattered his calves, and his spine tingled with a lust so crazy he could barely control it. "It was too windy to be out there."

She gave him a defiant look. "I don't like people telling me what to do."

Or she wasn't used to it. No one in her family seemed to bother with her. "I'm not going to apologize for worrying about you."

"Why?" Her voice sounded thin, shaky. Water beaded on her skin.

He was so hard he hurt, but even though he could barely think, he knew she deserved an answer. "Because I *like* you."

She let out a shaky breath.

"Fuck, Sophie." Leaning in, he watched the desire in her eyes turn fiery. Her fingertips traced a path down his chest, making him shudder. He licked the water droplets off her lips, and she sighed into his mouth.

He kissed her—*fuck, yes*—tongue stroking into her mouth, fingers sliding into wet hair, shoving it off her face. Cupping the back of her head, he shifted her so he could kiss her more deeply. Her mouth, so lush and hot, opened to him, and he lost himself in all the lusciousness that was Sophie Valentine.

Her hands pushed under his arms, moving restlessly over his back, gliding across skin that awakened to her touch. His body hummed. And then she cupped his shoulders, drawing him tightly against her.

Lifting the heavy hair at the back of her neck, he tugged the tie of her bikini top and pulled it down, exposing her gorgeous breasts. *Oh, Jesus.* Full, plump, round. Her nipples puckered, beaded, and he had to have them in his mouth.

When he cupped her, the bounty of her breasts overflowing his big hands, she sucked in a breath. He caressed her, gently rubbing his thumbs over the hard nipples. Her eyes went all soft with desire, and her back arched, offering herself to him. And so he kissed her, all the while caressing and gently squeezing those plump mounds.

He was losing his mind. "You feel so good, Sophie." He spread kisses along her jaw, down her neck, and then he pushed her breasts together and licked her deep cleavage. His tongue flicked out, sucking first one nipple and then the other. Her hands clutched the back of his head, holding him tightly to her.

He took his time, savoring the feel of that hard nipple in his mouth, the generous mound in his hand. Those sounds she made—erotic whimpers—and the way her hips rocked with such urgency made him wild.

God, she lit him up. She *woke* him up. He was aware of everything, the smell of wet concrete, the sting of spray on his ankles. The scent of her body, so feminine, so blatantly Sophie. A little salty, a little floral, a lot sexy.

He reached for her hand and brought it to his dick.

"Okay, okay." Yanking out of his hold, she pushed at his shoulders. "We have to stop."

No. Jesus. Ryan closed his eyes, the loss of contact with her body hitting him with a painful jolt. He squeezed his dick to alleviate the unbearable pressure.

"I want this…I mean, obviously I do, Ryan. But I…God, I know myself. I can't just have sex with you and then…"

The anxiety in her voice tore him out of the sheer, blazing pain of blue balls.

Her hands came up to cover her breasts, her wet hair streamed down her creamy skin, and she looked completely torn apart. "Just…please just go."

The mix of aching desire and wild frustration overwhelmed him. But he understood. He had nothing to give her beyond a hot fuck in a shower stall. Yeah, he got it. He had to get out of there. Keep away from her, because she drove him out of his mind. Turning, he jammed his hands into his hair, pulling it off his face.

Christ. He could go so fucking hard in her.

But she didn't want to be used like that. And she shouldn't. She deserved so much more.

With a shaky hand on the lock, he lowered his head. He was out of control, no question. And it scared the shit out of him. Because it wasn't getting better. He'd been dealing with this building frustration and aggression for months now, and it wasn't going away. It was getting worse.

Breaking up with Emma hadn't helped. Taking this break? Only made it worse.

Chancing a look at her over his shoulder, he found her hands behind her neck tying the bikini. "I'm sorry." And then he walked out.

CHAPTER SEVEN

All Sophie could think about was Ryan's mouth. The wet, heat of his kisses, the *hunger*. Pushing him away had been the hardest thing she'd ever done. Because she'd lost herself in him completely.

So hot.

A lovely breeze fluttered the edges of the umbrella sheltering their table on the terrace. Mixed with the briny scent of the ocean, she caught a whiff of the exotic flowers hanging off the trellises surrounding her.

Honestly, this resort couldn't be more beautiful. And she was with two of her best friends in the world. She forced herself to tune back into their conversation and just *be here now*.

"Did you guys see the picture I put up on my Facebook page?" Laura Denham, her friend since fifth grade, speared a piece of chicken and shoved it in her mouth. She chewed quickly.

See, this was good. The perfect way to take her mind off Ryan. "I'll look it up right now." She pulled her phone out of her bag and swiped the screen.

But as she opened her Facebook app, all she saw was Ryan's face as he'd kissed her breasts in the outdoor shower.

85

His expression—the utter ecstasy—had given her such a charge. She'd come so close to going all the way. And when he'd brought her hand to his erection…of *course* she'd wanted him as much as he'd wanted her. Her mind had jumped ahead to pulling his board shorts down. She would've loved to feel him in her hands, all hard and hot and soapy slick.

Heat burst in her chest, coursing in fiery pulses along her nerves.

But what he'd said just before—that he liked her? Well, she liked him, too. And giving him her body…she couldn't do it. Just couldn't give her whole self like that and then walk away unscathed.

It would kill her. She'd feel used—like he'd had his fun with her and then moved on. She wasn't cut out for that.

"What do you think?" With her long blonde hair and toned body, Laura had never had an insecure moment in her life. Until now. "Does it look like we're having a great time together?"

Sophie focused on the picture of Laura with some guy, both looking pretty wasted. "I guess."

"Let me see." Kat took the phone from her. After examining the screen, she let out a sigh. "He's cute. Do you like him?"

Laura shrugged. "I don't know."

Sophie hated Laura's mission to make her ex jealous. Since her recent break-up, she'd been on-edge and brittle. Normally the most confident person she knew, Laura now doubted her choices.

"Look at those guys." Laura watched a group of men heading toward a table nearby.

"The tall one's yummy." Kat's shoulders pushed back, and she gave a toss of her glossy hair.

Just like that, the guys turned to look at her. Sophie smiled. Yeah, that's all it took. Kat was a magnet for hot guys.

"Okay, do your magic." Laura made a sweeping motion. "Laugh or something. Get them to come over here."

"You guys crack me up." Sophie set down her fork.

"What?"

"You are two *gorgeous* women." She motioned to Laura. "You play volleyball for UCLA. You got recruited to play professionally in Italy." Then, she gestured to Kat. "You've got it going *on*. Looks, brains, everything. You guys don't have to work so hard to get a guy."

"I don't want a guy," Laura said. "I just want my ex to think I have one."

"Well, I want one." Kat blazed her bright white smile. "And I don't have a problem admitting it."

"Okay, well, you're not going to find true love at Isla de los Amantes. I told you last night the guys who come to this place are looking for hookups not future brides."

"Oh, come on," Kat said. "When it happens it happens. We know plenty of hot guys with serious girlfriends." She drew in a breath, gazing out toward the sea. "What *is* it about me?"

Laura and Sophie looked at each other. Sophie wasn't about to lie to her closest friend, so she reached for Kat's hand. "There's nothing wrong with you. You're beautiful, and you have a great personality. But I think you're expecting sex to turn into love. And it hasn't. So maybe you should change your expectations."

"I can't be like you," Kat said. "Come on, if Ryan wanted me the way he wants you, I'd dive right in. That's just how I am. I'm not going to pass that opportunity by because…you just never know."

"Who?" Laura looked away from the guys settling in at their table. "You met someone?"

"The hottest guy in the resort last night wanted her, and she turned him down." Kat pushed her plate away.

"He's not looking for a relationship."

"That's what they all say," Kat said. "What guy says he's looking for a relationship? But it happens. Look at Dan Archer."

For three and a half years, the quarterback of the football team had been a total man-whore. But then he'd fallen hard for a pretty freshman from Iowa. No one would've expected Dan to be in a serious relationship.

And what if his girlfriend had shared Sophie's attitude? What if she hadn't given him a chance? Not that this situation was the same. She and Ryan didn't even go to schools in the same state. *God, listen to me.*

He doesn't want you like that.

"It happens all the time, but you have to be open to it," Kat said. "And in this situation, you have nothing to lose and everything to gain. I would never have turned a guy like that away."

"I didn't." Her friends looked confused. "Not exactly."

Kat stilled. "What?"

"Wait, what happened?" Laura set her fork down. She'd powered through her salad in the seven minutes since it'd been deposited in front of her. The girl was *stressed out.*

Sophie let out a breath. "I almost had sex with him."

"When?" Kat said. "I saw you turn him down. You went to your room, and he went to the bar. I saw him partying with a bunch of women in the hot tub."

"I know. But I came downstairs to, you know, get some air."

"Some air? Is that what we're calling it now?" Kat smiled.

"Okay, maybe I wanted to see if he was around. I couldn't stop thinking about him."

"I *told* you there was something between you two."

There was. There really was.

"Guys, who're we talking about?" Laura drained her glass of ice tea.

"The guy who helped get me out of the bar last night."

"That guy? I thought *you* wanted him?" Laura asked Kat.

"You met him?" Sophie asked.

Laura shook her head. "No, but she told me about him. She *really* wanted to get with him."

"He didn't want me. I flirted like a hooker, and he was all charming and fun, but he wound up leaving with his friends and some other girls." Kat pressed her lips together. "And what do you mean you almost had sex with him? How does that work exactly?"

"I got a little carried away, but then I shut it down."

Laura motioned to Sophie's phone. "Do you have a picture of him? I have to see this guy."

"Oh, you'll see him around," Kat said. "You can't miss him. Imagine Zac Efron in board shorts."

"That hot?" Laura asked.

"Hotter." Kat didn't look happy. "And *Sophie* got him."

"What's that supposed to mean?" She supposed Kat would be hurt that Ryan had rejected her, but she didn't have to be surprised that he'd go for Sophie.

"I didn't mean it like that. I meant because you're the one woman at this resort who *wouldn't* do him."

Laura shrugged. "Maybe that's why he wanted her."

The idea struck Sophie hard. "Maybe." That made total sense. A guy like Ryan wasn't used to rejection. "But it doesn't matter. Nothing really happened. We made out. That's it." *Well, and he might've licked my nipples a little, too.* She pressed her thighs together as the memory sent a sizzling jolt through her.

Laura reached for a roll, but then tossed it back in the silver basket. "He's probably not all that great in bed. The hot ones usually aren't."

Heat shot up her neck, spread across her cheeks, burning the shells of her ears.

"What? He was good?" Laura said, at the same time Kat's eyes went wide. "You liked it?"

"I loved it."

Both of them stared at her.

"Then why didn't you seal the deal?" Laura asked.

Pain at the base of her finger had her looking into her lap. She'd clasped her hands so tightly one of her rings had dug into her skin. God, she was a mess. "It's not what I want."

"Oh, come on," Laura said. "It doesn't make you slutty to have some fun with a hot guy."

"I don't think it's *slutty* to hook up with a guy. That's not it at all. I just…I get too emotionally involved." Look at the conversations she'd had with him. No small talk, no flirting. It was real. They connected.

Because I like you.

She knew it meant something to him, too.

"Soph, he's into you." Kat reached for her hand. "I was there. I saw. And if you don't go for it, you'll never know if something great could come of it. He could be the one for you. Just put yourself out there. If it doesn't work, so what? You're not made of glass. You won't shatter if it doesn't work out. But what if it does? What if it turns into something?"

"Oh, my God. It *won't*. Guys, let's stop talking about it. He doesn't want me that way. He's here for spring break. He just wants to party and go wild."

Laura's hand closed over hers. "Would that be such a bad idea for you?"

"She's right," Kat said. "You could stand to have a little fun yourself."

She hadn't dated anyone since breaking up with King. And, even though she had lots of friends in the sorority and on a campus of over fifty-five thousand people, she did get lonely.

"You obviously really like him," Laura said.

"I do like him. But he's messed up right now. He just broke up with his girlfriend of six years." *He came here for sex.* And after he got it from her, he'd get it from someone else.

She really had to stop listening to Kat.

"Oh. Forget it." Laura leaned back in her chair, raising both hands in warning. "Don't go there. Six years? That's, like, the worst. He'll get back with her ten times, screw as many girls as he can, and then wind up marrying her."

"Wow, Laura," Kat said. "Way to write a happy ending."

"No, she's probably right." Sophie didn't want to talk about it anymore. "He's got a lot of stuff going on. And it doesn't matter anyway. I didn't come here for that. Besides, I've got my whole week planned out."

"But it was good, huh?" Laura asked.

"It was…I've never…"

Her friends burst out laughing. After a moment, Sophie joined them. "Okay, God. I mean, it was good with King, but this…this was like…" She let out a breath, remembering the blazing look he'd given her in the outdoor shower. "You guys, no one's ever looked at me the way he does. I mean, it's like he *has* to have me."

"Oh, that's hot." Laura gave a sad smile. "I miss that. You know? In the beginning, Blake and I were all over each other like that. It was so hot. So fun."

"Aren't all hookups like that?" Kat said. "Hot and fun?"

Disappointment slammed her. *Of course* hookups were like that. She'd never had one, so she'd misunderstood. She'd thought his hungry gaze meant he'd wanted *her*. Not just raunchy sex in a shower stall.

Okay, so that really put things into perspective. She'd needed to hear that.

"Yeah, well, mine wasn't." She'd never seen Laura so torn up. "Mine sucked."

"Then stop doing this," Sophie said. "You're beautiful, sexy, and smart. You're an elite athlete, for goodness sake. You and Blake had a great time together for two years. Just...move on."

"I can't. I want him to see those pictures on Facebook and regret dumping me."

"Would you take him back if he did?" Sophie asked.

"Of course I would. I love him. I didn't...I had no idea anything was wrong. And now? I just want him to hurt as much as I do. You know what's killing me? He's completely happy to be done with me. Like..." She brushed her hands together. "Done. Moved on. I saw him the night before we left. God, I never should've gone over there, but Deb and Lise were going to the frat party Friday night, so I went with them. He was laughing, having the time of his life. That skank, Alyssa?"

Everyone knew Alyssa. She'd probably done more frat laps than any other co-ed in UCLA history.

"She was all over him."

Sophie shook her head. "He's not like that."

"He is now. I saw him put his hand on her ass. I swear it gutted me. I wanted to throw something at him. Here I am dying inside. I can barely get out of bed, and he's hooking up with *Alyssa*."

"You know what I think it is?" Sophie looked at her friends. "We're seniors. We graduate in two months. I think we're all freaking out."

Kat pulled a tube of lipstick from her straw clutch and swiped it across her lips. "I know I am. Have you really thought about it? We're all going off in different directions. No matter what anyone says, we'll get busy with jobs, make new friends, date people. It's going to be different, and I don't want to do it alone. I want a boyfriend. Even if it doesn't lead to marriage, I just don't want to go out there alone."

"We're doing it with you," Laura said.

"You're going to *Italy*. We're not on the same path at all. I mean, I love you, and we'll always be friends, but you're not going to be my roommate anymore. You're not going to come over after work and get ready to go clubbing with me."

No one could argue that point. "I'm still around."

"You don't party, Sophie. You're probably my favorite person in the world, but I'm not going to be spelunking with you on the weekend."

Sophie burst out laughing. "I know what you're saying. We're all freaking out for different reasons. I'm just saying that Blake is, too. I know he looked like he was having fun with Alyssa, but I think it's easier for guys to compartmentalize. He puts his feelings over the break-up in a box so he can party with his friends."

"Did he respond to the picture you posted?" Kat gestured to Sophie's phone.

Laura shook her head. "No, but he wouldn't. We're trying to ignore each other. That's what exes do, right?"

Sophie wouldn't know. She and King had remained friends. "I know you don't want to hear what I have to say, but I'll say it one more time. I think you should forget about trying to hurt Blake. Forget about school and Blake and start thinking about this whole new chapter in your life. I mean, *Italy*. Come on, what an adventure."

"I think our definitions of fun might be a little different," Kat said. "I like to play with boys, Laura likes to play with balls, and you like to play with boats."

"Really?" Sophie said. "Because since I got here yesterday, I've made out with a really hot guy in an outdoor shower stall. And it was the most fun I've ever had."

There was a moment of silence when her friends just stared at her, and then they burst out laughing. All three of them lifted their hands and high-fived each other across the table.

See that? She could handle her brief little hookup with Ryan.

Next time she passed him in the hot tub with half-naked women she wouldn't even look twice.

******

A shock of cold had Ryan jackknifing up. Sleep still had a grip on him, so it took a moment to get his bearings. Where was he?

Sophie. Forcing himself fully awake, he looked for her, but the chaise next to him was empty. Only after taking in the pool, the blue umbrella shading him, and the hum of conversation did he realize he'd been dreaming about her. In the shower stall, his hands cupping her breasts. Jesus, he could feel the hard bead of her nipple in his mouth.

Lust surged through him hard and fast.

Enough already. *Jesus.* He had to cut this shit out. Lusting after some girl he'd just met? Come on, he had a resort full of women to choose from.

Besides, he'd put it off long enough. He pulled out his phone, ready to listen to Coach's message.

His mouth tasted nasty, and his throat felt dry, so he grabbed the beer sitting on the table beside him and took a swig before punching in his password.

"Ryan. Checking in with you." His coach's voice sounded full of compassion.

Regret weighed hard on his chest.

After a pause, his coach continued. "Worried about you, son."

Son. He was a piece of shit for lying to his coach. *No more.* Immediately, he hit the man's speed dial.

"Ryan?" His coach answered on the first ring.

"Hey, Coach."

"How's it going? You all right?"

Ryan took in the row of palm trees, the train of clouds skittering across a brilliant blue sky, and blew out a breath. "I'm fine."

"Talk to me. How's it going?"

Ryan drew in a breath, his fingernail scraping at the damp beer label. "Coach. I lied to you. There is no emergency."

A rush of breath hit the receiver. "Come again?"

"There's nothing wrong. I bailed on the team."

"What the hell's going on here?"

Ryan sat up fully, legs straddling the chaise, and scrubbed his jaw. "I need a break."

"There is no break. We're in the middle of the season. So what exactly's going on?"

If Ryan had an answer, he wouldn't have lied in the first place. "I don't know, Coach. I just…don't know."

"You sick?"

"No."

"This about drugs?"

"Of course not."

"A girl?"

"*No.*" As if he'd ever fuck up his life over a woman.

"Ryan, goddammit. I told the scouts you had a family emergency. And you're taking a break now? This week of all damn weeks?"

"Yeah. Pretty stupid."

"Where the hell are you?"

"I'm in Santa Grenada with some friends."

"You're fucking off in Santa Grenada with your friends when your agent and I have arranged scouts from major league teams to fly out here and see you play against LSU. Do I have that right?"

"Yes, sir."

The beer in his otherwise empty stomach churned. Sweat popped out on his forehead and over his lip. He needed to give his coach a reasonable answer. Something to make him understand that he…that he what?

He didn't know.

"You gotta think real hard about what you're doing, son. Does your dad know about this?"

"Yeah. I called him this morning."

"What'd he have to say?"

"Told me to figure out my shit."

"You done yet?"

"No."

"Well, Ryan, I'll tell you what. You're going to have a couple hours to do just that, as you pack your bags and head back to the airport. Because you're going to come back here and be on the field for Tuesday's game. I'll be goddamned if I blow my credibility with the scouts because you need a damn break."

Nausea sent a sting of cold fluid through his veins. *This isn't just about me.* A whole community had helped him get here.

"Do you understand what I'm telling you?" Coach snapped.

Of course he understood. And he wanted to snap out of it. He did. But panic had a grip on his mind and body.

"I'll arrange your plane ticket. All you have to do is get to the airport. Where are you?"

"Santa Grenada."

"Flying out of where?"

"San Juan."

"You gonna be on that flight?"

"I don't know." And yet he did know. A flare of awareness flickered through the numbness. He wanted to do what his coach asked, but his gut gave a firm *no*.

He wasn't going to be on that flight.

Because he knew with absolute certainty if he showed up for tomorrow's game, he'd fuck up again. He couldn't go back yet.

"I'm calling you back in two hours. Be ready for my call." Coach disconnected.

A bark of laughter drew his attention to the pool. Jake chased some woman in the shallow end. Lunging, he wrapped his arms around her waist and pulled her toward him. The woman shrieked, arms and legs flailing. People around them laughed. Everyone carefree, having a blast.

Apparently, his buddy had been with two women last night. He'd woken up in someone's bed. Then, when he'd gotten up to take a piss, he'd found her roommate in the shower. She'd invited him in.

That's what I should be doing. Going wild. Getting this crazy energy out of his system.

Tipping the bottle back, he appreciated the cool liquid sliding down his throat.

He closed his eyes, seeing the face of his barrel-chested

coach. Damn. He hated letting him down. No, he didn't want to get on a plane. Everything in him rebelled against the thought. But his coach had done well by him the last four years. Ryan wouldn't be a first-round pick had it not been for Coach Harding's training and interest.

Ryan glanced down at the black flip flops he'd kicked off. He sat around by the pool in Santa Grenada, while his coach worked his ass off to get him drafted. *Nice.*

Of course he should go back. Ryan got up.

What was with this wall of resistance in him? Why couldn't he just do the right thing and get back to his team?

He didn't know. But he did know he always worked his shit out in the gym.

He headed inside to change.

In two hours he'd be ready for his coach's call.

After a hard work-out, Ryan found his friends still at the pool. They'd commandeered a couple of tables near the hot tub and drawn a large crowd of women. Jake was telling a story, his hands moving fast, the women around him laughing. The table held pitchers of beer and glasses.

His friend looked up when Ryan approached. "And this, my friends, is Ryan O'Donnell, soon to be shortstop for the Yankees."

Carrie, the woman he'd met in the bar the night before, shot off the chair. "Are you serious? That's so awesome."

An invisible fist shoved right up under his sternum. "I have no idea where I'll be playing."

Dix handed him a glass of beer, shrugging his brows and tilting his head toward Carrie. A silent thumbs-up to go for the hot brunette. Ryan looked away.

When someone vacated a nearby chaise, he grabbed it, lifting the back so he could get a better view around the pool.

His gaze swept the area, and he found himself looking for Sophie.

Idiot.

He needed to get Coach's call over with. Then he could relax and have a good time with his friends. With the phone in his hand, he lifted a knee, braced his wrist on it, and took in the action around him.

A woman hoisted herself out of the pool, this one topless. A guy had her bikini, waving it over his head and cracking up. She just laughed, completely comfortable with her body—something he appreciated after so many years with Emma.

As she got out of the pool, her gaze flicked over to him, stopped, and held. Her smile turned seductive. Sashaying over to him, she leaned back, gathering her hair to squeeze the water out. The guy sent the bikini top winging right at her, hitting the side of her head with a wet splat. If that had happened to Emma, she'd have been hurt and embarrassed. But this woman? She burst out laughing.

Swinging around, she shouted, "Nice," and shot the guy her middle finger. Then, she turned back to Ryan, still smiling. She held the wet suit out to him. "You want to help me put this back on?"

"Sure." When she sat on the edge of his chaise, she positioned the cups over her breasts and tossed the ties over her shoulders.

"You got it?" She glanced at him, licking water droplets off her lips. This woman was hot. Where Carrie came on too strong, this one was pure sex. The way she moved, the look in her eyes. She had a great attitude, she was comfortable with her body, and she was obviously down to have a good time.

Lifting her wet hair, he pushed it over her shoulder and tied a bow at the back of her neck. Just as he grabbed the bottom ties the woman held out to him, he caught sight of a guy in board shorts wheeling a cart of surfboards toward a large shed. A group of people followed behind, everyone in swimsuits and wet hair.

Sophie. Electricity sparked in his chest. In her red bikini, she laughed with the others.

Ryan's hands stilled on the woman's back.

"Everything okay?"

"Yep." But he fumbled with the skinny ties.

The woman shifted around to face him. "Your hands are probably too big." Swiftly, she reached behind her and tied it herself. "There's nothing sexier to a woman than big hands. You know that, right? We love it."

But he barely heard her. One of the guys got Sophie in a playful headlock. Her good humor flattened, and she tore herself away from him. And then the guy grabbed her. *Smooth. Chicks dig headlocks.* Sophie struggled out of his arms. Ryan may not know her well, but he recognized a woman who wasn't amused.

"That your girl?"

He tore his attention away from Sophie. "What? No. I don't have a girl."

"Well, I'm going to grab myself a gin and tonic. See you around?" She got up, just as the guy hoisted Sophie over his shoulder. Twisting, Sophie tossed her phone onto the nearest empty chaise, as her body went sailing into the pool. The asshole who tossed her just stood there laughing.

Ryan got to his feet, ready to dive in after her, but a woman cut into his path. Toned and tall, she put her hands on her hips.

"Ryan, right?"

He didn't have time to deal with her, so he stepped around her. "Excuse me—"

"Hold on." She nodded to the pool, where Sophie stroked to the shallow end. "I'm Laura, and that's one of my best friends."

Ryan grew uncomfortable at the way she looked at him. "Okay."

"She's about the nicest person you'll ever meet. Did you know that the week after next, the mayor of Beverly Hills is honoring her at a dinner? Her mom may have hosted a lot of dinners and raised money, but Sophie's not like that. She doesn't just give money. She gets her hands dirty, figures out solutions, and organizes the community to actually give personal time to projects."

"Okay." He didn't need to hear about how great Sophie was. He already knew that.

"My point is that she's not like other people." She gestured to the people around them, everyone flirting and looking for hookups. "She doesn't play games, and she'll give you the clothes off her back. So, unless you're actually interested in her, leave her alone."

"I'm helping her out of the pool."

"She can get herself out of the pool, and I think you know that."

He really didn't need this shit. He cut sideways, but she blocked him again. "I'm getting her a towel."

"No, you're not. And because I can see how much you want to help her, I'm going to share a little secret with you. Her family treats her like the neighborhood babysitter. Her ex put his 'career' before her. The last thing she needs is some guy using her for booty calls. What she needs is someone who puts her first. You up for that?"

He didn't bother answering her, just reached around her for a towel. Of course he wasn't up for that. He'd just met her.

"You've got an entire resort full of booty calls. Stay away from Sophie." She pulled it out of his hands. "I'm not trying to be a bitch. I'm just looking out for her."

As pissed as he was, he recognized the truth in what she'd said. So he gave a curt nod, found a shaded area by the outdoor showers, and dialed his coach.

"You pull your head out of your ass?" Coach asked.

In the background, Ryan could hear the crack of a ball hitting a metal bat, followed by clapping and some shouts. And the thing was, Ryan didn't miss it. At all. Nothing in him stirred to be on that diamond with his teammates. "No, sir."

"Goddammit, Ryan. You gotta get this thing back on track. You understand that, right? We've come too far for you to fuck up now. Look, I'm going to have Marjorie buy you that plane ticket. I'll pick you up myself at the airport. I already talked to your dad. He's coming out here. We'll coordinate flights."

He wrapped a hand around the back of his sweaty, hot neck. "Coach."

"If you're drinking, stop right now. We'll give you a little exercise first thing in the morning."

His fingers dug into the muscles. "Coach." He said it more forcefully.

"Get you warmed up. It'll be all right. We'll pull out of this. But, listen, I haven't talked to the guys yet. I don't want them to know their captain fucked off at a time like this. You're the leader, Ryan. You get back here tonight, it'll be like nothing happened."

"Coach." He'd never raised his voice to his coach before. But plans were being made. Airports and pickups. His *dad* was involved. Jesus, his heart hammered, and his palms went damp. He felt like he was in a speeding car and couldn't find the brake. "Let me talk. I came here because I was having panic attacks on the field. I owe you a lot. I do. You're a great coach. And I lied to you because…" *Fuck.* "Because I need time away from it. I have to have this break."

"Panic attacks?"

"Yeah." Shame burned a hole in his gut. "This feeling's been building, and it's only getting stronger. I get that the timing sucks. I get that I'm letting down you and my dad and my teammates, and I'm sorry for the way I'm doing it. But I'm not coming back right now. I'm sorry about the scouts. I am. Believe me, I know what you've done for me. And I'm grateful."

"Don't be grateful, boy. Just get your ass on a plane and play some damn ball. Now is not the time for you to have a breakdown."

"I'm not having a breakdown. I'm not on drugs. I'm not drinking. And it's not about a girl." And then he calmed down and said the words slowly so his coach understood he meant them. "I just need a break."

"Okay, okay." His coach paused. "Okay. The most important thing is getting your head on straight. I can't tell you I'm not pissed. Just…take a day or two, okay? How about that? Two days, and then I'll expect you back here. You'll make it for the last game." His coach cut the connection.

Ryan stood there, his skin cooling, the noise in his head quieting. Leaning against the shelter of the outdoor shower, he took in the pool area—the half-naked bodies, booze, laughter…and couldn't work up a damn bit of interest in participating.

So what *did* he want?

CHAPTER EIGHT

After dinner, Ryan and his friends headed back to the outdoor bar. He'd meant to find the woman from the pool that afternoon, the one who'd lost her bikini top, but he kept forgetting to look for her.

Because...Sophie. A couple hours ago she'd taken off with her surfing group—which included that same asshole who'd tossed her into the pool. Ryan had only noticed her leaving because of the red dress. Who wouldn't have noticed a curvy woman in a red halter dress, her long, dark hair a tumble of waves down her back?

The dress flared around her hips, accentuating her waist and...damn did it work with her hourglass figure. From her apple cheeks to her round ass, Sophie Valentine was sexy as fuck.

He had—what? Forty-eight hours before he had to head back to Florida. So what was he doing watching the pathway, waiting for Sophie to come back from her night out, when he had a resort full of women who wanted to party?

Exactly. He pushed his chair back. He'd find the topless woman from earlier. Just as he left the table a beautiful woman brushed past him. "Hey." She gave him a sultry smile. "You heading over?" She gestured toward the crowded bar.

"Yep."

"Awesome. Want to grab me a chocolate martini?"

"You got it." As he pushed his way through the crush, he saw a flash of red. And, just like that, he lit up like a firecracker. His body tensed with anticipation, and he scanned the faces of the group coming out of the lobby. He recognized some of the people she'd gone surfing with that afternoon.

They headed up the walkway, approaching the bar, but he didn't see Sophie among them. She'd probably gone straight to her room. *No, wait.* Tonight was that music festival in town.

"Everything all right?" the woman beside him asked.

"Sure." But his attention was on Sophie's friends. They wouldn't have left her behind, would they? His body fired up at the idea of her alone in town in that red dress.

"Excuse me," he said to the woman, as he wove through the crowd. Out on the path, he met up with the group. "Hey. Did Sophie come back with you guys?"

One of the women gave him a slow look from his boat shoes to his mouth before answering the question. "She stayed in town."

"Is she with anybody?"

"What's up, man?" the guy who'd thrown her into the pool asked.

"He wants to know where Sophie is," the woman said.

The guy smiled. "Oh, yeah. She's at the festival."

Careless asshole. He'd left her alone in town. "Who's she with?"

"She's not with anybody. Why? What's the problem?" He seemed genuinely curious. Like he didn't have a clue how dangerous it would be for a woman alone in that rough crowd.

"Tonight's the festival, and you just left her alone?"

Now the guy just looked annoyed. "She wanted to see it. What's it to you?"

"She shouldn't be at that concert by herself."

"You're right about that," the woman said. "That's why we left. It's in the town square, and it's mobbed."

The guy stepped forward. "We tried to get her to come back with us, but she didn't want to. I don't get what your problem is. We're not her keepers."

"My problem, asshole, is you shouldn't have left her there by herself." Ryan shouldered past him and took off. He hated to think of her all alone. Pulling his phone out, he called her.

She answered right away. "Ryan? Hello?"

He could barely hear her over the loud music. So he ended the call and texted her instead.

Where are you? He headed into the lobby.

She responded right away. *In town.*

Are you okay?

Of course. Why?

You alone? At the valet desk outside, he motioned for a cab. The guy nodded and picked up a phone.

Not exactly.

What the hell did that mean? *Your friends said you were alone.*

You talked to my surfing buddies?

Soph. You alone or not?

I'm with a couple thousand people. Why???

Looking up from the phone, he asked the valet, "How long before the cab gets here?"

The guy tilted his head toward the long driveway, and Ryan caught headlights approaching. *Be there in twenty.*

You're coming to the festival?
I'm coming for you.
Ryan, I'm perfectly fine.
Don't want you alone.

The cab pulled under the portico, and Ryan handed a folded bill to the valet. "Thank you."

As they drove off, Ryan checked his phone. Nothing more from Sophie. *Tell me where you are exactly.*

No response. With every minute that went by, his impatience grew.

Answer me, Soph.

Nothing. He shifted in the uncomfortable seat. How come he could feel his skin? He started to perspire, and his shirt felt too tight. And why the hell was this driver being overly cautious? The roads were empty. He didn't have to drive like he was transporting a truck full of bottles.

He texted her again. *I'm almost there.*

His phone buzzed. *Ryan, I'm fine. So unless you're dying to hear electronic music don't come!*

Coming. Need to know exactly where you are.

She sent him an emoticon of a smiley face sticking its tongue out.

Cute. Jamming the phone into his pocket, he watched out the window, waiting for the first sign that they were nearing the town.

What was taking so long?

Just like the night before, the moment traffic slowed to a crawl, Ryan paid the driver and jumped out of the cab. Electronic music throbbed in the air, and a steady stream of people flowed in the direction of the town square.

Once the stage came into view, he got his bearings. People around him thrashed and banged into each other like it was one giant mosh pit.

Sophie had sent a text about five minutes ago, letting him know where she was, so he stopped to reread it.

On San Gabriel, across the street from Hotel Abac, in the park. Standing right behind a bench.

Ryan pushed his way through the throng. The deeper in he got, the more worried he became. The square was jammed with people. Bodies pressed, slammed, and undulated together.

Imagining her alone in this crazy crowd, her curvy body in that red dress, got his blood pumping. If anyone touched her...He pushed through, trying to read the storefronts and finally spotted Hotel Abac.

Thank Christ. *I'm here. Wave or something.*

Waving. Crowd's insane.

His nerves fired up, and if he didn't get to her soon, he'd start dropping bodies. Where the hell was she?

At the corner of San Gabriel and Monuments Boulevard, he stood on the base of a streetlamp to give him extra height. Every spot of red spiked his pulse.

A fluttering white scarf caught his attention, and once he saw it led to a red dress, he took off, shouldering people aside to get to her.

Finally, she was within his reach. He grabbed her hips from behind and hauled her up against him, immediately surrounded by her sweet, floral scent. She gasped, whipping around with fear in her eyes. But then she saw him, and happiness bloomed across her features. Her mouth moved, but he couldn't hear a thing she said. Turning in his arms, she wrapped a hand around his neck and lifted up on her toes to bring her mouth to his ear. "I can't believe you're here."

He didn't know if she meant to, but her nose nuzzled his neck. Desire kicked him hard. He lowered his face into her hair, breathing her in, painfully aware of her breasts pressing against his chest through the cotton of his Polo shirt and her hand on his neck, holding him close.

Desire streamed through him in a fierce, hot wave, making him so hard he pushed himself against her stomach to relieve the throbbing pressure. He felt a shudder run through her body, and then she looked up at him. She was so beautiful, and that mouth, so lush, so pink, was right there. Her expression turned heated, mirroring the same crazy need burning through him.

He kissed her. And the moment he pressed his mouth to hers, she squirmed against him, returning his kiss with equal fervor.

She made him hot and wild. His tongue licked into her mouth, his hands slid down the bare skin of her back to cup her perfect ass. Fuck, he'd missed her. He didn't understand it—he certainly didn't *want* to feel this way—but he was powerless to stop it.

Bodies knocked into him, causing him to tighten his hold. He kissed her more deeply, needing more of the slick heat of her mouth, the slow, seductive tangle of her tongue.

She grabbed a fistful of hair at the back of his neck. Her hips pushed up hard against him, and the kiss turned voracious.

Fucking hell. Too much need and want and desire. He was losing his mind. He wanted her naked in a bed, her body completely bared to him. He wanted to touch and kiss her everywhere. When she reached between them and stroked his dick, when she clasped it through his shorts and squeezed, he about jumped out of his skin.

Need had a grip so tight on him he had a hard time taking a full breath. They had to stop or he'd take her right there, in front of everyone.

Jesus Christ. Grabbing her hips, he turned her away from him so he could get a hold of himself. But it was impossible when her scent clung to him, when her hips shifted restlessly over his painfully hard cock. She leaned back against his chest, and it thrust those gorgeous breasts out. He'd never seen anything hotter than the view into the silky V-neck of her dress to the lush mounds of her cleavage.

With a hand low on her stomach, he held her firmly to him. The crowd jostled him, and he caught an elbow to his ribs and an unintentional hip-chuck, but nothing distracted him from the warm, luscious body in his arms.

As her hips swayed to the beat, her breasts undulated in the silky top. He wanted to slide his cock into the deep valley of her cleavage.

He scanned the people around him, everyone dancing and singing, lost in the ecstasy of the music. Not a single person paid attention to them. So he reached into her dress and filled his palm with her plump breast. Lust pounded in his veins and roared down his spine. Arranging the scarf—wrap, whatever she called it—around her shoulders, so no one could see, he caressed all that smooth, supple flesh. Her back arched, her ass swaying over his hard dick, and she moved sinuously against him. Oh, Jesus, she felt so good.

The look she gave him, eyes glazed, mouth opened softly, pleaded for more. So, he cupped her chin, tilted her head, and kissed her. Jesus, he couldn't get enough of her. He squeezed her breast harder, pinched her nipple. Her other arm went around to his ass and pulled him to her. She made him wild.

Out of his mind with need, he lifted the back of her dress and cupped between her legs. The wetness sent a spike of electricity through his limbs. He pushed aside the thin lace of her panties and slid a finger into her tight, slick heat. Her body shuddered, and her hips rocked in rhythm with his easy thrusts.

She felt so good, all honeyed heat, quivering breasts, and that round ass moving assertively over him. With a hand on her stomach, he held her tightly as he pumped, adding another finger and working hard to keep as still as possible.

With the skirt of the dress draped over his arm, and her ass pushed up tightly to him, no one could see what they were doing. Everyone around them was drunk, high, and mesmerized by the DJ's electronic music.

Ryan moaned, letting out all his pent-up frustration. Fuck, he wanted this woman. More than he'd ever wanted anything. And then he slid a finger up to her hard nub, drawing circles around it. She closed her eyes as her body shuddered and her knees buckled.

He caught her around her waist, pulling his hand out and smoothing down her skirt. Winding his arms around her, he held her against his chest.

They stood like that for long minutes. Until he'd had enough of noise and strangers. He wanted her all to himself. He dropped his mouth to her ear. "Stay or go?"

"Go."

He wrapped an arm around her shoulder to hold her close and maneuvered them out of the crowd. The air smelled of cooked meat, body odor, and a clash of perfumes and colognes.

As they made their way down the boulevard, away from

the square, the crowds thinned. Each bar they passed pulsed with music, and he had to skirt around drunken revelers.

She tugged on his hand. "Slow down. I can't go this fast."

He glanced to her shoes. "Sorry." And then he saw her flushed cheeks, reminding him of what they'd just done in a crowd of people, and concern flashed through him.

Was she pissed?

With a lock of hair spilling across one eye, she gave him a naughty smile. "Do you think anyone saw?"

Apparently not. And the relief was so sudden it felt like taking a full breath after being underwater too long. "Nah. That crowd was wild." He wouldn't have touched her like that if he'd thought anyone was watching.

"I know. What an event."

"Are you okay?"

"Okay about the festival? Or okay after you ravished me at concert in a town square in Santa Grenada?"

Lust slammed him all over again, as his body remembered every sensation of her body pressed tightly to his. He leaned down and pressed a hard kiss on her mouth. "About everything?"

"I'm good. A little confused." They continued walking, as he kept watch for an available cab. "Why'd you come all the way out here?"

"Your friends came back without you." The words hurtled out of his mouth. "They shouldn't have left you alone." But he was lying.

"They didn't do anything wrong. They wanted to go back to the resort, and I wanted to stay." Her jaw tightened, and she drew in a deep breath. "I told you I was going to this festival. It's not that big a deal."

"I was worried." He gestured to her dress. "Look at you."

"What about me?"

"That dress."

"I wore it for the nice restaurant we went to, and I covered up with *this* when I got to the concert." She waved her wrap. "I'm not stupid."

"No, you're gorgeous. And sexy. And I didn't want you alone in a crowd of drunk, aggressive men."

"Remember this morning, when I told you I hate when people tell me what to do?"

She had no idea how fucking hot she was. None. But he kept his mouth shut.

"I'm not some wild child looking for attention. Did you see me taking hits off a blunt? Taking drinks from strange men? No, you didn't. Because I'm smart. I grew up in a big city."

"You can't compare Santa Grenada to Beverly Hills."

"Oh, my God, my life isn't what you see in the movies. Do you think I got chauffeured to school in a silver Bentley? A butler answering the door, a manservant fetching my lattés for me? God, Ryan. We had a housekeeper, that's it. The minute I could get my license I did because I couldn't stand asking my friends for rides all the time. I've been taking care of myself a long time."

Why did that make him sad? He'd never been alone. Ever. Surrounded by family, teammates, coaches, his girlfriend, he'd never had a break.

A flash of insight struck him. He'd always been surrounded by people who had expectations for him. And he'd always met those expectations. Sophie had none. She could've been some wild, rebellious teen, but she'd chosen instead to make the best of her isolation by pursuing her interests.

He grabbed her hand, kissed her palm. "I know you can

take care of yourself. I just don't want you to always have to."

She drew in a breath, gazing up at him with pure affection. But then she looked away. "You're a dangerous man."

He didn't know what to say to that, so when a cab turned the corner he flagged it. It pulled right over.

Once inside, they buckled themselves in. With her elbow on the windowsill, one hand covering her mouth, she looked pensive. She must think he was crazy, the way he kept coming after her.

The thing was, he was known for his self-control. He'd excelled at baseball because of his discipline. While his friends partied, drank, cut class, and ignored curfews, he'd always towed the line. He knew that if he screwed up, he got benched. If he showed up to practice hung-over, he didn't play his best and Coach limited his play-time. He'd been *trained* to control himself.

So, what the hell was happening to him? Yeah, his attraction to her was off the charts, but why couldn't he *control* himself?

You need to fuck and fuck hard. Then he shouldn't be spending time with the one woman at the resort who didn't want a simple hookup. The only one who didn't want to fuck around. She wanted to surf and rent boats. Jesus—it hit him right then—she'd just wanted to see the festival, and he'd charged into town, mauled her beautiful body in front of everyone, and then dragged her off with him.

Fucking caveman. He looked over at her, the white wrap balled-up in her lap, streetlights dancing over her features. She deserved the truth. "I came because I missed you."

Her eyes flared.

"I spent half the night looking for you. I tried to get into it, the drinking and partying, but…" He shrugged. "I just wanted to be with you."

She watched him a moment before shifting her gaze out the window. "You slay me." She sighed. "You really, really slay me."

He hoped like hell she didn't feel disrespected by what he'd just done to her in the middle of the square. "I'm sorry if—" Her expression had his jaw snapping shut.

She let out a huff of breath. "Do you have any idea how offensive that is? Do you think you're just taking advantage of some helpless girl who has no say in what you do to her body? What just happened in the town square was my choice. I *liked* it, okay? It was fun and exciting, and it was my choice. God, Ryan."

Happiness ignited in his heart, sending heat and light everywhere inside him. He leaned over and released her seat belt. Sliding one hand under her ass, the other under her legs, he dragged her onto his lap.

Burying his nose in her hair, he breathed her in. "I'm out of my element here."

She didn't fight him, just exhaled. "It's bad enough that I keep wanting you, but if you apologize every time we get funky you make me feel worse."

"I don't want you to feel bad at all. I don't want to hurt you."

"Well, I don't want you to hurt me, either. And if we don't knock this off, I *will* get hurt. I know you don't want to hear this, but I'm already getting emotionally involved. I'm sorry, but I can't separate my mind from my body. I actually like you, and that fuels my interest in you physically. Do you know what I mean?"

"Of course."

She looked at him. She was so fucking beautiful, that sexy

mouth and warm, intelligent eyes. "Is this…I mean, is it because of the challenge?" When he didn't answer, her gaze cut away. "You can have any woman you want, but you keep chasing after me. Is that what gets you all fired up?"

"Not at all. It's you."

"Were you like this with Emma?"

He shook his head, barely able to think past the rush of heat flooding him. "No. It's never been like this for me. What about you? Was it like this for you and your ex?"

Her brow pulled in. "How'd you know about King?"

He couldn't keep his laugh from bursting out. "King? His name is *King?*"

"His name is Richard. But he was a really good snowboarder, and the press dubbed him King. It stuck."

"Trust me, he didn't have to keep the nickname."

"Why do you say it like that?"

"Because I play ball. They're always coming up with nicknames for me."

"What'd they try to call you that you didn't like?"

"Lots of things."

"Like?"

"Like Hollywood."

"You are pretty gorgeous."

"Whatever. I'm saying you don't have to put up with that shit."

"He likes it. Not so much now, since he didn't pass the Olympic trials. So what do you let them call you?"

"Six." He had a grip on her thigh over the silky fabric, and he had to restrain himself from shoving it up to get to her skin.

"Six? What does that mean?"

"I play shortstop. It's my position."

"That's boring."

"Exactly."

She leaned back, taking him in. "You don't want them to see you."

"No, I'm controlling *how* they see me." Ryan cupped her chin, forcing her look at him. "Now get back to the sex."

"I'm not talking to you about my sex life with King."

He gripped her, pulling her closer to him. Those blue eyes widened, her jaw slackened, and her tongue came out to moisten her lips. "I want to know…" His jaw snapped shut. He couldn't believe the shit about to come out of his mouth.

She shifted to face him fully, cupping his chin. "You want to know what?"

In the dark of the cab, it felt like being under the covers with her, the two of them in their own little world. He felt like he could say anything with her. "I want to know if you respond like this with other guys." *Am I in this alone?*

"No," she whispered.

"Did you love King?"

"Of course. But it was complicated with us. We had history."

"Meaning?"

"He's from Utah. My parents had a winter house down the street from him. My family likes to ski, so we spent a lot of time there. He was an only child, and in some ways I was, too. So we hung out with each other and, I guess, we fell in love."

"You guess?"

"Honestly, I remember the bad more than the good at this point."

"When did you break up? For good?"

"Junior year of college. Right at the beginning. So, a year and a half ago. He was going to the Olympics and he wanted to be free. To…you know…"

"To bang other women?"

She nodded.

"What a dick."

She shrugged. "He's not a dick. He was honest with me."

"You can't break up with someone so you can fuck other people. That's bullshit. You either love someone, or you're fuck buddies."

A gentle smile lifted the corners of her mouth, and she scratched the scruff on his jaw. "You're a good guy. I thought you were like your friends, all man-whorish, but you're not. I think you're trying to be something you're not." And then she wrapped her arm around his shoulders and pressed a sweet kiss to his cheek. "King and I were on and off a lot. He doesn't come from a good family, so I was like home for him. He could go out into the world and do stuff, but he always had me to come home to. I'm sure I needed him in the same way. Dating sucks. I'm in a sorority, and I think you have a pretty good idea what frat boys want, so it was nice to have him there for me."

"Did he try to get back with after he didn't make the Olympics?"

She nodded.

"But you didn't take him back."

She ran her fingers through his hair, her voice soft. "I was done. I want to be more than someone's fallback."

His nerves thrummed from her touch. "What do you want?" He watched the rise and fall of her chest, the gentle way her teeth sank into her bottom lip. Gave her a minute to get her thoughts together.

"I guess...don't we all want someone who sees us? The real us. But likes us anyway? I guess I want to be completely myself around someone and not worry I'll bore them or...not be enough for them."

"No one's going to get bored of you. Not in ten lifetimes."

She drew in a breath, and the prettiest pink flush spread across her cheeks. "When you look at me like that I can almost believe you."

His restraint snapped. Drawing up the material of her dress, his hand slid up her thigh and squeezed. "Good. I mean it."

"The thing is…" She put her hand on top of his. "I think what gets me the most about you is the way you pay attention. I mean, as much as it pissed me off that you cut my boat ride short—well, and my concert—it excites me that you notice what I'm doing. You're at the resort, surrounded by sexy, willing women, and yet you notice that I didn't come back with my friends. That just makes me go all gushy inside."

"I can't stop thinking about you."

"You're nothing like what I thought." A slow smile warmed her features. "When I got to the bar last night looking for Laura, I noticed you. Of course I noticed you. You're gorgeous. But it was such a turn-off."

"Hey."

Her smile lit up the cab. "Yeah, because you need more women stroking your ego. My point is that you've got his movie star smile. It's all fake, like, *I am Ruler Thor, and with my smile I knight you.* But when you touched my leg? You weren't that cocky charmer. You were…I don't know, almost scared. No, not scared. You were in awe. And then the more we talked, the more I saw who you really were, and the hotter you became."

He leaned closer, heading for her mouth, but she leaned back.

"I love the way you want me."

Cupping the back of her head, he took her mouth and

tasted all her sweetness. But just as he deepened the kiss, she pushed him away.

"What about you and Emma?"

"What about us?"

"You know. Was it ever crazy like this?"

"Hell, no." The words shot out of his mouth with such aggression he surprised himself.

Sophie smiled. "I'm listening." She settled back against the door.

He reached for the lock, pushed it down. "I told you I don't like to talk badly about her." Besides, he'd much rather kiss her than talk about Emma.

"So it was bad?"

"It's just sex after sleeping with the same person for six years."

"I told you about the offer to buy Crazy Hearts. Do you know how bad that could be for me? If you told even one person, I could blow the deal for my family. I think you can tell me a little about your ex. And, besides, this time you really won't see me again. I'm going away tomorrow. So you can stop being my watch dog and move onto...other things." She wiggled her eyebrows.

But he wasn't amused. She was *leaving*? "Where you going?"

"There's a three-star restaurant here. Did you know that?"

He shook his head. From this position, he could see all of her, just how he liked it. The smooth skin of her thigh, her feminine hands. It was driving him crazy. And her mouth. Her expressive, beautiful mouth. He wanted to kiss her, reach under the fabric and hold the weight of her breast in his hand.

"Well, there is. It's part of a resort on the other side of

the island. It's so famous you have to make reservations months in advance. I can't wait."

"You can't wait for what? To eat in a fancy restaurant?"

She laughed. "To try the food. The chef makes a hybrid of Spanish, Caribbean, French, and Portuguese cuisine. I asked for the sampling menu." She shifted on him. "Now, let's go, cowboy. Back to the sex."

"I already told you. Sex was exactly what you'd expect after being with the same person for six years."

"You never slept with anyone else in all those years?"

"Of course I did."

She looked so disappointed in him. "You *cheated* on her?"

"No, but we broke up a lot. I went off to college, and she moved to Europe. We spent a lot of time apart. And, you know, we don't have a lot in common." Other than her dad, what *did* they have in common? Growing up in the same town used to be enough, he supposed.

He had to admit it felt good to get this shit out. Like opening a valve and letting off some of the pressure. "The sex was polite." He squeezed her thigh. "And I don't want to be nice all the time."

"So she never got to see Ryan Unleashed?"

"Never."

"Shame."

"I don't want to talk about Emma."

"Because you still love her? On some level, I mean."

"Maybe. On some level."

"You're being polite."

"Of course I am. She was my girlfriend for six years."

"But I don't know her. I'll never know her. So you don't have to be polite with me."

"I'm not going to disrespect her."

"By opening up? Venting? Ryan, if you want to get

anything out of this week, then at least open up. Tell the truth to yourself. Or are your feelings for her too complicated?"

"Of course they're complicated. Her dad practically raised me."

"Your feelings for *her*. That's what we're talking about. If it's so hard for you to talk about her, maybe you still love her." She smiled at him, obviously enjoying provoking him.

Only, it *did* provoke him. Stirred up an angry nest of shit. "I told you I don't love her. Not like that."

"But you have feelings for her."

"Of course I have feelings for her. What kind of an asshole would I be if I didn't have feelings for someone I've known most of my life?"

"Are you angry with her?"

"No. Jesus, Sophie."

"Are you happy with her?" Her smile broadened.

"Cut the shit."

"Are you frustrated with her? Afraid of her? Sad about her?"

"Sophie…"

"Are you displeased with her?"

"Knock it off. I'm not talking about Emma."

"I'm leaving tomorrow morning. You'll never see me again—well, you might see me, but I'll have a restraining order, keeping you ten feet from my adventures at all times."

He didn't like the sound of that, the not seeing her again part. His hand flexed on her bare leg. She looked down—her red dress rucked up, his big hand covering her thigh.

"Embarrassed by her? Suspicious of her?"

"None of those things, okay? I'm just sick of her. I need a break from her, from everyone. From every-fucking-thing."

"Because you're sick of doing what everyone else wants you to do?"

"How would I know what Emma wants for me? We only ever talk about Emma. She doesn't ask about me."

"Or do *you* not talk about you? I mean, is she totally self-involved or are you not the kind of guy who talks about yourself?"

"Both."

"So, if you open up a little, she'll have things to ask you about."

"Are you trying to fix my relationship with her?"

"Do you want it to be fixed?"

Fuck, no. "I want her to leave me alone."

"See what I'm saying? A second ago you said you have feelings for her since you've known her most of your life, and now you're saying you want her to leave you alone. You need to get it out, Ryan. Let it rip. Just say it. I swear you'll feel better. I don't know your friends, your family, I'll never meet Emma. So just say it."

He tapped her knee with his fist, anger rising, roiling, until he wanted to punch something. Instead, he looked into Sophie's hazel eyes and just fell into them. She wanted him to let it rip?

Brace yourself.

"She's neurotic. Her hair is too flat, she's too fat, nothing fits her right. She needs to know I love her all the time. She texts me every five minutes to see what I'm doing. She wants me on a leash, just to know I'm there so she can go out and party and have fun and know that I'm standing there waiting for her at home plate. Because the people she hangs out with? Fuck her over again and again. But me? She knows I'll never hurt her. She wants to keep me in line, and I can't fucking stand it. It's not...I don't want this kind of relationship. I don't want *any* relationship. I want to be free. That doesn't mean I want to fuck anything in a skirt. It means I don't want to feel obligated to check in with someone, take care of someone, be on my best behavior all the fucking time. I want to eat what I want, go where I want, and do whatever I fucking want. I don't want people telling me what to do all the fucking time. And I don't want to worry about someone's fucking feelings every minute of the fucking day."

Breathing heavily, he closed his eyes.

She drew a finger over his lip, wiping away the beads of moisture. Then, she leaned in and kissed him. "Now doesn't that feel better? And, look, you're still here. Nothing blew up. Your world didn't implode. And all you did was tell the truth."

Affection for this girl rolled through him in big, fat waves.

She leaned into him, the top of her dress gaping, revealing plump cleavage. "I'm glad you skipped your baseball games."

His fingers tightened on her thigh. He chased her mouth, wanting more.

But she pulled away. "We're here."

He looked out the window, only then noticing they'd turned into the long driveway that led to the resort. He didn't care. All he wanted in the world at that moment was her sexy mouth. So, he took it.

He got one hint of her sweetness, as his tongue touched hers and her fingers curled into his shoulder, before she pushed him away. Leaving him desperate, raw, and unfulfilled. She crawled off his lap, gathering the wrap and her little purse.

The cab pulled under the portico, and she pulled cash out of her bag. "I got this one."

At the same moment, the valet opened her door, and she slid out of the taxi, heading into the lobby. "I'm going to check in with my friends before I go to my room," she called over her shoulder.

Oh, hell, no. He caught up with her and grabbed her hand. He wasn't letting her walk away from him. She'd gone distant, all that intimacy they'd shared drifting away like smoke. They headed up the path, the sound of steel drums growing louder. Just as they reached the bar, just when her hand relaxed in his, like maybe she'd stay with him, Carrie stumbled onto the path and into his arms.

Sophie dropped his hand.

"There you are." Carrie slurred her words, gazing up at him with her hands on his chest. "I wondered where you'd gone. One minute you were hanging out with us, the next." She tried to snap her fingers, but she was too drunk. "I want you so bad. Let's go to my room."

The look on Sophie's face flayed him. He shook his head at her, letting her know he hadn't been with this woman. But then Carrie's knees gave out, and she burst out laughing, collapsing against him. His arms banded around her waist to keep her upright. "Hang on—"

But when he looked up, Sophie had gone.

CHAPTER NINE

Reeling from the sight of that woman in his arms, Sophie skimmed the perimeter of the dance floor looking for her friends. But she wasn't really seeing anything.

The woman had obviously felt comfortable—*familiar*—enough with Ryan to throw herself at him. It made her wonder if they'd spent time together.

What does it matter? That's who he should be hanging out with. Come on, he'd just unleashed a whole tirade about not wanting to take care of someone, check in with them…all the things she wanted. *Needed.* As attracted to her as he might be, this was just the wrong time for them to be together.

And she needed to stop caring about a guy she couldn't have.

All this angst and doubt was too reminiscent of her time with King. As close as she'd felt to him when they were alone, she'd always wondered what he did in their time apart. King was charming and charismatic. Their shared history—well, honestly, their shared isolation within their families—had forged a bond between them. But when he was at large in the world, he was everyone's buddy, a spontaneous, impulsive guy. And, truthfully, when he'd dumped her to go to the Olympic trials, she'd been devastated. For an occasion so momentous, when she'd been with him every step of the way since they'd become friends as kids, it had sucked to be dumped right then. And it had driven home how much she'd lived on the periphery of his world.

So, to be so close to Ryan, so trusting that she'd let him touch her intimately in public, and then to see him with some other woman—well, it just had peripheral written all over it, didn't it?

Sophie didn't want to see her friends after all, so she texted to let them know she was back at the resort. Too restless to go to her room just then, she headed for the beach.

She needed to stop obsessing over some guy she met on spring break. She'd come to this resort to deal with her family issues, her *future*. Last night she'd gotten good information from Barry, and now it was time to figure out the next step. She'd already sent messages to her brothers to see if they were a hundred percent on board with Abby's plans.

Surely one of them would side with her. It seemed impossible that all four of them wanted to sell Crazy Hearts. They'd grown up in a house filled with framed photos dating back to the eighteen-hundreds. History mattered to the Valentines.

From the framed sepia-toned photos her mom had hung on the walls, Sophie had conjured up images of a kitchen, an iron stove, her grandma pulling a batch of cookies out of the oven.

Originally, they'd been round cookies with a raspberry jam thumbprint. But when the family bakery had hit on hard times, her grandmother had the fabulous idea to take advantage of their last name and turn a staple into a special Valentine's Day treat.

Her heart seized at the idea that her grandma's cookies would become a Nestlé product.

But the offer? Honestly, how could her siblings turn down that kind of money? They wouldn't.

At least they couldn't sell it without her consent. Which was great—it gave her a sense of power—but, really, it put her in a terrible position. Withhold her consent and keep her siblings from a payout of a hundred million dollars or go along with it and lose her family legacy?

And she was worried about seeing some guy she'd met yesterday flirting with other women? A guy who, after this week, she'd never see again?

Heading down the walkway, toward the ocean, she ignored the text that had just come in from Ryan. She needed to call her sister, tell her to put a hold on her talks with Nestlé while she did a little more research. Sitting on the edge of a chaise, she smoothed the skirt of her dress, as she waited for the call to connect.

"Hey, Soph."

The baby screaming in the background and her sister's exhausted voice made her question the timing of her call. "Not a good time?"

"There's no good time. Let me hand her off. Just a second."

Sophie waited. Maybe she should talk to her sister another time. On the other hand, it had to happen now so Abby could deal with Nestlé right away.

She dreaded Abby's reaction.

One hundred million dollars.

"So what's up?" Her sister sounded on edge.

But it wasn't about the money. She had to keep focused on what truly mattered. "Not going well, huh?"

"I don't know what the hell I'm supposed to do. I feed her, change her…I mean, God, what does she want?"

"Is she colicky?"

"It's not like she's drawing her legs up. She doesn't seem to be in actual pain. Nothing I do calms her down. I'm officially the worst mother in history."

"The worst mother wouldn't care. She'd leave the baby to cry it out, and you're not doing that. You're a good mom. Besides, it's a phase, right? It'll pass. She's not going to be crying like this when she's twelve."

"I know. You're right. So what did you need?"

"Maybe now's not the best time." On a good day what she had to say would set her sister off.

"Soph…" She drew the word out like she was at the limit of her patience. "Spit it out."

"Okay. Well, I don't want to sell Crazy Hearts."

"I know that." She bit each word out.

"I talked to Barry."

"You *what*? Why would you talk to our lawyer?" But before she could say anything, her sister blew up. "You're going to take us to court?"

"Calm down. Of *course* I'm not taking my family to court."

Abby swore under her breath. "I do not need this right now."

No, Sophie suspected she didn't. That didn't change the fact that she had to deal with it. "But I am going to see what I can do to make *all* of us happy."

"I've gone over this with you. Selling processed food is a thing of the past. We're looking *forward*. We're taking this company into the *future*."

And Sophie heard the unspoken words. *With or without you*. And that just hurt. "I get it, Abby. I know where you're coming from, but I want to look into this a little bit more. I want to talk to everyone, see where everyone stands."

"I know where we all stand because there's nowhere else

to stand. One hundred million dollars, Sophie. We'd be stupid to turn that away for any reason, let alone a product that no longer fits our brand. We'll never get another offer like this so, trust me, we're definitely on the same page."

"I don't think it's unreasonable for me to talk to our brothers and hear their perspectives. But I'm letting you know I'm going to do everything in my power to keep Crazy Hearts in the family."

"What does that mean, exactly? If the four of us want to sell it, then that's what's going to happen. We make the majority."

"Right, but in this case the majority doesn't matter. As I said, I talked to Barry. We need one hundred percent agreement of the beneficiaries of the trust in order to sell any part of the company."

"Oh, my God. Why are you doing this? You don't even work here. And, I'm sorry, what were you before you decided at the last possible second to become a business major? Oh, right. A *dance* major. And before that, I'm pretty sure it was photography. And then before *that*? English Lit, if I remember correctly."

Every word hammered her deeper into the cushion of the chaise, making her feel smaller and flakier and more immature.

But deep in her gut Sophie knew she was right. And she wouldn't let her sister bully her. "I'm telling you the terms of the trust. I'm not talking about my life choices. But you need to know that I'm going to look into my options."

"There are no options, Sophie. Crazy Hearts is an old school product with a shrinking market."

"Well, it can't be that bad if Nestlé wants to buy it."

"This is a strategic deal for them. They're giving us some of the value they expect to create. It's a stupid offer, one we'll never get again, and I can promise you every one of us is in perfect agreement."

"You're talking about money. I'm talking about preserving the very foundation of the company. The history. I'm sorry, but I'm not giving my consent to sell Crazy Hearts."

"Do you even hear yourself? You want to hold this company back because of sentimental value. It's a good thing you're talking to *me* right now because I can't imagine what kind of response you'd get from our brothers."

"I'm not trying to hold you back. I'm holding onto our family legacy. Of course I get the business side of things. I'm not stupid. But I think I can find growth in Crazy Hearts."

"You don't work here, and you don't know the marketplace at all. And the bottom line is they're giving us a stupid price, and there's not a chance in hell we're turning it down."

If Sophie blocked the deal, they'd have no choice. But she didn't need to say that. Not yet. "I'm not stopping you from changing our brand. I'm on board with organic products and environmentally-sustainable production facilities. That's all great. But I'm not giving my consent to sell Crazy Hearts. That's why I'm looking into options. And one of them is me buying it from you."

"You don't have a hundred million dollars."

She knew her sister was exhausted, but she hated the condescending tone. "I don't have to have that much. I can simply block the sale, remember? But I'm not a bitch, and I don't want to alienate myself from you, so I'll see what kind of offer I can make that will satisfy everyone. But that's just one option. When I get home I'll look into others. It's possible one of the guys will want to run it with me."

"No offense, Soph, but you don't know what you're talking about."

"Okay." She kept her voice pleasant, even though she wanted to tell her sister exactly what she could do with her attitude. Bullying her into going along with their plans might've worked when she was a kid, but it didn't work now.

Or maybe she'd never cared about anything enough to fight for it. But they weren't selling Crazy Hearts. No matter how much Nestlé offered.

An image of her great grandma, her gray hair in a bun and a white apron wrapped around her belly, smiling into the camera popped into her head. Whether she'd actually met the woman or not, that grandma was real to her. She could feel the heart of that woman. And she wouldn't destroy the legacy her great grandparents had started.

Sophie could hear the baby wailing, and her sister let out an exasperated growl. "Look, I really can't deal with this right now."

"Okay." Sophie took in shallow breaths, fisting the material of her skirt. "You get back to the baby. We'll talk more when I get home."

But thanks, once again, for shoving my nose in the fact that it's the four of you against me.

Tossing her overnight bag into the backseat of the Jeep, Sophie glanced to the clear blue sky. *Another perfect day on Santa Granada.* She couldn't wait to explore more of the island. And, frankly, to get away. She needed a chance to clear her head.

A twenty-four hour reprieve from Ryan O'Donnell.

She waved to the concierge, who'd arranged the car for her overnight trip, then climbed into the driver's seat. Sliding the key into the ignition, she looked for the gear shift and then startled when she saw the car was *manual* transmission.

Oh, no. Quickly shutting off the engine, she got out of the car. "Sir? Excuse me?" She caught him right before he entered the lobby. "I'm so sorry, but I don't drive stick." She held out the keys.

The older man cocked his head. "Excuse me?"

"It's a stick shift. I only know how to drive automatic transmission."

"Ah. I see. Unfortunately, this is the only car left today."

"But I can't drive it."

"I'm so sorry about that, ma'am."

"No, I mean, I have to have a car." Frustrated, she glanced around, but the only other cars under the portico were a van and two idling cabs.

"I can check for availability tomorrow, if you like."

"No, I need it today. My reservation's for tonight in La Marca. I can't miss it."

"I'm afraid there's nothing I can do."

Dammit. "There must be something we can do. I lucked out and scored a last-minute reservation at Très Palmeras. I have to get there."

He pulled up the paperwork in his hand, scanning it. "I see no mention of automatic transmission."

Well, no, she hadn't specifically asked for it. It would never have occurred to her. "I didn't know I had to specify."

"We only have five rental cars. Three of them are manual, ma'am. Again, I can see if an automatic is available for tomorrow."

"No, thank you. I need to get there tonight. Can I hire a car service?"

"To take you to La Marca? I'll check, but it will be hard to find anyone who'll go that far. Not with the festival this week." He started to go.

"Wait, could you possibly give me a quick lesson?" How hard could it be?

He looked like he was going to tell her no, but then he sighed and said, "Let me see if Jorge can help you." He strode to the valet station and spoke quietly with the attendants. Three heads turned to her. One of the guys snickered. And, of course, that was the one who jogged over to give her a lesson in manual transmission.

"Hey." He stuck out a hand. He couldn't have been older than eighteen. "Jorge."

"Hi. Sophie." They shook. "Thanks for helping me."

"No problem. Okay, let's do this." He gestured for her to get in the passenger seat.

Settling in, she focused on his instructions.

"See how there are three pedals instead of two? This one on the far left is the clutch. It's what you'll use when you're shifting gears." He motioned to the center console. "And this is the gearshift. To start, you'll put your foot on the brake, then your left foot on the clutch. Then, you'll shift into first."

After detailed instruction, she switched places with him. One attempt resulted in a stalled engine. The second attempt ended in a horrible screeching sound.

The guy gave her an apologetic smile. "Hey, man, I'm sorry, but I've got to get back to work."

No, no, no. "I understand."

He reached for the keys.

But her hand shot out to guard them. "Wait. What're you doing?"

"I'm signing you out of the car."

"No. I'm still going to go."

"You can't drive it."

"I will. I'll keep practicing. I'll get it, you'll see."

Jorge looked back to the valet station, clearly unsure. She hated to put him in a bad position, but she was going to figure out how to drive the Jeep. He gave a deep sigh. "Okay, let's try this one more time."

She made it about halfway around the golf course, stuttering and stalling, when the car jerked and died. Sweaty with frustration, she smacked the steering wheel with her palm. "Dammit." Some golfers nearby froze, watching her. "Sorry."

Just beyond them, she noticed a group of three guys and two women. Ryan, wearing aviators, khaki shorts, and a white Polo shirt, stood out among them. His height, his stance, his *presence*, made him the focal point on the green.

And he was watching her. Lowering his head, he rested a gloved hand on top of his golf club. Around him the others laughed, all clearly flirting with each other.

When one of the women took her position to swing, her hips gently swaying as she sized up her shot, the tallest of Ryan's friends came up behind her. He wrapped his body around hers, as if to give guidance. But then he grabbed her hips and did a sensuous dance with her. The woman dropped her club and turned in his arms to give him a kiss.

Laughter rang out across the golf course.

But Ryan never took his gaze off Sophie. God, did he look good. She couldn't stop thinking about the way he'd touched her in the town square the night before. He'd been wild with need, yet totally in command. *That was hot.*

Okay, focus. Once she got manual transmission down she could leave the resort and not think about Ryan O'Donnell anymore.

Ready to give it another go, she started the engine, put her foot on the clutch, and drew the gear shift down to first. The car lurched forward, and she slammed on the brake. It stalled again.

"Oh, man," Jorge said. "Look, I'm sorry, but I really have to get back."

"I know you do. You go, and I'll keep at it. I've almost got it now."

"I'm not sure they're going to want you driving it, you know?"

Perspiration prickled under her arms, and she cut a look toward the golfers. Tossing his club on the grass, Ryan jogged toward her.

She had to get out of there. "You go. I'll get it right, I promise."

Jorge jumped out of the Jeep, watching Ryan approach. "Is he gonna help you?"

If saying yes was the only way for Jorge to leave her with the car, she'd pretend. "Yeah, he is. He's a friend."

"Okay, then. Take it easy." And then he took off.

A quick glance across the vibrantly green course showed Ryan nearing. Hell and damnation, she did not need an audience. She had to block everyone out and just calm down.

Okay, what had he said? Step on the clutch and the brake, put the car into first...*oh, awesome. Movement.* The car jerked forward—jerked again—but continued moving forward. What the hell was she doing wrong? She had to get it in second, but when she tried shifting it made that horrible screeching sound.

"Stop. Just stop." Ryan reached into the car and cut the ignition. "What the *hell* are you doing?"

"Driving."

He gave her a dull look.

"They gave me a stick shift. I've never driven one."

"I see that. Jesus, Sophie. You're killing the car."

"Do you know how to drive a stick?"

He stood there with his aviators and Lord of All Things Mechanical smile.

"Of course you do. Well, do you think you could teach me?"

With his broad chest right at eye level, he gazed down at her. "I'm in the middle of a game."

"All righty then. Please move along so I can figure it out on my own."

"Why the hell would he let you take out a car you can't drive?"

"Because I've almost got it."

"So you're not actually stalled here?"

"Yes, I'm stalled, Ryan. That's why I asked for your help. But if you don't want to teach me, then go back to your game."

"I don't have time to teach you how to drive a stick."

Ignoring his presence, she started the car, stepped on the clutch—

"Ryan." In a loose silk blouse, breasts bouncing, the brunette from last night hurried toward them. "You're up." When she reached them, she hooked her arm through his and smiled at Sophie.

Ryan pulled away. "Hey, Carrie. This is Sophie."

"We met last night." Sophie smiled.

Carrie cocked her head. "I don't remember." But then she gave an apologetic smile. "I think I was pretty wasted." She reached for Ryan's hand. "Come on. It's your turn." And then she gave a pleasant wave to Sophie. "Nice to meet you." She tugged on Ryan's hand, but he pulled free.

"I'm helping Sophie with something, so I'll have to catch up with you guys."

The happiness slid right off the woman's face. "Everything okay?"

"She needs help with her Jeep."

Carrie leaned toward the window. "Anything I can do?"

"No, thanks," Sophie said. "It's not that big a deal. And it won't take long at all."

"It might take long." Ryan gave her a hard look.

"I'm a quick learner." Sophie held his gaze in challenge, and sparklers went off in her chest. God, this was crazy, this snap-crackle of connection. She almost felt embarrassed by her body's reaction to him—until half his mouth curled, making her realize he felt it, too.

"Okay, well, hurry up." Carrie's gaze lingered on him for a moment before she turned and left.

Sophie reached for the key in the ignition.

"Move over."

"Excuse me?"

Tearing off his sunglasses, he stuck his face into the Jeep, forcing her to lean back. "Move over. I'm getting in."

Struck by all that masculinity, the scent of sun-warmed cotton, soap from his shower, and whatever shampoo he'd used, it took her a moment to answer. He was a formidable presence, and the energy rolling off him overwhelmed her. "You can teach me from the passenger seat."

"I'm not going to teach you. I'm driving you."

"You can't drive me to the other side of the island."

"Wanna bet?"

"Why?"

"Because you're going to get twenty minutes down the road, stall out, and then what? You'll be stuck on the road in the middle of nowhere by yourself."

"Why are you staring at my mouth?"

His jaw clamped shut. "Because I fucking love your mouth. I can't stop kissing it, remember?"

Heat rushed up her neck, burning her cheeks. "Yes, I remember. That was very rude of you to bring it up."

His arms reached over his head, hands clutching the roll-over bar of the Jeep. "Move over, Soph."

"This isn't a good idea."

"It's happening."

"I'm not coming back until tomorrow."

His nostrils flared, but he remained silent.

"And you don't want to see the volcano."

"Not really."

"I'm not missing the waterfall with magical properties." She gave him a meaningful look.

"No." His lips twitched. "I wouldn't expect you to."

When she didn't budge, he finally looked her right in the eyes and gave her the most searing look she'd ever seen. The heat, the intensity, ignited a flurry of explosions in her chest. Holding her gaze, he said, "I think you know I'm going with you."

She may have been a lot of things, but she wasn't a game player. And she loved the idea that he wanted to be with her. "Okay, but just to put it out there, I don't need you to drive me. If I really can't drive this car, I'll find someone to drive me. The car services might be busy because of the festival, but I'm willing to pay whatever they ask. I don't need to be rescued."

"No, but I do." He sighed. "Are you going to move over or do I have to pick you up and toss you into the passenger seat?"

Why did that idea send a thrill shooting down her spine?

He looked at her. And his restrained expression drew a smile to her lips. "One...two..."

"As hot as it sounds to be manhandled, I'd probably just wind up with a gearshift in my butt, so I'm going to pass. Plus, I just can't see myself coming out looking all that attractive sprawled over the seat." She opened the door, jumped out of the Jeep, and then stood before him. "You know this probably isn't a good idea, right?"

The intensity of his gaze thrilled her. "Buckle up."

Warm island air blew her hair around her face. As they traveled up the mountain, Sophie watched the land between the road and the ocean grow wider, the cliffs higher. Thunderous waves crashed against the shore. If she'd been alone she would've stopped a while back to walk down to the sand and experience them in all their powerful glory.

Ryan hadn't spoken much since they'd left the resort, leaving her to babble on. She couldn't help wondering what he was thinking. "Second thoughts about coming with me?"

"None."

She smiled at the certainty in his tone. But then…why so quiet? "Missing your golf game?"

"Golf's boring."

"Okay. Regretting time away from your friends?"

"My friends are swapping drinking stories."

Then what was troubling him? *Oh, whatever.* She wasn't a mind-reader. If something was bothering him, he could spit it out.

She turned her attention back to the map she'd printed out. Since there were no road signs to get to the falls, she had to watch carefully for the landmarks. They wouldn't see the path to the waterfall until they'd driven further inland.

After another mile of quiet, she couldn't take it anymore. "What're you thinking about?"

"I'm not."

"You're not thinking?"

"Nope."

"Who doesn't think? You're driving along, but you're not thinking?"

"Nope. I'm just enjoying being with you."

Warmth flooded her. She looked away from him, letting it spread through her, thick and sweet as caramel. He'd seemed at peace when they'd first started out and she'd told him about the island, the superstitions. She'd even told him about her conversation with her sister. He'd gotten angry at

Abby's attitude, and she'd appreciated his support.

Up ahead she noticed a stand of trees. "Here we go. It's getting more wooded. We're close." She read the information she'd printed out. "Pretty soon we're going to see a big rock with some graffiti on it, and then we enter a forest." She leaned into him, their arms brushing, as she reached for the control panel.

"What're you doing?"

"Reseting the odometer." She looked for the button. "The path's exactly two point four miles from the rock."

He batted her hand away, leaned forward, and hit the button.

"Awesome. I can't wait." She gestured to his lap. "You can go in your shorts."

"That's okay."

"Oh, you have to go in. The water has magical properties."

"So you said."

"You don't believe in it?"

He shrugged. "I believe telling people water has magical properties is a great way to get tourists to come out here and spend money. Do they sell it in bottles in roadside kiosks?"

"Well, hello to the itty bitty cynic who lives inside you. Does he come out often? I don't think I've met him before."

He slowly leveled her a look that said he wasn't amused.

So she met his with one of her own. "This isn't a *tourist* attraction. The islanders actually believe in it."

"And a tourist guide book told you that?"

"I didn't buy a tourist guide book."

"You learned it from an islander?"

"I got it from the Internet."

And then that serious face blew wide open with laughter. "Okay then." And that right there was the man she'd fallen for.

And, yep, no doubt about it. She'd fallen for this

complicated, moody, sexy man. "You can fester in your cynicism. I choose to believe in magical properties."

"And what do you hope to get from the magic?"

She quickly turned away from him. "I don't know."

"Wait, did you just blush? Are you...*embarrassed?*"

"Just drive the freaking car. I'm not embarrassed."

He took his foot off the accelerator, shifting gears. "Not until you tell me what you want the magic for."

She shoved his thigh. "God, Ryan. I want to eat whatever I want and not gain weight. I want to meet the man of my dreams and drive off into the sunset in a convertible. I want to find my passion and earn a living out of it. What does anyone want?"

"I love your body, so cut it out."

"I'm not going to stop eating. Besides, if I lose weight, I lose my boobs."

"I love your boobs."

She laughed. "Really? Huh. I didn't get that."

"I thought your passion was Crazy Hearts."

"I'd like that to be my *business*. But it's not my passion."

"But you love the business so why do you need more?"

"I don't love business at all. I love that my great grandma and grandpa turned a favorite cookie into a Valentine's Day treat that millions of people enjoy. It makes me happy to go into the store and see a whole display of Crazy Hearts. It makes me smile when I see faces light up when people eat one. But *I* don't make them. I don't dig my hands into dough and knead it and roll it out and cut it into hearts."

"What do you love?"

"I like travel. I like food. I like cooking. Dance. Reading. Hanging out with my friends."

"So drive a food truck and dance while you cook and read recipe books with your friends."

"Now you're making fun of me."

He smiled. "You're twenty-one. Why do you think you have to have all the answers?"

"Says the man whose future is completely set."

His features froze. The humor drained out of him completely. And then one second later he slipped his impassive mask back on.

This man needed to let it all out. "If you couldn't play ball, what would you do?"

"I'm playing ball." His flat tone told her the topic was not open for conversation.

"But let's say—for shits and giggles—that you weren't going to. Let's say the League of Ball Players got shut down in a nation-wide steroid sting—"

He shook his head like she was crazy, but she ignored it. "And you were forced out on the street, suitcase in hand. What would you do?"

"I'm a business major with a computer science minor from Mich U. I could get a job."

"Oh. Well, then. That's exciting. Who wouldn't give up the Yankees for a *job*."

He blew out a frustrated breath. "I write apps."

"You...*apps*? Like Twitter?"

He cracked a smile. "Yes, exactly." He gave her a deadly serious look. "I invented the Internet."

"Okay, smart ass. Guess what? I'm not a computer science major. Explain."

"You want to get baseball stats? I'm working on an app for it."

"Have you made any money on them yet?"

He shook his head, looking uncomfortable.

"Well, do you have anything ready to go?"

He nodded. "I've got one out there, but it's free. I did it for a class project."

"So…? What is it?"

"At school, you know how there's food at every meeting? Every department has luncheons or breakfasts, every committee meeting…food everywhere right? Well, at Mich, once the meeting's over, anyone can come in and polish off what's left. So I made an app to let people know when and where to find the free food. There's so much free food on campus, you'd never have to pay for a meal plan again."

"That's so cool. I love that."

His smile told her all she needed to know.

"You love it, don't you?"

He nodded.

"You love the challenge."

The smile faded, and he looked caught. Why was it so hard for him to face the truth?

"Is baseball still challenging?"

"Of course. Well, maybe not right now. But it will be. Going into the majors is a whole other level. It's much tougher."

"Nothing you can't handle."

"Probably not, no."

"And you've spent your life doing it, so…"

"Sophie."

"Yes?"

"I'm going pro."

"Of course you are. I'm just thinking how lucky you are to have something to do when you retire. That must be the biggest issue for professional athletes. Figuring out what comes next."

"I'm sure it is."

"What does the odometer say?"

"Two point one."

"Yay. I'm so excited." She reached into the back seat,

unzipped her travel bag, and pulled out a towel. "I only brought one towel, but we can share."

"I'll wait by the Jeep."

"You trust me to go all by myself into those deep, dark woods? To get near a body of water by myself? Because, Ryan, I didn't bring my water wings."

One half of his mouth kicked up, and she absolutely loved that she could make him smile.

She nudged him. "You're not losing interest in me already are you?"

"No." The word rang out like a shot.

She smiled at his intensity, trying hard to ignore the zing in her chest. He had no idea how passionate he was. He really didn't. "Well, good. Then you better come with me. I'd hate for a merman to yank me down and whisk me off to his underwater castle."

He slowed the car, edging onto the shoulder of the road. Leaning forward, he looked into the woods for a path. "Is that it?"

"Must be."

He eased into a stand of trees and cut the engine.

Her bare thighs stuck to the leather seat as she got out of the car. "Oh, it's beautiful here." The air smelled so fresh, like pine, a hint of ocean, and sun-baked earth. "I'm so excited." She turned back to find him leaning against the Jeep, watching her. She motioned for him to join her.

He pushed off the Jeep, blew out a breath like he was so put-out, but fell into step beside her.

"You know, I'm thinking those magical properties might do you a world of good."

CHAPTER TEN

As they descended the rocky path that followed the falls, Sophie had to stop and shake out the dirt and pine needles from the bed of her flip flops.

When Ryan turned and offered a hand for balance, the whole world quieted, narrowed, to just the two of them. She reached for him, their gazes catching, and her pulse quickened.

Something about the density of the forest, the shelter of the tree canopy, made her feel him intensely. In that long, intimate moment, she let it sink in. That he'd chosen to come with her, knowing she'd be gone overnight.

He could be with his friends, he could be with all those willing women, but when his hand curled around hers, his grasp so warm and secure, she couldn't help feeling that he belonged *here*. With her.

"Ready?" he said softly. And maybe she was reading into it, but the look in his eyes made her certain he felt the same way.

She nodded, sliding her foot back into the flip flop. Just as she started to pull her hand away, he tightened his grasp and headed back down the path.

When they got to the biggest pool, Sophie set her towel

down at the foot of a big pine tree. Pulling off her gauzy white tunic, she tossed it on the ground and then turned to find Ryan staring at her.

It still surprised her, how much he liked her body. She didn't wear skimpy swimsuits. Her bottom and boobs needed coverage, so there really was nothing provocative about her bikinis. Certainly nothing like what the women at the resort wore.

But every time Ryan looked at her like that—all hungry and lustful—it thrilled her. She had no idea what about her rendered him so speechless, but she loved it.

At the water's edge, she turned to him. "You coming in?"

He reached behind his neck for the back of his Polo, the muscles in his arms bunching. "Sure." Pulling off his aviators, he tugged the shirt over his head.

Holy cow. That muscled chest, the bulging biceps…God, he was gorgeous. She'd never been so aware of a guy's physique before. Sure, King was cut, but she'd never felt this intense, powerful attraction. It unsettled her.

Only when he reached out to her did she realize she was just standing there, staring at him. He gave her a sweet smile, so unlike what she'd expect from a guy like him. She figured he'd be all cocky about her drooling over him, but he wasn't. He was kind.

She wanted to run her hands all over him. She wanted to *lick* that smooth, golden skin. Was that weird? She couldn't remember ever wanting to lick a guy before. "Let's do this."

And then she jumped into the warm water, her feet landing on soft, silky mud. The pool came up to her ribcage, so she dove under, swimming out a few feet. Bubbles streamed out of her nose, as she rose to the surface. She found him watching her. "Come in. It's warm."

He shucked off his boat shoes and crouched at the edge of the water.

She ducked under again, swimming away from him. When she popped up, she found Ryan buck naked in the clear water, coming for her. "Do you feel it?"

Gaze trained on her, he broke into a slow, sexy smile. "Oh, yeah. I feel it."

"Why do I think we're talking about totally different things?"

"What're *you* talking about?"

"Magical properties."

"Nope. We're definitely talking about the same thing." Never taking his gaze off her, he took long strides towards her, the water swirling around him. Her chest tightened, her fingers tingled, and she held her breath until he reached her. Lifting her, he hitched her leg over his hip.

He lowered his face into her neck, breathing in deeply. "Hell, yeah, I feel it." And then he cupped the back of her head, lifting her mouth to his and kissed her.

******

Jesus. He couldn't get enough of her. Gripping her ass, he lost himself in the slick heat of her mouth. The low roar of the falls, the rush of water around his legs, and the clutch of her hands around his neck, sent a pulse of electricity through him.

With her body pressing against his, struggling to get closer, she grabbed a fistful of his hair and pulled. Hard. He walked her across the pool, lifting her onto the rock ledge.

"Fuck, Soph. I can't stand it. I want to be with you."

Foreheads touching, breathing uneven, her fingers stroked roughly through his hair. He knew she wanted him the same way, but she'd shown a hell of a lot more self-control so far than he had.

"Okay." She said it so softly he had to pull away from her.

Excitement struck his heart, and he couldn't catch his breath. "You sure?"

"Yes." She shifted forward and wrapped her legs around him.

He kissed her again, harder this time. *Oh, fucking hell.*

Desire roared like a bullet train through him, and he brought his mouth back to hers, his hands cupping her face, angling her so he could deepen the kiss.

Tongues stroking, he untied the back of her bikini, pulling the straps down to reveal her breasts. He cupped them, pushing them together, loving the weight, the hard nipples in his palm, and the way her body shuddered from his touch.

When he sucked a nipple into his mouth, she gasped, and he yanked the tie at the back of her neck, tossing the top onto the dirt.

Fingers dipping into the elastic of her bottoms, he tugged. "Off." She lifted one hip, then the other, as he peeled them off her wet skin and threw them.

Hands on her knees, he pressed soft kisses along her inner thigh. Her legs trembled, and her hands clasped the back of his head. Reaching for her ass, he drew her closer to his mouth, and his tongue stroked into her folds, seeking her slick heat. She gasped, shifting restlessly against him, her hands fisting in his hair.

Fuck, she drove him crazy. Everything about her. He loved the way she whispered his name, loved the way her thighs cupped his head, and he fucking loved the way her honey coated his tongue. Her response to him drove him wild.

He wanted to fuck her more than he wanted to breathe,

but he needed to calm down and take the time to make it good for her. So he focused on the sounds she made and the way her body stiffened when he licked her hardened nub. Her back arched, and her fingers dug into his scalp. When his tongue swirled around her clit, she let go of him, arms bracing behind her on the rock, ankles clasped behind his neck. "God, Ryan. Oh, *God.*"

As she rocked her hips against his face, her cries grew louder, more insistent, letting him know how close she was, and it fueled him, made him bury his face deeper between her legs, made his tongue flick harder and faster. He wanted her to come apart from his touch.

Her legs tightened around his shoulders, muscles tensing. "Ryan." She gasped, one hand coming back to grip his head.

Fuck. *Fuck.* He needed her so badly. Couldn't wait to get inside her, to feel all of her. And then her body jerked, and he knew she was there. She cried out, hips twisting and clutching his head to keep him in place.

When she settled, she lay back on the rock. "Oh, my God, Ryan. I just...that was...*God.*"

As much as he loved her dazed, satisfied expression, he couldn't take not being inside all that soft, wet heat. Heaving himself onto the ledge, he scooped her limp body into his arms. His bare feet crunched pine needles, as he snatched her towel off the ground. He tried to shake it out, but his cock throbbed, and the feel of her bare breasts against his chest made him wild. Jesus, he'd have her against the tree if he couldn't manage to lay the damn towel down.

As he fumbled with it, she laughed into his neck, then pulled free of him. Grabbing the towel, she bent over to lay it on the ground. Her round ass, the cheeks all pink from the cool rock, sent a shot of lust so intense through him, his knees went weak. Christ, he had to have her. *Now.* "Come here."

"Just wait a second."

Hands on her waist, he swung her around to face him, kissing her, reaching for that pink ass and hauling her up tight against him. He groaned into her mouth. He loved the feel of her, the way her hands moved restlessly over him. But then she reached between their bodies and palmed his cock and need burst into flames.

Enough. He couldn't take it anymore. He lowered to his knees, rolled onto his back, and grabbed her hips. "Birth control?"

She nodded, straddling his thighs. When he tried to pull her forward, to position her over his aching cock, she resisted. "Slow down."

"Can't." Jesus, she had no idea, as she sat astride him naked, those breasts bouncing with her every move. "Clean."

"Yes—"

"No, me."

When she shifted back his cock thrust up between the juncture of her pale thighs. She clasped both her feminine hands around him.

He jerked, his dick ready to explode. "Now, Sophie."

She gave him her mischievous smile. "Can't I have a second to appreciate you?" Her hands slid in a twisting motion around his length. "You are so beautiful. Every part of you."

"Jesus, Soph."

She leaned over and slowly licked around the sensitive head, her wet hair sprawling across his stomach.

He gritted his teeth and arched his neck, out of his mind with need. "*Fuck.*"

Her tongue swirled, and then licked under the ridge, one hand gripping him firmly at the base. Without warning, she sucked him deep into her mouth, and his hips lifted off the towel, fingers curling into fists from the decadent pleasure.

"Soph." He pushed her hand away, grabbed his cock, and pulled it out of her mouth. Gripping himself to ease the pressure, he watched her sit up, eyes all sexy, lips parted and wet. With a hand on her hip, he tried to position her over his cock. "Let me in, Soph."

"I just want to savor you." She fell forward, planting her hands at either side of his head, breasts at his chin. "I want to lick you from your mouth to your—"

He rocked his hips up, wedging his cock along her slick opening. He thought he might explode just from the slight friction and lush heat.

She closed her eyes, features softening. "Oh."

"Savor later. Need you now."

Slowly, she rocked on him. His cock sank deeper between her hot folds.

His eyes rolled back in his head, the tension in his body unbearable as her slick heat rubbed along the length of his cock. "Let me in."

She licked his nipple, let her tongue swirl around it, while her hands caressed his shoulders, his biceps, all the way down to his wrists.

Muscles bunched and coiled tight, he thought he might explode. "I want to fuck you, Sophie Valentine. Like I've never wanted to fuck anyone in my life."

"God, Ryan." Her expression turned hungry and feral, as she sat up, gripped his cock, and guided him inside her hot, slick body. "*Oh.*" Her shoulders hunched, and her head tilted back. "So good."

His hips jerked up, plunging him deep inside her, and it felt so unbelievably good. He grabbed her hips and held her in place. Jesus, nothing had ever felt like this. Nothing.

Hands on his chest, she lifted and sank back down, closing her eyes and sighing.

"Faster, Soph." He grabbed hold of her hips, fingers digging into her flesh, and lifted her. He thrust his hips up hard as he slammed her down on him. She cried out, the look of rapture on her face letting him know she liked it just as much as he did. So he did it again. And again. And, Jesus, did it feel good.

She was a goddess, with her dark hair all wet and wild around her, her shoulders pushed back. She reached behind her to grip his thighs, and it thrust her breasts out. They bounced—so fucking erotic—and he jerked up to cup one, sucking the nipple deep into his mouth. She swung forward, clutching the back of his head, riding him just as fast and hard as he needed. Her desperate sounds only fed his frenzied need for her.

"Fuck, Soph, *fuck*." A hand on her back, the other on her ass, he toppled her onto her back.

He powered into her, his cock swelling, spine tingling, and her eyes went wide as she let out a cry. She planted both feet on the towel and bucked her hips up to meet him. "*Ryan*."

She looked so beautiful, her features lost in ecstasy, her wet hair sprawled around her, those sexy lips parted.

His orgasm bore down on him. Clamping his hands on her hips, he held her to the ground as his hips pumped into her. Fuck him, her tight grip on his cock, all slick and hot, made his body yearn for more—more friction, more…more *her*. He needed to get deeper, go harder. God, he just needed her so fucking much he couldn't stand it.

And then electricity raced across his skin, making him burn. "Fuck, oh, fuck." He came hard, not letting her move as he snapped his hips again and again, out of control, through burst after burst of raw, wild pleasure. He didn't want to ever come down off this high.

Still planted deep inside her, he wrapped her in his arms, breathing harshly in the curve of her neck. His body shook from the power of his orgasm. "Did I hurt you?"

She scraped her hands through his hair. "Stop it. Would I let you hurt me?" She held him tightly. "I *love* when you let go with me. It's hot and real and…God, Ryan, it's amazing."

She was amazing. Everything about her.

He fell onto his back, and they lay side by side, looking up through the dense tree cover, sunlight spearing through the branches.

As his skin cooled and his mind settled back into his body, the tension slowly coiled through his muscles again.

He could tell himself he'd bailed on his friends because he didn't want to party all day and night like they did. He could tell himself he didn't like golf or hanging out by the pool. But the truth was he was falling for this woman.

Only, he couldn't have her. He had one objective: to go back to school refreshed and ready to face his future. Nothing was more important than getting back to the time when he was confident and sure of himself, of his life.

He sat up. "Let's get you to your three-star dinner."

Back on the road, Ryan ignored the phone vibrating in the cup holder. He knew Sophie thought he wasn't checking it because he was driving. But the truth was he suspected it was Emma, and he had no interest in dealing with her.

Last night, after he'd gotten Carrie safely to her room, he hadn't gone back to the bar. Instead, he'd showered and turned on the TV, trying to find his world-class discipline and block out all thoughts about Sophie.

But then Emma had called. He'd told her to back off,

that he'd talk to her after spring break. And he'd kept the conversation short because he didn't want to engage her.

But, of course, she wouldn't listen. She didn't like when he withdrew.

When his phone buzzed again, Sophie said, "You want to pull over and get that?"

"Don't want to make you late for your reservation."

"It could be important."

He wouldn't let Emma on this trip with him. "We'll be there soon enough."

"You afraid it's your coach?"

He shot her a look. "I'm not afraid of anything." And he wasn't. He knew he'd earned a consequence for bailing on his team. He was the captain, for Christ's sake.

Besides, it wouldn't be his coach texting. He'd given Ryan forty-eight hours to get back to his team. He had nothing else to say. The next move was Ryan's.

Houses started springing up, letting him know they were approaching the town of La Marca. When he got to the resort, he'd check his messages. They couldn't all be from Emma.

"Do you think it's your ex?"

"I don't know, and I don't care. Whatever it is can wait until I get to the resort."

"Then maybe you should turn off your phone. You can't relax when it's blowing up like that."

It buzzed again. Something *was* wrong. Too many texts coming in. His fingers gripped the wheel. "We getting close?"

She nodded, looking ahead. "The resort's on the outskirts of town, so we should see a sign coming up soon."

"I'm sorry for jumping down your throat."

"Don't be. I'd be freaking out, too."

"I'm not…" He blew out a breath. "Yeah. Something's going on."

She put her hand on his thigh. "We can pull over. Better to face it than make stuff up in your head."

"We're almost there."

The road descended, and the area grew more populated. An automotive shop, a gas station. And then he saw a billboard, set against a backdrop of trees, announcing the resort and its three-star Michelin restaurant. "Here it is."

He glanced at her, taking in the wide smile. She practically glowed with energy. And just like that the thick cloud hovering around him dissipated. Just being with her made him happy.

At nearly six o'clock, the sun was still bright. He pulled under the portico of the resort and handed off the car keys to the valet. Grabbing Sophie's bag out of the back seat, he met her on the pavement.

When she looked up at him with a serious expression, he worried his mood had ruined her trip. "I'm going to check in and change, but I wanted to point out the obvious. You don't have to stay with me. I know you don't care about Chef Tomas's sampling menu or the volcano I'm going to see tomorrow. And it was really nice of you to come with me today, but I know you've got other things you'd like to be doing."

He looked away from her, only aware of his sunburned neck when the collar of his shirt scraped against it. She was giving him the out he knew he should take. Because he *should* go back to the resort. He flexed his toes inside the leather shoes.

"Go on and head back. I'm in a thousand-dollar a night resort. If I ask for a car, they'll find me one. Or I'll hire a driver. You've been awesome, but it's okay. You can go."

She stepped closer to him. "Look, I know you've got this thing about not upsetting the people that matter to you, but I'm not your alcoholic mom or your dad who couldn't handle things. Besides, I'm super boring. I'm just going to eat my sampler meal, walk on the beach, take a shower—"

"I'm in."

She laughed. He loved when she did that. It lit her up, made her eyes sparkle. "What?"

"You had me at shower."

"I didn't say I'd shower with you."

"Didn't you? Sorry, my mind must have made the leap."

The energy crackled between them, and he felt the joy of it sink into him like a hot coffee on a cold day. "Go check in. I'll grab our table before they give your reservation away."

The look she gave him—so happy, so unabashedly joyful—made him happier than he'd felt in a very long time. "Sounds perfect."

Even though she'd only booked the reservation a week ago, she'd managed to score the nicest table in the room. Ryan breathed in the salty air, as he gazed out the open window overlooking the sea. With the steady crash and drag of waves the only music in the low-lit room, he started scrolling through the text messages.

He had three from Emma.

I hated that phone call. Nothing's right between us.

We've been apart too long. We need some time alone. It'll be better when we're together.

I'm coming to see you. Already booked my ticket.

Jesus, why wouldn't she let up? He didn't know how much

clearer he could be. He wasn't getting pulled into her drama.

The best thing about Sophie was her straight-up, in-your-face honesty. It made him see how hard he worked to manage everyone's feelings and expectations.

What Sophie had said earlier—that not everyone was like his alcoholic mom or frazzled dad—hit him. Really, his only childhood memories were of irate parents. They'd gotten into physical fights—his dad prying the bottle out of his mom's hands, restraining her when she threatened to off herself. And all because of Ryan's temper. His demands.

He'd always caused trouble. Demanding food, rides. Always wanting something.

The same wild frustration that drove him to this island was what he'd grown up feeling in his home. The countless times he'd wanted dinner but had found his mom passed out in bed. He'd shake her, demanding to be fed. Then, when his dad came home, Ryan would nearly attack him, all sweaty and angry. He'd never forget the way his dad's complexion would get all mottled and red, how he'd push Ryan aside, storm into his mom's bedroom, and slam the door. Not only would Ryan still not get dinner, but he'd cause yet another screaming match between his parents.

So, yeah, maybe he did work to avoid confrontations. All that chaos of his childhood? He'd instigated it. And while nothing had bothered his younger brother, Ryan would never forget the haunted look in his little sister's eyes. She'd seen everything.

I did that. By demanding so much, he'd created the chaos.

He hadn't thought about it before, but he suspected Sophie was right. Not everyone would react the way his dad and mom had. And even if they did, it was slowly killing him trying to keep everyone happy.

He wished he'd told Emma flat-out that it was over

between them. Staying friends was only preventing her from moving on.

And damn if that didn't hack a wide swath of relief through him. *Should've done it months ago.* Tucking his phone into his pocket, he looked up and did a double-take on the stunning brunette heading his way. His heart pounded, and he gripped the cloth napkin in his lap. *Sophie.* Jesus, when she smiled his heart actually hurt.

"Hey, handsome." She slid into the seat across from him. Her smile faded. "You all right?"

She'd put on make-up—a touch of raspberry on her lush mouth, a brush of pink across her cheeks, mascara to frame those startling blue eyes. He had to force himself to breathe. "You're gorgeous."

"Oh." She looked away, unrolling her napkin, spreading it across her lap. "I didn't have time to shower, so I probably smell like sun tan lotion."

But she didn't. She smelled like she always did—that soft hint of sweetness that stirred his blood.

The server approached the table. "Good evening. Miss Valentine?"

Sophie beamed her dazzling smile. "Yes."

"I see you've brought a guest. Will he be having the sampling menu as well?"

Ryan didn't have a clue what was on the menu, nor did he care. "Sounds fine."

Sophie reached across the table for his hand, the action plumping her breasts in the round neck of the slinky, sky blue dress. "You don't even know what's on it." Then, she smiled at the server. "Can you please leave us the menu, and he'll decide what he wants?"

"Absolutely." The woman set a menu down. "I'll give you a few minutes."

She left, and Ryan pushed the menu away. "I really don't care. Whatever you're having is fine."

"What's the fun in fine?" She crooked a finger, beckoning him to her side. "Come take a look at the menu with me."

He couldn't have cared less about the menu, but he wouldn't miss the chance to sit next to her.

As soon as he slid in beside her, she opened the menu. "So, what looks good?"

Candlelight flickered over her features, accentuating her rosy cheeks. Her hair had dried all wavy and loose and smelled like sunshine and flowers. Her skin glowed with health and vitality, and that lower lip, so plush and dark pink, stirred his arousal.

"Do you like shellfish?"

What had she said? "Sure."

"Really? I hate it. Why do people even eat oysters? Aren't they like eating globs of snot? And mussels?" She shuddered. "I don't get it. And that's all they have tonight, shellfish. Do you want hocked-up loogies?"

He wanted to kiss her mouth. Instead, he laughed. "No, Sophie. No loogies."

"Then pay attention because that's what you'd get if you let someone else decide what you're eating tonight. What do you like?" Her blue eyes glittered with humor. "How about venison?"

"Sure."

"Great. Because it's not on the menu. Can you please pay attention?"

"I promise I'm paying attention."

"No, you're not."

"I'm paying attention to the only thing in the room that matters." He placed his hand on her thigh, felt the soft material of her dress and the heat of her skin underneath. He gave her a squeeze, and he loved the way her eyes heated.

"Trust me. This is a once-in-a-lifetime experience tonight. You should really choose the kind of food you like."

"I'm pretty easy."

"Yes, we know. But being easy isn't making you happy."

"I'm happy."

"Is that why you're here instead of playing shortstop with your team in front of the scouts?"

Ouch. She hit hard.

"You know, expending all your energy trying to keep everyone *else* happy is a losing enterprise. Why not expend it on figuring out what makes *you* happy?"

"You make me happy." Her lips parted, her eyes rounded, and color rushed into her cheeks. He shrugged. "You do."

"Ryan." Doubt fell across her features, and she grew uncomfortable. "Sometimes I can't tell if you're being charming or real."

"I'm real with you."

"Yeah. I think you are." She reached for his hand. "Were you real with Emma?"

"I never really thought about it."

"Okay, well, if you pay attention to your life, maybe you won't wind up in any more six year relationships that drag out long past their end-dates. Now, let's figure out what you like to eat."

He pulled his hand away. "Fine. Give me the menu."

She handed it to him. "Why would you ever just eat for fuel? Eat because it tastes delicious. Because it makes you happy." When she leaned closer to look at the menu with him, her breast grazed his arm, and all the blood in his body rushed to his cock. "Look at the desserts. They're supposed to be out of this world."

"Gruyere donuts with maple syrup? That sounds disgusting."

"Yeah, it does."

"Ginger-flavored panna cotta with poached pears?" Was she joking with this shit?

"Keep going."

"Honeycrisp apple Napolean with caramel custard, cider syrup, and vanilla spice gelato. That sounds okay."

"I like the chocolate cake."

"You're showing me all this crap, and all you like is the chocolate cake?" He slammed the menu closed.

"At least I've looked at the other choices and eliminated them. If you'd taken whatever they gave you, you'd be biting into a gruyere donut."

"True."

"So, if you don't want roasted kitten with caramelized onions and a sherry lime sauce, you should look at the menu."

But he couldn't take his eyes off her. He wanted to suck that plump lower lip into his mouth. He wanted to press her down on the banquette and feel her soft curves under his body. He was so hard right then he didn't give a shit what the waitress brought him to eat.

The heat of her hand at his temple, the scrape of her nails across his scalp, made him turn his mouth to press a kiss to her wrist. But she pulled away. "You should probably order." Her gaze slid past him to where the waitress waited.

The last thing he wanted to do was pay attention to the menu, but for Sophie he'd do anything. Scanning it, he saw he had three choices. The tasting menu, the prix fixe, and the sampling one Sophie had ordered. When he saw that it included a bite of every item on the menu he gawked. "That's what you're getting?"

She nodded with a mischievous smile.

"You can't eat that much."

"It's literally a *bite* of everything. Just to show off the chef's cuisine. It's awesome."

"Fine. I'll have a bite of everything." He handed the menu to the waitress, who also took their drink order, before disappearing into the dimly lit dining room.

His hand found her thigh, gathering up all that slinky material and sliding it higher to expose her creamy skin. His heart raced, and he needed more. "You're not going to eat that much."

"Maybe. But I want to see it. It's going to be a beautiful presentation."

His hand glided higher. "Beautiful, huh?"

"Am I too hard on you?" Her words came out on a soft gust of air.

He brought her hand to his hard-on. "Yes."

She gripped him, looking all hungry and needy. That pink tongue came out and wet her lips. "I'm sorry. I just feel like I can see the stuff in your life that maybe you can't right now." The heel of her palm pressed down, as she slowly rubbed his cock.

Sparks fired in his blood. His pulse skyrocketed. "Fuck, Soph." Tipping her chin, he pressed his lips to hers, licking the path her tongue had just taken. She leaned closer to him, her scent filling his senses. His kiss turned carnal, as he stroked into her mouth. When her hand closed around his cock and squeezed, his knees hit the table.

He pushed her up against the half-wall of the booth, pressing that sexy as fuck body as close to him as he could get. He needed to feel her skin, needed her body wrapped around him. God, he wanted every inch of her bared to him. Fuck the menu, he wanted *her* to be his feast.

Smoothing out the material of her dress, he slid his hand between her legs. When he felt dampness on her inner thighs, his skin prickled with anticipation. And then, when his fingers brushed her damp curls, electricity flashed through him. "You're not wearing underwear."

Her hands cupped the back of his head, and she whispered in his ear, "I was in my bathing suit. I only brought one pair, so I thought I'd save it for tomorrow."

"Sophie," he breathed, before taking her mouth. She opened right away, her hand sliding to the back of his neck, pulling him closer. Fuck, he couldn't help himself. He had to delve into her slick heat.

She shifted restlessly, parting her thighs, letting him inside. Between her hot, wet mouth and the honey between her legs, his pulse spiked and blood pounded in his cock. He kissed her hard, licking into her mouth, tangling with her tongue, his fingers plunging inside her slick channel.

Fucking hell, she felt so good, so soft and lush. He pressed against her, pushing her back, his hand so far up her dress he'd exposed the tops of her thighs.

"What're you doing to me?" His blood surged and his body roused with the imperative to sink inside her, pound into her until he finally relieved this constant ache, this powerful drive to fuse with her.

"And here we are." The waitress's voice tore into his lust-driven state of mind.

He quickly withdrew his hand, pulled her dress down, and sat up. Dragging his palm over his mouth, still wet from their kiss, he had to shake some sense back into himself.

"Your drinks." The waitress poured sparkling water into the glasses and then left the bottle on the table.

After she left, he said, "I'm sorry." Jesus, he'd mauled her in a restaurant. If the waitress hadn't interrupted him, he would have absolutely taken Sophie all the way over the edge. No question.

He'd completely lost control.

He *never* lost control.

Sliding out of the booth, he scrubbed his jaw. "Excuse me."

Needing air, he stalked away. He pushed through a side door that led to a garden. Immediately, the warm, flower-scented air cleared his head. A fountain with tinkling water drew him further in.

He was more screwed up than he'd realized if he'd just about finger-fucked Sophie in a three-star Michelin restaurant.

Needing a slap of reality, he pulled out his phone to find dozens of texts.

Jake. *Where are you?*

Another. *You left with that chick hours ago. When you coming back?*

A third. *Are you still with that girl? What're you doing?*

A fourth. *Six years with one chick, and you jump into the next relationship that comes your way?*

He didn't need to read anymore. Of course Jake was right. Stepping around the fountain, he stood on a teak deck overlooking the ocean. Gas lamps lit a path to the beach. A couple strolled hand in hand along the shore.

Of course he wasn't in a *relationship* with Sophie. He was...what was he doing? He didn't know, but the idea of being a couple again...fuck, no. He didn't want to be tied to someone. Relationships required time and attention he absolutely couldn't give. Forget that. Attention he didn't *want* to give. Compromises. Jesus, the compromises to make

Emma happy had nearly driven him out of his mind.

He checked his voicemail and found one from Doug Saunders.

A chill blew through him. *What the hell did you think? Your agent wouldn't have something to say about you taking off without telling him?*

This one he had to hear. He jammed a hand deep into his pocket and waited for his agent's voice.

"Hey, Ryan. Doug Saunders here. Heard about the family emergency. Let me know as soon as you can whether you'll be at the next game. I can reprogram the scouts if you're not, but I've got to tell them something. Hope all's well. Let me hear from you soon."

Ryan thumbed the pad, ending the message. He stood there in a dark corner of the garden, sick to his stomach.

His coach, his teammates, his agent, the scouts…he'd lied to all of them.

He'd never been more ashamed of himself.

He'd worked hard to be the guy coaches counted on. First kid at practice, first to pitch in to help. It had taken a lifetime of good decisions to earn his great reputation.

And in one stupid moment, he'd blown it all to hell.

His dad was right. It *had* taken a whole community to make him into the player he'd become. A player good enough to make the majors.

He'd failed them, and he'd failed himself.

It all bore down on him. He had a good enough relationship with his coach that he could be forgiven for this one aberration in his behavior. But his agent? Every year Doug had a roster of up-and-comers from colleges around the country. If he came clean, Doug wouldn't hesitate to dump him. Knocking Ryan O'Donnell off the list wouldn't mean shit to him.

He shoved his hair back from his temples, gripping his skull. *What the fuck are you doing?* Very few draft picks started out in the majors, but Doug thought Ryan had a shot. But if the truth came out that he'd bailed on his team to spend spring break in the Caribbean, he'd be toast. Dread pinched his nerves, making them sting.

His forty-eight hours ended tomorrow. Going back for the next game would clean up his mess. His agent would never have to know about the lie. Ryan would stay on track.

Either way, this thing with Sophie had to end. Tomorrow, first thing, he'd head back to the resort and make his travel plans.

His life was careening out of control. And he had to fix it.

No more fucking around.

CHAPTER ELEVEN

Since he'd come back from the bathroom—or wherever he'd gone—Ryan hadn't taken his attention off his phone. Sophie watched from across the table, as he shoveled food into his mouth while reading the screen.

She couldn't gauge his mood. He just seemed... distracted. "Is everything all right?"

"Hm?" His fingers tapped on the keypad.

"Ryan?"

Her sharper tone had his gaze flicking up. "Yeah?"

"Is everything all right?" She gestured to the phone.

"Sure. Yeah. Just...catching up with everybody. You know."

"No, I don't know." And what did that mean, *catching up with everybody*?

His brow creased as he read a text that just came in.

"Did your teammates find out?" She couldn't think of any other reason his phone would be blowing up.

"What?" His impatience felt like such an insult.

She understood if he was dealing with his friends finding out about his lie, but he didn't have to be so rude. It wasn't like him. "If there's something going on, just go and deal with it."

He stilled, phone propped in one hand, fork in the other. "Sorry." He let out a long-suffering breath. "Let's just eat."

"We can get it to go. Would that work better for you? Doggy bags for my three star Michelin-rated dinner?" Her sarcasm went unnoticed. Okay, he had a lot going on. She'd give him the benefit of the doubt. "Did you hear from your coach?"

"No." Terse, cold. The man had shut down. "So. Any news on your business situation?" With that tone, he might've been talking to the waiter about settling the bill.

She studied him a moment. He'd been all over her before the waitress had brought the water—had that freaked him out? He wasn't used to losing control. Or maybe he'd talked to Emma. Maybe she was pressuring him to get back together.

You know what? It doesn't matter what happened. You don't treat someone like this no matter what you're going through. He wanted to change the conversation? *Fine.*

Toying with the pecan-crusted Chilean sea bass, she set her fork down. "Not news, really. I talked to my brothers. They're all on board with Abby's plan. Which, of course, I expected." Although, truthfully, little butterfly wings of hope had beaten underneath that *expectation.* She'd wanted at least one sibling on her side.

"What did they say?"

"I didn't actually talk to them. I emailed Mark and texted the other two. So we didn't get into it. They just said the offer was too good to pass up. Anyway, I've been thinking about it a lot, and it just seems like if I move forward with my effort to keep Crazy Hearts, then I pretty much lose my family."

"That's one way to look at it."

"It's the most important way to look at it. My family means more to me than a business deal."

"I thought Crazy Hearts was about a great grandmother in England who'd made a cookie that was so good it was passed down for generations. When did it become a business deal?"

Right. She'd forgotten that for a moment there. "You're right." She sat back. "You're totally right." She picked up her fork, driving the tines through the soft white fish. "My sister just had a baby, and she's having a hard time. She's not getting much sleep, so she's kind of…"

"Selfish?"

Her gaze snapped up to him. "Emotional."

"Whatever. Your life, your choice."

"Yes, that part couldn't be clearer to me."

"What's not clear is why they can't do their organic thing, while maintaining Crazy Hearts. It's the reason Valentine's has a reputation. No one cares about the other crap you sell."

She hadn't told him what Nestlé had offered. "It's a stupid amount of money."

"How much?"

"A lot."

He shrugged. *Whatever.* "At least you'll all be set for life."

"That's a stupid thing to say." Why was he talking like this? "I should be happy with the cash, live a life of leisure?" Anger rippled beneath her skin. "Besides, I'll be sick knowing someone else is running Crazy Hearts. Maybe even changing it."

"Well, Sophie, it's really not that complicated. You either give your consent and get on board with their new brand of organic and sustainable products and stock up on Crazy Hearts at CVS every February like the rest of the world, or you figure a way to buy out your siblings and run it yourself."

Irritation blasted through her. "Not complicated?" Why

was he being such a jerk all of a sudden? "Right, of course. Such a simple choice between buying a company I have no clue how to run and alienating my siblings, or kissing my family's legacy goodbye."

"And enjoy a lifetime of financial freedom."

"I already have that. It doesn't buy nearly as much as you think."

He held her gaze, and for a moment she thought she might have broken through. That he'd come back. He had that look in his eyes—like he was really seeing her.

Joy bloomed in her heart. She *wanted* him to talk it through with her. She needed his perspective. "I know nothing about running a business."

But just when she thought he was leaning toward her, that he was about to reach for her hand, he pushed back in his seat. "You should talk to my buddy Jake. His family runs Cellular Integration. They started out making cell phones, but they've expanded into other businesses. It's family run, just like yours. Jake's been involved since he was a kid. In fact, you and Jake have a lot in common." A smile crept over his features. "I'll have to hook you two up when we get back."

Her fork clattered on her plate. "What the hell does that mean?"

"Just what I said." He shrugged. "He can talk to you about running Crazy Hearts, give you a chance to see if it's something you can handle."

"You said *hook me up*. With a stupid smile."

He looked *so* put-out. "Can we not do drama right now? I'm saying my friend can help you. That's it, okay?"

"You made it sound like you were setting me up with him."

"No." His shoulders went rigid. "That's not what I

meant." He huffed out a breath. "You know what? Why the fuck not? I'm leaving, so it really doesn't matter who you hang out with."

"Why are you being like this? Just talk to me."

"Jesus Christ, Sophie. Would you give me a break here? The last thing I want to do is talk. Can you just leave it alone?"

"That's kind of hard to do when you're passing me off to your friend. Look, obviously something happened when you went to the bathroom."

"Nothing happened." He sounded like he was placating her, and the idea that he would treat her like his needy ex— or all the other people in his life that wanted something from him—drove her crazy.

"Cool. So I imagined it then? That you went from practically having sex with me at the table to setting me up with Jake?"

His gaze, fixed on something just over her shoulder, narrowed, and he sat perfectly still. After a tense moment, he exhaled roughly.

And then, as if looking into a camera lens, he let loose his signature smile. *Oh, my God.* All that was missing were the damn aviators. "Not passing you off, babe. Just trying to help you out."

She thought she'd known him. That they'd had some kind of special connection. God, was she stupid. *You don't know someone in three days.*

She looked at the third course samplings set before her. Not even halfway through her feast, and she'd lost her appetite. She'd so looked forward to the desserts. "Are you going to snap out of it any time soon?"

He maintained that stupid smile. His phone buzzed, and he read the screen. He snickered and then started tapping away.

This was not her Ryan. Her Ryan wouldn't engage in a text conversation at the dinner table of a three-star restaurant.

She'd had enough. "I don't know what happened in the fifteen minutes you left the table, but I do know I'm not going to sit here and let you treat me like crap." She reached for her clutch, slid out of the booth, and took off.

Eyes stinging, she blinked back the tears.

This was why she didn't sleep with guys right away.

Had she held off a couple days, she would've seen his true colors.

"Can you keep a secret?" Cradling the phone between her shoulder and her ear, Sophie pushed the elevator call button.

"You know I can, sweetie." Even though only eighteen months separated her mom and her aunt Georgie, the sisters couldn't have been more different. Where her mom had lived in Beverly Hills, presiding over charitable organizations and running a corporation, her aunt lived on a ranch in Montana. She rode horses, hiked, fished, and skied.

Sophie hadn't known her aunt well until she'd moved in after her parents had died. In those two years, Aunt G had felt more like a mom to her than her own. Maybe because she'd been older, and her aunt had spent so much time with her. In any event, she knew she could trust her with the news. "We have an offer to buy Crazy Hearts. And Abby and my brothers want to take it."

"Really?" After a moment, her aunt said, "How do you feel about that?"

"I hate it." Tears blurred her vision. The bell dinged, and the doors parted. She stepped inside.

"And you've talked about it with them?"

"Yes." She blinked several times to clear the moisture so

she could see which button to push for her floor. "I even called Barry, just to see if I had any say in this."

"Oh, my love, you absolutely have a say. What did you learn?"

"That, according to the trust, it isn't about a majority rule. All five of us have to agree."

"And you shared this with your sister?"

Interesting how she didn't include her brothers. "Yeah."

"I'm going to guess that didn't go over well."

"She thinks we'd be stupid to pass up an offer that not only isn't even close to the value of the business but will never come our way again." She let out a shaky breath. "I know they think I'm an unsophisticated businesswoman for not understanding why this money—and, Aunt Georgie, it's a lot—is so much more important than a cookie. And I'm sure I am. But, come on, *Crazy Hearts*? I have to do something."

"Of course you do."

"I'm not going to take my brothers and sister to court or anything, but I do want to explore my options."

"And what does Barry say about that?"

"He told me I can use my shares to buy them out, but…do you think I can run Crazy Hearts on my own?"

"Sweetheart, I don't know enough about it, but I think you can do anything you set your mind to." She paused. "And, most importantly, I think you can hire the people necessary to run it, so yes, I think you *can* run it on your own."

"God, when I think about the amount of money. It'll basically set up a Valentine dynasty." She forced a laugh.

"What do you think your parents would've done?" her aunt asked quietly.

And just like that her rocked world settled comfortably

back into place. "They wouldn't sell. They would never even consider the offer." She knew it without a doubt.

"I'm pretty sure that's why they set up the trust the way they did, sweetheart. That's what your mom told me. So one generation can't undo the work of the ones before it."

"That's exactly what Barry said. But, um, there's something else. Abby and my brothers want to rebrand the company. Become sustainable and organic, which would mean they couldn't produce Crazy Hearts in the same facility."

"Ah. That would be a problem."

And here's the tricky part. "It would mean I'd have to build my own plant. Unless I wanted to change the cookie. You know, make it organic."

"Is that what you want? To go in the same direction as Abby and the boys? Or do you want to keep it the same?"

"I could look into changing it, but I can't see the harm in a cute little cookie. We're not talking about a staple food of the American diet. We're talking about a beloved Valentine's Day treat."

"I agree. So we're talking about a new facility." She paused. "Which would mean you'd have to split off completely from your sister and the boys."

The idea of her siblings hating her sliced deeply. "I have no idea if I could afford to build a new one. Plus, hiring people, taking on all the administrative stuff. I mean, God." Pressure built inside her chest. "It's too much, right? It's way beyond what I can handle."

"Well, hang on. I don't know how you feel about living in Montana, but I happen to have that big events building just sitting here on my property. What do you think about that?"

The car settled and the doors parted. Sophie strode out

into the softly lit hallway. A fuse lit deep in her belly, sending warmth along her limbs. "I like it."

"Building's yours if you want it. You know the house is plenty big enough for you to live here with me, too."

"I think I'd want to live on the mountain." *Oh*. Living in *Montana*. She'd never even imagined living there, but it would be perfect for her.

"Yeah. I can see that."

"But I don't want my family to hate me."

"Sweetheart, you've waited an awfully long time for your sister and brothers to bring you into the fold. Maybe it's time you lived your own life. Take some chances, see how things turn out."

Fishing her card out of her clutch, she swiped it and let herself into her room. "If I move away, I won't ever get a chance to be included in their lives."

"And how much longer are you willing to wait for that to happen? You're almost twenty-two." Her aunt went quiet. "I had the impression you didn't exactly love living in that house."

The ache of that loneliness filled her. "I hate it." Sophie had grown up there, and it had never felt like a home. Sixteen-thousand square feet of high ceilings and huge rooms just highlighted the fact that she lived there alone. Her siblings didn't want to sell it, but that was because they had memories of big Christmases and birthdays and their friends making use of the game room and theatre, the pool and tennis court. But Sophie didn't have those memories.

She could distinctly remember sitting at the kitchen table dying her Easter eggs, while Dorothea, the housekeeper, kept her company as she cleaned the kitchen, humming some tuneless song.

"Then let it go. Stop waiting for them to finally see you and start living your own life."

"It's hard."

"I know. But when you've reached your limit, it won't be hard anymore. Is there anything I can do?"

"You've just done it. I have a lot to think about. Thanks, Aunt Georgie. I'll talk to you when I get back."

"Love you, angel."

"Love you, too."

Sophie unzipped her dress and let it drop to the floor. She kicked off her shoes, one flying under the desk, the other to the foot of the bed. As she headed into the bathroom, she peeled off her bra, flipped on the lights, and started the shower.

Her thoughts immediately went to Ryan. He must be on his way back to the resort. He couldn't possibly think she'd welcome him into her suite, not after he'd tried pimping her out to his friend. What a jerk.

As she stepped into the tiled shower stall, closing her eyes as the water streamed down her body, she thought of his exasperation when she'd pressed him in the car.

I don't know, and I don't care.

Not a half hour later, he'd tried to get her off at the table. He wanted to have fun. Sexy times. He wanted to get away from his problems. *And you just won't let up.*

Mortification slammed her hard.

No matter how many excuses she came up with for Ryan's bad behavior toward her—his coach, his ex, practically having sex at the table—one thing she had to face was that she hadn't let up on him since she'd met him. Why did she keep pushing him so hard?

Maybe he was finally just pushing back. His way of telling her to mind her own business. Because he sure wouldn't come right out and say it. *Not his style.*

She lowered her head, letting her hair stream down,

curtaining her. She could keep telling herself she was just having fun with a guy who made her feel like a goddess, but it wasn't true.

The truth was she had hope. Hope that he felt the same way—that he wanted more.

Stupid, stupid girl.

A gust of cool hair whisked around her legs, and she jerked up to find the shower door open. Ryan stood there. *Her* Ryan. He looked miserable. She turned off the faucet. "What the hell are you doing?" She shoved the hair off her face and covered her breasts with an arm.

Snatching the towel she'd placed on the lid of the toilet, she quickly wrapped up in it. He stepped inside the shower stall, fully clothed, and tugged her into his arms. Turning into her neck, he said, "I was a dick."

Her anxiety finally crashed. "Yeah, you were." She didn't lift her arms. "You done now?"

He tightened his hold. "Yeah."

"What happened?"

He sat on the bench that ran the length of the stall, reached for her arm, and tugged her closer. Settling her on his lap, he pressed kisses to her cheek. "Got a message from my agent. He wants to know if I'll be back for the next game." He leaned back against the tiled wall. "I feel like shit for letting everyone down."

"So go back."

"I am." Each word snapped out of his mouth loaded with anger and frustration.

"But?"

"But there's this fucking wall of resistance in me."

"Come on, Ryan. You're a smart guy. You know exactly why you pulled a runner *this week*."

He stroked wet tendrils off her forehead, her cheek, her

shoulder. "I couldn't have picked a worse time to start questioning my choices."

"That's the first time you've admitted it."

He exhaled roughly. "I can't let everyone down."

"You also can't live your life to make them happy."

"You don't get it. My life *is* baseball. It's a great life, and I don't want to fuck it up."

"But you *are*. Ryan, you are messing it up. Instead of thinking how you don't want to mess up what you already have, why don't you think about what you'd really like? If you could take Emma, your dad, your coaches, your teammates, and your friends out of the picture, what would you want to do?"

"I can't take them out. They've made me who I am. They're part of this whole show."

"You don't owe—*Oh*. You feel *guilty*." She pushed back a little, as clarity hit her. "You had to be on your best behavior, right? With all the chaos in your house, you weren't allowed to be a little boy who had tantrums. I'll bet your mom couldn't even handle you in a bad mood."

Something changed in him. His features clouded, tensed. "She shouldn't have had to."

And then he fixed those topaz eyes on her. "I made everything ten times worse. All the time. I never let up."

The worry and fear in his eyes killed her. "What'd you do?"

He looked stricken. "I went nuts over something stupid, and my mom left. Because of my bullshit."

"Wait, you're not blaming yourself for your mom's drinking, are you?"

"No. Well, partly."

If he'd been a good boy his mom wouldn't have had to drink. *Is that she'd told him to justify her neglect?*

179

"I knew she was an alcoholic, and I never let up on her. Everyone else left her alone, but I kept pushing."

"You can't blame yourself for their divorce." *Oh, Ryan.*

"Yeah, I can. She, uh, she didn't pick me up after a tournament. We'd won the Little League championship for the third year in a row, which was a big deal in our town. Most of the parents had come to the game, so the kids went home with them. There were only a few of us on the bus, but they all got picked up. I was the only one left in the parking lot. My mom didn't come. And it pissed me off because everyone was meeting at Brazzo's Pizzeria. We were celebrating. And I wanted that damn pizza and Coke. I wanted to be there with my friends. And…" He glanced at her with a rueful expression. "Fucking *pizza*." He forced a laugh. "I was a whiney bitch."

"No, you weren't. Your mom *should've* picked you up. You should've celebrated with your team. You should've had that pizza and Coke. You were a *kid*."

"Believe me, it was nothing new. Anyhow, I needed a ride. And I knew Coach would take me because, of course, that's what he always had to do. But that day I said, *Screw it.* And I left. I walked, man, I don't know how many miles home. And the whole way, I was just building up this rage. I walked in and saw my mom drunk in front of the TV. And I lost it. I just fucking lost it. Yelled at her for not picking me up. It was the *Jerry Springer* show. I'll never forget it. She didn't come to my game, didn't pick me up, so she could watch *Jerry Springer*? So, I'm yelling at her and she just starts screaming at me. *Why can't you leave me alone? Why do you always have to be such a pain in the ass?*"

He looked tortured, and she knew there wasn't a damn thing she could do to make it better.

"Usually, once she'd start on her rant, I'd go to my room.

Or go to Jake's house. But that day I was so pissed. I took her bottle away, threw it out the sliding glass door, and she just lost her mind." He closed his eyes, brow furrowing tightly. "*I hate you, I fucking hate you. Why can't you leave me alone?*" When his eyes opened, he drew in a sharp breath. "She ran after her bottle. Right into the sliding glass door. I guess she didn't see me close it. I don't know, but she hit it hard. Her nose was bleeding. I mean *gushing*. I freaked out, all that blood. And she was on the floor screaming and thrashing. I called my dad at work. It was…it was bad."

The way he stared at the glass door made her feel like he was back in that moment, reliving it, and she wanted to say something so badly, but she knew he wasn't finished.

"She didn't come home from the hospital. I never saw her in our house again. She and my sister moved into an apartment. At some point, my parents got a divorce. I don't really know. We never talked about it." He shifted her on his lap. "I mean, obviously I knew she was a drunk. She rarely picked me up. She hardly ever cooked or bought food. My dad did all of that. So I don't know why I was on her all the time. Yelling and throwing tantrums."

She couldn't take it anymore. "Ryan." She cupped his face in her hands. "It wasn't your fault."

"I was old enough to know. I should've ignored her shit like everyone else did. Hell, *I* should've made dinner for my brother and sister. Instead, I pushed so hard I made my dad get rid of her. And when Nicole, my little sister, came back to us?" He lowered his head, eyes closing for a moment. "She was a mess." He shook his head. "I fucked everything up."

"No, you didn't. You didn't do anything wrong."

He didn't look like he believed her.

"How old were you when she walked through the sliding glass door?"

"Eleven."

"You were a kid, and a kid doesn't have the maturity to understand his emotions, let alone the crazy dynamics between his parents. Ryan, you reacted like any pissed-off eleven-year-old. If anyone's to blame it's your parents. I wasn't there, but it sure sounds like your dad should've divorced her years earlier. A nanny would've taken better care of you than your mom did."

"I wish I'd shut my mouth that day."

"I think you've made up for it." When he looked confused, she said, "You've spent the rest of your life keeping your mouth shut, trying to be the good boy who doesn't cause trouble. Look, you have to let this go. What happened to your family is not your fault. It was a messed up situation, and you kids took the brunt of it. But you're not that little boy anymore. You don't have to hold everything in. You can stop worrying about upsetting the balance and just let yourself be whoever you want to be."

She felt too much for him. Every time they talked, the bond deepened, and she couldn't do this—keep getting closer to someone who would leave her in a day or two and never look back. She started to get off his lap, but he held her tighter. "You know I don't want you with Jake. Not like that. But I do think he can help with the business stuff. You should talk to him to figure out if taking over the business yourself is something you want to do."

"Okay."

When he leaned in, like he might want to kiss her, she pushed him back. "Why did you shut down on me at the table?"

"I just ended a six year relationship. I can't...I just can't get back into another one."

"I'm not asking for one."

"No, you're not. You're great. You're perfect. But look at me. I came after you at the concert. I commandeered your boat *and* your Jeep. It's not your fault, it's *mine*. But I can't go right into another relationship. Especially another long distance one." He shook his head. "I want you to distraction, but I can't *have* distraction. I have to face my shit."

"You do." Holding the towel more tightly, she got off his lap. "And I don't need to be jerked around while you decide whether you want me from one moment to the next, so let's just go to sleep. You'll take me back to the resort tomorrow, and we'll just do our own thing, okay? Like none of this ever happened."

When she came out of the bathroom, she found Ryan sitting on the edge of the bed, looking at his phone. "Bathroom's all yours."

Bare-chested, wearing only his boxers, he got up, dropped his phone on the nightstand, and nodded as he walked past her. She'd brought her toiletry bag out with her, so she tossed the towel on the bed and began slathering on lotion. As long as she could hear the water running, she figured she was okay being naked.

She was trying hard not to be hurt that he'd called her a distraction, but it wasn't working. She had a lot to deal with in her life, too, and she didn't think of him that way—

"Oh, shit, sorry."

Heart leaping into her throat at the sound of his voice, she snatched the towel and quickly covered her body. Although, seriously, why bother? Like he hadn't seen her? Touched and kissed her in the most intimate places? Silly to feel modest at this point.

He looked utterly miserable. "Is your deodorant unscented? I didn't bring anything."

She *really* needed to stop staring at that powerfully cut chest. "Yep, unscented. Help yourself to anything in my toiletry bag." She gestured to it on the nightstand.

He grabbed it and returned to the bathroom.

When she finished moisturizing, Sophie reached into her overnight bag for something to wear. Normally, she slept in the nude, but she certainly hadn't imagined sharing a room with a guy. So she pulled out her gauzy cover-up. Once she got under the covers, Ryan wouldn't see her body through the sheer material.

Her phone danced on the nightstand, and she picked it up to find a text from her aunt.

Glad we talked. Why don't you come out to the ranch next weekend, before things get too hectic with school? We can talk about moving Crazy Hearts out here. See if you could be happy in Big Sky country!

A thrill shot through her, quickly replaced by fear. She typed out her reply. I already know I love it there. Just not sure I want to leave my family. Will talk to them first, see if we can find a way to make all 5 of us happy. But I love knowing it's an option. Thank you!

"You look happy." Ryan came out of the bathroom in nothing but his boxers. His hair looked like he'd scrubbed a towel over it. It made him even hotter—less movie star and more boy-next-door approachable.

"I am."

"What's going on?" When his gaze roamed her body, she remembered the naughty view offered by her cover-up.

She quickly peeled back the covers and climbed into the bed. "I talked to my aunt."

"The one who lives in Montana?"

She nodded. "She's got this huge ranch right outside Bozeman. It's a great town. Montana State University's there, so it's lively and fun, lots of restaurants. Anyhow, she's got a big events building on her property. The former owners used to show horses."

"Are you talking about moving Crazy Hearts there?"

"Maybe. It's just a thought. I have to figure out if it's even feasible for me to consider running a business."

"Damn. You work fast. Yesterday you thought you'd lose your family's legacy, and today you're moving to Montana." He sat in a chair, looking at her in awe. "You impress the hell out of me." For a moment, he looked lost in thought. And then he gave his head a slow shake. "You sure you want to live there?"

"I think so. It'd be so great to live where I could hike and ski. Yellowstone's right there, and Jackson Hole's just a few hours south. There's so much to do out there."

"What about your family?"

"Well, that's the point. I don't want to leave them. I hope they'll want to compromise with me." But, of course, she knew they wouldn't. Maybe a few months from now, when her sister had settled into being a mother. But by then it would be too late. "At least I have an option."

Leaning forward, elbows on his knees, he looked like he was really giving it some thought, and to know this guy she just met had become so invested in her...it twisted her heart. Because she couldn't have him. Forget the timing. He'd never live with her in Montana, and she'd never be the tag-along girlfriend in his professional baseball career.

A knock broke the uncomfortable tension between them. He got up, opened the door wide, and stood back to let the room service cart in. Handing a bill to the server, he closed the door behind him.

She sat up. "What's this?"

"You didn't finish your dinner."

Heat bloomed across her cheeks. "Oh, I ate enough." But maybe he hadn't finished his, either. "Are you hungry?" The way he looked at her told her what he was really hungry for.

"I didn't order dinner." Wheeling the cart to her bedside, he started lifting the silver dome lids.

Happiness washed over her like sunshine. "Dessert?"

"One of everything."

She had no words.

"You game?"

She sighed. Wasn't that just the problem with him? "Totally."

She shouldn't have had sugar right before bed.

The sheet bunched under her legs, so she yanked it out and drew it over her. Still uncomfortable, she threw it off entirely and rolled to her side. And…still wide awake. Her suite overlooked the ocean, so maybe if she opened the French windows the steady roar of waves would lull her.

"Can't sleep?" Ryan asked.

"No." Of course *he* was awake. She'd banished him to the couch.

Yes, because I knew what we'd do if we shared a bed.

"I can make you some tea. They have chamomile."

Seriously? Mr. Pro Baseball Hottie wanted to make her tea? After he'd ordered her dessert, since she'd missed it at dinner?

I could fall in love with this man.

"Thank you, but I don't think that'll help."

"What will?"

She didn't answer right away, torn between wanting him

under the covers with her and knowing it was best for them to keep their distance. She should just stick with the plan they'd already made—go to sleep and in the morning go their separate ways. If she could only ignore that annoying voice that kept reminding her she was on spring break. She should be having fun, letting go. They'd already slept together. Why not do it again? What had Kat said? *You're not made of glass. You're not going to shatter.*

But it was complicated enough. They didn't need to make it worse by having sex again. "Ryan?"

"Yeah?"

"You obviously can't sleep either. That couch is way too small."

"That's not why."

"What is it, then?"

"You."

She sucked in a breath. Did he mean it like she think he did? Or just that her restlessness had kept him up? "I'm sorry. I'll keep still."

"I want to be where you are."

Oh, my God. The things he said. "Ryan."

Material rustled. She looked over to find him sitting up. Shirtless. In the shard of moonlight streaming through a break in the curtains, she could see the tension in his muscles. She could feel her own restraint like a pressure bearing down on her.

"Do you want to sleep in my bed?" she asked.

"Yes." He sprang off the couch and climbed in beside her, keeping a good distance between them on the king-size mattress. "Don't worry. I'm not going to jump you. Go to sleep."

"Okay." *Sleep. Right.* She lay back down on her side, facing away from him.

Except sleep was impossible. Because he was *right there*. Her body was strung so tightly if he touched her she'd twang. She wanted him so badly, but after everything he'd told her in the shower? He had nothing to give her. He had to figure out his life. And when he did, she still wouldn't fit into it. They had nothing beyond this one night.

"This is worse." His voice sounded strained.

It *was*. Maybe she was making it too complicated. They'd already had sex—what would be so bad about doing it again?

Just one more time.

Every cell in her body shuddered with glee and shouted, *Yes. That.*

"I'm going back to the couch." Bedding rustled, as he started to get up.

Her heart pounded, and she reached for him. "Stay."

"Soph…" He exhaled in what sounded like unbearable frustration.

One more night. "Please?"

With a big sigh, he eased back down. On opposite sides of the big bed, she couldn't even feel his heat. She shifted backwards, closer to him. Reaching behind her, she held out her hand. He clasped it, and she drew it over her waist. He pushed right up against her, tucked his face into her neck, and breathed her in. His hand flattened on her stomach, and he pulled her up against him.

He kissed her cheek, and then settled in behind her, spooning.

Wide awake, her nerve-endings sparked and snapped like live wires. The heat of his body, the pressure of his palm, and the clean, masculine smell of him drove her crazy.

She couldn't take it. Rolling over, she faced him. In the faint light, she looked into his eyes and took in that handsome face. The scruff couldn't hide his movie star good looks. "I know we just met, but I really like you."

His fingers flexed on her waist. Heat poured off him, and tension strained his muscles to the point she could see the tendons in his neck. "*Fuck*." With a pained expression, he pulled away.

She reached for him, her hand tugging on his shoulder. "Don't go."

"I can't do it. I can't keep my hands off you."

What did it matter, the things that kept them apart? So what if she never saw him again if she wanted him so desperately right now?

Her heart thumped heavily, as desire rose from a purr to a roar. "Then don't."

His features tensed at the same time his mouth softened, lips parting. The vulnerability in his eyes, the *hunger*, was her undoing.

"One last time." Everything in her rebelled at the thought of never having him this close again.

He shifted towards her, until they lay facing each other. Brushing a lock of hair off her cheek, he tucked it behind her ear. Gentle fingers cupped her chin, as he pressed the softest kiss to her mouth. "You taste good." He licked the seam of her lips. "You smell good." Pulling away, he gazed into her eyes. "I feel different around you." A sexy smile curled his lips. "And I like it."

An electrical charge heated her blood. Her body trembled. "I like it, too."

Pushing up on his elbows, he sat back against the headboard and reached for her. "Get up here."

The moment she rolled over and climbed on top of him, he tugged on the cover-up, urging her to lift her arms so he could pull it over her head.

He let out a hiss of breath, letting his gaze travel from

her mouth to her bare breasts to the junction of her thighs. A hand at either side of her waist, he drew her forward, until he settled her right over his hard, thick erection. She let out a moan of pure pleasure and rocked her hips.

Those big hands glided up her ribcage, thumbs brushing the undersides of her breasts. "Sophie Valentine." He whispered her name with reverence. Brushing the hair off her shoulders, he ran his fingers across her collarbone, between her breasts, and then gently cupped them. "You are magnificent."

He leaned forward, pressing feather-soft kisses to the corner of her mouth and the curve of her neck. He licked the dip in her collarbone, while those big hands caressed her everywhere.

"More. I need more." Hands on his shoulders, she pushed him back, leaning forward until her hair spilled around them.

He took possession of her breasts, cupping them, caressing them, his fingers tweaking her nipples. She thought she'd go crazy with need. Her hips rocked, but the layer of lace between them only frustrated her. She sat up on her knees and pulled off her panties.

But then he pushed forward, tumbling her onto her back. He kissed her, fingers skimming up the back of her thigh, stroking the curve of her ass. "Softest skin I've ever felt."

"Ryan." The word came out a whisper, paper-thin.

He moved over her, an arm wrapping around her waist, his mouth pressed to her neck. With his thighs bracketing her hips, he locked their bodies together.

"Sophie. My Sophie." He trailed hot, wet kisses to her collarbone, one hand cupping her breast. "Mine." His voice turned to a growl just before his lips closed over her nipple.

Her back arched, and she gasped at the warm suction.

Fire blazed a path straight to her clit and burst into radiant desire. She loved the heat of his skin, the flex of hard muscle.

She needed more. Reaching for his bottom, she grasped the hard globes and pulled him to her.

"Soph, fuck." His hips rocked into her.

And then, God, he was claiming her, *devouring* her. He kissed her with his whole body, with every fiber of his being, drawing her out, stroking her senses to life.

She felt him everywhere. On her skin, in her senses, and in her heart.

Tomorrow, she'd let him go. Tomorrow, she'd get off this crazy ride. But tonight? She wanted him. All of him.

Yanking down his boxers, she pushed them off with her toes. He groaned, whispering her name reverently, as his mouth pressed wet kisses into her neck and onto the tops of her breasts.

And then his mouth closed over her nipple, his tongue swirling sensuously. She arched, fingers scraping into his hair, holding him right there.

Oh, yes, *right there*. Desire pulsed in her clit, enflaming her. Need tore her open, exposing her throbbing center.

"Ryan." She pulled at his arms, but he didn't take his mouth off her nipple, his tongue worshiping it, as his hips pressed down. His hot erection pressed against her stomach, and she lifted her hips, lodging it between their bodies. When she reached for him, he pushed her hand away.

"Let me, Soph. Let me have all of you."

He pressed wet kisses down her stomach, his hands caressing her flesh, leaving a glowing trail in their wake. And then he parted her thighs, his tongue dipping into her aching core. He licked into her, his hands sliding under her ass and lifting her to his mouth. His tongue stroked through her folds, making her body burn.

She *loved* the way he made her feel. Loved the way he seemed to care so much about pleasing her. His tongue took long, decadent licks, while his thumb lightly circled her clit. Her hips rocked, and she grabbed the back of his head.

Delicious sensation rolled through her, spreading and enflaming her. Just as she cupped her breasts, he reached up and knocked her hands away, gently squeezing one and rubbing his thumb over her nipple. God, that just lit her up. That he wanted her pleasure to come from him.

"You make me feel…" His tongue licked up her length, swirling around her clit, and her back arched off the mattress. Everything in her sizzled, turned electric. She'd never felt so alive, so in touch with her body. "You make me feel *everything*."

Oh, God. His palm scraped back and forth across her nipples, his fingers pinching with each pass, until her body lit up, and the first rush of sensation clutched her. She didn't want it to end. Never, ever wanted this feeling to end. Head thrashing on the pillow, hips thrusting against his mouth, she cried out, her climax rising, tightening, flashing through her.

And then she burst free. "Oh, God." His hands held onto her hips, as he licked hard and fast. "Ryan!" It was so intense, so wild, her body wouldn't stop convulsing. Even as she settled, even as he lifted away from her, she still trembled from deep within.

But he didn't give her a moment to come back into her body. He kissed her voraciously, a hand under her ass, as he pushed into her. Each stroke lit her up, and before long he was pounding into her with a force that pushed her down the bed.

Grabbing her knee, he lifted her leg, tilting her hips, and he eased in even deeper. "Ah, fuck. Oh, fucking hell. Jesus,

Sophie, I…fuck." He slammed her so hard, her teeth knocked together. Nothing had ever turned her on more than his wild, primal need for her.

Sensation bloomed deep within, as his body stiffened, his movements turning erratic, jerky. She kept herself still, as he passed over the same spot that ramped up her desire into a wild, uncontrollable burst of fire that spread through her limbs, locking her muscles as another climax lit a scorching path along her limbs.

Panting harshly, his hands gripped her hips and held her down, as he pumped into her in short, desperate stabs. And then he collapsed on top of her, breathing harshly at her ear.

He kissed her cheek, before slowly rolling off her, a hand rubbing over his face. "Jesus, Soph."

How the hell are we supposed to walk away from this?

CHAPTER TWELVE

Light flickered behind his eyelids. Flashes of brightness that pricked at his consciousness, until a growing sense of alarm awakened him. He lifted his head, disoriented.

What the hell?

Sophie stirred in his arms, making him aware of his hard dick prodding her ass. As his eyes adjusted to the dark, he could make out the feminine slope of her shoulders, the fall of dark hair on the white pillow, and the bare skin of her back.

So beautiful.

Last night—*fuck*—last night he'd loved her so hard. How was it possible to want someone so much? He'd touched and licked every inch of her smooth skin. And he still needed more.

The light flashed again, and he saw the phone on the nightstand. It struck him that he'd never checked in with Jake and Dixon. After listening to his agent's voicemail, he'd forgotten to tell his friends he wasn't coming back to the resort.

Careful not to wake her, he gently lifted his arm off her body. She made a sound of protest, before curling her hand under her pillow and burrowing deeper into it.

Sliding off the mattress, he moved as quietly as possible to grab the phone.

Twenty-three text messages, a pile of missed calls, and voicemail messages.

Setting the phone down, he stepped into his shorts, zipped them up, and then headed out onto the balcony. The salty, moist air hit him right away. Waves crashed on the beach. It was dark, just a thin, glowing band of dawn on the horizon.

He sat on the edge of a deck chair and swiped the screen. A half-dozen messages from Emma. Jesus Christ, why wouldn't she leave him alone? But then he saw texts from some of his teammates.

Instead of reading each one, he'd call Mike, his closest friend on the team. Find out what was going on.

"Yeah?" Mike sounded sleepy.

"I wake you up?"

"Yeah, we got a game coming up, man. Where the hell are you?"

"Why's everyone blowing up my phone?"

"Your girlfriend's been messaging us." His voice sounded sleep-roughened. "At first she just wanted to know why you weren't calling her back. I told her you weren't here. You had a family emergency. She backed off, but now she's at it again. I guess she called your house, and no one knew of anything wrong. So now everyone's goin' nuts trying to find out where you are."

"I'm in the Caribbean."

Silence. Ryan lowered his head into a hand. *I'm such a dick.*

Mike let out a breath. "You…Wait, what?" He sounded much more awake. "You skipped out on our games for spring break?"

"Yeah."

195

"You lied to Coach."

He got the deeper message. Ryan had lied to *him*. His teammates. "Yeah." He felt like shit.

"What about the scouts? I don't get it, man. What're you doing?"

"I just…" He straightened. *Own it.* "Everything was closing in on me. I needed to get away."

"Now? You needed it now, you dumbfuck?" He blew out a breath. "I can't believe I'm hearing this. Why didn't you tell me? I'd have talked you out of it."

"I didn't want to be talked out of it. Look, I know I did a shitty thing, but I'll take this time, and when I come back, I'll be ready to kick some ass."

"For what? Our final season at Mich U? Who gives a rat's ass about that when we're talking about the Bigs? I'd give my left nut for that chance. I mean, serious as shit, man. If I had a tenth of your ability, your fuckin' discipline, I'd be all over this shit. You think I'd piss my opportunity away if I was considered the best short stop in the country? Jesus, Six, I never would've expected shit like this from you."

"I took a few days off. It's not like I killed somebody. Jesus."

"Yeah, well, just to put a cherry on top, guess what? Your girl's on her way to Florida. She thinks you're here."

Damn her. "I'll take care of it."

"You gonna tell anyone else where you're at?"

"No. And I'd appreciate it if you'd keep it to yourself for now."

"Yeah, sure, man." His friend blew out a breath. "I think you're fuckin' up, but if anyone can pull out of it, it's you."

"Thanks, Mike."

"What do you want me to tell Emma if she messages me again?"

"You don't have to tell her anything. It's none of her damn business."

"She's makin' it everybody's business."

"Then I'll make her stop. See you soon."

The line went dead. He opened Emma's last text.

Just landed at JFK.

And the one before that.

Boarding. I'm so worried about you. God, I wish you'd just talk to me.

And one more.

Your dad won't answer his phone. I'm worried about you. Talk to me!!!

In the past he'd tolerated her drama. Balancing school, sports, and a social life kept him busy enough to not care too much. But this time? He was done. He tapped out a response.

You're out of control. Leave my friends and family alone. I told you not to come out and see me and that I'd talk to you next week.

She wrote back instantly.

OMG, where r u?

He needed to shut her down without creating more drama. But he was running out of patience.

I said I wanted space and I meant it. Now back off.

You're not acting right. This isn't you. Is something wrong?

Nothing's wrong. I'm serious, stop stirring up trouble. You need to stop texting me. I'm fine. Shutting off my phone now.

But she got in one more text before he powered it down.

I'm totally freaking out. Ur not with ur team. Ur not talking to me. I no something's wrong.

He shot off the chair, stalked across the balcony, and gripped the rail. Honestly, he couldn't blame Emma for his problems. *He* chose to bail on his team. *He* chose to lie to his friends and coach.

He didn't doubt for a second that even if he'd had a real emergency that coincided with spring break, the scouts would question the timing. They'd seen it all. But if they found out he *had* lied...forget it. He'd come across as immature, arrogant. Like he thought a first-round pick didn't need to show up.

Of course, he didn't think that way at all. He thought the opposite. All he did was train and play. His entire life was about his diet, exercise, and being a role model for his teammates. And the majors? Come on, training would be harder and more intense than anything he'd ever done.

Fuuuck. Baseball would become his life. Well, of course, it already was his life. Which was why he'd bailed in the first place. Because for a few days he hadn't wanted it to be.

He thought about Sophie and realized one of the things that drew her to him was the way she lived her life. Her spirit of adventure. Her passion to experience everything. He didn't do that.

I don't have passion.

The thought jolted him. He did everything he was supposed to do—get up on time, drink a protein shake, work out, get to class, study, practice, lights out—*lather rinse repeat*—to the point that it had become a mindless routine.

Earlier, at dinner, she'd pushed him to pay attention to the menu. To actually decide what he liked, instead of just taking what was offered.

Okay, enough of this shit. This wasn't some fucking existential crisis. He did love baseball, and he wasn't going to blow up his life because he didn't know if he liked shellfish or not.

No, what he needed was balance. Going forward, he'd play as hard as he trained. Meaning every vacation and every break, he'd travel, see the world, get laid, have fun. Sure, he'd keep up his work-outs—he needed those for his sanity—but he needed to build breaks into his schedule.

If he did that—balanced fun with training—he'd look forward to playing again. Drawing in a deep breath, he felt better. More settled about things. He just had to manage the situation he'd created.

Intending to call his agent, he wound up hitting his dad's speed dial.

"Yep. Yello. This is Bill." He sounded groggy.

"Dad?"

"Oh, hell, son. Hang on a minute."

Ryan could hear fumbling, some grunts, and then his dad came back on the line.

His dad barked out a laugh. "Phone scared the crap out of me. Okay, I'm up."

"Sorry to wake you."

"You sure stirred up some trouble."

"I see that."

"So, Emma's been callin' the house."

"I know."

"You talk to her?"

"Yeah, I talked to her. Told her I wanted her to back off."

"Break-up's been hard on her. She loves you."

"Well…" He needed to say the words out loud. "I don't love her. But she doesn't get that it's actually over."

"You've broken up a lot. She figures you'll take her back."

"I'm not." Not after Sophie. He hadn't known a relationship could be like that. *Ha*. A relationship. *See what I did there?* Jake was right—he'd traded one girlfriend for another. He shook his head, forcing his thoughts back on track. "So, yeah, she told the guys there's no family crisis. Now everyone knows."

"Why would she do that? Never mind. Forget I asked. The girl loves her drama. So, what're you gonna do? You figure your shit out yet?"

He knew he should tell him about the forty-eight hours. That he was heading back to Florida. But resistance pulled. Maybe his dad would see his perspective. "I'm not doing anything right now. I'm taking my break."

His dad went quiet. Ryan braced.

"You think your coach doesn't want a break?" His dad sounded hard, angry. "He's got a wife, kids, an athletic director, and a bunch of players who think with their dicks, get drunk, don't keep up their grades, and give him attitude every day of the week. Life closes in around all of us, but we don't skip out on it."

"I know that, Dad. It's not like I do this all the time. I did it *once*. And I don't regret it."

"Will you regret it if you get pulled from the next few games?"

He didn't even have to think. "No."

"How about if he tosses you off the team?"

Ryan felt the kick of that one. "I want to play."

"And what if it affects the draft? You gonna regret that?"

"Yes." His ego would. Being a first-round pick? Hell, yeah. If he was going to—

Wait, *if* he was going to play? Damn Sophie for putting ideas in his head. Of course he wanted to play pro ball.

What did he know better than the soft, worn-in leather

of a glove? Oiling it, the smack of a ball hitting the inside pocket? The heat of the sun bearing down on him, the camaraderie of teammates? *I like that.*

But if he were honest it didn't excite him. And, truthfully, nothing beat the high he got from brainstorming ideas, working on apps. His brain never shut down. From the moment he'd seen the Crazy Heart ink on Sophie's wrist his mind had been spinning with possibilities for a game app. If she went through with her idea to run the company on her own, he could create a website devoted to Crazy Hearts for her with all kinds of game.

But could he make a living out of writing apps? Few people did.

"Son, what do you want?"

"I don't know." It was Monday. His coach expected him back for tomorrow's game. But he wasn't ready. He just...He wanted to crash his fist through a wall.

Just go back. Jesus.

"How about this? How about while you don't know what you want, you keep on doing what you're doing so you don't blow up the path you've worked so hard to clear. Because once you blow it up, there's no getting it back."

"Yeah."

"Baseball worked for you. Got you on the right path. And it's gone well for you all these years. I'd hate for you to pull your first rebellious act at a time like this."

After his mom left, his dad had sent him to a therapist. She suggested sports as an outlet for his anger. And from the moment he'd chosen baseball, he'd gotten the kind of positive feedback he'd never had before. Including a whole community supporting him. And he didn't want to let down all the people who'd worked so hard to get him to this point.

He should get on a plane that afternoon, head back to

Florida, and finish out the week. The scouts would believe he'd had a family emergency. Since he'd continued his workouts, he could do it.

But his gut pulled again. He didn't want to go.

Sophie sprang to mind. Was she what held him back? Because that would be beyond stupid, to fuck up his life over a woman he met over spring break.

"Look," his dad said. "Is this about Emma? The way it ended?"

"This has nothing to do with Emma."

"You sure about that? Crappy thing she did."

"It's not about what she did. I don't care about that." Which was the problem. He should care. "I think she's just part of all the things I'm stuck with."

"Stuck with? You're *stuck* with baseball? That's how you feel? You could've played any sport. You were a phenom. But you chose baseball."

"I chose Coach Banbury."

Silence.

Funny how they'd never talked about it. "He brought me into his home, Dad. He…" Christ. "He fed me, helped me with my homework."

"Oh, hell." His dad exhaled into the receiver.

"I'm not blaming you. Life sucked. But it didn't suck at his house. I chose baseball because of him."

His dad cleared his throat. "And now you don't want it?"

"Of course I want it." But then he wondered…had he done all he could with baseball? Maybe he wanted a new challenge. The idea thrilled him, and at the same time scared the shit out of him. "What if it's enough, though? Enough that I was All American in high school and MVP in college? What if I trained and worked hard so that I could be all those things, but I don't have to make a career out of it?" Was he actually quoting Sophie Valentine?

"You *don't* have to make a career out of it. But since you're not sure what you want, how about you don't close any doors just yet? Keep your options open. We're not talking about a *job*. You lose a job, you'll have a dozen others to choose from. We're talking about Major League Baseball. I'm not telling you anything you don't already know, but people would kill for what you've got. And you've got it all. Not just natural talent, but drive, determination, focus. You're an elite athlete." He could hear his dad swearing under his breath. "Was I that much of a fuck-up? After the divorce, I tried so damn hard to make things right for you kids. Baseball worked for you. Did I get it all wrong? I thought you wanted all the training camps and private lessons."

"Nah. I wanted to go to the Bahamas with you guys." Spring break of eighth grade, his family had gone on vacation. His dad had dropped him off at a special training program in Florida. "But most of all, I wanted to major in computer science." But given the number of away-games, he couldn't take the core classes offered in spring semester. His schedule hadn't allowed it.

So why did he think he had enough knowledge to make a living in the field?

"I didn't know it was that important to you."

"It was." He thought of Sophie again. Of all the things he wanted to talk about, she mattered most. He was all kinds of messed up about her. "I met a girl."

"Oh, hell, no. Is *that* what this is about? You're there with some girl?"

"I didn't come here with a girl. I came to get away."

"And now you've met some girl, and she's putting ideas in your head. Is she an athlete? Does she understand how few people ever have an opportunity like yours? Not just to be drafted, but to be a first-round pick?"

"I'm sure she doesn't."

"Look, I can't get into your head, but I can tell you it's a mistake to walk away when you're so damn close. See it through. If you don't like it after a year or two or three, quit. But at least hit a home run. Don't stall out at third and wonder the rest of your life what would've happened if you'd gone for it."

Great image. Everything snapped into place. "You're right."

Energy poured back into his body. His purpose returned. He knew just what it felt like on third, muscles twitching to make a run for it. Keeping an eye on home plate, wanting it so badly he could taste the dust he'd kick up once he got there.

And he *didn't* want to be that guy at forty, thinking back on what might've been. Knowing he'd walked off the field before touching the bag just because he'd gotten a little burned out.

That would suck.

"And this girl? You just got out of a six-year relationship. Do you really want to get tied up with another woman so soon after you just got your freedom?"

"No. I don't." His dad was right. Everything he said was right.

"My advice is to get back to school. Knock it out of the park. Play in the majors and *then* reevaluate."

"Yeah. I hear you."

"You want me to get you a flight back to school?"

"I'll take care of it." He'd bought his own ticket. He'd be the one to change it.

"I'm here if you need me."

"I know. Thanks, Dad." Ryan disconnected and sat there, letting it all sink in. After months of being twisted up and frustrated, he finally had clarity. He'd played baseball so long, of course he needed to pull back and assess before taking the plunge into the big leagues.

And, thanks to Sophie, he could admit that maybe he didn't want to be a shortstop the rest of his life. But his dad was right. He *should* cross the finish line. Get drafted and play in the majors. All the while, he could be developing his apps. Easy segue into a different career.

Anything else was just stupid.

******

The curtains yanked open. Bright light flooded the room.

Sophie jerked up. *What the hell?*

"Hey." Ryan stood at the foot of the bed looking at his phone. "Time to hit the road."

Oh, wonderful. Jerkface was back. "What's going on?"

"I'm going to grab a coffee and meet you downstairs."

She tossed the sheet off, got out of bed—*naked*—and he didn't look at her once. *Right.* The same man who turned feral at the sight of her bare shoulders wasn't even looking. *Well, screw you, Mr. Hyde.* "I'm going to shower. I'm also going to eat breakfast. Furthermore, I'm going to stop at the volcano. I think I made my plans clear yesterday."

His gaze flicked over to her, did a slow glide from her eyes to her mouth to her breasts, all the way down to her toes. Color stained his cheeks, his jaw tensed, and his Adam's apple bobbed.

There he is. Well, at least she still turned him on. She didn't know what was going on with him, but she wished he'd talk to her instead of shutting down like this.

She'd heard him go out onto the balcony in the middle of the night. He'd been out there a while. Something had obviously happened. "Is everything all right?"

"Everything's great." He gave her his signature smile, which clued her in that something was *wrong*. "But it's time to get going."

"Okay." No longer comfortable naked around him, she reached for the cover-up that had landed on the ottoman. "But that doesn't mean you have to be a dick."

"I'll order you breakfast. Hurry down."

"You don't even know what I want to eat."

"Pancakes, hash browns, sausage patties, bacon, coffee— black—and a tomato juice."

It wasn't anger so much as hurt that flared up. "No, I—"

But he smiled—a genuine one—and for one moment he was the Ryan she'd come to like so much. "Okay, how 'bout a spinach and cheddar omelet, whole grain toast, strawberry jam, a mango and a papaya juice?"

Shocked that he'd gotten it so completely right, she didn't even confirm it before he walked out the door.

Sophie spotted him at a small table at the back of the grand dining room. French doors opened to a wide veranda with outdoor seating, but he'd chosen a table just to the side of the heavy, pale blue drapes. He faced her, a newspaper open and covering most of the table. "You ready to eat?"

"I—" The moment she sat down, he motioned the waiter to bring her food.

Then, the paper rustled, and he went back to reading.

Are you kidding me?

Okay, whatever was going on with him, he was not going to ruin her time on this gorgeous day in Santa Grenada.

Pushing her chair back, she got up, found a waiter, and asked him to bring her breakfast outside on the terrace.

Reaching into her bag, she pulled out her sunglasses and took in the magnificent view. With its bougainvillea-draped balcony, the terrace overlooked acres of trees and an endless swath of frothy gray ocean. She breathed in the scents of sun-baked stone and bacon and forced her thoughts away from the butthead behind the newspaper in the dining room.

The busboy cleared a table for her, the waiter snapped open a fresh, white tablecloth, and then she sat down.

Oh, yes. This was lovely. Perfect, cloudless sky, sharp, pine-scented breeze. The clink of silver on china. So much better than sitting in that stuffy room.

The waiter set her plate down so quickly Sophie had to assume they'd made it a while ago and had just kept it warm for her. Well, Ryan could screw himself. If her toast wasn't crisp she'd order a fresh batch. He would not rush her.

But, no, the omelet tasted fluffy, the cheese melted just right—not congealed as though it'd been warming. She slathered a good amount of butter and strawberry preserves on a triangle of toast and bit in. *Delicious.*

"Enjoying your stay?"

Even with her sunglasses, Sophie had to shield her eyes to see who'd spoken to her. An older man sat a table nearby, smiling warmly. "I am. I love it here. How about you?"

"We're having a wonderful time. Ever since I retired, my wife's been planning these trips." He leaned forward, cupped the side of his mouth. "And if she didn't, I'd be on my boat on the lake with a fishing pole and a couple of egg salad sandwiches."

She smiled. "I can see why she plans these trips."

He laughed. "Yes, I do, too. I traveled every week for nearly forty years, so living out of a suitcase is the very last thing I want to do in my retirement. But she stayed home, raised our kids. She deserves to go wherever her heart desires."

Warmth suffused her. "That is so sweet."

A shadow crossed over her, and then a big body blocked the older man from her view. A chair scraped back, and Ryan dropped into the seat opposite her.

The man leaned around Ryan. "Enjoy your trip."

"Thank you. You, too."

Tall, broad-shouldered, Ryan leaned forward in his chair. "I like you." The force of that mega-watt smile only served to piss her off even more.

"I'm so pleased." She reached for her juice, wondering if she should tell him to go wait for her somewhere else. She wanted to enjoy her meal in the sunshine.

"You do exactly what you want to do. You don't worry about hurting my feelings—"

"Why would I worry about your feelings when you have this really neat switch you use to shut them off?"

The grin dropped away. He sat back, toying with the linen napkin arranged like a swan in front of him. She bit into her toast, but she didn't taste it. What was he thinking? That after last night's intimacy he could throw up a wall this morning, and it wouldn't hurt? Well, it did. A lot.

You know what? She was sick of him. "Well, aren't you just the perfect diet plan." She'd lost her appetite again. Draining her juice glasses, she pushed back from the table. "I'm going to brush my teeth and check out. I'll meet you at the car."

They drove in silence. She had no idea what he was thinking, only that each time his phone buzzed his fingers flexed on the steering wheel.

As they sped along the empty road, they passed by endless meadows of tall grass sprinkled with wildflowers. She wouldn't let herself get all worked up over some guy she met on vacation. Maybe one day she'd hear his name on the news or see his picture in the paper for some scandal with an underage pop star, and he'd just be some vague memory, no more potent than an old photograph.

His phone vibrated in the cupholder yet again.

"Oh, my God, would you just pull over and answer it already? Either that or put it on silent."

"I can't. I'm working on some travel arrangements."

"Well, it's just annoying." She wanted to ask him what was going on but, of course, she was done getting into his head.

"My teammates found out." His tone was flat. Dead.

She sat up. That would be awful for him. "What did they say?"

"That I'm a dumbass."

"And you told them where they could shove it?"

He let out a short laugh. "I might've worded it differently. But I'm back on track now."

"Meaning?"

"Meaning break's over. I'm heading back today."

"When?"

"Soon as I'm done swimming in water with magical properties and dining in three-star restaurants." She saw no humor in his eyes.

"You're obviously not happy about it."

"I shouldn't have come out here to begin with." His features shut down, and he stared at the road.

"Just talk about it, Ryan. You're going to have an aneurysm. You can't keep everything inside. Pull the car over and just let 'er rip." She gripped his forearm. "Lose your shit for once in your life."

But he didn't. He just kept driving. And so she pulled out her notes for finding the turn-off for the volcano and watched the scenery unfold.

Sophie stood at the edge of the cliff, looking down at the forest below and the ocean beyond. A breeze made the skirt of her dress flutter around her thighs. She breathed in the sulfur-tainted air.

Strong arms wrapped around her, and a familiar scent filled her senses. She tensed, moving to shrug him off, but Ryan held tight, his mouth at her ear.

"I did it again. I'm sorry."

"I'm sure you are." Again, she tried to pull away, but he wouldn't let her go.

He let out a breath, resting his chin on her shoulder. "I want you, Soph. More than I've ever wanted anything. And I'm really good at denying myself—I'm the fucking king of self-discipline. But I've got none when it comes to you. And I don't know what to do about it. I don't know how to stop wanting you." He nuzzled her neck. "Jesus, just the way you smell. Everything about you drives me out of my mind."

"I feel the same way. Minus the whole self-discipline issue."

His grip tightened, and he nuzzled the hair away from her neck and kissed it. "I want this." His mouth opened, his tongue drew a sensuous circle on the skin just under her ear, and then he bit her lobe. "*Us.*"

"Ryan." She smiled, but she totally understood. She understood everything. The reason he'd closed down, the reason he'd put up the wall of newspaper, and the reason he wouldn't look at her.

"But I can't have it. I have to get back to my team. I've come too far, sacrificed too much, to flush this opportunity down the toilet."

"You don't want to have regrets later."

"Exactly."

"How many games are left this week?"

"Two."

"Are the scouts still there?"

"They're not just there to see me. It's a big week of games, so yeah. They are." He shifted his legs. "And my agent will tell them I'm back. So instead of being the arrogant prick that bails on his team, I'll be the disciplined player who races back after a family emergency."

"Don't be so hard on yourself. You're allowed to be imperfect."

Finally, he let her turn in his arms, and she saw the calm in his eyes. He was okay. Happy with his decision.

"I've never…" He snapped his jaw shut, then tried again. "I want…" His gaze dropped to her mouth.

She pushed on his taut stomach, laughing. "Yeah, I know what you want. But here's what you don't want. To become a fifty-year-old insurance agent with a red Corvette who bangs his secretary instead of being a Major League Baseball player all because you couldn't resist some girl whose name you can't even remember from thirty years ago."

His hands gripped her ass and hauled her up against him. "Sorry what was that? I heard something about your ass and my brain shut down."

"*You're* an ass." She wrapped her hands around his neck, swaying against his body. "I don't know if you can base your decisions on what may or may not happen in the future. I'm pretty sure if you stick with your gut you're going to be okay."

He smiled. "But what if my gut keeps leading me to you?"

When she didn't answer, he kissed her.

This is not a good idea. Not when her body went hot, and desire rolled through her in thick waves. Not when she wanted nothing more than to take him deep inside her body and relieve the unending ache he stirred up.

So she pushed him away. "Let's get you back to the resort, okay?"

CHAPTER THIRTEEN

Something lumbered across the road, snapping Ryan out of his thoughts.

"What the hell is that?" He swerved the Jeep around the animal, who disappeared into the forest. It had a barrel-shaped body and a head shaped like a fat bullet.

"I don't know." Sophie had swung around, trying to get a look out the window. "It's gone."

"That was the weirdest looking animal I've ever seen."

"Might've been a giant hutia."

"A what?"

She settled back in her seat. "It's a rodent."

"Damn." He hadn't been paying attention to his surroundings.

He kept trying to focus on his plans—changing his ticket, getting a ride from the airport. But, all the while, the restlessness seeped back in as steadily as a tide.

He'd been so good at shutting shit down all these years, why couldn't he do it now?

A warm hand stroked his thigh, squeezing just above the knee. "Please tell me what you're thinking."

"Four ideas. That's all I've ever had. That's not exactly a career."

She cocked her head, confused. "Are we talking about baseball?"

Yeah, he had pretty much blurted it out. "Sorry. I was thinking about making a living writing apps. Even if one of them took off, it wouldn't be enough to live off of."

"You told me about the baseball stats and the free food. What else do you have?"

Excitement rushed through him, and it seemed bizarre that he'd never talked about his ideas with anybody. "I told you about Jake's family business?"

She nodded, turning in her seat to face him better. It meant a lot that she always gave him her whole self.

He really didn't want to lose her.

"So, one of the biggest issues they have is billing. The big stores like Walmart and Costco have their own purchase and delivery systems. But the smaller companies, like Jake's, have to go through independent contractors who buy wholesale from them. I want to make an app that would streamline it for them. Cut out the middlemen, saving them a ton of money. All small businesses could use it, so it'd have a pretty wide application."

"That sounds like a good one."

The energy coursing through him was something he only felt when he talked about his ideas.

She laughed.

"What?"

"Look at you. Your eyes are all bright and shiny. You look happy."

Her smile ignited little explosions in his chest. And he couldn't deny it. He did feel happy.

"So, there *is* life outside of baseball. What else would you do with your time, other than write apps?"

Now, see what she did there? She carved a path wide

open inside him. Gave him breathing room. "I don't know." He'd travel. Bike across the States, backpack in Europe. All the stuff he'd never done because he was going to camps and getting private coaching and training.

She stroked his thigh. "Okay, take away everything you're supposed to do. I mean strip it all away. If you had free time what would you do?"

"Go to Montana to visit you." Her look of surprise made him smile.

She turned in her seat, facing forward again. "God, Ryan. The things you say to me. You're such a charmer."

"But I'm not. I'm not like this with anyone else."

She let out a sigh. That pretty pink mouth, those bright blue eyes, and her feminine scent swirling around him. He wanted to bundle it all up and take it with him everywhere he went.

I don't want to lose her.

There it was again, that want, that hunger bearing down on him. But it was so much more than just wanting to fuck her. "You make me...happy. In a way I've never been before."

He wanted *her*. All of her. Checking the rearview mirror, he eased off the road and maneuvered the Jeep between trees.

"What're you doing?"

"Backseat. Now."

She didn't hesitate, just unsnapped the seatbelt and climbed into the back. He cut the ignition, got out of the car, and climbed in beside her. His hands slid under her thighs and ass and he shifted her onto his lap, lowering his face into her neck and breathing her in.

Yes. Oh, fucking yes.

"I want you." He grabbed a fistful of hair at the back of her neck and tugged so he could see her face.

"I know."

"No, I want *you*. You're amazing. I like your independence, your strength…I like the way you make me notice my life in a way I never have before. I've never liked anyone the way I like you."

"Oh." It came out less a word than a soft exhalation.

He smoothed the hair back from her face and off her shoulders. His thumb traced her plump lower lip, and her tongue flicked out. The contact sent a jolt of electricity right to his balls.

He kissed her, his hands sliding under the peach sundress, up her smooth thighs, pushing under the elastic of her panties, and he squeezed her bare ass. She surged into him, her mouth opening for him.

"Ryan." Her voice, needy, her tone, urgent, shook him to his core.

This is it. Their last time together. Because no matter how he talked about writing apps and backpacking around Europe, he knew he'd be a complete asshole to walk away from baseball. Not when he was this close to signing a major league contract. Who did that?

He loved the way she kissed him, the way she couldn't seem to get close enough. His hand slid up her back until the material of the dress tightened and cut his access.

He wanted her body bared to him. Oh, fuck, just the anticipation of his cock sliding into her slick heat sent a shudder through him.

Gripping his shoulders, she shifted on him, straddling his lap, the urgent rocking of her hips making his heart thunder and his blood burn. "Dammit, Sophie."

She reached between them and rubbed his dick, and he nearly bucked her off his lap. He kissed her deeply, holding her so tightly he didn't know if she could take a full breath.

Her fingers went to the top button of his shorts, and she pushed back on his lap, giving her room to unzip them. And then she shoved his boxers down and got hold of his cock. Rising onto her knees, she held him at the base and then slowly sank down on him.

"Jesus," he cried out. Nothing ever felt as good as the tight fist of Sophie Valentine on his cock. But sensation pulled him under as she moved on him, her eyes glazed, hands clutching the seatback behind him. Her hips rocked, grinding on him every time she came down. The noises she made let him know she needed more. She was frantic, desperate, so he unzipped her dress, peeled it off her shoulders, yanked down the cup of her bra, and sucked her nipple deep into his mouth.

She cried out, thighs tightening around him, her movements becoming jerky. "Ryan. Oh, my God."

His tongue flicked over her taut peak, and he shifted slightly, tilting his hips so that he ground over her clit with each thrust.

Her head reared back, her mouth open, as she gasped. "Oh, *God.*" And then her entire body jerked, stiffened, and held like that for long moments while the climax ripped through her. Finally, she collapsed onto his chest.

Clamping his hands on her ass, he took over. With each thrust up into her, his body tightened, his balls pulling up, his spine tingling. Shoving the other cup of her bra down, he freed her breasts. Holy fuck, it was so intense, *too* intense. His head rammed back into the seat, as he powered into her hard, fast, fierce. He didn't want it to end. It was too good. Too fucking good. Until pleasure spiked so hard and fast it bordered on pain. His release came hard, and he shouted. With every burst from his dick, a jolt of bliss shot through him.

And when he finally settled down his whole body thrummed.

Hands on her thighs, head tilted back, he let his breathing even out. As he watched her fix the cups of her bra, he felt his heart shrink, his world collapse. Because this was it. They were done. He had to get to the airport.

Taking a deep breath, he leaned forward, cupping her chin and pressing a kiss on that mouth he loved. "We need to go."

She just nodded, turning away from him, as she pulled up the strap of her dress. She got off him and climbed over the seat.

Time to get back to his real life.

Ryan didn't know how to say goodbye. After fucking her in the Jeep on the side of the road, what could he say? See ya? Thanks for a great three and a half days?

As he waited for the valet to check the mileage, images kept slamming him.

That first night on the chaise, lying side by side, the ferocious desire he felt for her even then…Jesus, his cock pulsed remembering how badly he'd wanted her.

And the waterfall? Holy shit. He could see being that fifty year old man, waking up in the middle of the night remembering the way Sophie had looked straddling him, taking him in her hot, luscious mouth.

"You're good to go." The valet handed him the paperwork.

He signed off on the rental and handed over the keys. "Great, thanks."

Maybe he'd fly out to Montana this summer. Spend some time with her. The idea sent a rush of happiness through him. *Why not?*

But when he swung around the front of the car, she

wasn't there. And as he strode into the lobby, hoping to catch up to her, he didn't see her anywhere.

A wisp of peach fabric flared out before disappearing around a corner.

Sophie Valentine was gone.

Ryan found his friends at the pool, surrounded by their posse of loud, partying women.

The moment Jake spotted him he jumped out of his chair. He met Ryan at the side of the building. "Where you been, man?

"Long story. Checked out the other side of the island with Sophie."

"You spent the night with her?"

He gave a tight nod.

"Was it wild or what? You get what you came for?"

"I had a nice time. Listen, I have to talk to you. I'm heading back to Florida."

"You in trouble?"

"No doubt. Just don't know how much."

"What can I do to help?"

"Nothing. I just have to get going. But I wanted to thank you. For pulling me out of that game before the scouts…"

"Yeah, man. I get it." He clapped a hand on Ryan's shoulder and they shook hands.

He started to go, when Jake said, "Hey, you gotta know. Emma's been blowing up my phone. Dix's, too."

"Yeah, she's hit up just about everybody I know."

"She asked about you a few days ago, but today? She's out of her mind."

Dammit. "What's she saying?"

"Wants to know where you are, what's goin' on with you."

"What'd you tell her?"

"We didn't tell her shit. But I'm about two seconds away from blocking her ass."

"Fine with me. Listen, I have to pack and get myself on a flight."

"Yeah, but you should talk to her. She's pretty worked up."

"I'll deal with her later. She's the last on my list of shit I've got to clean up."

"I don't get it, man. What's up with you and this Sophie chick?"

"Nothing, why?"

"Come on, Ryan. You spent the night with her. Either she fucks like a champ or—"

Ryan shoved his oldest friend so hard he stumbled back.

"What the hell?" More than anger, Ryan saw hurt in his friend's eyes.

"Don't talk about her like that." He wasn't even sorry he'd gone after his friend. He was done going along with shit that didn't sit right with him. "Don't talk about *any* woman like that."

"What's the matter with you? You're like a fuckin' prisoner who steals a box of cigarettes so he can get back in the slammer. You want to be tied down so bad, stick with Emma."

"I don't want to be tied down. That's the last thing I want."

Jake studied him a moment, anger slowly giving way to shock. "Oh, shit. This isn't about Emma at all, is it? I thought you were freakin' out 'cause of that shit she pulled over winter break. But that's not it, is it?" And then clarity struck so hard his shoulders pushed back. "Oh, fuck, man. Is this about *ball*? The draft?"

Ryan didn't have time for this discussion, so he pushed past his friend and entered the building.

"You don't want to play ball, don't play ball. Is that what this is about? It's not like I'm playin' for the Knicks."

"It was never an option for you."

"Even if I didn't have to go into my family's business, I still wouldn't be a ball player. It was fun. I got laid a lot. But it's done. I just thought it was different for you."

"Why?"

"Because you've got a gift. You're a natural. That means something. Plus, isn't it what you've wanted to do since you were, like, eleven?"

Eleven. The year his mom moved out. "Of course."

"You know what I think?" Jake followed him into the hotel. "I think you're hiding behind this chick. You don't deal with your shit, man. You just don't deal."

"I'm dealing with it right now." He punched the elevator button. "I'm going back to my team."

"Look, man, I know you're messed up, and you asked me to back off so I did, but I figured at some point you'd talk to me, let me know what's goin' on in here." He rapped on his head with his knuckles. "But instead you're hanging out with some chick."

"That's the thing." The elevator opened, and he got on. "She's not just some chick."

Jake curled his hand around the door, not letting it shut. "Yeah, she is. In the scheme of things, that's exactly what she is. You're never gonna see her again, so let it go."

He knocked Jake's hand away and let the doors shut.

He didn't need to hear any more. He'd already made his choice.

******

Sophie entered her room and tripped over her carry-on bag. "Dammit." Breathing hard, palms damp, she closed her eyes and stood there for a moment, trying to get a hold of herself.

Blinking back tears, she tossed her purse on the bed and headed to the French doors. She stepped onto the balcony, inhaling warm, tropical air. From the sixth floor, she could see blue umbrellas dotting the beach, white sails speckling the lagoon, and groups of people gathered around tables at the pool.

Her heart hurt. Yeah, she got that she'd had wild monkey sex on spring break—just like ten thousand other college girls. It was a hookup. She got it. Whatever. She'd live.

But if spring flings felt like *this*, forget it. She didn't want to do it ever again. It hurt too much when it ended. And some stupid part of her couldn't help thinking what she had with Ryan was special. *He* was special.

He sees me.

She couldn't imagine feeling this kind of passion for anyone else. Of course she got that he had to get back to his team, but they could've kept in touch. Neither of them had even suggested it. They'd both just run from whatever these feelings were—and they were strong. She knew he felt it, too. It was just the wrong time.

Stop thinking about it.

Heading back into the room, she dug her phone out of her bag and called her sister. While it rang, she glanced at her list of activities. *Oh, good.* She'd forgotten about scuba diving this afternoon. That would be fun. And tomorrow she had paragliding. *Awesome. See? This is what I came here to do.*

"Hey, Soph." Abby yawned.

"You sound exhausted."

"You have no idea. What's up?"

"I just wanted to let you know that I talked to Aunt

Georgie. If you're really sure you want to sell Crazy Hearts—"

"We're sure."

Oddly, the *we're* hurt more than her sister not caring about what mattered to Sophie. "Okay, well, she totally respects your interest in taking the company in a sustainable and organic direction, but she brought up a really good question. She asked me what Mom and Dad would want, and I just know in my heart they'd never sell Crazy Hearts. Not for any amount of money."

"Are you seriously dragging our dead parents into this?" She blew out an angry breath. "I can't believe this. Our *parents* could never have imagined a global food corporation showing up out of the blue and offering us twice the value of our company. Trust me—since *I* actually worked with them—they'd be laughing all the way to the bank."

In her gut Sophie knew Abby was wrong. "But they *did* imagine it, Abby. Why else would they have given each of us a blocking vote? If they hadn't, they'd have set up a majority rule—or even a super majority rule. No, I have no doubt they set up the estate the way they did to protect the company. They wanted to protect Dad's family legacy. I don't believe they'd even consider the offer."

"Yes, because in their wildest dreams they couldn't have imagined someone offering them *one hundred million dollars*. You just don't turn an opportunity like that down."

"Look, if we were struggling, if we needed liquidity…if Hannah wanted for anything, then I could see this from your perspective." Not really, though. No matter what, she'd still try to come up with an alternative. "But we have more money than any of us can spend in our lifetimes. Why on God's earth would we get rid of our family history for more?"

"This is a *business* decision. The money will create

opportunity for us, Sophie. You don't grasp that our products are outdated. There's no future in them. This money will enable us to develop new products—food that people will actually want to eat. You want to preserve the legacy? Then we need to change our brand to fit the new market. People want healthy. They want foods created and marketed in sustainable ways. You want to keep the family business going? Then you change with the times. You *grow*. And that's what we're doing. Instead of fighting us, get on board and join us."

Sophie crossed an arm over her stomach. Having always wanted to be included, she'd never fought with her sister. But that gap she'd hoped to close with age only loomed wider than ever. And had become impossible to bridge.

Of course she wanted to join them. More than anything. Well, obviously not more than *anything*. Because Sophie wouldn't go along with their plans. She just didn't believe in her heart that selling the company that meant so much to generations of Valentines was the right choice.

Abby let out a huff of exasperation. "God, I hope you haven't talked like this around Mike and the guys. I don't know what kind of job they'll give you when you sound this naïve."

Something snapped in her. "I don't care what I sound like to you." And it was true. For the first time in her life, she didn't care what her sister thought of her. And that was incredibly liberating. It gave her the courage to go on. "You know, in two months I graduate, and I've been so worried about what job you guys would give me. Can I do it? Will I even *want* to do it? But this week I've realized it all comes down to one thing for me. What do I want to spend my life doing? And now I know. I want to spend it continuing this incredibly beautiful tradition our family started generations ago. This is my connection to our ancestors, my family, and there's nothing I'd rather do with my life than run Crazy Hearts." And, wow, that felt good. Not just saying it but *understanding* it.

"Okay, you know what?" her sister said. "I can't deal with this right now. I don't want to fight with you, and I don't want to hurt you. But I'll tell you the truth. This isn't about what you want to do. This is about what's best for Valentine's. Once you've worked with us for a while your input will carry more weight, but right now you're going to have to trust that the rest of us know what's best for the company. And we certainly know our parents a hell of a lot better than you ever did."

Way to plunge the knife in and twist. "Not to be a bitch or anything, but you don't have a deal without my vote. So it's time to move the conversation past that. You don't care about Crazy Hearts, and you want the money from Nestlé to fund development of new products and build organic factories, so that's going to be our starting point for future discussions. I can't pay you a hundred million dollars, but I've talked to Barry and, between my savings from distributions and bank financing, I know I can pay you enough to allow you to pursue your objectives. And since Crazy Hearts doesn't fit the new Valentine brand, then I'm asking for a shot at running it on my own. Because it *matters* to me."

"Okay, stop it. Just stop it. We'll talk about this when you get home. As a *family*."

"I think we're done talking. But I hope you've put a hold on your talks with Nestlé like I asked. Have you?"

"Sophie, what has gotten into you? We're a family. And instead of talking to *us* about all this, you're talking to Barry and Aunt Georgie?"

"I've tried talking to you. You keep telling me I'm an inexperienced outsider, which is good because it's forced me to face the truth and explore options I never would've considered before. And one of those options is using the event building on Aunt Georgie's property. She said I could use it for Crazy hearts."

"You're going to take Crazy Hearts and move to Montana and live with our crazy hermit aunt?"

Sophie'd never heard her sister sound so distraught. "She's not a hermit. She's very involved in her community. Always has been. And she lives near Bozeman. It's a fun college town."

"Your life is here, Sophie. Your family's here. This is all you've ever known. You really want to start over in some remote mountain town? Think about where you live. My God, why would you ever want to leave?"

"What do I do in LA? Go shopping, go out to dinner? I don't even like shopping. I hate the traffic, and I have to leave the city every time I want to have some fun." She drew in a breath. She'd never told her siblings this, but she had to do it. "And I *hate* living in that house all by myself."

"How can you say that? That's our home." Was Abby crying?

"It doesn't hold the same happy memories for me." A thousand flapping wings burst out of the cage in her heart. She couldn't believe she was finally voicing thoughts she'd kept hidden for years. God, did it feel good.

"What are you talking about? We have all of our parties there. Christmas, Thanksgiving, birthdays. All five of us, our spouses, our children. We're all there more than we're in our own homes. And if you leave, we'll wind up selling it."

"I'm not staying so you can keep your childhood home."

"That's not what I mean, and you know it. What happens

when you get married and have kids? You'll want it, too. You can't leave, Soph. Hannah will grow up without you."

"It's an easy plane ride away. I'll come home all the time."

"See? You said it yourself. This is home. *We're* your home."

"Oh, come on, Abby. I hardly you see you guys. Unless I'm babysitting."

"Is that what this is about? I'm sorry if I rely on you too much, but I'm not sorry that you're Hannah's babysitter. You're the only one in the world I trust to watch her."

Her heart swelled. *This* is what she needed to hear. That she mattered. That she meant something to them.

"Don't you want to watch her grow up? Don't you want to be there for her? Taking her to swimming lessons, taking her to her first haircut, teaching her to put on make-up? You can't miss out on all that. She needs you. *I* need you."

"Of course I want to be there for all that. But I…" She'd waited a long time for Abby to need her.

"I love you, Soph. I don't know what I'd do without you." She could hear her sister weeping. "You're my *sister.*"

"I love you, too. But we have to talk about this. You can't keep dismissing my ideas. Let's just think about it, okay?"

"No. Don't think about it. You're not moving to Montana. We're not selling the house. God, all I wanted was to build a company we can be proud of that will live on for future generations, and now I'm losing my sister and my family home? Is it worth it, Soph? Just to hold onto some processed, unhealthy cookie that doesn't fit our brand anymore? Family first. *That's* what mom and dad would've wanted."

"Okay, okay. We'll talk in person as a family. Listen, I'll be home on Saturday, and I'll take Hannah for a few hours and you can catch up on your sleep, okay?"

"Oh, thank God. I'm dying."

"I know you are. Give my little punkin a big kiss on that gorgeously fat cheek."

She hung up, letting the feelings settle in. Her sister loved her. Her family needed her.

But did they love her enough to hold onto Crazy Hearts for her?

She wasn't sure she wanted to find out.

******

Dropping his duffle bag at his feet, Ryan looked up at the monitor to see five names listed on the standby screen. His came first. A quick scan of his gate made him think he had a good shot of getting on the flight. Not too many passengers. If he got in tonight, he'd be on the field for tomorrow morning's game.

The band around his chest tightened, and anxiety raced through him.

Block it out. Grabbing the handle of his pack, he headed for the plate-glass window overlooking the tarmac. A baggage handler wheeled a cart, a plane rolled back from the terminal, and a man in a neon yellow vest read the screen of his cell phone.

When he closed his eyes, he saw Sophie. Riding him in the back of the Jeep, her silky hair brushing over his arms. Everything in him pulled to go back to the island to be with her.

What was it about her that drove him so crazy? She was feisty and fun. He loved her spirit and her sense of adventure. He loved the way she cared enough to push him. Everyone saw what he wanted them to see—and built their expectations based on that. Not their fault—he didn't let them in. But that shit didn't fly with Sophie. She dug deeper with him. She got him.

Just thinking about her made his skin heat up, his blood simmer. He wanted his hands on her. Her mouth—kissing had never felt like that before.

Dammit. Shut it down. Enough about a girl he'd never see again.

In fifteen minutes they'd start boarding his flight. He'd get on that plane and go back to his life. He wouldn't crap-out before he got his home run.

Pulling out his phone, he sent a text to his coach.

At airport, hope to get on standby. Should be at game tomorrow.

There. It was done. He touched his forehead to the cool pane of glass. He'd just sealed the deal. No going back to the island now.

Restless energy kicked up his pulse. And not the good kind. Not the kind that pushed him to work out instead of partying with his friends. Not the kind that gave him the will to shove down his impulses and call on that prized self-discipline.

No, the kind that caused him to jump on a plane for a singles resort and bail on his teammates.

Pushing off the window, he headed to the row of stores. He'd grab a drink and something to read on the flight. But not two minutes later he heard the announcement for his flight. The sound of his name over the PA system shrieked like a whistle in his ear.

His phone buzzed. *Coach.*

Where are you?

He dropped his duffle to reply. *San Juan.*

Meet in hotel dining room tomorrow at 7:30 AM.

See you then. Adrenaline pumped through his system. Wiping his damp palms on his shorts, his vision narrowed, and he went light-headed.

Fucking face it, man. You don't want to go back.

He reminded himself of his dad's advice, about staying the course, sliding into home. Make the majors, play a few seasons. *Makes total sense.*

When he reached the desk, he found a soldier and a harried woman with a baby in a car seat waiting for the gate attendant to get off the phone.

When she did, she looked up. "Mr. O'Donnell?"

"Yep."

"We've got a seat for you." She gave him a smile that told him he'd won the lottery.

When he glanced up to the monitor, he saw Lt. James Wilson in the second waiting position.

Hands clammy, he handed over his boarding pass. Beads of perspiration popped out on his forehead, and his stomach rolled. If he took this flight, he'd redeem himself in the eyes of his coach, team, and scouts. He'd recover from his lapse in judgment.

As the woman typed, the soldier beside him tapped the keypad of his phone.

"You need to get on this flight?" Ryan hoped like hell he'd say the family he hadn't seen in eight months was waiting for him.

"It'd be great, but I can't say I *need* to."

Ryan nodded, ridiculously disappointed not to have an excuse to give his seat away.

But something the guy said struck him. *Can't say I need to.* Because Ryan *did* need something. Strip away the expectations, the guilt, the fear of repercussions, and Ryan knew exactly what he needed. Jesus Christ, what was he doing going back? He'd risked everything for this break and instead of taking it he'd listened to messages, responded to texts, and taken phone calls. He should've powered down his phone and locked it in the hotel room's safe.

He knew in his gut if he woke up tomorrow and walked onto the field, he'd be just as fucked up as when he'd left. Not only would he let his teammates down, but the scouts would wonder what the hell had happened to Ryan O'Donnell.

His dad thought he should see it through—and, yeah, that rang true, and he would. But right now, for whatever reason, what he needed to see through was this week. This break that he absolutely needed.

"Hang on."

The attendant looked up.

Was he really going to do this? He'd just told his coach he was on his way back. He had a chance to recover from his one and only act of rebellion. He had a chance to slide right back into his life as though nothing had happened. He doubted his coach would give him much of a consequence if he showed up tomorrow.

But if he took the full week?

If he gave himself the gift of Sophie Valentine?

Elation spread through him like fresh, clean air. "Give him my spot."

His room had been taken, but he'd upgraded to a suite for his remaining two nights. He'd changed his ticket back to his original flight, though he'd lost his seat beside his friends.

Now he just needed her.

Rougher sea made for a rocky ride, but Ryan's focus was on the glittering yellow lights of the resort, the palm trees swaying in a semi-circle around the beach. He'd texted her several times since giving away his seat, but she hadn't responded. He wouldn't let it wind him up. She could be off on another adventure.

When his phone vibrated in his pocket, he whipped it out. But it wasn't Sophie.

A stab of guilt hit him when he saw his coach's name. But, fuck, when had he ever taken something for himself?

Damn the consequences, he was going to take his tiny slice of happiness by spending two more days with Sophie.

As the engine decelerated, and the boat bumped into the dock, Ryan reached for his duffle bag.

A deckhand stopped him. "We'll bring it to your room, sir."

He pulled a bill out of his pocket and handed it to the guy. "Great, thanks."

And then he jumped off the boat and headed for the hotel. Once he reached the pavement, he shook the sand out of his boat shoes. He checked the time on his phone. Eleven-fifteen. She'd probably be back in her room. Or on the beach—in a chaise? But a quick scan of the area—a couple strolling along the shoreline, a group gathered around a bonfire—came up empty. He doubted she'd be at the bar. Her friends partied, so she never stayed with them this late.

That meant she'd be in her room. He hurried around the pool and entered the hotel. Once at the elevator he texted her again.

Here. On my way to your room. U there?

He boarded the car, then jabbed the button for the sixth floor. She didn't respond. He didn't care. He'd find her.

She wouldn't have gone back into town, would she? Why the hell hadn't he asked her plans? He couldn't believe he hadn't tried to stay in touch.

He strode down the hall and knocked on her door. While waiting for her answer, he checked his phone. Nothing.

He'd find her friends. He pounded one more time, waited, and then took off.

Instead of taking the side exit that led directly to the bar, he went out towards the pool. The humid air clung to him, as he passed by a bunch of people in the shallow end, their bodies rippling silhouettes against underwater lights. On a chaise, a woman sprawled atop a man. He had his hands under her short skirt, squeezing her bare ass cheeks.

No sign of Sophie or her friends. He checked the beach one more time, but he still didn't see her. So he entered the bar. Right away he saw Jake with a blonde, her arms slung around his neck, her body swaying against his.

He'd leave his friend to it. Shooting another text to Sophie—*Looking 4 u. Where r u?*—he pushed through the crowd of grinding bodies on the dance floor. Recognizing the height and toned body of Sophie's friend, he tapped her shoulder.

She pulled away from the guy she was kissing, and it seemed to take a moment for her vision to clear. "Ryan? What're you doing here?"

"Where's Sophie?"

"She went up to her room about an hour ago. Why?"

"I need to see her." He started to go, when he felt a hand on his shoulder tug him back. "What?" he snapped.

"Did you come back for *her*?"

A slow smile spread through him. "Yep."

Heading to the elevator bay, he found a crowd of people, laughing, drinks in their hands, but he didn't want the company. So he ducked into the stairwell and took the six flights up to her floor.

Once there, Ryan banged on her door. "Soph? Sophie?" Where was she?

A door swung open down the hall, and a guy with a towel

wrapped around his waist leaned out. "What's going on?"

Ryan raised a hand in apology. The guy shook his head and retreated, closing the door.

Turning his back against the wall, he scrubbed his face. He'd shaved before taking off for the airport, wanting to show his coach and teammates he'd cleaned up his act. Was back to being the guy they'd always known.

But he wished he hadn't.

Because as much as he'd like to be that guy, he just wasn't.

CHAPTER FOURTEEN

With her French doors thrown open and a strong breeze riffling the bed skirt, Sophie danced like a wild thing all over her suite. Pharell's song *Happy* played in her earbuds, and she lost herself in the ocean-scented air and uplifting beat.

Spinning around, she hit a high note and her face cracked. The weird sensation made her burst out laughing. *Guess it's time to wash off the mudpack.* Flipping on the bathroom light, she turned on the faucet and let the water warm up before splashing it on her face.

With her eyes closed, Ryan came to mind. He'd still be on a plane. Was he happy to be going back?

Did he feel relieved he'd pulled out of this tailspin?

It didn't feel good to get so close to someone and then never talk to him again. They could have at least kept in touch through social media. But, no, she really didn't want to see pictures of him with other women. Or back with Emma. That would hurt.

But for now she could send him a text. Just to see how he was doing. Would he like that? Or had he already moved on?

Yeah, probably moved on.

Actually, she'd like to get Jake's contact information. She

wouldn't talk to her sister again about Crazy Hearts until she had an actual plan. And to make one she needed to find out whether or not running the business herself was a viable option.

Quickly rinsing off the mud, she patted her skin dry, smoothed on lotion, and then went to grab her phone off the nightstand.

The moment she popped the buds out, she heard pounding at the door. Grabbing her phone, she caught the robe in a fist at her collarbone and peered through the peephole.

All she could see was a light blue button-down stretched across a broad, muscled chest. "Ryan?"

"Soph? Open the damn door."

Joy sparked and crackled under her skin. That deep, sexy voice thrilled her. She unlocked the door and threw it open.

He barreled inside, lifting her off the ground. Feet dangling, she had to grab onto his shoulders. He breathed her in. "Why didn't you answer?"

He was back. He'd come back. "What're you doing here?" Had he missed his flight?

But instead of responding, he closed and locked the door, and then walked her back into the room. Licking into her mouth, hands gripping her ass, he tumbled them down onto the bed. Immediately, he rolled to his side, bringing them face-to-face.

She scraped the hair at his temples, tucking it behind his ears. "You're here." Leaning in, she rubbed her cheek across his smooth skin. "You shaved."

"Yeah. Wanted to show my coach I was back."

"You're too gorgeous to walk around like this, you know."

Lifting the back of her thigh, he draped it over his hip.

Then, he cupped her chin and kissed her in the sweetest, most desperate way. Like he'd missed her. Like he couldn't believe he had her back in his arms.

He pushed the robe off her shoulders, but the material caught between them. "Get this off." His gruff voice heated her.

Leaning away from him, she yanked at the silk, throwing it off her shoulder and pulling her arm out. He skimmed a hand slowly down the dip of her waist, the rise of her hip, and around to her ass. "You feel so good." He pressed into her, kissing her cheek, her temple, and then nuzzling her neck.

Caressing her ass, he hit the elastic barrier of her panties, and then he sighed, pulling back. "How long have you been in here?"

"My room? A while." She ran a hand up his chest, undoing the top button of his shirt.

"You didn't open the door or answer my texts."

"I was listening to my iPod. I had a spa night. I took a bath and gave myself a facial."

"Yeah? I wondered what you were doing. You look all flushed and sweaty."

The next button popped open, and she got a better view of his gorgeous, lightly-haired chest. "I was dancing."

He licked a path from her neck to her collarbone. One hand cupped her breast, plumping it, and he swiped his tongue over her nipple. "Oh." *God.* "Ryan, what're you doing here?"

"Shit." He pulled away from her, sitting up. Digging into his pocket, he pulled out his phone. "Hang on."

Was there anything sexier than a man's forearm, all strong and tan, the sleeve of his shirt rolled to his elbow? She waited while he typed out a text, and then tossed the phone onto the couch.

"What was that?"

"Had to tell my coach I didn't make the flight."

"Why fly all the way back to Santa Granada when you could've just stayed the night in San Juan and caught the first flight out in the morning?"

"I don't want to go back yet. So I'm taking my break. I'm seeing it through."

"You're such a rebel. And you are so going to pay for it."

"You know, one of the things my dad said to back his argument is that he didn't want me to regret coming this far and then bailing before I had a shot at the majors. Well, I don't want any regrets here either."

"Yes, I can see how cutting short your hedonistic vacation might one day trigger a midlife crisis."

"If I get on that field tomorrow, I'm going to fuck up. It's just where I am right now." He lay back down beside her, his hand stroking the slope of her shoulder and resting on her hip. Tugging at the robe half hanging off her, he said, "Take everything off and welcome your man home."

She laughed against his mouth. "You sure you don't want me to fry up some bacon for you first?"

"I want you naked."

"And what do I get out of it?"

"You get to see my impressive man-meat."

Laughter burst free from her belly. She hadn't expected him to say anything like that.

She shifted off the bed, letting her robe fall to the floor. "I don't know, buddy. You're gonna have to step up your game, offer me a little more than just your man-meat if you want some of this." She brushed the hair off her shoulders and shimmied playfully. He watched her, his expression hungry, hard, and it sent a thrill down to the soles of her feet. She stepped out of her panties.

"I came back for you." He lunged for her, grabbing her arm and tugging her onto the bed. Once he had her under him, his mouth at her ear, he said, "I'm nowhere near finished with you."

Desire burned under her skin, and happiness flooded her.

He kissed her slow and sweet, letting their tongues tangle deliciously. He palmed her breast, rubbing across her nipple. "I'm happy. Right here, right now. I'm happy. That's why I came back. I just want this time with you." He gave her breast a lustful squeeze, gently sucking her bottom lip. "Will you be mine for the week?"

******

Strapped into their life jackets and harnesses, Ryan reached for Sophie's hand. He brought it to his mouth and pressed a kiss to her palm. He'd never gone paragliding before. As the boat picked up speed, their sails flapped, opened, and together they rose, climbing higher and higher into the air. Legs dangling, body weightless, he took in the sandy shoreline, the forest, and the turquoise lagoon.

He shouted as they climbed steadily, floating higher in the air. Sophie squeezed his hand. She smiled at him, and their gazes locked. He couldn't remember ever feeling this kind of happiness before.

Their friends hollered and hooted at them from the boat, and Sophie waved. She seemed so content in her own skin. He wouldn't know what that felt like, but she made him want to know. Being with her—it made him...fuck, he just felt so much. He couldn't believe he'd only known her four days.

Fear sliced through him at the idea of losing her. Going back to his life, as if he'd never had this connection, this happiness.

He drew her hand to his mouth again, held it there in a lingering kiss. She watched him, almost warily. *I love you.* His body thrummed with more emotion than he could handle. *I fucking love you.*

To his surprise, she didn't look away. She took in a deep breath, and a sense of peace seemed to spread over her, relaxing her body. He could've sworn he saw it in her eyes. *I love you, too.*

The moment the boat hit the dock, Ryan grabbed her hand and towed her up the beach. While the staff unloaded the boat and packed up the van, he wanted to steal a few moments alone with her.

"What're you doing?" She glanced back at the others talking and laughing together.

He yanked her to him and kissed her cheek, gliding his tongue down to her neck and biting the tendon. Her hands tightened on his forearms.

"Ryan." Her voice sounded thin and needy.

The ocean had carved caves into the rugged cliffs of this cove. He towed her into one, the dark and cool of it only igniting his need for her. He pulled her into his arms and kissed her, his hands smoothing down her back, sliding under the elastic waistband of her bikini bottoms, and gripping her flesh. He was so fucking hard for her.

He ground his dick against her stomach and kissing that hot, wet mouth. Sliding his hands lower, dipping between her legs, he grazed the dampness beneath her curls. She sucked in a breath, moaning into his mouth.

"I want you, Soph." He spun her around, yanking her bottoms down, jerking her hips up high.

"Ryan, dude?" Jake called from somewhere down the beach. "Where'd you get to?"

"Maybe they went to the parking lot already," one of

Sophie's friends said, voices getting closer.

"Fuck," he whispered harshly, pulling her bottoms back up. As she turned around, he kissed her mouth hard. "*Fuck*."

And then he took her hand, leading them out of the cave. "Here." He gave Jake a menacing look.

"Ready to go?" Jake gave him a shit-eating grin.

As they started off, Ryan leaned into her ear. "When we get back to the resort, let's go to your room. I want to spend the rest of the afternoon alone with you, okay?"

Energy radiated between them like shimmering heat. Color suffused her cheeks. "Yes."

******

The van idled in the parking lot, waiting for them. Jake and Laura ran for it, slamming into each other as they fought to get into the back row. By the time Sophie and Ryan caught up, she found only one seat left in back and one up front beside the driver.

Disappointed she wouldn't get to sit with him, she took the passenger seat, while Ryan took the window beside Dix.

Her body still buzzed from the way he'd looked at her, the intensity. For a minute there, up in the air, all weightless and giddy with excitement, it had almost felt like he was trying to tell her something. Ridiculous to even think it, but the way he'd held her gaze with such...intention...it had made her feel like he loved her.

Could Kat be right? Could what she had with Ryan actually turn into something real? Something that lasted?

He'd come back to the island for her.

Affection rushed her hard, and she glanced back at him, wanting him to know she felt just as strongly for him.

But she found him with his cell phone in his hand, features tightened in...shock. She turned more fully to observe him. He looked stressed, almost angry. Jake leaned over the seat and said something that riled him, and he shouldered his friend away.

What was happening? The only thing she could think that would make him react this way was if his coach had gotten tough with him. Not taking the flight home last night had to have been a game-changer. Had he kicked him off the team?

Ryan set his phone down, gazing out the window. She wanted to crawl in his lap and comfort him. No matter how bad things were, all problems had solutions. He just had to talk about it. Not keep it locked inside.

She couldn't stand to see him so unhappy, so she unbuckled her seat belt, climbed over the console, and sat on his lap.

"Seriously, Soph?" Laura said.

Ryan's arms banded around her, and he pressed his lips to her temple, not saying a word.

She loved his scent, all hot sand and clean cotton. She loved his body, his strength, and the possessive way he touched her.

"You all right?" she whispered in his ear.

He didn't answer.

Sensing eyes on her, she looked up and found Jake regarding her with barely disguised impatience. What the hell had *she* done?

Once they arrived at the resort, everyone filed out of the van. But she didn't budge.

She leaned back against the door, her legs draped across Ryan's lap. "What happened?"

"Nothing."

She cupped his chin, tilted him towards her. Oh, that look in his eyes—filled with anger and frustration. It killed her. "Ryan."

He drew in a deep breath. She thought he might say something, but his jaw snapped shut.

"Talk to me."

"I don't want to talk about it. I shouldn't have to talk about it. It's not my problem, and I don't want it fucking up my last few days here."

"But—"

"Two days, Soph. That's all I'm asking for. I want these two days for myself. With *you*. Okay?"

What could she say to that? She answered with a kiss. She'd meant a simple kiss, a touch of affection, but as always it ignited into so much more. *Oh, yes.* She fell into the slide of his tongue, the grip of his big hands.

"Uh, excuse me?" a voice called.

She tore her mouth off his to find the driver standing outside the van.

"I'm sorry, but I've got another group to take out."

Ryan's hand squeezed her thigh, like he wasn't ready to let her go. But she just smiled. "Of course. Sorry."

His hips flexed hard, grinding his erection into her bottom. Without even thinking, she pushed back down.

"Let me grab my bag." She launched forward, hands on the seat, ass in the air, as she grabbed her tote from the floor of the passenger seat. Ryan's hands clamped down on her, giving both cheeks a hungry squeeze.

She couldn't wait to get back to her room and be with him. As she stepped into the cool of the lobby, Ryan reached for her hand. While the others headed for the bar, he steered her toward the elevators.

But a hand touched her shoulder, stopping her. She turned to find Jake standing there, tall and imposing.

He gave her a chin nod. "Ryan said you wanted to talk to me about your business?"

"I do." She did need to talk with him. But something else was going on. She could've sworn she saw Ryan shoot his friend an appreciative look.

"Why don't you guys hit the café?" Ryan held up his phone, and she understood he had to deal with something. "I'll catch up with you later."

Well, if his coach needed to talk to him, Ryan had to face it. "Sure. Come get me when you're ready."

An hour and a half later, after two cups of coffee and a Rum Baba, their friends appeared at their table.

"We thought we'd join you for lunch." Laura slid in beside her. "Are we interrupting?"

"Not at all," Sophie said.

"You get your business stuff worked out?" Laura swiped a finger through the whipped cream left over on the plate.

Dixon flopped down next to Jake. "Don't get him started. He could go on about business shit for days."

Jake gave him a quelling look, but Dixon just picked up a menu. "What's good?"

"Believe it or not, we've been talking the whole time," Sophie said. "We haven't even ordered."

"Hey, guys." Kat slid in next to Laura.

Just then Ryan arrived. He looked hard, tense, as he motioned for her friends to get out. "Let me sit next to Sophie."

Kat scooted out and went to sit beside Dixon. Laura got out, too, and Ryan pushed in until he was right up against her. He rucked up the material of her dress, and his big hand clasped her bare thigh.

She was about to ask how everything had gone with his coach, but he spoke first. "You get the help you needed?"

"I did." She smiled across the table to Jake. "He had great ideas."

"Like?"

"Well, first off, he said to leave all the administrative stuff in LA and only move production to Montana. That in itself makes it much more do-able."

"You're moving to Montana?" Kat looked more upset than surprised.

"I'm not doing anything." She hated deceiving her friends, but she couldn't risk exposing the Nestlé deal. "Jake's family runs a business, too. I'm just asking him about theoretical situations."

"But it's a possibility?" Kat asked.

"Who wouldn't want to live in Montana?" Jake said.

As Jake turned the conversation to all that Big Sky had to offer, Sophie shared more with Ryan. "He also had a great idea about incenting the current workers with a profit-sharing model." She said it quietly, while Kat argued against living in a tourist resort full-time. "That way they're invested in the company and might not mind moving with the business. It'll make it easy for me to keep things going smoothly."

As wound up as he was, Ryan's tight smile let her know he was happy for her. "Sounds good, Soph."

"Oh." Laura dug into her bag and pulled out her phone. "You guys, let me get in next to Jake so I can get a picture."

Jake reeled back. "What the hell for? Get one with Dixon."

"I already have one with him."

Sophie set down her menu. "What happened to one guy for the whole week?"

"Yeah, well, that didn't work out. I'm just doing a bunch of guys—"

Jake snorted.

"Not like *that*. Just me having a great time."

Jake watched as Kat and Dixon got out of the booth. "What does that have to do with me? I'm not part of your good time."

"Today you are." Laura got in beside him, handing off the phone to Kat.

Ryan wrapped a curl around his finger and tugged to get Sophie's attention back. "Sounds like he had good ideas."

She nodded, as he stroked her inner thigh.

"What's the big deal?" Laura gave Jake a little shove. "I'm putting pictures up on Facebook with me and hot guys. You should be flattered I'm including you." Laura leaned against him. "Now smile."

Jake pulled away. "What's the point?"

"To make her ex jealous," Kat said.

Jake looked completely disgusted. "Count me out. That's stupid."

"It'll be on my social media accounts. It's not like any of your friends will ever see it."

"What'd he do to you?" Jake asked.

"You seriously won't take a picture with me?"

"That's right."

"Fine." Laura dropped her phone in her tote.

Ryan's hand inched higher up her leg. She wrapped an arm around his shoulders, sifting her fingers through the silky hair at the back of his neck. "Do you want to order something?"

He shook his head tightly.

"Why bother with your ex? It's over." Jake looked completely clueless.

Kat handed Laura a menu, but she waved it away. "He broke up with me."

"He fuck you over?"

"No, he was really nice about it."

"So why try to hurt him?"

"Because we had a *plan*. He just...God, he just dumped me."

"By text?"

"No. He was really good about it. He called and asked if he could come over. He wanted to take a walk with me."

"Which was especially cool of him that he didn't do it in the house," Kat said.

"We live in the sorority." Laura flicked a glance at Jake, who actually seemed interested. "Anyhow, he took me to a bench behind the library and told me he wasn't going to Italy with me." She stopped talking, tears glittering in her eyes. "That was our plan. We both signed with teams in Italy. But all of a sudden he doesn't want to play soccer anymore."

"So?" Jake said. "Lots of division one players don't go on to play professionally."

"Okay, well, I'm sorry, but I planned my life around it. Instead, he tells me he's got a job lined up in *Michigan*. What about me? I'm just supposed to go to Italy alone?"

"Yeah." Jake sounded incredulous. "That's how it goes."

"Are you serious? He tells me now? In March? Two months before graduation?"

"What was he supposed to do? Go ahead with something he doesn't want to do because you don't have the balls to go through with it on your own?"

"I didn't say that."

"You didn't have to. You're spending spring break trying to make him jealous by putting up pictures of you with strange guys. You're lying to him. And what'd he do? Break up with you. Look, after college...shit changes. You're not in that bubble anymore."

"Word." Dixon lifted his fist, bumping with Jake's.

"And if he's not going to Italy with you, then what's the point of staying together?"

Sophie totally agreed and hoped hearing it from an outsider would help.

"We have two more months. If he loved me, he wouldn't have broken up with me."

"So, he doesn't love you anymore. You gonna punish him for that?"

"Back off, Jake." Ryan said.

"No, it's all right." Laura seemed hopeful for the first time. "I actually want to hear it." She drew in a breath. "I just…it hurts that he doesn't want me anymore." She looked embarrassed. "Sorry. I'm not usually like this."

"Like what?" Jake said. "A guy blew up your world. It's understandable. Just don't take it out on him. That's not cool. Deal with it and move on."

Ryan placed a soft kiss on Sophie's mouth. "You okay?"

Was she *okay*? Between the sensual assault of his stroking hands, the heat of his body, and the unsatisfied sexual energy coursing through her, she wanted to climb on his lap and make out with him. She almost didn't care that she was in a café, surrounded by her friends.

He kissed her again, going deeper. *God.* Desire rolled through her, sending pulses of electricity through her. "Let's get out of here."

Oh, yes.

He turned to Kat. "Can you let us out?" Grabbing Sophie's hand, he practically pulled her out of the table. "We'll see you guys later."

"Hang on." Jake had never sounded so serious. "Got a quick question for you."

For one moment Ryan's grip on her tightened, but then he let out a resigned breath and let her go. "Yeah. Sure."

She knew he had to deal with whatever was tearing him up, so she pressed a kiss to his cheek. "Talk to your friend.

I'm going to shower and take a nap. I'll catch up with you later, okay?"

One terse nod without even looking at her, and then Ryan strode out of the restaurant, Jake on his heels.

She watched until she couldn't see him anymore, dread creeping through her.

What wasn't he telling her?

CHAPTER FIFTEEN

"Emma's on her way." The words crashed like cymbals in Ryan's head. "*Here.*"

The normally chill Jake cringed.

"How the hell did she find out where I am?" Standing under a hot sun by the pool, Ryan crossed his arms over his chest.

His friend scrubbed a hand over his mouth, looking remorseful. "Alyssa must've told her."

"Your *sister* knows where I am?" And why would she tell Emma?

"She wanted to know why Emma was blowing up everyone's phone. Lys loves you, man. She was worried. I told her we were hangin' out for a few days at this resort. She wanted to know if you were all right, if you were havin' fun like me and Dix, and I said, of course not. Ryan's doing his usual monogamous thing."

Ryan scraped his hands through his hair. "You told Lys about *Sophie*?"

"I didn't mention her name. Just that you had a girl. It was no big deal."

"Well, it turned out to be a big fucking deal because Emma's flying out here." *Dammit.* "No one was supposed to know, remember?"

"How was I supposed to know your ex was gonna go psycho and start interrogating everyone you've ever known?"

"Jesus, *that's* why she's coming here. Because she found out I'm seeing someone."

"Seeing someone? Do you hear yourself? This is spring break. You're supposed to be fucking around. No ties, no obligations. And don't blame anyone but your nutjob ex. She's the one stirring up trouble for you. Not me, and definitely not Alyssa."

"We're leaving the day after tomorrow." There were no direct flights, so he'd spent the last hour trying to get a message to her. Get her to turn back around in San Juan. He'd tried to get a hold of her mom, her dad, anyone he could think of. "I don't want her here."

"You tell her that?"

"Every day since I got here."

"Tell her to fuck off. Tell her if she shows up you're gonna ignore her bony ass."

"I'm not treating her like that. I've known her most of my life."

"See, that's just it. You think you're doing the right thing by not hurting her feelings, but really you're stringing her along. God forbid you ruffle some feathers." Jake watched him for a moment. "Why are you even staying friends with her?"

"We're not friends. We're friendly. That's how you end long-term relationships."

"Yeah, I see how well that's working out. You should write a book about how to end relationships."

He didn't give one fuck about Jake's sarcasm. The only thing he cared about was getting Emma to change her flight. "Jesus, I just want my last two days here. She's not my problem anymore."

Jake looked at him, all quiet and intense. "That's the

thing, man. She *is* your problem. You should've made a clean break. But you didn't. You kept her hangin' on. And now you gotta deal with it."

"There you are."

That familiar voice made every muscle in his body clamp down. He was in no mood. But it wasn't her fault. "Hey, Carrie."

The realtor slinked up to him in a bikini that was nothing more than three slashes of material. "What're you guys up to?"

He couldn't deal with her right then. "I'm heading up to my room."

"That's a great idea. We can order some food, get out of the sun."

"Yeah, I think I'm just going to catch some of the game."

"March madness? Oh, hell, yeah." She turned to a group gathered around a table. "You guys want to go to Ryan's room? It's Mich U versus UConn."

"Fuck, yeah." Dixon came out of the hotel with Laura and Kat.

"Actually, you can head up to Jake's room." Ryan turned to go, but Jake was right behind him.

"Nah, you got that big suite. Ryan's room it is."

"I said no." Ryan got right up in his face.

Several people surrounded them, already making plans. "I'll order some booze."

"Get ice, too."

"What's your suite number?"

"Look, man, it's over." Jake shrugged. "Emma's on her way, and we leave the day after tomorrow. Let's just have some fun."

As soon as the door opened, Carrie went straight for the phone to call room service, Jake found the basketball game on the big screen, and people got busy at the mini bar.

They could have his suite. Ryan didn't care. He'd text Sophie to let her know he was going for a run.

Someone offered him a beer, but he brushed it away and headed for his room to change into running shoes.

A hand tugged on his board shorts. He turned to see who it was when fingernails scraped into his scalp. Carrie licked her lips, eyes half-lidded.

"You want some company in there?" As she reached for him, he caught her wrists.

Time to set the record straight. "No, I don't. Look, Carrie, I'm seeing someone."

She laughed. "Oh, come on. I told you. What happens in Santa Grenada stays in Santa Grenada." She pressed closer to him. "Your girl will never know."

"No, I met her here. About twenty minutes after I got here."

"You mean that girl I've seen you with?"

He nodded, but his phone buzzed and he checked it. Because if it was Emma, he was going to—*Fuck.* It was Coach. "I have to take this."

She gave him a gentle smile. "Seems like you've got a lot going on."

"Yeah. Excuse me." He brushed past her, answering the phone. "Coach?"

"Ryan. I got a team to run here, a whole roster full of players who need my attention. I'm going to ask you one question, and I want a straight answer. Did you choose to miss the flight last night or did you not get off the standby list?"

Ryan turned his back on the room. "I chose to miss it."

"Right. You know there are repercussions to your choices in life."

"Of course." Ryan braced.

"Here's your first. I'm removing you as captain of this team and replacing you with Mike Wilder."

Ryan stepped out onto the balcony, into the glaring sun.

His coach exhaled into the receiver. "We'll talk about you being part of the team when you get back." The line disconnected.

Ryan stared out to sea, the noise from the television, the laughter and clinking of glasses in the room only making it harder for him to think.

Having his captaincy taken from him would definitely impact the draft.

But kicking him off the team? Even right then, he had to do a gut check. But, yeah, he definitely wanted to play his final season.

Would Coach actually do it—kick him off the team?

He quickly texted his dad. *Coach called. Not captain anymore.*

He was so fucked.

An hour later, when Ryan opened the door to his suite, his body still slick with sweat, he found three times the number of people he'd left behind.

And what the hell? Most of the women were now topless and everyone was drunk. Looked like they'd turned the kitchenette into a full-scale bar with liquor bottles, silver buckets of ice, and high ball glasses.

In the chaos he made a quick scan for his buddies. On the couch, Jake had a girl straddling his lap, her tits in his face, his hands kneading her ass. Dixon danced on the terrace with three girls.

"Hey, handsome." A topless girl stood unsteadily before him, eyes glazed. She tipped her beer toward him, the cold bottle a shock to his heated skin. "Are you for real? Or are my drunk goggles turning you into a Greek god?"

The door opened, and a flash of red caught his eye. Red heated his blood because it called up Sophie's bikini. And then energy rushed through him when he remembered he'd never sent her the text letting her know he'd be working out. He hadn't taken his phone with him, so he had no idea if she'd tried to contact him.

Through the crush of bodies, he'd lost sight of the spot of color. But, fuck, if it was Sophie, she'd get the wrong idea about what he had going on in his suite.

He stepped around the girl, but she caught his arm.

"Wait, wait, wait." Her small breasts wobbled with her movements. She dribbled her beer onto his chest and then leaned forward to lick it.

"Jesus Christ." Just as his hand shot out to push the girl away, he looked over and caught the horrible look in Sophie's eyes as she stood a few feet away, watching.

And then she shut down. Her features just slammed closed. Turning, she disappeared into the crowd.

Oh, hell, no. He shot after her. Pushing through the press of bodies, he caught up to her at the door. "Hang on." She ignored him, opening it. But he caught her around the waist.

"Let go of me." She tried to wrench free of his hold, but his fingers tightened.

And now he had to explain why a drunken, topless girl was trying to lick him. "Soph, come on. You don't think I was actually hooking up with that girl?"

"*Shut up.*"

She looked somewhere over his shoulder, eyes flaring, and he turned to see Carrie doing a striptease for a couple of guys.

"I have nothing to do with any of this. I just got back from working out."

"Go to hell, Ryan." Again, she tried to pull away.

Anger so fierce and volatile swept over him. His whole fucking life was spiraling out of control, but her? *I'm not giving her up*. Not until he absolutely had to. He hauled her against his chest. She was *not* leaving him. Bending his knees, he lifted her and strode into his bedroom. He slammed the door and locked it.

"Jesus fucking Christ." Setting her down, he threw his head back and let out a shout. "I can't believe this shit."

"Yeah, it must be so awful getting caught."

"I didn't get caught. I wasn't *doing* anything."

"So I saw."

"Look at me, Sophie. I just got back from working out. See this? It's sweat."

"You're wearing the same board shorts you had on this morning."

"Yes, and now I have on gym shoes. Why am I arguing with you? You want to make drama? Be my fucking guest. I sure as hell can't stop you."

"Oh, my God, you jerk. I am *not* Emma. You don't get to put me in the crazy girlfriend box."

"I didn't say you were Emma. But can you stop for a minute and think about the situation before you shut me out?"

"Oh, right. I forgot for a second there that I'm the fun spring break fling." She turned to the door, but he lunged for her, pulling her back. She looked so fierce and wild, shoving her arms at his chest.

"Just stop it. Can you calm down and let me talk to you?"

"I walked in on your orgy, Ryan. You had a topless girl licking you. Things like that don't just happen. You weren't some victim."

"Look at me, Sophie. I just got back from a run. I was going to my room to shower."

"And a topless girl just happened to lick your chest. I know. It happens to me all the time." She turned away from him, but he kept her trapped in his arms. "Just let me go. I don't need this crap."

"You're *creating* it. I know what you saw, but I didn't do anything." The anger drained out of him, replaced by the heavy weight of exhaustion. He really should just let her go. Emma was on her way, and everything he'd hoped to get from this break was over. With everything else going on in his life, the one complication he absolutely didn't need was Sophie.

He loosened his hold. Jake was right. Not the part about fucking other women or partying, but he had to let Sophie go.

She must've seen the change in him, because a look of understanding lit her eyes. Without a word, she headed to the door.

Jesus, his chest—it felt like a hand punched through his breastbone and caught his heart up in a meaty fist.

Hand on the doorknob, she turned. "Good luck with everything, Ryan."

Pain…no, desperation burst free from his chest. "Sophie." He shouted her name, making her flinch. She stilled. "Don't leave, Soph. Just…don't."

"What do you want from me? God, Ryan? What the hell do you want?"

She was not going to make him say it. "You know what I want."

"No, actually, I don't."

"Get back here."

"Why? So we can have sex again?"

"Yes, Sophie, I want to have sex with you. I think you know that."

"Well, guess what, Ryan?" The fierceness came storming back in. "I'm not really interested in being marginalized in yet another person's life. In yours, I'm the girl you screw on spring break. I'm the escape. And you know what? I was cool with that for a while, but it's not really working for me anymore. If the only thing I'm getting out of it is feeling like shit, then it's time for me to take my beach ball and go home."

"I don't want to be with anyone else but you. I've made that clear."

"Okay, let's stop playing games. I know you're keeping something from me. I saw it in the van on the way back from paragliding. I saw the look you gave Jake when he offered to take me off your hands when we got back here. Did something happen with your Coach? Or is it Emma? Is that what's making you so tense?"

"I don't want to talk about Emma. I especially don't want to talk about her with you."

"See, this is what I'm talking about. You want to keep me in the little spring fling box. Well, I'm not your spring fling. I'm Sophie Valentine. I have a heart and a brain. I want things. And I feel things. And all those issues you're sick of in relationships? I expect them. And, sorry to say it out loud, but this *is* a relationship. Even if it's got an end-date, it's still a relationship. And since it's just moved past the fun phase, I think that's my cue to leave."

She had her hand on the doorknob, when he caught her around the waist and tugged her hard against him. "Don't fucking leave me."

"Just let it go, okay? It's over the day after tomorrow anyway." But she didn't struggle. She just leaned her head against his shoulder. "I don't want to do this anymore."

"I get one more day with you. Don't take it from me."

"Why?" Her pleading tone gutted him. He knew he should let her go, but…he couldn't. He just fucking couldn't.

His palm on her stomach, he lowered his face into her neck, breathing in her sweet, subtle scent. "You make me happy. The rest of my life is fucked up, but you're my happiness. Come on, you know I wasn't fucking around out there. They came up here because I've got the suite, but I didn't want to party with them, so I went for a run. I wasn't in the door two minutes before you came in. I don't want anyone else, and you know that. I've proven it to you. Every single damn time, I've come after you."

He saw the moment she relaxed, the moment she heard the truth in his words.

Her hand covered his, and her hips pushed back. His cock surged as it pushed between her legs. She swayed against him, lighting him up.

"Goddamn, you make me crazy." Turning her in his arms, he lifted her, pressing her against the wall. Her legs wrapped around his waist, her arms around his neck. And then he kissed her.

The heat between them flared instantly. Desire whipped through him, and he flexed his hips, needing to feel her sweet body against his. Grabbing a fistful of hair, she pulled his head back, turning the kiss carnal.

Hot, raging lust swept over him. Lowering her, he ground his cock against her, and that was it. Grasping her ass tightly, he carried her into the bathroom, not even setting her down to turn on the faucet. Cold water blasted them— both fully clothed—and she shrieked, laughing. He kicked off his shoes while reaching for the bottom of her cover-up and tugging it over her head.

Laughing, she wiggled out of his arms and stepped away from him. "I got it."

"Now, Soph." The laughter in her eyes, the way it made her sparkle, did something to his heart. Made it hurt. Made his pulse beat too quickly in his neck. He yanked down his board shorts, tossed them out of the stall.

He grabbed her hips, tugged her closer, and reached for the tie at the back of her neck. Blood roared in his ears as he pulled. Jesus, he could barely draw a full breath in anticipation of revealing her lush breasts. As she reached behind to untie the bikini, he cupped her, stroking his thumbs over her nipples. She drew in a breath, her lids lowering, and her back arching. She was the sexiest woman he'd ever seen.

Steam covered the glass walls, closing them in, making him feel like they were the only two people in the world. *She's mine.*

This sexy, strong, fierce, gorgeous woman is all mine.

She reached for the soap and lathered up her wet hands before setting the bar back on the shelf. With sweeping strokes, she caressed his shoulders, his arms, his chest.

He trembled with restraint. That look in her eyes was killing him. All sweet and soft and devastatingly sexy. Taking a step back, but never taking her gaze off him, she slid those soapy hands all over her luscious body. She stood before him naked, bubbles streaming down her smooth skin. The sexy flare of her hips, the feminine slope of her shoulders. *Jesus.*

Sophie was beautiful no matter what, but turned on she was fucking radiant. And there was no mistaking the flush in her cheeks, the hard beads of her nipples, or the heat in her eyes.

Taking her hips in his hands, he claimed that mouth he would never stop wanting. He loved the way the soft, wet heat of her kiss swept him in and yanked him under. He couldn't keep his hands from sliding down her soapy back to grab the firm globes of her ass. Jesus, he loved her ass. He kept squeezing, drawing her harder up against him.

"Ryan." She said it with her mouth against his ear, and when her tongue licked the sensitive shell, heat exploded within him. She reached between their bodies, and he jerked when those warm, soapy hands clasped him.

Both hands tugged, swirling, pulling in opposite directions. Holy fuck, what was she doing to him? He was losing his mind. It was at once wildly sensuous and fucking erotic. He didn't want to come. He wanted it to last forever. Watching her feminine hands move on him, he leaned forward, bracing his arms on the wall behind her. Electric heat pulsed through him, making his legs tremble.

She was so fucking gorgeous, so bold, and sexy.

Her grip tightened on him, and she pulled harder, squeezing the head with each pass. His body burned. He needed release so fucking badly, but he didn't want this to end. He never wanted it to end.

And then she let him go. With a hand on his hip, she turned him into the spray, washing the soap off him. What was she doing? "Sophie, I can't—"

She dropped to her knees, hands on his ass, and brought his painfully engorged cock to her mouth. In one fluid motion, she sucked him all the way to the back of her throat.

Every cell in his body exploded in pure, scorching pleasure. *"Jesus Christ."*

Her tongue flicked along his length, as she sucked him hard and fast. His blood hammered in his veins, heat flashed across his skin, and his balls drew in so tightly they hurt. She pulled him in even deeper, as the wet heat of her mouth consumed him.

His hands went to her head—Jesus God, he needed to

fuck her mouth so badly—but he quickly dropped them, not wanting to hurt or degrade her.

She pulled off his dick and gazed up at him. "Don't hold back with me."

The determination in her voice made him roar. "Fuck." He'd never let himself go so completely with anyone before. But that gleam in her eye...fuck, yes. He cupped the side of her head with one hand and guided himself back into her mouth with the other. Oh, Christ, she took him so fucking deep. This time, he didn't hold back. He held her head still, gliding in and out of that perfect mouth, watching to make sure she was all right. But she just moaned, sucking him harder, deeper, and when she gazed up at him, her eyes glittered with pure lust. That was it. He completely lost it. Bliss soared through him, a sensation so explosive his entire body convulsed in pure ecstasy. He came so fucking hard— pulse after hot, shuddering pulse—into her hot, eager mouth.

When he finally finished, knees weak, body depleted, he helped her to her feet. Pulling her in close, hot water raining down on them, he nuzzled her neck. "Let's stay here forever."

"I'm down for that." She peered up at him through a tangle of hair. "I'm sorry for overreacting."

"I wouldn't have reacted any differently if I'd walked into your room and found that shit going on."

"I hadn't heard from you, and when I walked in and found you had an orgy going on in your room, I got scared. Scared that I misread you. That you were finally getting caught up in the freedom you'd come here for. I mean, you should've done that from the beginning. It's just I thought..."

"You thought right. Look, Soph, for the first time in my

life, I'm doing what I want. Not what Jake thinks I should I do, not what my coach or my dad or anyone else thinks is right. I'm doing what *I* want." It was a revelation to him, and it made him soar. He reached for her hand. "I didn't know what happy was until I met you. I just want to hold onto it as long as I can."

She gave him a funny look. "Ryan, you can have happy. It's yours to have. You just…you don't seem to get it. You're so worried about disappointing the people you care about, but what you don't get is that your happiness is the best gift you can give them."

He kissed her, brushing her hair off her shoulder. "Come to bed with me. I want to make *you* happy."

CHAPTER SIXTEEN

After dinner, Sophie watched Jake pull Ryan aside for yet another private discussion.

She hated secrets, so she wandered down to the beach. Toward the end of her relationship with King, she'd spent most of her time suspecting him of cheating. He kept making plans, but none of them included her. If snowboarding didn't work out, maybe he'd work for a merchandising company. Or he'd design sunglasses for one of his sponsors. Not only didn't his plans include her, he'd often shut down a conversation if she walked into the room. She could never figure out why he wouldn't want her involved, but it drove home the fact that she was his home base, which was nice, but she wasn't his partner.

And, of course, why wouldn't he want her hearing his conversations if they were just about business plans? It made her wonder if he was talking to other women.

She didn't believe he'd ever cheated on her, but still, she'd lived with the constant, nagging doubt. She'd never again live with her gut twisted in knots all the time.

But Ryan *did* talk to her. He said he'd shared more with her in four days than he ever had with anyone before. But, while he continued to tell her about his baseball-related issues, he'd definitely stopped talking about his ex. And the way he and Jake kept giving each other looks—it just made her feel like whatever he was hiding must somehow affect her.

But, really, why was she obsessing over something that would end the day after tomorrow?

Saturday night she'd be home. And she'd have to face Abby and her brothers. Blocking a hundred million dollar deal meant they'd be geared up for a fight, and she'd have to hold her own against the four of them.

Anxiety ripped through her at the thought of her siblings ganged up against her like that. Holding her stance would cause an irreparable chasm.

Of course, she *could* let this issue go. Just to keep peace in the family, she could back off and—*Oh, hell, no*. She wasn't going to sell Crazy Hearts no matter what.

So, then, how did she handle it so that they didn't hate her? Maybe she should get Barry to meet her at the house.

You know what? Just talk to Abby. She needed to hear her voice. Get a sense of their attitude towards her.

Kicking off her heels, she dug her toes into the still-warm sand and dialed her sister's number. A few yards away a bonfire popped and crackled, the group around it laughing and flirting. Sophie closed her eyes to let a breeze wash over her. The hiss of waves dragging back into the sea soothed her frayed nerves and the cool water felt good on her bare feet.

"Hey, Soph. What's up?" Her sister hadn't sounded this upbeat in months.

"You sound good."

"Yeah, well, Leslie took Hannah for a few hours so I could nap."

"That's so nice of her. Did you actually sleep?"

"Not really. I don't want Hannah around all that craziness. I don't like how she raises her kids."

She was about to say their sister-in-law was a great mom, but the last thing she needed to do was antagonize Abby. "So, my flight gets into LAX around five on Saturday. Do you want to pick me up?"

"You want me to drive all the way to the airport? With a baby? No, just get an Uber."

Funny, because Abby always asked for a ride home from the airport. "Yeah, I guess so. It's always nicer to have someone pick you up."

"So hire a car. I'll hire the car. Just give me the flight information. There's no reason for me to go all the way out there."

"Right. Okay, then. So, I'm just checking on you. How're you feeling?" Crossing an arm over her stomach, she looked out over the ocean.

"I'm freaking out. All I want to do is go pick up Hannah. I can just imagine her getting stitches when Carson throws a block at her face or shoves a Lego up her nose. What about you? You sound funny."

"Oh, I've…" Should she talk to her sister about Ryan? They didn't have that kind of relationship, but she wanted it. It was just that Abby tended to be a little sharp and not hugely sympathetic. But she supposed if she wanted it, she had to make the effort.

Just go for it. "I met a guy."

"At the resort?"

"Yeah. He's really great. But he goes to school in Michigan, and he's going to play baseball professionally. The draft's in three months."

When her sister didn't respond, she continued. "I like him, but we live so far apart, and our lives are completely different."

"That's right. So, what's the problem?"

"I like him in a way I've never liked anyone before."

Her sister let out a sigh of exasperation.

"What?" The sound of giggling had her turning around to see a couple making out on a chaise.

"How many years were you with King?" her sister asked.

"Over three." She headed back up the beach toward the pool area.

"And how many of those did you live in the same state?"

"Never." Unless you counted the times he'd crashed at her place, which she didn't. Because every time he'd done that, he'd been plotting his next big move. She half-suspected he'd considered her family's company his fallback if snowboarding didn't pan out.

"Do you really want to do this again? With King, it was all about boarding. Now, you want a baseball player? At least with King, he never made it, so he always came back to you. But if this guy's signing with a team right out of college, what hope do you have?"

She hit the pavement and leaned over to wipe the sand off her feet. "I guess I don't." Beer bottles littered the area around the hot tub. The water bubbled and frothed, as people hung out.

"You live *here*, Sophie. That's never going to change. This is where your family lives. Your business. Unless he's going to play for an LA team…I mean, come on. Why are we even having this conversation? Are you looking for forever? Forevers don't come out of hookups."

"Well, that's what I'm saying. It feels like more." So much more. "We have this bond, this connection…it's different, Abby."

"I'm sure it is, but the moment your planes land and you get back to your real lives, don't you think these feelings are going to fade? And even if they don't, realistically, as soon as he graduates, he's not going to have time for you. If you couldn't make it work with King, imagine how it's going to feel with this guy. He's never going to be around. And you know about the groupies. They lurk around these guys, popping up in their cars and breaking into their hotel rooms."

Entering the air-conditioned building, she headed for the elevator. Talking to her sister agitated her even more. Not sure if it was because of her sister's attitude or the truth that rang out in her words. But she really wanted to forge a real relationship, so she'd listen to her sister's advice. Appreciate the time she was giving her.

So, she gave a little more. "And he's just coming out of a six-year relationship." Three women stood waiting, the button already lit.

"Six years? Oh, Soph. Come on. He's your age?"

"Yeah." She turned away from the women, keeping her voice low.

"Okay, that's his entire dating life. No offense, but he's probably having the time of his life with you."

"Yeah. But he could be with lots of women here. And he's not. He's only with me. We both feel it. He keeps telling me—"

"He'll tell you anything you want to hear. I know you're not that naïve. Come on, the guy's been with the same girl for *six years*. He goes on spring break…of course he's going to go wild. I'm not saying you're not special. I'm saying he's probably bingeing on a new girl."

How could she argue with that? Ryan was absolutely bingeing on her. But it was so much more than that. If he'd only wanted to have sex with her, sure, she could see what Abby was saying. But he talked to her. And the way he looked at her? She knew she affected him.

"Guys aren't like us, Soph. He knows he's going back to school and onto bigger things. I'm not trying to be mean, but I'm on the outside looking in, and I can see things you might not be able to. Go ahead and have fun with him but don't get your heart involved. And for God's sake, don't be someone's consolation prize again."

Mortification burned through her. "What does *that* mean?" The elevator dinged, and all four women boarded.

"I'm not saying King didn't love you. Only you know for sure about that. But he always chose boarding first."

"He had to. He was competing."

"And when he broke up with you before the Olympic trials? Was it about competing then? Or did he just want to be single?"

"He didn't know how long he'd be away. He didn't want to tie either of us down."

"Right. And it was a smart choice. You guys were so young. But you're older now, and maybe you want more. I mean, *don't* you want more than that?"

"Of course I do."

She could tell from Abby's tone that she was being sincere, but why did she have to be so freaking condescending?

"Look, I have to go. Hannah probably has a Barbie purse in her mouth right now, and if I leave right this second I can save her from choking."

"Anxious much?" Just as she stepped onto her floor, she saw Ryan leaning against the wall outside her room, reading the screen of his cell. He looked up, pocketed the phone, and headed toward her.

"Hey." He kissed her mouth.

Abby laughed, but it didn't sound real. "You have no idea the scenarios I come up with. I have to check on her every few minutes during a nap because I think she's smothered in her own spit-up. I'll see you when you get home. And Soph?"

"Yeah?"

When they reached her suite, Ryan pulled the key card out of her hand.

"Put yourself first for a change, okay?"

"I am." Continuing to be with Ryan was a gift she'd given herself. "Okay, I'll let you go. Give my love to Hannah."

"Oh, wait. I forgot. When's that philanthropy thing again?"

That philanthropy *thing*? The mayor of Beverly Hills was honoring her at a dinner. It was a big deal. "It's Saturday, April third."

"Right. Damn. I can't go."

Ryan swiped the card, opening her door. When she just stood there, stunned, he lifted her off the ground and carried her into the room.

"Abby, you have to go. You're speaking."

"I know, but it's Lexi's engagement party that night. I have to be there."

"No, Abby, you said you'd come to my event. I can have two people speak about me. You're one of them."

Once inside, Ryan set her down, then turned and locked the door, tossing her key card on the desk.

"I'm so sorry, but I'm the matron of honor, and I have to be there."

"Abby, seriously? You can't bail on me."

"I'll get someone else to do it."

"What're you talking about? You can't just *hire* someone for this, Abby. This is about people who know me well. Who *care*." Why did she think she mattered to her sister? Other than babysitting—and that was for the past six weeks—when had her sister ever even tried with her? Abby was all about Abby. "You know what? Forget it. I can't believe you'd bail on me."

"It's Lexi's *engagement* party."

"That she can have any day of the week. But the mayor is honoring me *that* night. That one night. And it's a big deal. You committed to me first—months ago." Ryan had gone out on the balcony, and she appreciated that he'd given her the space because she was absolutely devastated.

"I know that, and I feel terrible. But there's nothing I can do. I have to be there."

"You mean you don't want to miss out on the fun. Forget it. I don't know why I bother. Like I said, I'm pissed that you'd bail on me, but I can't say I'm surprised. Go get Hannah, and don't you dare ask anyone to take your place at the ceremony. It'll just be Laura." Kat's family went to Hawaii that week every year to honor her dad, who'd passed away eight years ago. She could ask another of her friends, her brothers, even, but she didn't *have* to have two people, so she wouldn't bother. "Bye." She stabbed the End Call button and let the disappointment bear down on her.

"Everything okay?" Ryan came in and sat beside her on the edge of the mattress.

"No."

"What'd your sister bail on?"

"Oh, just an award thing. No big deal."

"Yes, I see that." He took her hand, engulfing it in his huge one. "Talk to me."

"Like you talk to me?"

He flinched. She didn't care. She got up, tossed her bag on a chair, her sandals onto the floor outside the closet, and headed straight for the bathroom. "I'm going to shower. Give me about twenty minutes and then I'll be in a better mood."

Shutting herself inside the large, white room, she peeled off her dress, panties and bra, and then turned on the shower.

Abby *always* let her down. Sophie considered what she would do if she had to choose between honoring her commitment to Abby and going to *Laura's* engagement party. She'd hate to miss her best friend's big moment, but her obligation to her family came first. And wouldn't she simply ask Laura to change the date? She assumed she'd be in on the planning of everything—Laura would tell her every detail, so she'd have some kind of say.

More likely Abby had gotten carried away with her best friend's plans and hadn't bothered to check her calendar. Abby and Lexi talked every day—Sophie didn't have that kind of relationship with her sister. So, maybe—

Yeah, sorry. Nope. She didn't understand. Abby had a choice to make, and she'd chosen Lexi's event over honoring her commitment to Sophie.

Whatever. She was totally overreacting. Two speakers bragging on her seemed over the top anyway.

Funny, though, how she accused Ryan of living to make other people happy, when her own happiness was so tied to her siblings. If they included her, she soared. When they excluded her, she crashed.

She had to stop doing that. Letting them make her feel invisible. Inconsequential.

A memory hit her. Middle school graduation. Not a big deal, of course, but she'd been invited to a couple of parties. She'd turned them down because her sister had graduated college that same week. Her family had a huge event planned at the house.

Her whole life, her mom would set up balloons and crepe paper for all the family birthdays and celebrations. So she'd assumed she'd come home from graduation to a house decorated in her school colors. But she hadn't.

The balloons out front of the house were blue and

gold—UCLA's colors. Abby's school. Her mom had had the event catered, transforming the backyard into a festival with food stations, a DJ, and a dance floor covering the pool. Presents filled the dining room table—all the cards made out to Abby.

No one even mentioned Sophie's graduation. She'd gone up to her room, thinking she'd find a present on her bed. Balloons. *Something.*

But, no. Nothing. No acknowledgement.

The sharpest memory, though? Her brothers had stayed for Abby's graduation party. At that point, they rarely came home. They were involved in their own post-college lives. But they'd come for Abby's graduation—and stayed for the party. And she'd been so freaking jealous. And *hurt.*

As much as she'd wished she'd gone to Laura's party that night, some perverse need in her had kept her pinned right there on her balcony, watching the fun below.

Hoping her brothers, her sister, her parents—*someone*—would come in and congratulate her. But she'd never even seen her parents that night. They'd gone to their room, leaving the caterers and housekeeper to take care of serving and cleaning up.

Why was she thinking about that party? She'd been in *middle school.* Hardly worthy of a catered event. She really had to let this stuff go.

Steam filled the bathroom, erasing her image in the mirror, so she stepped into the shower.

She didn't usually dwell on this stuff. The whole issue with Nestlé had brought it up, throwing her back into those uncomfortable feelings from her childhood. Uncomfortable? *Come on.* She'd been painfully lonely. Made all the more acute because she'd been surrounded by her large family.

Tipping her head forward, she let the hot water stream down her body.

The door opened and Ryan came in, watching her carefully. "What did you mean? *Like you talk to me?*"

"You're keeping something from me."

"I talk to you more than anybody."

"Oh, cut it out. You're obviously upset about something. Something happened in the van. I saw your face."

He yanked her towards him. "No one pays attention to me the way you do. I don't know whether I like it or if it drives me crazy."

But the way he looked at her, with so much affection, told her how very much he liked her attention.

"When you keep things from me, I build it up in my head."

He wrapped his arms around her, drawing her out of the spray. "I'm not captain of the team anymore."

"Oh. Wow. That's...that's big."

"If I'd taken that flight, nothing would've changed. I'd be back for the game, and everyone would've forgotten what I'd done."

She loved that about him, that he was honorable enough, strong enough to tell the truth.

"Do you regret it?"

"No." He looked completely baffled.

"So what does it mean? How will it affect you?"

"I've been talking to my dad about that."

So, that's what he'd been dealing with. And why would he share that with her, since she had no frame of reference for it? She couldn't offer advice. It wasn't her world. "What does he think?"

"We don't know if it'll affect the draft." He shrugged, looking a little lost. "We'll see."

"God, you just wanted a break from your life. Shouldn't be such a huge price to pay."

"Sure it should. I'm in the middle of my season, and I bailed on my team. I fucked up."

"I like how you own it." She turned in his arms, cupping the back of his head. "You say you don't regret it, but I can see how upset you are."

With a stricken look, he sighed. "I needed to walk off that field, but I earned my captaincy. I earned my reputation. And I lost it because I'm not right in the head. It just…it sucks." His hands slid up her rib cage, cupping just beneath her breasts. "On the other hand, I'm not sure I'm going to feel the impact until I'm back at school on Monday. I'm in a whole other world right now, and I like this one. A lot." His hands hooked under her arms, slid up her back to her shoulders, and he pulled her closer, kissing the corner of her mouth.

Why did she find that so sexy?

He brought his mouth to her ear. "I don't want to leave it."

The look in his eyes made need churn inside her. "Me neither."

Abby was wrong. He did feel the same way she did. "Do we have to? I mean, we graduate in two months. And if I take over Crazy Hearts, production is only from October to February. Do we really have to go our separate ways? I'd be willing to see how it goes."

"Yeah?" He flashed her that god-awful Hollywood grin.

Oh, God. Could she be more humiliated? She'd gotten carried away in the moment, with all his panty-melting words. But he obviously hadn't meant them. Not really.

And that just gutted her.

She pushed back. "You don't have to get all phony with

me. I just got excited. I know how impossible it is."

But he kept his arms around her. "Of course I want to be with you. But I'm going to be drafted in three months. I don't know what my life will look like then. We've both got a world of shit to deal with."

"I understand." But she didn't. Not really. Because none of that had anything to do with his feelings for her, and if he felt anything like what she felt for him he wouldn't even consider all that nonsense. He'd just want to be with her.

Intellectually, she understood. They'd both done the long distance thing for years. And it didn't work. Besides, neither of them should be tied down when their lives were about to change so dramatically after graduation.

God, was that why she wanted to hold onto him? Was she as scared as Kat and Laura? She honestly hadn't even considered it until this moment. But it made sense. Because the truth was, she *didn't* have a job. Her brothers and sister had yet to figure out where she fit in at Valentine's. And if she blocked the deal with Nestlé, she'd be in for a real battle. One that would hurt her relationship with them irrevocably.

What relationship? Waiting around the house for the next family party? Hoping they'd find a job for her? Continuing to feel slighted as they negotiated with Nestlé without consulting her?

She started to pull away. "We're wasting water."

But he held her firmly, not letting her go. "You know I want to be with you."

"I know."

"Soph."

"What? I get it. You just got out of a six-year relationship. You should be single for a while."

He didn't answer, just held her gaze. She had no idea what he was thinking, and she just felt like a fool.

God, he'd asked for a *week*, not a lifetime.

If he didn't look at her like he…well, come on, like he *loved* her, it'd be so much easier for her. But he did. Which made it so damn confusing.

His hands ran down her back to her ass. "Of course I should be single. But, Christ, Sophie, I didn't know I'd find you. What the hell am I supposed to do about that?"

That phony smile he'd flashed her? Answer enough. "We don't have to figure it out right now." Breaking through the resistance of his arms, she punched the faucet off.

But he reached for her, turning her toward him. "Fuck, I'm sorry I didn't give you the reaction you wanted. My life is blowing up, and I'm handling the fall-out as best I can.

"I know that."

"No, I feel like the worst piece of shit for losing my captaincy. I let my coach and my teammates down, and I take their respect seriously. But I did it to myself, and I have to deal with that. I also have a real shot at being a first-pick in the draft—that's a huge honor—and if the scouts figure out what I've done, then I'll blow that, too. So, I'm fucked up at the moment."

"It's okay. I understand."

"Do you? Because I sure as hell don't. I'm trying to hold it together to pull through this tail-spin, because I've never been out of control before. But you know me, Soph. You know me well enough to know when I'm hiding behind a smile. You also know how crazy I am about you. So, yes, of course I want to keep seeing you, but I don't know how the hell that's supposed to happen."

"I know. I told you I got carried away."

"I did, too. I got so carried away I turned down my seat on a flight back to Florida so I could get more of you. So don't think I'm rejecting you. I'm not. I *want* to be with you right now. But, honestly, I can't see beyond that. Can you?"

Of course not. And, yes, she understood where he was coming from.

But her gut told her a connection like this didn't come along all that often. And it also told her that if they didn't hold onto it they'd fade away from each other.

And that would be a huge mistake.

CHAPTER SEVENTEEN

Sophie was used to sleeping alone in her king-size bed.

But sleeping with Ryan—the heat from his big body, his hands always reaching for her, pulling her closer—was awesome. His insatiable need to wrap himself around her made her feel wanted. Loved. Something she'd never felt before.

And she'd figured something out last night. She needed to pay attention to his actions. Not his words. His actions proved he needed her, wanted her. They *did* have a chance.

Like he said, he'd proven that to her again and again by coming after her. He couldn't keep away.

She opened her eyes, the room still completely dark, and realized there was no wall of heat. Jolting up, she patted the space beside her and found it empty.

She didn't hear him in the bathroom. The dampness and fresh tang of the hotel's soap permeated the room, so she knew he'd recently showered. She got up and whisked open the curtains. He was gone.

She spotted something on his pillow. A note. On hotel stationery.

Back soon.

The clock on the nightstand read eight-forty-two.

Seemed too early to meet up with his hard-partying friends. Whatever. She was just surprised. He hadn't mentioned his plans last night.

Ah. The gym. That made sense, actually. He'd want to get it out of the way so they could spend the day together.

Still, with all the secrecy, she couldn't fight the uneasy sense that something else might be going on. It pinged her because of King. But Ryan wasn't King, and he'd told her he'd been talking to his dad about losing his captaincy and his shot at being a first-round pick.

But *Back soon*? If he'd gone to the gym he would've said so. Whatever. She wouldn't make a big deal out of it. She had loads of things to do on her own. She'd check her list to see what she had on tap for the day. They'd meet up when they were both free.

But when she looked at her list, she found she hadn't made any plans. Her last day, after all. She'd planned on spending it with her friends. It was nice to have a whole day of freedom.

First up, a shower. Then, she'd head down to the restaurant and have breakfast on the terrace.

Ryan should be back by then.

As expected, the dining room didn't have many patrons at this early hour. Sophie waited for the hostess to seat her, her gaze scanning the pretty room, decorated in pale blues and creamy whites. A woman breezed past her, her long hair streaming behind her, her white shorts highlighting long, tan legs. She joined her companion at a table, leaning down to kiss him right on the mouth.

Seeing that easy connection, that intimacy, made her miss Ryan. And her heart clutched because this was it, her last day. She'd never in a million years expected to meet someone here, but she had. And, oh, what a someone.

"Just one?" The hostess appeared at the podium and reached for the stack of menus.

"Yep. I'd like to eat outside, if that's all right."

"Of course. Give me one second to set a table for you."

"Sure. Thank you."

She thought about Ryan at the gym, sweating away. Maybe Jake and Dixon were there, too, swapping drinking and hookup stories—which he hated. No doubt he was thinking about her, too, wondering what she was doing and coming up with excuses to end the work-out early so he could get back to her.

In a corner booth, a man ate alone, scarfing down scrambled eggs. A group of women clustered together around a table, laughing, looking a little drunk. She doubted they'd gone to bed last night.

And then her gaze swept over—and jerked back to—Ryan.

No.

But, of course, it was. How could she mistake that build, that movie star face?

The jolt to her heart made her limbs go weak.

She looked across the table to his companion.

Female companion.

Ryan was having breakfast with a woman.

Long buttery hair tumbled down a slender back. They leaned toward each other across the table.

Heat rushed up Sophie's neck, her heart pounding so hard it hurt.

What had she missed? How could he have conned her? It made no sense, for all the time they'd spent together, how could he possibly have been with other women? *When* would he have been with them? She thought of the dark-haired woman that hung around him, always so comfortable with him. Such an easy rapport. Had he slept with her?

But, no, no, no. How did that make sense? Even last night, Sophie had encouraged him to go off with Jake, but when she'd gotten off the elevator, he'd already been waiting outside her door.

When could Ryan have been with other women?

Had he had *unprotected* sex with them like he'd had with her?

She could barely breathe, let alone form a clear thought. Her feet started moving, fear whirling, taking form, whipping into an anger so vicious it shook her whole body.

He looked up before she reached the table, his eyes going wide. He shot up, knees banging into the table. "Sophie."

But she didn't care about him in that moment. She wanted to know which woman he'd left her alone in bed for. And—no surprise—she was gorgeous, big eyes, plump lips. She looked like a...*oh, God.* A model.

This was Ryan's *girlfriend.*

She could scarcely breathe, let alone activate her vocal chords.

"Sophie, this is Emma. Emma, Sophie Valentine."

Eyes glassy, the woman gave her the softest, sweetest smile. "Hello."

"I don't understand." She had no words. She literally had so many thoughts jamming into her brain she couldn't read them fast enough to figure out which one to say first.

"She flew in yesterday." She heard exasperation in his tone—or was it desperation? Too much noise in her head for her to evaluate clearly.

This is his secret. "Yesterday?" How could that be? All those hours yesterday she hadn't heard from him. Oh, God, had Emma been part of that orgy...*Wait.* The woman who'd spilled the beer on his chest? Had that been Emma? It had all happened so quickly, the way he'd ushered Sophie into the bedroom. Her stomach balled so tightly she thought she might throw up. "Was she in your suite yesterday?"

"No. She got in last night."

"So you knew she was coming?"

Color roared up his cheeks. "Yes."

"Why would you *do* this?" He'd played her. No matter what, he'd played her.

"Hold on." His hand closed around her elbow. "It's not what you think. Let me talk to you."

She pulled away. "No." *God.* "You can't talk to me *now*. You've had every opportunity. But now?" She shook her head. "It's too late." She fled. Literally raced out of the dining room.

He caught her, of course. Just outside the restaurant, in the carpeted hallway, he grabbed her arm and spun her around. "You're jumping to the wrong conclusion."

"Fuck you." Her cheeks burned. Her scalp itched from the rush of blood.

And then the gorgeous model came out, looking concerned. "Is everything all right?"

"No, *Emma*, it's not." He was clearly irritated with her.

Those big eyes rounded, that plump mouth formed a pucker, and she looked wounded. "I'm sorry."

Sophie glanced at Ryan, who looked like he might jump out of his skin. But she didn't care what he was going through. "You are disgusting."

"No. First of all, I didn't find out she was coming until yesterday. Secondly, I told her not to come. And, come on, Christ, I didn't think she'd actually *do* it. Fly all the way out here for one day, after I told her I didn't want to see her? I mean, what the fuck?"

"Ryan, stop." The woman's voice sounded so sweet, so gentle. "Don't drag her into this."

"Into *what*, Emma?" He sounded exasperated.

Emma turned to Sophie with an apologetic—no, pitying expression. Then she turned the full force of her attention on Ryan. "You have to stop trying to hurt me back. I'm sorry, Ryan. I regret what I did every minute of my life. But at some point you have to let it go. And you can't hurt other people just to get back at me."

She gave Sophie a compassionate smile. "I'm so sorry."

"What's she talking about?" Sophie fired the words at Ryan, but it was Emma who answered.

"I cheated on him, and he can't get over it."

Oh, my God. This gorgeous creature had cheated on him. *She* was the reason he was blowing up his life. She was the reason he'd become so obsessed with Sophie.

"It was a mistake." Emma's voice was filled with regret. "I got swept away in the moment." And then she approached Ryan. "I'm so lonely over there. And I met him, and it was crazy, and it all happened so fast, but I knew right away that I'd made the worst mistake of my life. Ryan, you have to forgive me. You can't keep…" She gestured to Sophie without even looking at her, as though Sophie was just residual damage from her error in judgment.

Sophie couldn't listen to another word. She jerked out of his hold and took off.

"Goddammit. Sophie!" He chased her, but she spun around.

"Don't come near me. I'm serious. You…you…" Tears blurred her vision. Inexorable pain bore down on her with such force she thought she might collapse right there in the hallway. "Leave me the hell alone."

"She's got it all wrong."

"I saw you in there. I saw your expression. She's not wrong. Stop torturing your ex and get your damn life back on track. Or don't. Continue to screw it up. I don't care. Just don't come near me ever again."

"I've told you everything. You know I don't love her anymore."

"You've told me what you wanted me to hear. Go back to her, Ryan. You make the perfect couple."

"I'm never going back to her. It's not my fault if she's not getting it."

"No, Ryan. I think the only one not getting it is you." She turned and raced off to the elevator.

"Fuck." He chased her down the hall. "Stop it, Sophie. I told you everything about Emma from the beginning."

"Except the part that she was coming here." She stabbed the call button.

He loomed over her, as if he wanted to touch her but couldn't. "I found out yesterday."

"And you didn't think to tell me?"

"I should've told you. But I didn't want her invading our time together. I shouldn't *have* to deal with her. I've told her repeatedly that it's over."

"But you didn't really do that, did you? You tried to make nice with her. Instead of telling her the truth, you wanted to keep everything on an even keel. God forbid you upset anybody by owning how you feel. So you played her with your charming smile and your evasive answers."

He looked uncomfortable, hands digging into his pockets. "Yes, I probably did that."

"So let's see if you've learned your lesson. What about me, Ryan? Do you want to continue to be with me after we leave here? Or do you want to move on with your life and leave me as your one and only spring break fling?"

"We've been over this. You're not a fling. But I do have to get back to school. I have to play my ass off the rest of the season to make up for this week. And I have to earn back the trust the scouts had in me."

"And…you've learned nothing. Still evasive. Let's try one more time. Do you want to be with me?"

"I've shown you how much I want to be with you, but I—"

"It's a yes or no answer. That's all a woman really wants to hear. Yes or no. We don't want to be strung along. We don't want to waste time trying to figure out what you're thinking or what you really want. Yes or no, Ryan?"

His eyes shuttered, the man she'd fallen for gone. He drew in a deep breath, gazing down the long hallway. And then he looked back at her. "No."

The elevator dinged, the doors parted. The only sound in her head was her heart shattering. "Goodbye, Ryan."

"He's not a sociopath." Stretched out on her bed with a pillow on her lap, Laura reached for another strawberry off the platter delivered by room service.

Sophie had awakened her friends for an emergency meeting. They gathered in Laura's room because she didn't want to risk Ryan coming to hers. Of course, he was with *Emma*. But, honestly, she didn't know which would be worse. Him showing up at her door to win her back or knowing he hadn't come at all.

Laura offered her a berry, but the very thought of food made Sophie sick. "Sure seems like one to me."

"Soph, he's crazy about you. Anyone can see that." Laura bit into the strawberry and chewed. "But that's not the issue."

"Give him time," Kat said from the chair she'd dragged

close to the bed so she could prop her feet on the mattress. "If anyone's crazy it's the ex. Can you imagine showing up at Blake's resort over spring break?"

"God, no." Laura shuddered.

"He doesn't need time. He's already decided."

Kat nodded slowly. "I don't think he knows what he wants. Look, we're all in a really weird place right now. I don't have a clue what I want to do with my life because I was so sure everything would magically fall into place." She gestured to Laura, who grabbed a handful of grapes. "*She* thought she'd be on the adventure of a lifetime with Blake, playing the sport she loves and seeing the world with her boyfriend. *You* don't know what job your family's going to come up with. And I don't know Ryan's story, but I know he's got one. He wants you, but he doesn't want to make commitments he might not be able to keep."

But it wasn't about that at all. Only she wouldn't betray the jerk's trust. "God, I'm so stupid." She could still see the pleading look on Emma's angelic face. *Don't drag her into this. You can't hurt other people just to get back at me.*

Pain sliced through her. Emma had cheated on him. That explained everything.

"You're not stupid." Laura patted her leg. "You fell for a really hot guy. So what?"

Kat reached for her coffee. "I came here looking for a boyfriend. How stupid is that? But you know what? I figured something out this week. Like you said at lunch the other day, I work so hard to get a guy's attention. Of course he's going to give me a chance to rock his world in bed. I *dazzle* him. I thought it gave me power, you know? You look into his eyes, and you see you've got him. You think you can *win* him with that power. But what I didn't get is that I only have that power while I'm on my knees with his dick in my mouth."

"Oh, sweetie." Sophie started to get up to give her friend a hug, but Kat waved her away.

"No, it's good. I get it now. I mean, four years and a lot of frat parties later...I feel like an idiot. All those times I thought I was sweeping the guy away with lust or whatever, but really he's just thinking how he has this hot girl blowing him and how, as soon as he's done, he's got to study for that test, but maybe he has time for one more beer before he heads back to his room. That's...that's...God." She nodded with a determined expression. "But, like I said, I'm glad I figured it out."

Laura wiped her fingers on a linen napkin. "Well, look at me. The only reason I came here was to hurt my boyfriend of two years. At least I thought that's what it was, but you know what? I don't think that's it at all. I was trying to make it look like I found someone else first. I was *competing* with him. And you know what hit me? Being competitive is awesome. It got me a full-ride to UCLA. And in business, whatever I do for a career, I'm going to kick ass. But in relationships? It's *terrible*. I mean, seriously, spending my spring break finding hot guys to pose with me so I can *outdo* Blake? I wouldn't even want to know someone who did that."

"All righty then." Sophie forced a smile. "Looks like this trip turned out awesome for all of us. 'Cause, you know, in spite of how it ended with Ryan, I got epic sex."

Laura smiled. "Exactly. The most gorgeous guy on the island gave you the best sex of your life. You are the winner of spring break. And we all go home with a whole new outlook. It's not about guys. It's about *us*. It's about figuring out what we want. And making kickass lives for ourselves."

Kat shrugged. "I don't know, Soph. I don't think it's over yet. Give him time. If I were you, I'd keep in touch with him. You never know."

"Here's what I do know," Sophie said. "He's going to play professional baseball. He'll be traveling, training, doing interviews, all that same stuff King did only on a way higher level. I'd be on the periphery of his world. And I'm not going to be waiting around for him. I'm just not."

"You're in the center of ours," Kat said. "You're the reason we all stay in touch and get together as often as we do. We may go off with boyfriends and sports and whatever, but you'll always bring us back home."

Home. Where the hell was home? The house she'd grown up in hadn't felt like home in years. Her sister said she'd feel differently when Sophie had kids of her own, but the age difference would never change. They'd always be in different phases of their lives.

She finally got it. She sat up, shoving the cart aside to get out of bed. "I'm moving."

"What?" Laura held a grape in front of her mouth.

"I haven't told you guys the truth. And I have to trust you to keep this completely confidential."

"Of course," Laura said.

"You know you can trust us, honey," Kat said.

"My sister and brothers are negotiating to sell Crazy Hearts."

When her friends started to protest, she continued. "I'm working out the details of whether or not I can buy it and manage it on my own. Jake gave me a ton of information, and I think it's really do-able. That's why I was talking about Montana. I love it out there. I'm going to get a place right on the mountain. I can ski, hike, fish, boat...I mean, it's perfect for me." Her friends looked a little sad. "It's the biggest ski resort in the country." She leaned over and shook Kat's foot. "I'll get a big house so you guys can visit whenever you want."

"I want to say you're being a selfish bitch leaving me all alone in LA, but I'm a little turned on by this whole idea." Kat smiled. "I don't know about the fishing thing, but a cool ski town? That sounds fabulous."

"Oh, shut up. You can't make a decision like this when you're upset." Laura tossed a grape at her. "Go home. Finish school. See how you feel this summer. You've got all the time in the world."

"Time?" *Ha. Good one.* "Do you know how long I've waited to start living my life? I've been waiting for everyone—for King to move to LA to be with me, for my family to include me in their little circle of exclusivity. I've stayed in that damn mausoleum because they don't want to lose their childhood memories. Well, guess what? I want to make happy memories of my own." She slid her feet into her sandals and leaned down to buckle the straps.

"Where you going?"

She hadn't been this sure of anything in ages. "Don't be mad at me, but I'm done here. I want to go to Montana before I head back to school. And, come on, you know there's no way I'm going to risk running into Emma and Ryan hanging out together."

"How many times does he have to tell you he's over her?" Laura shoved the cart aside and got up.

"It doesn't matter what he says. The only thing that matters is what he does. He knew Emma was coming, and he didn't tell me. Me, the woman he's sleeping with. How awful is that? And if he really doesn't want to get back with her, why would she fly out to Santa Grenada? He's playing both of us because he doesn't have the balls to own what he wants." And she understood why. She really did. With all the chaos of his childhood, she could understand why he'd need to placate everyone. Look what had happened the last time he'd upset someone. His mother had gone to the ER, and his family had blown up.

"It's weird that he didn't tell you."

"Yeah, it's weird. And you know what? No matter how great we are together, he's not ready to jump back into another committed relationship. Of course he isn't. You guys are right. We had great sex." She drew in a sharp breath because it hurt. It hurt so badly, but she was finally moving forward. "I had a great time with him, but it's over. And I want to move on. I want to start my life."

Her friends walked her to the door. "I'm going to talk to Jake. He's frustrated working for his family. His dad and older brother won't listen to any of his ideas. I'm going to see if he wants to help me with Crazy Hearts."

"I don't know whether you're truly happy or just racing off on another adventure to cover up Ryan's assholery," Kat said. "But I don't want your sister steamrolling you, so go. Figure out your shit. Just let us know how it's going."

"Take lots of pictures and put them up on Facebook so we can all be jealous of your exciting plans for after you graduate," Laura said.

"Did you just hear yourself?" Sophie asked, and all three burst out laughing.

CHAPTER EIGHTEEN

"You can't stay here." Ryan looked at the woman he'd grown up with and understood she'd lost her way.

"They're booked, Ryan. There's nowhere else for me to stay."

He didn't feel even the slightest inclination to give in. "That's not my problem. I told you not to come out here."

"After I was on a plane." She used her soft voice, the one that usually made him feel sorry for her.

Only, this time he didn't feel much of anything. He was done. "Why are you here? Why would you come all the way out here for one day? I told you I didn't want to see you."

"I thought you were upset." Tears welled. "I thought you needed me. I came here to help you. Your teammates are worried about you. Everyone back home is freaking out."

"*You* did that. No one knew anything. Jake, Dixon, and my dad were the only people who knew what I'd done. And then you went and stirred up trouble. What the hell?"

She cocked her head, eyeing him carefully. "You're different."

"I sure as hell hope so." He needed to get to Sophie. Ironically, he'd been ending his relationship with Emma when Sophie had shown up in the restaurant. He hoped his ex finally got it, that they'd never get back together. But even if she didn't, that was her issue. He'd hurt Sophie, and that killed him. "Look, I have to go." He tried to usher her out the door, but she stayed by her luggage.

"I'm not going anywhere." Tears spilled out of her big, brown eyes. "I'm not giving up on you, Ryan." Her breath hitched. "I can't believe I did this to you. I'm sorry. I'll never forgive myself."

Was she serious about this shit? How did he even address it? With the truth. "Emma, listen to me. I don't care that you cheated. I really don't. We should've ended things a long time before that. Now, come on." He lifted her suitcase— Jesus, what had she packed for a weekend on an island?

"Look, baby, just talk to me. We never talked. You saw the tabloids and you just shut me out. And now look at you." She held prayerful hands over her mouth. "God, you were so perfect. You had everything. And now...You're spiraling out of control. Sit with me, talk to me, just let it all out. Even if you still don't want to get back with me yet, at least let it all out."

"Let what all out? What're you talking about?"

"Ryan, baby, it's me. No one knows you better. No one gets you like I do. Come on, your mom let you down all the time, your dad wasn't there for you. I know. Why do you think my dad started bringing you home with him after practice? Because of me. Because I couldn't stand that no one came to pick you up. And then you gave me your whole heart and what did I do? I trashed it. For a stupid fling with some guy in a boy band."

Clarity struck like the flare of a match. Why had he never seen this before? "I never gave you my heart."

She flinched, as though he'd slapped her.

"I'm sorry, but I didn't." He got it. He got it so clearly.

"I liked going to your house. It was peaceful. Everyone got along and laughed with each other. But I was on my best behavior. All the time. I was so polite, so careful not to say the wrong thing. I didn't want to be kicked out. And believe me, after all the trouble I caused at home, I locked my shit down for your family. I wanted them to like me." A terrible feeling crawled up his spine. Some kind of understanding shifted like a shadow at the back of his mind, but he didn't have time for this. He needed to get to Sophie.

"It's not true. Nothing you're saying is true. You had a terrible home life, and you got to be yourself around us. You're only saying this because I hurt you. I wish I could go back in time. I hate myself. I hate what I've done to you."

"Emma." He shook his head, holding her gaze. "I've *never* been myself around you. I've always been polite, a gentleman."

"You *are* a gentleman. You're such a great guy. The best. I've never met a guy as kind and gentle and sweet as you. Everyone loves you. *I* love you."

"I don't love you, Emma. Not that way."

"Are you saying you love that girl? You just met her."

"I'm not talking to you about Sophie." *She's mine.*

"You're using her to hurt me. You can't love her."

"But I do." *Oh, holy hell.* The truth hit him like a body blow.

He stopped in the doorway, letting it sink in.

He was completely and totally in love with Sophie Valentine.

This wasn't about escaping his troubles or going hard for a week. This wasn't about lust.

He fucking *loved* her. Everything about her—from her independent and fiery spirit to her warmth and sensuality to her sense of humor and adventure. He loved her.

293

And he had to have her.

Opening the door, he set Emma's suitcase outside and waited for her to pass. She stood immobile, looking dazed.

"But she's not your type at all." Her frail chest heaved with rapid, shallow breaths. "God, Ryan, she's...*fat.*"

Ryan grinned. "I think the word you're looking for is voluptuous." For the first time, he felt free of Emma, free of the guilt. "Do you have any idea how refreshing it is to be with a woman with no body issues? Come on. I gotta go."

"*Wait.* You can't dismiss me like this. Six years, Ryan. And years of friendship before that. Can you at least be my friend? You've always been there for me." She reached for him, but he took a step back.

"Friendly, yes. Friends?" He shook his head. "I already told you that's not going to work."

"I don't think I can do this anymore." Her voice sounded so faint.

"Do what?"

"Live overseas. I'm so lonely. I know it looks like I'm living this crazy life of parties and clubs and magazine shoots, but it's not like that. I have no one to talk to most days. Yeah, I get invited on trips or out to clubs, but it's empty. I don't really have friends. Except you."

"Then come home."

She perked up. "I'm thinking about that. But come home to what?"

The hopeful look in her eyes made him uneasy. He had to quash it. "To a fresh start. What do you want to do?"

"I don't know. All my friends from home are graduating college this year. They've got jobs lined up. If I come home, I'll have nothing. I'll live in my parent's house and have nothing."

"You've got money. You've been working for more than six years."

"I don't have any skills. I don't have an education. There's nothing for me besides modeling, and I'd only get catalog work in the States."

"Then take the time to figure out what you want to do."

"I want to build a life with *you*, Ryan. I thought my life would be with you. That's what you led me to believe. That we'd be together."

An electrical current skidded across his skin, lifting the hairs at the back of his neck. "What're you talking about? We never talked about marriage. You were doing your thing, and I was doing mine."

"With the assumption we'd wind up together. That when you got drafted, I'd come with you."

Holy shit. "We never talked about that." *I never wanted that.*

"We didn't have to. We've been together six years."

"Emma, it's not going to happen. I broke up with you months ago. I've moved on."

"Bullshit. This is all such bullshit. All this talk—this isn't you. You don't just give up because of one mistake. You owe us the chance to see if we can make it."

"You know what I owe you? The truth. I don't love you, Em. I'm not angry that you slept with someone else. You know what I felt when I saw those pictures? Relief. I don't want to hurt you, and I'm sorry you're lost, but I'm not your answer. And, as hard as it's going to be, you're going to have to figure out your own life. Because it's not going to be with me."

She looked horrified, almost shriveling with each word he said.

"I can see I'm hurting you now, so I'm going to stop talking." He took her by the arm and pulled her out of his room. "If they don't have a room for you here, you're going to have to find one in town. You can't stay with me. Not only because I don't want you to, but because it wouldn't be right. It would hurt Sophie, and I've done enough of that."

"My dad is going to hate you."

The arrow hit its mark. But it didn't sting the way he'd feared. "He might. But do you really want me to be with you because I'm worried what your dad will think of me? You deserve better than that."

In the past he might press a soft kiss on her cheek. But he didn't want to do that. He just wanted to go. And so he stepped out of the room, shut the door, and raced to the elevator.

After covering every square inch of the damn resort and still not finding her, Ryan had had enough. He needed to find her and let her know what she meant to him. He needed to wipe that *no* out of her head and turn it into a *hell yes*. He sure as fuck did want to be with her.

He strode into the dining room, where he found Laura and Kat with a large group. He strode right up to them. "Where is she?"

"Who's this?" one of the guys said.

But Ryan never took his gaze off Laura. She set down her fork. "She left."

Reeling back, he scraped a hand through his hair. "Fuck." People from other tables turned, but Ryan didn't care. "Where'd she go?"

"Excuse me." Laura pushed her chair back and took his elbow, guiding him away from the table. "She left. That's all I really want to tell you."

"What does that mean? All you *want* to tell me?"

"Are you serious right now?" And then she leaned into him. "What do you care?"

The image of Sophie's face when he'd told her they were

done punched him hard in the gut. "Just tell me where she is. I need to talk to her."

"Leave her alone. She gets it, okay? She gets that you guys had fun together, and now you both have to get back to your real lives." Her gaze narrowed. "Let her go."

"Not gonna happen. And this isn't any of your business."

She gave a snort. "When my closest friend in the world comes to me at nine in the morning, her world in a million ugly, little pieces, it becomes my problem."

"I want to fix it."

"Guess what? She fixed herself." She said it like it was the most obvious thing in the world. "So you don't have to worry about her. You're free to go on with your life. You two have no future anyway, right? Isn't that what you told her?" When he didn't answer, she continued. "I promise you, she's not a mess. She's good. In fact, she's happier than I've ever seen her. Leave her like that."

"Dammit, Laura, when did she go?"

Laura looked thoughtful for a moment. "Couple hours ago."

"Did she go home?"

Laura pressed her lips together.

But he knew. "She went to Montana?" He saw it right away. A flicker of joy, like he'd impressed her. "Where?"

Laura got right up in his face. "I'm telling you she's fine. She's happy, so why would a guy who doesn't want a relationship with her want to find her and hurt her all over again? Do you even know what you want? Because until you do, stay the hell away from my girl."

"Oh, I know. I know exactly what I want."

He'd known what he wanted the moment the word *no* had left his mouth. The second anguish had flashed across Sophie's features. Even as she'd taken off, he'd known he'd lied to her. Lied in the never-ending effort to keep everyone who'd supported him for so many years happy.

Standing on his balcony overlooking the ocean, black sky flickering with blazing stars, Ryan knew it was time to go after what he wanted.

Turning back into his room, he pulled his duffle out of the closet, eager to get going. As he tossed his belongings into the bag, he had a moment of panic when he thought about Sophie somewhere out there in the world thinking he didn't care enough to be with her.

He did. And now he'd show her.

It was too late to get a flight out, of course. Between looking for her and ending things with Emma, he'd wasted the day. But he'd leave first thing in the morning. He knew the ranch was just outside Bozeman. So he'd fly there and then what? Magically find her aunt's ranch? He didn't know, but she'd find it hard to ignore him when he texted her from the Bozeman airport. He'd have a day and a half to make it right with her before school started.

He couldn't miss school or another game, obviously, so he had to get to her before then.

His phone buzzed. *Soph?* He'd left her a dozen texts throughout the day, but she'd ignored them all. Was she finally getting back to him?

But it wasn't her. "Hey, Dad, what's up?"

"Ryan, when's your flight back?"

"Tomorrow night." But he'd head to the airport anyhow. He'd take the first standby flight he could get.

"You'll need to change your ticket. I'll have a car waiting for you at JFK."

"Actually, I'm going to Montana. But then I have to go straight to Michigan. I'm going to be back on campus and ready to go Monday morning."

"No, you're not." His dad sounded tired, worn…a little freaked? "Brandon's in the hospital."

The shock of it rang through him. "What happened?"

"Alcohol poisoning."

Ryan dropped onto the edge of the mattress. "Is he all right?"

"He's unconscious."

What the hell? "What does that mean? Is he at school? Are you at Yale Hospital?"

"Okay, slow down. I don't know anything yet. I wasn't going to call you, but…you should be here."

"Of course I'll be there."

"He's here. In Greenwich. I guess he came home for Parker's birthday. Look, I'm sure he'll be all right, but I needed to let you know…in case…"

In case his brother *died.*

His *brother.*

"I didn't see it," his dad said. "Sure, he drinks. What college kid doesn't? But this much? I…didn't see it."

"Dad, this isn't on you." His dad had talked to them a lot about booze, warning them about a possible genetic predisposition. "He'll be fine." But Ryan's stomach twisted hard, making him sick. Because he didn't know that at all.

"I didn't know he had a problem. Is this normal for him? This much drinking?"

"I don't know what's normal for him." And in that moment Ryan hated that he didn't know a damn thing about his brother's life. He exhaled roughly. "I'll be on the first flight home. Keep me updated, okay?"

"Of course."

He ended the call and just stood there, letting it sink in. Brandon, lying unconscious in a hospital bed. The image sacked him.

What a selfish fuck. All those years hiding out in Emma's family, it hadn't even occurred to him that he should've been taking care of his brother and sister.

He drew in a deep breath. He had a hell of a lot to make up for.

CHAPTER NINETEEN

When Ryan entered the family room, he found his little sister making out with some big, long-haired dude. The surprise of it had him slamming his shin into the edge of the coffee table.

At the sound, Nicole jerked away from the guy. Her boyfriend—Dylan, if he recalled—pulled his hand out of her shirt looking a little dazed but not the least bit embarrassed. His sister sat up—never leaving the guy's lap. "Oh, hey." She straightened her shirt. "Sorry."

One half of the dude's mouth hitched up in a smile. With an arm around her back and the other under her legs, the guy got up and set Nicole on her feet. He reached a hand to him. "Dylan McCaffrey."

"I met you over Christmas break, right?" He gave him a chin nod. "Ryan."

The guy didn't reveal much of anything. Just nodded. "How's it going?"

Hadn't Dylan dumped his sister on New Year's Eve? He remembered hearing something about it. Guess they'd worked it out. "Better, now that Brandon's home. That was some scary shit."

"It was." Nicole blew out a breath, and the guy wrapped

an arm around her waist, tugging her against him.

That possessive gesture made Ryan ache for Sophie. She'd only responded to one text, when he'd told her about his brother.

Sorry about your brother. Hope he's okay.

Even after he'd told her Brandon had come home, she hadn't responded. He needed to see her. Too much time was passing. "You guys good? School going okay?"

Nicole reached for Dylan's hand. "It's all right. I think we're heading back in an hour or so. We just want to make sure Brandon'll be okay."

Ryan nodded. "Looks like he's fine."

"Well, not *fine*." Nicole didn't look pleased with him.

"Is there a problem?"

"Of course there's a problem, Ryan. I just don't think dad's going to do anything about it."

"What's he supposed to do?"

She let out an impatient breath. "Brandon obviously needs help, and Dad's just going to let him go back to school like nothing happened."

He gave a broad smile. "Ah, come on. He's a junior in college. He's having fun."

"You can't mean that."

Oh, hell. He'd done it again. Flashed the phony smile. He shoved his hands into his pockets when he thought how Sophie would've called him out on his shit. "No, you're right. I don't mean that."

Nicole tilted her head. "I know Brandon has to go back to school for finals, but we have to do *something*. The next time this happens, he might not get so lucky." She looked up at Dylan, like the guy hung the moon.

Dylan squeezed her hand, brought it around his back, then lifted his arm and tucked her under his shoulder. "You want to talk to him before we hit the road?"

"He's sleeping." Ryan had left his brother's room a few minutes ago.

"No," Dylan said. "Your Dad. She's not going to relax until she gets it off her mind."

"Yeah," Nicole said. "I should probably do that."

"Do what?" Brandon came into the room, looking pale and exhausted.

"Shouldn't you be resting?" Nicole lurched forward, catching her brother on one side, while Dylan got the other.

"Guys, I'm fine." He eased himself onto the couch, stretching his legs out on the coffee table. Brandon shot Ryan an apologetic look. "Sorry you came all the way out here. If I'd known they were going to call you, I'd have told you not to come."

"Hard to do when you're unconscious, though, right?" His sister wasn't letting up.

"Hey, now," Brandon said, but Nicole had already left the room. "You gonna get in trouble with your coach?"

He flipped on his smile. "Nah." *Wow.* Empty words and a fake smile. That's what he had to give his brother who might've *died?*

Enough of this bullshit. His whole life his brother and sister had looked at him with so much expectation, but he'd barely acknowledged them. He'd been so wrapped up in baseball and school and...yeah. *Excuses.*

He couldn't change what he'd done, but he could be a different brother from now on. "Actually, I'm screwed."

Nicole returned with a glass of water. She stopped and stared at him. "For missing one day?" She pushed the glass at Brandon. "You have to stay hydrated."

"I bailed on the whole week."

She sat down on the couch. "I thought you had a big

tournament in Florida? Weren't the scouts supposed to see you play?"

He looked at his sister a little too long. She paid attention to his life, and he didn't know a damn thing about hers. He'd fix that. "I needed a break."

"*Now?*" Brandon choked on his water. "You needed a break now? When the scouts were coming to watch you? What the hell?"

"Yeah, well, like I said I screwed up."

Brandon looked concerned. "Gotta tell you, man. This isn't like you. You never screw up."

His mind quickly processed a way to spin the story, but before he could spew more bullshit, he shut it down. *Not doing that anymore.* "Yeah, I know. I think, uh…" *Just say it. Be real with them for once in your life.* "I guess I got all my screwing-up out of my system as a kid."

"What do you mean?" Nicole looked confused.

"You were too young to remember, but I pretty much drove Mom crazy."

"Everything drove Mom crazy," Nicole said. "She's an alcoholic."

"Yeah, but instead of leaving her alone, I made it worse. I challenged her all the time." With his thumb and forefinger, he rubbed his jaw. "And I guess I always felt pretty crappy that it was because of me that Dad kicked her out of the house. I screwed things up for you guys."

Nicole watched him steadily, but Brandon looked shocked. And then his sister got up and came closer to him. "You do realize divorce was the best thing that could've happened to us, right? So, if you're feeling some kind of guilt or whatever, you can just let it go right now."

And right then he regretted missing out on knowing his sister. Because she was pretty cool. No drama, no theatrics.

Just calm, collected. Real.

"I lived with her," Nicole said. "So I can tell you she didn't want to change. You guys stopped visiting her, but I didn't. I couldn't stand the idea of, you know, *abandoning* her. But then I figured out that she didn't *want* us around. She wanted to be left alone with her disease. It's not your fault."

"Yeah, but…I don't know. I feel bad about it." He blew out a breath. "I wish I'd been a better brother to you."

"What does any of this have to do with you blowing off the scouts?" Brandon brought the glass to his mouth and chugged the water.

Ryan noticed neither one addressed his apology. But then what could they say? He had been a shitty brother. "I don't know. I've been restless. Just kind of fucked up the past few months."

"Is it because Emma cheated?" Nicole said.

"No. It's because I'm goddamn tired of training and watching what I eat and…just missing out on life. I'm sick of working so hard trying to keep everyone happy."

"Well, they made you that way." Nicole leaned back into Dylan. "We had to be on our best behavior or it was screaming chaos."

"Nah," Brandon said. "That's not what it was. Dad sent mom away." He gave a chin nod toward their sister. "Sent Nic away, too. That's when you changed. Shut down. Probably thought, if you didn't, you'd get sent away, too."

Nicole looked pensive for a moment. "He's right. You did change. You became…well, you know, perfect." She smiled and whacked Brandon with the back of her hand. "Pretty deep for a bro."

"Ryan got his act together because of baseball." Their dad stood in the doorway, bottle of water in his hand. He tipped it toward Brandon. "What're you doing out of bed?"

"And look at that," Brandon said. "An O'Donnell family reunion. I should get hospitalized more often."

"Brandon…" Nicole looked upset.

"Too soon." Ryan held his brother's gaze, warmth seeping through him. He should've been there for his younger brother. *Damn.*

"Best money I ever spent was on that therapist," his dad said. "She said putting you in sports would channel all that aggression. And it sure as hell did."

But a memory struck him like a flash of light. "I didn't know."

His dad cocked his head.

"I didn't know she was a therapist." He stuttered out a laugh, as he thought about it from an adult's perspective. "I was eleven." He shrugged. "I thought her job was to decide what to do with me. She kept asking all these questions, making me out to be some kind of dangerous freak with anger issues, and when we talked about sports she got happy. Told me I should focus on one and get really good at it. That was my second year on Coach Banbury's team. He was really cool to me, so I figured I'd choose baseball." He looked to his dad. "You got really into it. It's like I went from pissing everybody off to being the good kid." He'd never seen it so clearly before. "You're right." He nudged Brandon's foot. "I did think if I stopped causing problems Dad wouldn't send me away, too."

"I would never have sent you away. I was trying to *help* you. Jesus, I can't believe you've been thinking that all this time."

"I never thought about it at all. All I knew is it worked. It kept everyone happy with me." But Ryan turned to his brother. "You nailed it."

"Fuckin' Dr. Phil right here." Brandon smiled.

"This got anything to do with skipping out on your games this week?" his dad asked.

"Maybe. I think I'm tired of dancing for everybody."

"You don't want to go pro?"

"No, I do. Of course I do."

"Okay, so you go back to school, show the scouts you're still the best shortstop in the country."

"But is it what you really want?" Nicole asked.

"He just said it is." His dad turned to her. "He sacrificed a hell of a lot to become the best at what he does, and now he's getting the pay-off." He came up to Ryan, slapped him on the shoulder. "I'm damn proud of you, son." He looked to Brandon and Nicole, his voice getting a little thick. "All of you."

"Thanks, Dad," Nicole said.

Big Bill pulled Ryan in for a bear hug, his beefy hands slapping his back so hard it stung.

When he pulled away, all that restless energy rushed back into him. Dragging his palms on his jeans, Ryan felt jittery.

"Ryan?" Nicole asked softly. "Is there something wrong? You seem…distracted."

"I met a girl. And I blew it." Panic welled, tightening his lungs. "I let her go." He didn't want to talk about it. He just… "I have to get her back." *Awesome*. He'd gone from never talking to suddenly spewing his shit all over the place.

"What'd you do?" Brandon asked.

"Emma showed up at the resort."

Nicole's eyes went wide. "That was bold."

"More like crazy," Brandon said.

"And then Sophie packed up and left." Just saying it out loud made him sick to his stomach.

Nicole gave him a thoughtful look. "Where does she live?"

307

"California."

The hand in his dad's pocket flexed, as he rocked back on his heels. "Why are we talking about some girl you just met? Come on, son. Your coach took away your captaincy. That's a big deal."

"Oh, shit," Brandon said.

"This isn't the time to worry about some girl you had fun with over spring break." His dad eyed him meaningfully. "You've got a lot to make up for when you get back to school. But you'll recover. This is your time, kid. You've worked your ass for it. Take it."

"Yeah, I know what I have to do, Dad. But I'm still going to get her back. She's…I'm not going to find someone like her again." If she'd only answer his calls.

"Ryan." The warning in his dad's voice didn't even faze him.

"I don't care what you think. I'm going to be with her." He turned to his sister, who was watching him all wide-eyed and jaw hanging open. "What? Why're you looking at me like that?" He was beginning to regret confiding in them. He didn't like the exposure.

"You've never shared anything before. In all my life, you've never been this…real." She smiled. "I like it."

She could help him. "So what do I do? I have to get back to school. I owe it to my coach and my teammates, but the way I left things with her…I told her I didn't want to keep seeing her. I didn't see how it could work—"

"Because it can't," his dad bellowed. "You live three thousand miles apart."

"I'll make it work. But she's not returning my calls. I don't know what to do."

"You go get her." Everyone's attention whipped to Dylan.

Big Bill looked at him like he was nuts. "Oh, no, you don't. You get your ass back to school and focus on ball. Jesus, Ryan, six years with Emma didn't teach you anything? Why the hell would you want to tie yourself to another woman?"

"Because nothing's going to be right until you do." Dylan held Ryan's gaze. "And then you figure out your shit together."

His dad carried his duffle bag outside. The driver grabbed it and shoved it in the trunk and then rounded the car to get into his seat.

Ryan gave his dad a hug.

"What'm I missing, son?" He pulled away. "I can't help thinking there's more going on. Lord knows I screwed up the first half of your life, I sure as hell don't want to mess with the rest of it."

"Nah. You did okay, Dad."

"Should've divorced her sooner, but I didn't want to take your mom away from you, you know? But you've always been so solid, so sure of yourself. You didn't need much parenting. I don't know what it is, but I'm getting a bad feeling I'm giving you the wrong advice."

"I'll figure it out."

"When you talk about the girl, you're happy. When we talk about baseball, you get all worked up. I can see it. Talk to me, Ryan. What's really going on?" When Ryan didn't answer, his dad crossed his arms over his chest, tucking a hand under each armpit. "You want to play, right? You love it?"

Ryan looked away. "Sure. I mean, I've always loved it. And it'll be fine—"

His dad's eyes went wide. "*Fine*? Hang on now. Playing pro ball is ten times more intense than college. The only people who survive the majors are the ones who want to play ball more than they want to breathe. This isn't something you do because it's fine. You gotta be driven. Up until now, you've played against some good teams, had your challenges, but in the majors everyone's the best, every game's the highest level of play. And *you* have to be the best all the time. You have to want this with everything in you."

"I know that."

"Tell me something. If you didn't play ball, what would you do?"

He'd never told his dad about his work. "I've been writing apps." He forced a laugh. "Me and ten million other people."

"Putting that computer science minor to use, huh?"

"Yeah." He felt this ridiculous need for his dad to understand him—and give him advice—something he'd never done before.

Big Bill blew out a breath, shoulders sagging. "Don't know if you remember this, but when you were a kid, you loved puzzles. More than anything. You'd get on your hands and knees and work on one puzzle board after another. Pieces all over the damn place. Your mom couldn't stand it, so she threw them all out. Then Gramps got you into Legos. And that was it. You remember? Always building shit. Pieces everywhere. Your mom went nuts." He barked out a laugh, his breath a white fog in the cold evening air. "She came into the kitchen one morning, a weird..." He circled a finger around his cheek. "Impression on her face. I thought she'd hurt herself. Turns out she'd passed out on a pile of your Legos. That was the end of that toy."

Ryan remembered. "Yeah. I was so pissed. I really lost it, didn't I?"

"Never seen anything like it. You were a wildcat, all right.

But, damn, Ryan, you had a right to be angry. She threw out the things you loved most."

All that crazy anger had died down after he'd started Little League. Well, after his mom had left.

"Thing is, you used to take everything apart. You didn't put anything back together, but you'd take apart radios and telephones. Man, you drove your mom batshit crazy. Not because you were doing anything wrong, of course. You were a kid. But because she couldn't deal with it." He shrugged, looking pained. "That's an alcoholic, right? No coping skills. But, anyway, it was no surprise to me you chose computer science. In fact, I can remember smiling when you told me you wanted to major in it. It just felt...right."

"I like it."

"Do you?" His dad seemed genuinely interested.

"I like the challenge. The mental challenge. Baseball..."

"Not so challenging anymore. Truth is, everything calmed down in the house after you settled on one sport. And I liked it. I didn't stop to consider if it was something you wanted or not. It just...worked."

"It did."

Bill gazed down at the slate walkway. "Maybe it's run its course. Shame to see you walk away from it. Damn, watching you play that field." His dad blew out a breath. "You're a fine athlete, son. And a good man." He looked troubled. "Can't say I had much to do with it. That's not lost on me."

"Know what's not lost on me? My big decision is whether to enter the draft and become a Major League ball player or move on and get a job in computer science with a Michigan University degree."

His dad barked out a laugh. "Good point. *Hell* of a good point. You're gonna be all right, son."

CHAPTER TWENTY

The ballroom of the Beverly Hills hotel sparkled with bejeweled guests. Crystal chandeliers hung over white linen-draped tables and tea candles glowed and flickered in clear glass holders.

A waiter leaned in. "Finished?"

Leaning back, Sophie let him take her plate. She didn't bother eating food she didn't like, so she nodded. Dry chicken and limp, julienned vegetables just didn't do it for her.

Laura squeezed her hand, forcing her attention back on the podium, where King stood addressing the room of hundreds of philanthropic citizens of Beverly Hills. Her mom had been honored ten years ago. Of course, as an eleven-year-old Sophie hadn't attended, but every day as she walked the long hallway to her bedroom she passed the picture of her glamorous mom holding the plaque and standing between the mayor and the president of Head Start.

Sophie pushed her chair back to give King her full attention. With his tousled blonde hair and tan skin, he looked like a surfer. Boyish and charming, he'd made a wonderful first boyfriend. He'd loved her as best he could, which hadn't been easy for a guy who'd come from such a dysfunctional family.

When he'd found out her sister had bailed on her for this event, King had offered to come. She appreciated his loyalty and enduring affection more than she could say. For some reason, he'd been extra sweet all day. Nostalgic, even.

It had made her wonder if he was thinking of getting back with her. But that ship had sailed. If only...*nope*. Not going to think about Ryan O'Donnell. His relentless attempts to contact her boiled down to one thing. Guilt. He couldn't stand upsetting people. He'd upset her, so he needed to make it right. To make her like him again. Well, she liked him plenty, but she was looking forward—not back. He could just deal with it.

Her chest ached under the weight of her lie. It took everything she had not to answer his call. Return his text. She missed him with her whole heart.

King must've touched the microphone, because it screeched. He laughed, raising his hands in surrender. "Sorry. But, yeah, I mean, she never gives up, man. That's the thing about her. Sophie gives her heart to something and that's it. She's in. No matter what I was doing or where I was in the world, I always knew I had her right there for me. She's one of the nicest, most generous, people I know. So...I don't know, man, she listens, and she cares. And there's not a lot of people like that. And, you know, she was my best friend. I hope she still is. So, yeah, that's my Soph." He raised his champagne flute and gave her his lazy smile.

Applause cracked the silence, and all eyes turned to her. Heat washed through her, and she gave a little wave, just like her mom used to do when she was honored for her work. Only her mom loved the attention. Sophie wanted to slide under the table and make a tablecloth fort.

The mayor resumed her place at the podium. "Thank you, King."

Oh, good, her time in the spotlight was over. They could move onto the next honoree.

"I'm going to the ladies' room," she whispered to Laura.

But before she could push her chair back, a hand settled at the back of her neck. King collapsed into the chair beside her.

"Thank you." She reached for his hand, clasped it. "That was sweet. And thanks for coming here tonight."

"Anything for you, Soph." He smiled, his cheeks as pink as if he'd just come off the slopes. He looked at her a little too long. "I can't believe you're moving to Montana."

"I'm excited." Why did he look so sad? They hadn't been together in a year and a half.

"I'm gonna miss you."

"Are you kidding? I'm going to Big Sky, the biggest ski resort in the country. And I'm buying a house big enough to fit all you bums."

She was excited about the move. She'd narrowed her search down to a few houses big enough to accommodate all her friends when they visited, but she had so many things to get done—moving was overwhelming. At least it kept her mind busy, so she didn't waste time thinking about—

The mayor's voice broke through her thoughts. "…shortstop for the Michigan Devils, Mr. Ryan O'Donnell."

What? Sophie spun around in her seat to see Ryan climbing the steps to the podium.

Ryan.

She stared at him, those broad shoulders, that devastating smile. *What's he doing here?*

"Did you know about this?" She leaned into Laura.

"Of course."

"And you didn't tell me?"

"Nope."

She sat back in her seat, stunned. "I don't understand."

"Sure you do." King spoke close to her ear, and she turned to face him. And then she understood the sadness. He got that she'd moved on. For good this time.

She gave his arm a squeeze. They shared a warm smile, and then she turned back when she heard that deep, sexy voice.

"I haven't known Sophie as long as King or Laura, but in the short time I've had with her, she's done more to wake me up than anyone else in my life. I guess we all have our sad stories, but unlike the rest of us, Sophie doesn't let hers define her. And that's because she's the strongest person I know. She faces her issues head on, deals with them, and then goes out and lives life on her own terms. And in the process of living, she touches the people around her. And you can't *help* but be changed by her. As Helping Hands knows when she provides the material and organizes the making of blankets, socks, and scarves for the homeless. I mean, how many people would've thought to go into senior housing centers, mother's groups, and book clubs to see if they'd be interested in making blankets?"

He looked around the room. "She could write checks— she's a Valentine—but that's not enough for her. Some of us see a problem in the world and feel bad, but we carry on with our lives. Some write a check, hoping someone else will take care of it. Some even get their hands in there, showing up on Thanksgiving to serve food at the shelter. But how many people stop and think the problem through? Come up with viable solutions? Not that many. But Sophie does. Because people matter to her. Deeply. She's looking at me right now like I've lost my mind. But I haven't lost anything. I've found something. Some*one*. Sophie…"

In the weighted moment, Sophie could feel the tension

in the audience as they waited to hear what he had to say.

"I know we live at opposite ends of the country. We're both just graduating college and we have big life decisions to make. It seems like we've got too many complications for us to work. But the thing is, it's always going to be like that. We're always going to have big decisions to make. Life never runs smoothly. So, really, who do you want beside you at those turning points? When you find someone—the *one*—you grab hold of her."

Sophie stopped breathing. Her hand automatically went to her heart. "Did he just say I'm '*the one*?'" she whispered to Laura.

Her friend smiled, keeping her attention on Ryan.

"No matter the obstacles, you face them together. Because, ultimately, nothing else will ever matter as much as being with the people you love. And, Sophie, make no mistake, I love you." He drew in a breath that looked like it hurt, and he looked right at her. "I don't have any answers about our future, Soph, but I do know I want it to be *ours*."

Oh, my God. Her heart thundered. Was this really happening? Ryan was in Beverly Hills, declaring his *love* for her? And then she felt strong hands on her arms, lifting her. King gave her a little push, and it took a moment for her mind to fit back into her body, but once it did, she was off. Heart pounding, blood roaring, she moved around the tables, as the audience clapped and cheered. But she only had eyes for one man. The one jumping off the stage, racing toward her. Lifting the hem of her gown, she ran straight into that hard wall of muscle. He caught her up in those arms she'd never thought she'd feel again.

Oh, God. She was back in his arms, and nothing had ever felt so right.

She turned her mouth into his neck, breathing in his familiar scent. "You're here."

"The only place I want to be."

"But nothing's changed."

"Everything's changed. My whole life has changed, thanks to you." He let her go. Confused, she wondered at the odd smile on his face. Only then did she tune back into the sound of applause. She turned to find the entire audience on its feet, beaming smiles at her.

Heat rushed her hard. She wanted to hide in Ryan's arms, but instead she smiled her appreciation, waved, and mouthed *thank you* as she made a slow turn to acknowledge the room.

"Come with me." He took her hand and led her into the hallway. Towing her along in her four-inch heels, he turned a corner and pressed her against the wall. His big arms boxed her in, and she gazed up into that astonishingly handsome face.

Ryan O'Donnell in a black tux made her knees buckle.

She reached her arms around his waist, feeling the heat of him. "I can't believe you're here."

"I want to be with you, Soph. We might only have had a week together, but I know. I knew it the first time I saw you. I couldn't explain it then, but I can now. You're the one for me."

"Ryan, I'm moving to Montana. I'm buying Crazy Hearts from my family."

"Cool. I've never been to Montana. Can't wait to see it."

"What does that mean?" She *had* said she only needed to be there from October to February. "Do you really want a girlfriend when you're just starting your pro career? You're going to be traveling so much."

His smile broadened and his hands settled on her hips, drawing her closer. "I'm not playing pro ball. I'm done, Soph." He shrugged. "I want a new challenge."

"I'm not much of a challenge. You took me in the town square in front of ten thousand people."

His gorgeous face lit up in a way she'd never seen before. No shadows, no doubts. Just peace and pure happiness. "I love you, Sophie. Whatever else we do with our lives, I want us to do it together. You in?"

"Yeah." She let out a shaky breath. "I'm way in."

His big hands reached up to cup her cheeks. "Gonna kiss you now."

Oh, yeah. Just as her eyelids fluttered closed, she said, "We *are* talking about more than a week this time, right?"

"You're my heart, Sophie Valentine. So that means forever."

CHAPTER TWENTY-ONE

Just as Sophie hauled her bag off the carousel, a streak of black out the window caught her attention. A limo eased to the curb at the Bozeman airport.

Joy burst inside her. Unfortunately, an accident on the snowy Gallatin Road had held up traffic for miles. Ryan had expected to be late.

He's not!

She hadn't seen him in a week. Anticipation had her so wired she could barely stand it. The car hadn't even come to a full stop when the door opened and a big, built movie star of a man in black aviators climbed out with all the grace of a professional athlete. He stood to his full height, his delectable mouth curling as he caught sight of her through the plate glass window.

Willing the revolving door to move faster, she burst out of the building. Her boots crunched, making track marks on the fresh, powdery snow. Ryan moved toward her, muscles tight, coiled. That hungry, intense look hardening his features made her heart flip over.

Dropping the handle of her suitcase, she took off at a run and launched herself into his arms. He braced, bent his knees, and whisked her off the ground.

Bound inside those big, strong arms, she buried her face into his neck, breathing in his fresh soap and clean cotton scent. "I missed you so much." Nothing felt better than those strong arms wrapped around her.

He nudged her cheek, forcing her to turn toward his mouth. He kissed her, his tongue stroking inside.

While the driver grabbed her bag and carried it to the trunk, Ryan slowly walked her to the limo. He set her down. "Get in."

She slid into the leather seat, and he followed behind her, shutting the door. Between the closed partition and tinted windows, she felt cocooned inside with him. "Anyone at the house?"

"They should be skiing." But he glanced uncertainly out the window, craning his neck for a better view of the sky.

"More snow?"

He nodded curtly. "We should have the place to ourselves for a few hours." One hand slid under her ass, the other curled around her waist as he lifted her onto his lap. "I want you to myself."

Her hands met at the back of his neck, and she pressed her cold cheek to his warm one.

He stole her breath with a hungry kiss. No one had ever made her feel more loved, more completely wanted, than this man. His tongue tangled with hers, as he held her tightly to him.

Knowing she was alone with him for the forty minutes it would take to get home, she got onto his lap and rolled her hips over his erection. His sharp intake of breath made her smile. Three years together hadn't diminished their need for each other. At *all*.

His fingers flexed on her ass as he found her mouth again, his hips rocking up and grinding against her. God, she needed him. Needed him now. Sliding her hands under his long-sleeve T-shirt, she lightly scraped her fingernails up his warm skin, and then found her way to the button of his jeans.

"Did you have a good time?" His voice sounded strained.

"It was great. How 'bout I tell you all about it later?"

The rough thrust of his hips told her he agreed.

She caught handfuls of his hair and pulled, angling him for a deeper kiss. "I missed you." Desire streamed hot and wicked in her bloodstream.

"Good that you spent time with your family, though."

Her brothers had chosen not to let money tear apart the family, so they'd accepted her offer to buy Crazy Hearts. It had taken Abby longer to come around, though getting pregnant again so soon after Hannah hadn't helped her emotional state. All was good now, though, and Sophie traveled to LA to see them as often as she could.

Trembling, she had to shift back on his lap to finish unbuttoning his jeans, but in her urgency she fumbled. Impatience had her gripping his shaft through the denim instead.

He batted her hand away, tore open his jeans, and yanked down his boxer briefs.

She closed her hand around the hard, hot length of him, and a thrill shot through her. Tipping her forehead against his, her fingers sifted through his hair, grabbing handfuls when he drove her crazy with his sexy mouth.

"I missed you." His hands glided up her stomach, under her shirt and sweater. "Take this off. I want all of you."

She pulled the sweater off first, and then the long-sleeve T-shirt. Instantly, his hands closed over her breasts, and he lowered his face into her cleavage, pressing big, open-mouthed kisses. As she stroked his erection, he tore the cups of her bra down and licked a nipple. She squirmed on his lap, one hand at the back of his head, holding him to her.

"Pants off."

She fell to his side, unbuttoning her jeans and peeling them off her legs, kicking off her boots when the pants stuck around her calves. He shed his clothing, then reached for her, his mouth on her neck, her collarbone, and then back in her cleavage. He pushed both breasts together, licking first one nipple and then the other, back and forth, driving her into a frenzy of need.

When his fingers reached between her legs, every cell in her body sparked. She shuddered at the intensity of sensation. "Ryan," she whispered.

"I love when you say my name like that."

"Like what?"

"All soft and sweet, like you're melting, like I make you happy."

"You make me *so* happy."

His finger slid along her length, barely brushing her clit before pulling away. Driving her crazy.

"Except when you do that."

"What?" He glanced around the sensitive nub. "*That?*"

Chasing his fingers with her hips, she let go of him. She laughed at the look of panic in his eyes. "Oh, I see how it is. Only you get to play?" She leaned back into him, kissing him with all the desire and need streaming through her. Her hips rocked on his erection, slicking him with her desire, but not letting him sink in.

"Game time over." He gripped himself, one arm going around her waist and lifting her. When he brought her down on him, he thrust his hips up hard, sending him so deep inside, her body exploded in a shower of sensation.

Nothing felt as good as their bodies pressed together,

joined so completely. Nothing felt as satisfying as the intense, powerful connection they shared. And then he started moving. She had to grab onto his shoulders, as he lifted her and slammed her down again and again.

A cry escaped her throat, the pleasure building so hard and fast her eyes watered. "Oh, God, Ryan."

His tongue flicked out, latching onto her nipple and sucking it into his mouth, hands clenching her ass to move her up and down his hard length. "Fuck, Soph." She recognized that tone, and it always thrilled her. "*Fuck*. I can't...Jesus, I'm not going to last."

Gripping her bottom, he watched her with half-lidded eyes. "Look at you, Soph. You're so fucking beautiful." Hips thrusting hard, he surged inside her, holding himself there, grinding and gasping with his release. He finally sank back down, closing his eyes, and breathing hard. "My Sophie."

"It's only been a week."

They traveled together whenever they could, but between his work and hers, sometimes the timing didn't work out. She encouraged him to go on his own, though, believing the time spent with his friends, his sister and brother, was just as important.

Normally, he'd come with her to see her family, but this past week he'd had work to do.

His fingers gently caressed her hips, his head tilted back, and he looked deceptively relaxed. "Kat says I get cranky when you're not around."

"Yeah, but it's good for us to spend some time apart." She shifted her hips just a little and watched his eyes flare.

And when his hips flexed, and his hold on her tightened, her suspicions were confirmed. He wasn't relaxed at all. One hand on her ass kept him inside her body, as he shifted her onto her back, then dragged her down the seat so she was sprawled out before him.

He brushed a lock of hair off her cheek. "Don't pretend with me."

"I don't pretend." But he'd already started moving again, sliding easily in and out of her.

"Yeah? Kyle told me you've been a real witch this week."

Her brother, the traitor. "Two babies in the house. No one gets much sleep."

"Uh huh." He settled on top of her, one arm under her ass, the other reaching for the arm rest, as he slammed into her, making her gasp.

Oh, God, he felt so good.

"So, it's not because you missed me?" He eased out. "You're good traveling without me?"

"All the more room for me in bed."

He thrust in hard. "Sleep better without me, do you?"

"Well, of course, I'm *sleeping*, so I don't really notice." In the tight space, she could only wrap one leg around his hips, but he felt so good, she tilted her hips. Then, with each snap of his hips, he slid over the spot that made fire burn through her veins.

"Is that why Kyle found you in the kitchen at three in the morning?" He could barely get the words out. Perspiration dotted his forehead.

She gazed up at him and smiled. "Okay, Sherlock, yes, I miss you when we're not together. What do you want me to say? I'm trying to give you your independence. You never got the freedom to do what you wanted before, so I don't want to hold you back just because of my production schedule or family obligations. Now will you just finish me? Because I *really* can't take much more."

"It would be my fucking pleasure." With that he gave a

thrust so hard she jerked up the seat. And then he did it again and again. One hand worked between their slick bodies, reaching between her legs.

She cried out when he circled her sensitive nub, and then let herself fall into the pleasure seizing her body. "Don't stop. Oh, God, don't stop."

"Never going to stop, my Sophie. Never, ever going to stop."

"Oh, Ryan, oh, God." As sensation coalesced, her body succumbed to the dizzying rush of her orgasm. She wrapped herself tightly around him, arms and legs gripping him, burying her face in his neck, and then shuddering with her release.

As she calmed down, she ran her fingers through his hair. "I hate being away from you. I miss you more than anything."

"Yeah." He planted a soft kiss on her mouth. "We're done with that shit."

As the limo wound up the two-lane mountain road, they quickly picked up their strewn clothing and got dressed. Sophie owned over forty acres, so her driveway was the only one for miles. When they turned into her property, she yanked her boots onto her feet, smiling at the sight of all those cars parked haphazardly around the circular garden in the center. Having spent too many years alone in her family's house, she loved having her friends living with her here.

When they got out, the driver handed Ryan her bag and then took off.

The house was dark except flickering lights downstairs. "Looks like someone's home."

"Better not be." He grabbed her hand and headed up the recently shoveled walkway.

The house smelled delicious, like warm bread and sautéed garlic and onion. Lit candles glowed on every surface of the lodge-like living and dining area.

When Ryan dropped her suitcase in the foyer, Sophie noticed rose petals scattered on the wood floor. The path led to a café table set for two.

Candles, roses, home-cooked meal…her gaze flicked up to Ryan. "Is something going on with Kat and Marshall?" Her friend was dating a wealthy oil man from Texas who spent as much time out here as he could. "Oh, my God, is he *proposing*?"

"No, Soph. This is—"

"She's back." Jake strode out of the kitchen in ski pants and thick wool socks, a plate under his chin, and a mouth full of food.

Ryan tensed. "That's Sophie's."

"Mountain's closed. Massive storm coming in."

Ryan blew out a breath. "Is *everyone* home?"

"Sophie!" Kat hurried down the stairs, ponytail swinging. In her black yoga pants and plain white t-shirt, she flew into Sophie's arms. "I'm so glad you're back. Did you have a good time?"

"She's home?" Laura came out of the basement, still wearing her ski clothes. Dixon appeared behind her. Both looked flushed from the cold. They must've been putting the skis away.

"Hey, Soph." Dix joined the group hug.

"Guys." Ryan pried their friends away. "I know you have plans for the evening."

"Everything's shut down." Kat pulled Jake's wrist toward her. "What're you eating? That looks so good. Is there more?"

"Some chocolate shit." Jake shoved another forkful into his mouth. "This is fuckin' *good*."

Ryan's gaze narrowed on the small white plate with a swirl of raspberry sauce and a dollop of something dark and decadent-looking. His features hardened. "How about you give me and Sophie some time alone?" He jerked it out of Jake's hands.

"Hey." Jake spun around, watching Ryan set the plate on the counter. "You've got plenty of food."

"Help yourselves to the leftovers."

Sophie came up to him and rubbed a hand on his back. "What's going on?" She gestured to the candles and flower petals. "Is this for me?"

Ryan turned fully to her, his gaze softening. He opened his mouth to speak, when Laura said, "Oh, wow. Look at all that food." She, Dixon, and Kat headed into the kitchen.

"There's plenty for all of us," Dixon said.

Sophie followed them to see the oven light on and foiled-covered platters warming. A bowl of salad, a basket of bread, and a dozen little white plates with glorious desserts on them lined the counters.

Jake reached for one of the plates, and Ryan smacked his hand. "Why don't you guys order a pizza, watch a movie in the basement?"

"But there's so much." Sophie smiled at him, reaching for his hand and clasping it. "How about they eat with us and then we can go upstairs?"

Silverware clanked, plates clattered, and soon the dining room table filled with settings for all six of them.

Jake strolled out of the kitchen with a second slice of cake. "Best damn cake I ever tasted. Where'd you get this shit?"

Ryan grabbed the plate. "This is for *Sophie*. Don't ruin it for her."

"What got up your ass? She's back now. You've got all

the time in the world." Jake swiped his finger across the raspberry drizzle on the plate. "But the mountain's closed right now, so we're in for the night."

Laura, Kat, and Dixon brought out food. Delicious smells filled the room. Sophie's stomach rumbled. "I'm starving. I haven't eaten since breakfast." She peeled back the foil to see a platter of roasted tenderloin. "This looks amazing. Who cooked?"

There was something soft, sweet, and vulnerable in his eyes. "This is the sampling menu from La Fete."

"La Fête? In Sedona?"

He nodded, pulling out the chair and sitting beside her.

Chairs scraped around them, and everyone settled around the table.

Their friends started to serve themselves, when Ryan said, "Eat fast."

She stroked his thigh. "I don't mind. Really."

"I do."

Okay, something was obviously going on. "What am I missing here?"

"He's been a bear all week." Laura spooned pasta onto her plate.

"Where's Sophie?" Jake said it like a whiney girl. "I miss Sophie. When's Sophie coming back?"

Kat leaned into him, bumping shoulders. "No, he didn't."

"Couldn't even wipe his own ass. Sophie? Soph? Can you bring me the moist wipes?"

Everyone burst out laughing. Even Ryan cracked a smile, shaking his head.

This was the family she'd always wanted.

Laura had played for two seasons in Italy. She'd seen the world but ultimately decided it was time to come back and get a job. On a visit to Big Sky, she'd fallen in love with the outdoor lifestyle. She, Kat, and Dixon had started up an adventure company. She and Dixon did the tours, while Kat manned the office.

And Jake? He'd given up his family business to help run hers. For a hundred years, Crazy Hearts had remained the same—a stagnant, though charming, business. But Ryan had created a webpage filled with interactive games and social media. People from around the world sent photos of the cookies posed in unusual places for a game Ryan called *Where in the World is My Crazy Heart?*

Working together, the three of them had brought a whole new dimension to her family legacy.

"Oh, dude, great news." Jake gave Ryan a chin nod before pushing his chair back and grabbing a magazine out of the pile of mail on the coffee table. He tossed it on Ryan's empty plate. "Page twelve."

Sophie leaned over to look, but Ryan shoved it aside. "Later. Right now eat up. Quickly."

"Read it," Jake said in his commanding voice. "It's good shit."

"Can I see?" Sophie flipped the pages, stopping at page twelve. Just as she started to scan the article, his hand came up to her chin, turning her toward his mouth. He kissed her. Soft, sweet. Like he adored her.

"Can you keep your hands off her for five seconds and read the damn article?"

But Ryan didn't look away. "No. I haven't had my hands on her in a week. And tonight, as you know, I want to be alone with her."

"Not my fault, dude. Talk to the man upstairs." Jake pointed to the heavens. When Ryan still hadn't opened the magazine, his friend blew out a frustrated breath. "Oh, for fuck's sake." He pushed his chair back, stood up halfway, and lunged across the table. Snatching the magazine, he held it up so everyone could see the cover. "Dude's app won for most revolutionary idea in *HotWired* magazine's annual Best Of list."

Sophie leaned into him and wrapped her arms around his neck. "Look at you." She kissed him full on the mouth. "All revolutionary and shit." She pulled away and cupped his face. "I'm so proud of you."

Oh, my God. The way he looked at her? Like she was the only person in the room. In the house. On the planet.

"Are you okay?" she asked softly. He'd set up such a romantic meal, and it seemed like everyone was just getting in his way.

"That's my man," Jake said. "Fuckin' revolutionized the way sales are made. Cut out the middleman."

"Congratulations," Laura said. "I'm proud of you. Well, I'm jealous, but I can see through that and just be proud of you."

Sophie rubbed his thigh. "Ryan?"

"Aren't you going to eat?" Kat asked him.

"Later." Ryan leaned forward to pour some ice water in their glasses.

"Damn, dude." Dixon scanned the article. "I don't know how you come up with this stuff."

"Wasn't that big a deal." When he spoke, he covered her hand on his thigh. "I just copied the way the big box stores do it."

"Why you gotta be so modest?" Jake drank his beer. "It's not like Walmart handed their system over to you. You created your own."

"And sold it. You've got to be a billionaire by now." Kat looked at him hopefully.

Jake gave her a dull look, and then turned his attention back to Ryan. "Point is, no one else had created it for smaller businesses, which meant we had to go through distributors. Makes way more sense to do it this way."

He turned to Sophie, leaning in. "Come upstairs with me."

Dixon forked salad into his mouth. "This is good."

"It really is. I can't believe you had this delivered all the way from Arizona." She gave him a soft kiss. "Thank you."

"I love you," he whispered in her ear. And then a chunk of bread hit Ryan's forehead. He glared at Jake.

Jake shrugged. "I was talking to you."

"I don't want to talk to you. Not *tonight*." His eyebrows lifted, as if trying to reinforce a point. "Now can you eat your fucking dinner and go?"

"Go where? Even if we made it to town, we couldn't get back tonight. Gallatin Road'll be impassable."

"We're in a *chalet*, Jake. Seven bedrooms, a gym, a basement game room. Lots of places for you to go."

"I don't get why you're being so…" Kat's eyes went wide. "Oh. *Oh*. It's tonight?" She covered her mouth with a napkin and then pushed her chair back. "I can't believe I…You guys, come on."

Everyone kept eating.

"Guys, seriously," Kat said. "Help me in the kitchen. *Now*."

Heads popped up; everyone eyed each other inquisitively. Kat shot Ryan an apologetic look.

"Well, I'm not going to do it now." Ryan tossed his napkin on the table.

Sophie turned to him. "Do what now?" She looked at her friends. "What is going on?"

"Oh, Christ." Ryan jerked his chair back hard. Scraping

a hand through his chin-length hair, he stalked over to the kitchen and opened a drawer. "This is not how I wanted to do it."

"Do what?" Sophie said.

"What's he talking about?" Jake said.

"I don't know."

"You *guys*," Kat said. "All of you come with me right now."

"I'm in the middle of eating. Let me finish." But Kat yanked the back of Dixon's shirt. He rose out the chair, shoving a forkful of food into his mouth. Kat whispered in his ear. His eyes went wide. "Oh. Shit. Sorry, dude. I didn't know you were doing it tonight."

Ryan came back to the table…and then knelt beside her. "Soph."

Was he…*Oh, my God.* He was *proposing?* She couldn't breathe, she couldn't think. Heat spread through her, joy tripping along her nerves. *Oh, my God. Oh, my God. Oh, my God.*

Her man—her life—looked at her with pure adoration in his eyes. "I know we're young. We just turned twenty-four."

"Oh, shit," Jake said.

"I told you," Kat said.

Her friends hurried off, their voices fading.

"But I'm in love with you. And I know you're it for me. There's never going to be another woman that makes me feel the way you do. You make me feel alive. You make happy."

"Ryan, are you…is this…?" She shifted forward on the chair.

"I want to be with you forever. I want…" Love softened his gorgeous features. And then he pulled something out of his back pocket.

Electricity buzzed along her nerves. Her hands started shaking.

Ryan held a red velvet box in his big hand. "Will you marry me?" He cracked it open, revealing an antique rose-gold ring. A ruby bracketed by sparkling diamonds stood prominently in the center.

"Oh, my God," Kat cried from another room.

"Shut up," Jake said.

"They can't hear me."

"Russia can hear you."

"Excuse me, but my best friend just got *engaged*."

Sophie dropped to her knees, the chair skidding back, and threw herself against him. She climbed onto him, toppling him onto his ass. "Of course I'll marry you."

Joy flooded her, as she found his mouth and kissed him, her heart so full she thought she might burst. His hands cupped her bottom as he hitched her higher onto his lap. "Thank God."

He said it like he couldn't believe it. "Did you think I wouldn't say yes?"

"You're gorgeous. And kind and generous and smart. You're perfect."

"I'm not perfect."

"You actually are."

"You know I'm yours. I can't believe you'd wonder for a single second whether or not I'd marry you."

"I didn't know if you'd want to be tied down so young."

"Tied down? Ryan, you make me fly. I've never been happier in my life. I love you."

She started to kiss him again, but he set her back on the floor as he got on his hands and knees.

"What're you doing?"

"You knocked the ring out of my hand, and I want it on your finger right now." Reaching under the table, he pulled out the ring. Then, he turned to her and slid it on. It fit perfectly. The rest of their crew came running back into the room. Kat screamed and threw herself at Sophie. "I'm so happy for you. Let me see that ring."

Her friends surrounded them in hugs, kisses, and lots of squeals.

In the center of all that love and attention, an overwhelming feeling of happiness gripped her. She'd grown up in a house just this size, but it had felt cold, empty, and painfully lonely. Now, three years after Isla de los Amantes, her life was filled with so much joy. She had the greatest job in the world, the best friends, and laughter. Lots and lots of laughter.

And she had the greatest gift of all. She had the love of her life.

She wanted to freeze this moment in time.

But, then again, in about two minutes she was going to be alone in bed with the sexiest, most passionate man she'd ever known. So, yeah, no need to freeze anything.

She still had *so* much to look forward to.

Thank you for reading MINE FOR THE WEEK! It's the second book in the Wild Love series:

MINE FOR NOW
MINE FOR THE WEEK
MINE FOREVER

Have you read the Rock Star Romance series? Come meet the sexy rockers of Blue Fire:

YOU REALLY GOT ME
I WANT YOU TO WANT ME
TAKE ME HOME TONIGHT
MORE THAN A FEELING

I'm so excited about my next series, which debuts April 2018! The first book in The Bad Boyfriend series is THE WORLD'S WORST BOYFRIEND. You can learn more about it on Goodreads and, if you sign up for my newsletter, you can find out when it goes up for preorder.

I'd love to get to know you better, so please come find me on Facebook, Twitter, Instagram, Pinterest and Goodreads.

Newsletter:
http://erikakellybooks.com/contact.html

Twitter:
@erikakellybooks

FaceBook:
https://www.facebook.com/erikakellybooks/

Instagram:
@erikakellyauthor

Website:
http://www.erikakellybooks.com/

Goodreads
www.goodreads.com/author/show/7568925.Erika_Kelly

Pinterest
https://www.pinterest.com/erikakellybooks/

MINE FOR NOW
(Book 1 in the Wild Love series)

CHAPTER ONE

Bass pounded in the air, red plastic cups littered the table, and a half dozen students played beer pong in the dining room. Party time in the Scholar House.

Dylan McCaffrey strode right past them, heading for his room.

"Dude." A guy lifted his cup, waving him in. "Play with me."

He didn't recognize him, but it was only the second day of school. Breezing by, Dylan gave him a chin nod. "Later." And then it struck him.

No one knew him here.

For the first time in his life he wasn't *That damn McCaffrey kid*. He wasn't Lorraine's son. No one would glare as he passed by or watch his hands when he walked through a store.

He had a fresh slate.

Well, hell. That tiny glint of freedom sent a pulse of energy through him. But just as he turned back around to join them, his phone vibrated.

Anxiety tripped down his spine. He thumbed the button to take the call. "Hey."

"We're here." His uncle sounded calm. *Good sign.*

"You just land?" Okay, forget beer pong. He had to deal with his family first. He had plenty of time to get to know these guys.

"A few minutes ago. We've only got carry-on, so this should be quick."

Dylan raced up the stairs, only to find the girl across the hall from him pounding on her door.

"Let me in, Caroline. This is my room, too." In her bright yellow dress and red high tops, the girl swiped bangs out of her eyes.

"What's going on?" his uncle asked. "Everything all right over there?"

"Yeah. Someone's locked out of her room."

"Lost her keys already?" He chuckled. "I remember those days. Listen, we're heading for the rental car place. Should we swing by on our way to the hotel?"

"No. "He lowered his voice so the girl wouldn't hear. "I have to go into town anyway, so I'll just meet you there."

"You're worried."

He really needed to work on his knee-jerk reactions. His mom had done great the past several months, going to her job and AA meetings. She'd mostly stayed clean this summer. Just one relapse at the beginning, but she'd pulled it together. Gotten back on track.

Besides, his uncle believed in her. He wouldn't be back in her life if she'd been messing up. So, she *could* come to the house. Since she didn't need cash for drugs and booze, he didn't have to worry about her stealing from his housemates.

Relief carved a path right through him, giving him breathing room for the first time in...well, ever. "Yeah. A little, I guess." Eighteen years of living with an addict had made him cautious.

"I understand, but she's been terrific. Best I've seen her in years."

Dylan hadn't realized how wound up he was until the tension in his neck and shoulders suddenly eased. His uncle was right. Even her sponsor had encouraged this visit.

"Caroline." The girl pummeled the door with both fists.

When he got off the phone, he'd ask the residential advisor to come up and let her in. "I have to fill out some job applications in town anyway. By the time I finish, you guys should be at the hotel. We can eat there."

Of course he'd bring her by the house—that was the reason for her visit, to see his new life in college—but maybe he'd wait until everyone was in class. He'd only been away from home three days. And it was the first time they'd been apart in eighteen years. Exposing her to all these new people—kids who mostly came from boarding and prep schools—might be too stressful. Better to ease her into it.

"Sounds good." His uncle paused. "I know you've never understood why we cut her off, but we're just damn glad she's pulled herself together."

"I know you're in there," the girl shouted. "I can hear you moaning. Come on, Caroline, you're not going to lock me out every time you want to get laid." Tilting her head back, she blew out a breath. She wore something weird in her hair—a big bow of some kind.

"Let me talk to you later. This girl's—"

"We're so damn proud of you, son." His uncle sighed. "I know how hard it was for you, choosing this school...but it was the best choice you could've made. We want you to do well. And now that she's thinking clearly, your mom does, too. I think seeing you in college will give her peace of mind. And it might just give her that extra incentive to stay clean."

Accepting a scholarship to a school two thousand miles

from home had been the hardest decision Dylan had ever made. But how could he turn down a full ride to the best liberal arts school in the nation?

And having his family back in the picture would make it possible for him to stay. He'd done everything he could to set her up for success. Using his summer paychecks, he'd paid her bills for the next two months. He'd also marked the calendar when she needed to pay future ones. He'd even gotten her a job three towns over, where no one knew about her, just to give her a clear shot at reinventing herself.

Unlocking his door, he glanced over to find the girl jamming a metal nail file into the doorframe and jiggling the knob. He smiled at her perseverance.

"Is she there?" Dylan asked his uncle. "Can I talk to her?"

"She went to get us some water, but I'll bring the phone to her. Hang on a second."

He entered his room, checking for his roommate. Then, he caught himself. Shaking his head, he realized he'd done it again.

He didn't have to hide his conversations. He didn't have to *hide*. His mom was sober now. *This'll take some getting used to*.

"Dylan?" his mom said.

A rush of warmth spread through him at the sound of *this* voice. She sounded...well, like a normal mom.

That meant everything to him.

"Hey, Mom. How was the flight?"

"It's been so long since I've traveled anywhere, I guess I was nervous. But I'm so glad to be here. I wish...well, I wish I'd come with you. Helped you move in."

She'd told him she couldn't take the time off from work, but he suspected she'd wanted to punish him for choosing

Wilmington over Boulder—or any school in Colorado. AA was working, if she could apologize and see past her own needs. "There wasn't much to move in, but I'm glad you're here now."

"I can't wait to see you." He heard voices in the background. "Oh, okay. We're getting on the shuttle to the rental car place. I'll see you soon, sweet boy."

Emotion flooded him so hard his fingertips tingled. He couldn't remember the last time she'd spoken to him with such pure kindness. Christ, she really *was* going to be all right.

He disconnected the call and hurled his backpack onto his bed. Glancing out the door, he saw the girl trying to unwind the wire of a coat hanger.

"Do I seriously have to take my keys with me every time I leave my room? This is ridiculous." The girl let out a growl. Then, fingers curling into fists, she threw her shoulder into the door.

"Hang on."

She looked up at him—the first time he'd actually seen her face—and he felt a jolt in his chest. The intensity in her hazel eyes made everything inside him go quiet.

He slipped his phone into his pocket. "You want me to get Chase up here?"

She tightened the bow in her hair, smoothing her hands down her sundress. "I learned something. I'm not the Hulk. The door doesn't yield to my supernatural strength." She flexed her biceps. "These guns? Not intimidating in the least."

He eyed the slight rise in her slender arms. "Surprising, considering how impressive they are."

"Right?" And then she let out an exasperated breath, pushing the drooping bow out of her eyes. "This is the second night she's locked me out so she can fadoodle with a total stranger."

Fadoodle? He bit back a smile. "Yeah, well, how long can it take?"

"Really? Because I slept on the couch last night. And you know what? That is not gonna fly with me. This is my room. My only place on this whole freaking campus, and there's not a chance in hell I'm going to let some entitled heiress keep me out of it." She turned back to the door.

"Having fun in college yet?"

She had a mischievous smile and a warmth in her eyes that sent a surprising wash of heat up his neck. "Not yet, but I will. You can count on it."

"You need a hand?"

"And have you get sucked into the sexual vortex that is Caroline Thayer? No freaking way."

"All right, well, I'm gonna head into town."

"Enjoy. I'll be *in my room.* Planting my flag in the carpet." She gave him a dazzling smile, sticking her hand out. "I'm Nicole."

"Dylan." He needed to get going, but he knew Nicole wasn't getting into that room any time soon. And he also knew what it felt like to need a place for himself. "Let me see what I can do." He turned back and rooted around in his desk for his Swiss Army knife. Motioning for her to step aside, he quickly removed the screws that held the doorknob.

She pushed up behind him, her body brushing against his.

He stilled, aware of her heat and the scent of something sweet, clean. When her hair brushed over his arm, chill bumps burst out and spread along his skin.

He glanced at her over his shoulder, surprised at his reaction to her.

She gave him a warm smile. "I want to watch how you do it, so I can do it myself next time."

Didn't she notice how close she stood? Close enough to make his heart pound. He stepped back a little, giving her room to watch. Reaching into the hole, he removed the bolt that connected the knob to the strike plate and opened the door.

Light from the hallway spilled into the room, where he got a view of two people going at it on the bed. Caroline jerked up, hands covering her breasts. "Oh, my God, what're you *doing?*"

The room stank of pot, sex, and...

Nicole charged in. "You're eating my peanut butter."

...peanut butter. A locker sat open in front of the other bed, its contents spread all over the blanket.

Nicole grabbed her things and started tossing them into the trunk. "You can't just take my food."

"It's a few snacks. Get over yourself." Caroline reached for a silky robe, shoved her arms in it. "When the scarf's on the door, that's your cue to give me some privacy."

Well, that explained the droopy bow in Nicole's hair.

"Wrong. When you want to hook up with someone, you find a private place to do it. When you want to look jaunty, you wear the scarf."

Caroline narrowed her gaze to the bow. "Oh, my God, give that to me, freak." She made a grab for it, but Nicole ducked.

Jaunty? He smiled. Something about this chick. He couldn't figure her out. Caroline was easy to tag—hot, rich girl. Liked to party. But Nicole? She didn't look rich. Her hair—dark brown, no fancy highlights—looked choppy, as if she'd hacked it off herself. It had so many layers it shook and shimmied every time she moved. Her yellow sundress hid her shape, and the high tops did nothing to flatter her pale, slender legs. No manicure, no make-up, but a sparkle in her eyes that showed intelligence and a sense of humor.

But what hit him the most was her warmth. It got inside him. She wasn't his type at all—but then what was his type? He couldn't deny he'd stayed with Kelsi as long as he had because she knew his mom. His situation. And she'd handled it. Most girls wouldn't.

They shouldn't have to.

And then that wild sense of freedom whipped through him again. He had a fresh start here. That meant he could date whoever he wanted without his mom fucking it up.

The guy rolled out of bed and stepped into his cargo shorts. "I'm out of here."

Caroline got up, tying the robe's sash around her waist. She walked toward Dylan, not disguising her blatant interest. "Mr. Tall, Dark, and Dirty from across the hall. Finally, we meet."

Nicole closed the trunk and pushed it under the bed. "His name is Dylan, and he smells like clean clothes and cinnamon. So, yeah, not dirty at all."

Dylan smiled. He hadn't had cinnamon gum since that afternoon—funny now she'd noticed.

Caroline's eyes went hooded, and she smiled. "So glad to meet you."

"Oh, perfect." Nicole shot him a look. "Please don't be the reason she locks me out tomorrow."

"Don't worry." Dylan never took his eyes off Caroline's. "Never gonna happen."

The blonde's smile spread wider. The look in her eyes said, *Sure it will.*

The guy smacked her bottom. "Catch you later, babe."

Dylan stepped aside so the guy could leave the room.

Since Nicole was all set, he'd go.

"Slow down there, gorgeous." Caroline opened a drawer in her nightstand, pulled out a half pint bottle of vodka, and waved it at him. "Let's hang out."

"Oh, my God, what is wrong with you?" Nicole looked ready to rip her roommate a new one. "We signed a *contract*. No alcohol, no drugs. Do you want to get kicked out?"

Caroline gave him a look that said, *Can you believe I have to live with this?* "Wow, we are so not going to get along." She sat on her bed, letting the robe fall open enough to reveal her upper thighs.

"You do realize if Chase comes in here, I get in trouble, too, right? We share this room, so I'm implicated in your illegal activity."

"Um, okay. Uptight much?" Caroline held the bottle out to Dylan, then gave Nicole a careless wave. "Look, how about you give me and him some time to get to know each other, okay? Go find somewhere to study or something."

Dylan had had enough. He came up to Nicole. "Grab your things."

She looked at him, brow furrowed.

He leaned into her ear. "Crash in my room tonight. Talk to Chase tomorrow about switching rooms."

"Where would I sleep?"

"You want to stay here?"

"God, no."

"Then, let's go."

Nicole grabbed her toiletry bag, a pair of pajama shorts, and a T-shirt, and stuffed it all in her backpack. She unplugged her laptop and clutched it to her chest, ready to go.

Caroline watched them. "You're leaving with *her*?"

He ignored her, following Nicole out of the room.

"Wait a minute. You have to put my doorknob back on."

Dylan turned to her. "You gonna keep locking her out?"

"Are you kidding me? Like you aren't going to do the exact same thing when *you* want some privacy?"

"You know, I never was under the impression the world revolved around me so, no, I won't be locking my roommate out when I want to get laid." He joined Nicole in the hall, gesturing to his room. "You gonna be all right in here?"

"Sure. I'll just get ready for bed and read."

"Okay, then. I'm heading into town. If I'm not back before you go to sleep, just use my sleeping bag."

As he turned to go, a group of girls came sauntering down the hallway toward Caroline's room. Their diamond earrings, expensive watches and clothing…Jesus. Talk about temptation.

And there was that knee-jerk reaction again. His mom was in a great place. He didn't need to worry about her stealing things.

He let out a breath. He had to let all this shit go.

For the first time in his life, he was free.